Diary of a Madman

and Other Stories

LU XUN

Diary of a Madman
and Other Stories

Translated by

William A. Lyell

UNIVERSITY OF HAWAII PRESS

HONOLULU

Printed in the United States of America
90 91 92 93 94 95 5 4 3 2 1

Library of Congress Cataloging-in-Publication Data
Lu, Hsün, 1881–1936.
[Selections. English. 1990]
Diary of a madman and other stories / Lu Xun ; translated
by William A. Lyell.
p. cm.
ISBN 0–8248–1278–6 (alk. paper). — ISBN 0–8248–1317–0 (pbk.)
1. Lu, Hsün, 1881–1936—Translations, English. I. Lyell,
William A. II. Title.
PL2754.S5A25 1990
895.1'351.—dc20 90–36785
CIP

University of Hawaii Press books are printed
on acid-free paper and meet the guidelines
for permanence and durability of the Council
on Library Resources.

The illustrations for "Ah Q—The Real Story"
were done by the modern Chinese artist
Cheng Shihfa and published in 1962 in
*Ah Q—The Real Story, One Hundred and
Eight Illustrations,* Shanghai: People's
Art Press.

CONTENTS

Preface vii
Introduction ix
A Biographical Sketch ix
The Stories xxxi
The Translations xxxviii
A Note on Pronunciation xliii

Remembrances of the Past (1911) 3

CHEERING FROM THE SIDELINES
(1918–1922)

Preface 21
Diary of a Madman 29
Kong Yiji 42
Medicine 49
Tomorrow 59
An Unimportant Affair 67
The Story of Hair 70
A Passing Storm 77
Hometown 89
Ah Q—The Real Story 101
Dragonboat Festival 173
The White Light 184
Some Rabbits and a Cat 191
A Comedy of Ducks 197
Village Opera 202

Wondering Where to Turn
(1924–1925)

New Year's Sacrifice 219
Upstairs in a Wineshop 242
A Happy Family 255
Soap 264
The Eternal Lamp 279
A Warning to the People 291
The Venerable Schoolmaster Gao 297
The Loner 311
Mourning the Dead 338
Brothers 363
Divorce 377

PREFACE

Picturesque farmhouses with whitewashed walls; rivers and canals crisscrossing a lush green countryside; long narrow boats with telescoping bamboo roofs that can be closed against the rain; mist-shrouded mountains off on the horizon; well-fed and friendly peasants everywhere—such is the impression that Shaoxing, in Zhejiang Province, makes upon the visitor today. When, in 1881, Lu Xun was born there to a gentry family in decline, the mountains and rivers of Shaoxing must have had exactly the same beauty they have today. But the social system was archaic, riddled with cruelty and injustice, and hopelessly corrupt at a time when China needed to be strong to avoid being devoured by imperialist nations of both the West and the East. Lu Xun devoted most of his life to dealing with those problems.

He belonged to that in-between generation of intellectuals who had one foot mired in tradition while they tried to step forward into the modern world with the other. Very few of them would take that step as surely and unequivocally as Lu Xun. Theirs was a unique experience, at once painful and exciting. They lived on the edge of history in an environment that will never be seen again, an environment that produced many great men and women, and Lu Xun a giant among them. He was blessed with a quick, probing, and powerful mind, large enough to accommodate prodigious amounts of the old learning *and* the new. In another more stable age, centuries earlier, Lu Xun might have become a great Confucian philosopher, interpreting the classics in a way every bit as fresh as Zhu Xi (1130–1200) or Wang Yangming (1472–1528). But he was born in an age that fated him to destroy what those men had built so that he might find a better way for human beings to behave—a way for them to treat each other with honesty, compassion, integrity, and love.

* * *

The present translation is based on the stories as found in *The Complete Works of Lu Xun (Lu Xun quanji)* published by the People's Literature Press of Beijing in 1981. I am very grateful for the copious and helpful notes provided in this excellent edition. I thank my students, colleagues, friends, and family for helping me to understand and to love these stories; Stuart Kiang of the University of Hawaii Press for his encouragement and for his faith in my translations; and Grace Wiersma for her careful and creative copyediting.

William A. Lyell

INTRODUCTION

A Biographical Sketch

The year was 1905. At a medical school in Japan a twenty-four-year-old Chinese student stalked angrily out of a lecture hall and decided to abandon his medical training then and there in order to devote himself entirely to literature. That student was Lu Xun (1881–1936), who was to become one of the modern world's greatest writers.[1]

During the mid-nineteenth century Western traders and missionaries had flocked to China and Japan in search of easy profits and heathen souls. As the century drew to a close, China remained helpless before this alien tide while Japan, long since gripped by the urgent need to modernize, had begun to turn it back. So successful was China's eastern neighbor in this regard that in 1894, apparently emulating the rapacious greed of the Western powers, she declared war on China. In the treaty that ended the fighting one year later, Japan won control of Taiwan and the Pescadores, and also the right to open trade in seven Chinese ports.

Suddenly it was clear that, like it or not, China would have to modernize in order to survive. Once the need for modernization had been recognized, the next logical step was to send large numbers of students to study in Japan; closer by far than either Europe or America, Japan also relied on a language that was easier for most Chinese to acquire and use than any Western tongue. Of still greater significance, however, was the fact that Japan, an Asian nation, had been demonstrably successful in penetrating the secrets of Western wealth and power.

Lu Xun was one of those students dispatched to Japan in the wake of Japanese victory. Graduating from the government-sponsored School of Mines and Railroads in Nanjing during the winter of 1901, he arrived in Tokyo the following spring and was for the next two years a student at the Kōbun Academy. This school had been established by the Japanese government especially to teach overseas Chinese students the Japanese language skills they would need to enter institutions of higher learning in Japan.

1. Lu Xun is the pen name of Zhou Shuren.

While in Tokyo Lu Xun wrote articles and published them in overseas Chinese student journals, introducing various fields of modern science to his compatriots and simultaneously exhorting them to patriotism. He also found time to translate two Jules Verne novels into Chinese: *From the Earth to the Moon* and *Voyage to the Center of the Earth*. Making full use of the Japanese translations, Lu Xun brought these works of science fiction over into Chinese in order, as he grandly announced in the preface to one of them, "to sweep away inherited superstitions, improve thought, and aid the cause of civilization." As a young member of the up-and-coming intellectual elite, he was confident that he knew not only what ailed China (the backward, superstitious thinking of her people) but also what was wanted in the way of a cure (popularization of scientific thought). Within the next few years, however, he would come to reject this judgment.

Upon graduation in 1904, young Lu Xun left Tokyo for Sendai to attend medical school. He could well have picked a school closer to hand, in Tokyo proper perhaps, or across the bay at Chiba. Intense dissatisfaction with the majority of his fellow Chinese students, however, made him decide to get as far away from them as possible. In Lu Xun's eyes these students were at once frivolous, mindlessly adopting the outer trappings of Western civilization (mainly social customs such as ballroom dancing), and cynically practical, pretending to pursue their studies in order to "save China" while their actual motives were to earn high salaries in prestigious positions after graduation. Lu Xun would have none of this. Instead he went to Sendai, where he would be the *only* Chinese student.

Located in Miyagi prefecture about two hundred miles north of Tokyo, Sendai was something of a military town as well as a university one. The Second Division of the Japanese army reserves was stationed there. When Japan took up arms against Russia in 1904, the Second was immediately called up and dispatched to Manchuria. Hundreds of Russian prisoners were taken in Manchuria and sent back to Sendai, where their captured army capes came to be much prized among the local citizenry, who were imbued with a heady blend of patriotic jingoism and hometown pride.

These were not the best of times to be the only Chinese student in the town of Sendai. Though the Sino-Japanese War was now a full decade behind, an atmosphere of arrogance still lingered here: Chinese were often contemptuously referred to as *chanchan bozu* (roughly equivalent to "Chinks" in English).

Lu Xun's instructor in microbiology used a slide projector to introduce the various microbes to his students. If the lesson finished early, he would use the remaining time to show slides of natural scenery—or scenes of the war. On one such occasion, as his fellow students shouted one wall-shaking *Banzai!* after another, Lu Xun looked at a slide showing a Chinese on the verge of decapitation at the hands of Japanese military men in Manchuria. According to the caption, this man had been caught spying for the Russians. Lu Xun was not so much interested in the condemned "spy" as he was in the Chinese bystanders, shown gathered round to watch the execution. Though they appeared physically sound and in no need of medical care, he inferred from their facial expressions that, psychologically, they too were close to death. Suddenly realizing that China needed someone to doctor its people's spirits more than someone to look after their physical health, he strode out of the lecture hall that day and decided to devote himself to the creation of a literature that would minister to the ailing Chinese psyche.

Lu Xun returned to Tokyo in the spring, determined to spark a spiritual revolution through the written word. Although to outsiders such a melodramatic step may appear quixotic, one should remember that Confucian ideology, a tradition in which Lu Xun had himself been schooled, was preeminently an affair of books, of canonical texts endlessly memorized and commented upon in order to assure the moral authority and intellectual orthodoxy of the scholar-officials who ruled the land. Moreover, these officials ruled primarily through the power of the written word, whose magical force was assumed by those whose lives it regulated. Against this background, Lu Xun's melodramatic decision takes on a more practical meaning.

But in the summer of 1906 something happened that remains difficult to explain even today, something that has so puzzled Lu Xun's biographers as to tempt them to ignore or even suppress it. At his mother's behest and showing uncharacteristic passivity, Lu Xun returned to Shaoxing and submitted to a parentally arranged marriage with a certain Zhu An, a marriage that is said to have never been consummated. In effect, Zhu An spent the rest of her life living in the Zhou household as a "grass widow" whose main function was to wait upon her mother-in-law.

In the fall of 1906, not long after his marriage, Lu Xun returned to Tokyo with his younger brother, Zhou Zuoren (1885–1968).[2] Zuoren had won a government scholarship and was to remain in Japan until 1911. While there he would fall utterly under the spell of Japanese culture and would choose a Japanese woman, Habuto Nobuko, as his wife. Perhaps Zuoren enjoyed more freedom in his choice of a mate than did his elder brother, for in traditional China responsibility weighed most heavily on the shoulders of the eldest male. This background may be particularly salient in the case of Lu Xun's family, since his father, a man stalled in mid-career by alcohol and opium, had died in 1896 of a protracted illness that Chinese doctors had proved helpless to treat. Indeed, the circumstances surrounding his father's death had been one of the factors leading Lu Xun to study Western medicine in the first place.

During 1907, amid a flurry of other activities, the two brothers joined with another young man from their native Zhejiang Province, Qian Xuantong (1887–1939),[3] and a few others to organize a Society for the Promotion of National Learning. They invited the renowned scholar and highly respected anti-Manchu revolutionary Zhang Taiyan (1868–1936) to serve as director of their group and to lecture them on Chinese literature and philology. A political activist, Zhang had earlier broken with the constitutional monarchists[4] and had turned to openly advocating revolution. The Manchu government had jailed him in Shanghai between 1903 and 1906 for activities that were deemed "seditious." Arriving in Japan after his release, Zhang was a ready-made hero among the Chinese student population of Tokyo. This patriotic and highly individualistic scholar exercised considerable influence on Lu Xun.

In keeping with his resolve to use literature to minister to the ailing Chinese psyche, Lu Xun now banded together with a number of his like-minded countrymen in an attempt to launch a new literary movement. Their first visible step was to organize publication of a magazine entitled *New Life*. As the proposed date of their

---

2. Lu Xun, it will be remembered, was the pen name of Zhou Shuren.

3. His son Qian Sanqiang (b. 1913), a nuclear physicist, was instrumental in the development of China's atomic bomb.

4. This was the group that had advocated modernizing China while retaining the imperial system of government, a program that echoed the Japanese model.

inaugural issue approached, however, manuscripts and funds that had been promised in support of the new venture failed to materialize and the enterprise was abandoned.

Lu Xun later brought out a number of the articles he had prepared for the stillborn *New Life* in the magazine *Henan,* published in Japan by the association of overseas Chinese students from that province. One essay, entitled "On Breaking Through the Voices of Evil," revealed how drastically his thinking had changed since the time of his earlier stay in Tokyo. Far from blaming China's backwardness on the "inherited superstitions" of the common people, he now appeared to turn against members of his own class, asserting that the accusation of superstition was only a convenient slogan of hypocritical gentry scholars who hoped to absolve themselves of responsibility for the current national crisis by laying the blame for China's unfortunate plight at the doorstep of the common people.

In another essay, "The Power of Mara Poetry,"[5] Lu Xun called upon his fellow countrymen to become "warriors of the spirit," writers who would give voice to the sufferings of China's silent masses and articulate their hopes and fears, writers who would, at the same time, exhort the whole Chinese people to reform their society and stir them to resist oppression. Of the many foreign writers whom Lu Xun identified as warriors of the spirit (his term for all such writers was "Mara Poets"), he singled out Nikolai Gogol (1809–1852) for special praise: "His was a voice," Lu Xun remarks, "that broke a Russian silence of centuries, making the world aware of the hitherto invisible traces of tears on the tragic faces of a suffering people." We might observe in this light that Lu Xun's first colloquial short story, "Diary of a Madman," was inspired by Gogol's story of the same name; and when Lu Xun died in 1936, he was still at work on the second volume of his translation of Gogol's novel *Dead Souls.*

As he had done in earlier days there, Lu Xun continued to translate in Tokyo, pursuing what was to be his lifelong passion. But now, rather than the science fiction of Jules Verne, he worked on the stories of Leonid Andreyev (1871–1919) and Vsevolod Garshin (1855–1888). He combed the world literature that was available to

5. Lu Xun glossed the name *Mara* as meaning "devil," claiming that this epithet was first applied as such to the English romantic poet Byron.

him in Japanese and German—the only two languages, other than Chinese, he knew well enough to read easily—for stories created by authors from weak and oppressed nations that shared, he felt, the fate of his own homeland. For Lu Xun, the function of the translator was not less important than that of the creative writer.[6]

In an essay entitled "The Erratic Development of Culture," young Lu Xun argued that China's weaknesses and strengths all proceeded from the same cause—isolation. Because of her distance from the other centers of world culture, China had seldom been the target of cultural stimulation from abroad and the result, Lu Xun felt, had been gradual atrophy. Just as the creative writer could break through internal barriers of silence and give voice to the sufferings of common people, so might the translator break through external barriers of language and culture separating one nation from another.

Lu Xun's first efforts to tear down the cultural walls that cut China off from the world at large resulted in a two-volume collection of short stories, *Tales from Abroad,* consisting of works translated by himself and his brother and published jointly under this title in 1909. The production cost was defrayed by a Chinese banker who had traveled to Tokyo for an ear operation. His contribution paid for printing one thousand copies of volume one and five hundred of volume two, which were marketed in both Tokyo and Shanghai. We have no record of the Shanghai sales, but in Tokyo only twenty-one copies of the first volume and twenty of the second were ever bought. Lu Xun and his brother were plainly ahead of their time. The political revolution that would destroy the Manchu dynasty was only two years away, but the literary revolution, for which the two brothers were so well prepared, was to be a decade in the making, and the evidence of its beginning was still invisible to them.

Lu Xun might have stayed longer in Tokyo this time, despite the failure of *Tales from Abroad,* but in the end it was lack of money that drove him home. Not only did the family back in Shaoxing need his financial support, but Zuoren's family in Tokyo needed it too. On the surface, it almost appears that Lu Xun sacrificed his own interests to those of his younger brother, much as he had done a few years earlier for the sake of his mother when he mar-

6. Lu Xun's collected translations run to ten volumes.

ried Zhu An. In any case, he now returned to China in 1909 to assume a teaching position at the Zhejiang Bi-level Normal School in Hangzhou.[7] This job had been arranged for him by his fellow townsman and lifelong friend Xu Shoushang (1882–1948), who had just returned from Japan the previous year and was now dean of studies at the school.[8]

Upon landing in Shanghai and before proceeding to his teaching post in Hangzhou, the twenty-eight-year-old Lu Xun bought an artificial queue from a store that specialized in their sale to Chinese students returning from abroad.[9] To all but the most discerning eye, these fake queues were indistinguishable from the real thing. Nonetheless, Lu Xun gave up wearing his after only a month, because it occurred to him that to have the thing fall off unexpectedly or—worse yet—to have someone *pull* it off would be far more embarrassing than to appear without it.

Situated in the provincial capital of Lu Xun's native Zhejiang, the Zhejiang Bi-level Normal School had originally been an examination hall. When the Confucian civil service examinations were abolished in 1905, it had been rebuilt as a normal school patterned after a similar institution in Tokyo, and Japanese nationals had been engaged to teach some of the courses. Since many of the Japanese did not speak Chinese, classroom interpreters were needed. Aside from teaching one course in chemistry and one in physiology, Lu Xun also served as interpreter for the Japanese instructor of botany. In this capacity he was required to translate the lecture sentence by sentence and then to interpret between instructor and students during a question-and-answer period following the lecture.

The Japanese presence weighed heavily in Hangzhou, one of the ports Japan had forced open to trade under the treaty ending the

---

7. The school trained both primary and secondary school teachers, hence the term *bi-level.*

8. A native of Shaoxing, Xu was finally assassinated in 1948 by a Kuomintang (Nationalist Party) agent in Taibei because of his leftist sympathies, and also because he had tried to popularize Lu Xun's works among students at National Taiwan University.

9. After their conquest of China in 1644, the Manchus required Chinese males to adopt their alien coiffure, which involved shaving the front of the head while letting the hair grow long at the back and braiding this into a queue; cutting off the queue came to be considered a gesture of defiance against the Manchu regime. The government did, however, make some allowance for returning students since, it was thought, they *might* have cut off their queues while abroad simply in order to blend with the local population.

Sino-Japanese War (1894–95) more than a decade earlier. Just as the Western powers had done before her, Japan established enclaves of immunity within the treaty ports where foreigners were beyond the reach of Chinese law. In Hangzhou the Gonghuan Bridge and environs on the north side of town became such an enclave. Among the attractions of this area was a house of prostitution that some of Lu Xun's colleagues liked to frequent on weekends. Lu Xun is known to have admonished his colleagues on one occasion: "Gonghuan Bridge is a piece of Chinese territory occupied by the Japanese. It's *Chinese* women who are being violated in the brothel there. Isn't that shameful enough? Of all places, why do you have to go *there* to take your pleasure?"[10]

The twin afflictions plaguing all of China at this time were thus plainly evident in Hangzhou. While the Japanese of the Gonghuan Bridge area gave meaning to the word *imperialism,* the administration of the normal school fleshed out the concept of *feudalism.*[11] During Lu Xun's second year of teaching there, a conservative Confucian ideologue was appointed as new director of the school. He insisted that the dean of studies, Xu Shoushang, perform a ceremonial kowtow in honor of Confucius. Xu refused and resigned from the school in protest. Then one after another, the faculty, Lu Xun among them, tendered their resignations in support of their dean. Eventually the new director was himself forced to resign, while the former faculty were all reinstated.

Then in 1910 Lu Xun accepted a position as instructor and dean of studies at the Shaoxing High School. Traditional Chinese schools taught the Confucian classics and prepared their pupils to sit for the civil service examinations. Modern schools like the Shaoxing High School, on the other hand, taught *both* the classics and contemporary subjects such as natural sciences and foreign languages. Upon graduation from one of these schools a student could either move to an institution of higher learning and pursue, say, engineering or (until 1905) sit for the civil service examinations. Modern schools were also likely to be centers of revolutionary political activity, and those in Shaoxing were no exception. The Shaoxing High School had been established in 1897 as a grass-

10. See Lin Zhihao, *Lu Xun Zhuan* (A Biography of Lu Xun) (Beijing: Beijing Publishing Co.), p. 62.

11. The term *feudalism* here refers to the traditional Chinese society, following the usage now standard in the People's Republic of China.

roots effort at modernization by a certain retired government official, with the explicit objective of producing large numbers of "ideal citizens" trained equally in morals, intellect, and physical cultivation. When the school had first opened its doors to students in 1899, Cai Yuanpei (1868–1940), another of Lu Xun's lifelong friends and fellow townsmen, had been its first principal.[12]

In 1901 the revolutionary martyr Xu Xilin (1873–1907) had been engaged by the school to teach the Confucian classics and mathematics. Also a native of Shaoxing, Xu had been promoted to assistant principal by 1903. In 1905 he left with a large contingent of his students ("disciples" would perhaps be a better word) for Japan, where they were ostensibly to study under his guidance. While in Japan, however, they spent most of their time planning and organizing for the revolution at home. Upon returning to China Xu found a position as head of the Anhui Police Academy. When the governor of the province came to participate in the academy's graduation ceremony, Xu assassinated him in hopes this would be the spark to set off the revolution at last. Following his violent act, Xu and some of his students entered and occupied the police armory, managing for a while to hold off the governor's troops. Later the same day, however, they were all captured. The governor's bodyguards cut out Xu Xilin's heart, then fried and ate it along with his liver to give scope to their fury and demonstrate their loyalty to the dead governor. Later, the grisly circumstances surrounding Xu Xilin's death would find their way into the tenth entry of Lu Xun's first colloquial short story, "Diary of a Madman."

In a related intrigue, a female cousin of Xu's, Qiu Jin (b. 1879), took charge of the Datong Academy for girls in Shaoxing during 1907, having planned a coordinated uprising jointly with Xu so that while he was taking over Anhui Province, she was supposed to take control of Zhejiang. Shortly after Xu's execution, however, she was betrayed by an informer in Shaoxing and soon arrested; the local Manchu government officials subsequently dis-

12. Also a native of Shaoxing, Cai had received a traditional education and had won the highest degrees attainable within the civil service examination system by the time he was twenty-two. Despite his outstanding academic record and his bright prospects for an official career, Cai became a revolutionary. In 1902, along with Zhang Taiyan, he became a founding member of the China Education Society, a revolutionary group dedicated to overthrowing the Manchu regime.

covered that Qiu Jin had secretly commandeered almost fifty guns and more than six thousand rounds of ammunition. She was publicly executed in central Shaoxing two days after her arrest.[13]

Thus it was little wonder that the government distrusted the new schools. Teachers who had studied abroad, where they might have been tainted by revolutionary sentiments or even have joined one of the revolutionary secret societies, were especially vulnerable to suspicion. So when Lu Xun moved to the Shaoxing High School as instructor and dean of studies in 1910, the local Manchu magistrate kept a close eye on him. Every one of the thirty-two faculty members at the school, with the sole exception of Lu Xun, wore traditional Chinese dress (long gown and mandarin jacket) and made a show of the obligatory queue (whether real or counterfeit). Lu Xun, on the other hand, dressed himself in Western clothes, sported a moustache, and went scandalously bareheaded.

Years later Lu Xun would recall that the situation in Shaoxing had been even worse than the one he left in Hangzhou. In Hangzhou, at least, he had occasionally been able to pass as a "foreign devil," one of the many Japanese nationals that populated the city, but back in his own hometown, such anonymity was impossible. Some people cursed him as "a Chinese sellout to the foreign devils," while others opined that he probably had lost his queue as punishment for some crime—perhaps for making off with a girl from a respectable family.[14]

Among the students of the Shaoxing High School, Lu Xun earned the reputation of being inconsistent when he opposed some of them who threatened to cut off their queues too. He reasoned that although the government might make allowances in his own case (since he had studied overseas), it would be very unlikely to tolerate such activity among students. When the students went ahead with the plan and cut their queues anyway, however, Lu Xun staunchly defended them and even managed to protect them from punishment by either school or government officials.

---

13. In Lu Xun's story "Medicine," a young revolutionary is executed at "Old Pavilion Road Intersection" the real place, in fact, where Qiu Jin met her death. Today a monument stands close to this spot in Shaoxing.

14. One of the characters in Lu Xun's best-known short story, "Ah Q—The Real Story," is openly reviled on the street and nicknamed "Fake Foreign Devil" because of his absent queue.

When news of the Republican Revolution reached Shaoxing in October of 1911, most people in town, not knowing what to expect, were on the edge of panic. In this charged atmosphere Lu Xun emerged as a natural leader who did his best to restore calm and to educate people about the significance of current events. After Republican forces liberated Shaoxing and established the new military government, Lu Xun was appointed principal of the Shan-Kuai Primary Level Normal School.[15]

Like almost everyone else, Lu Xun had cherished extravagant hopes for the Revolution. Before long, however, the new "revolutionary" government at Shaoxing itself began to show signs of corruption, taking little visible interest in any governmental functions except the collection of taxes. Thus, when offered a position in the newly formed Ministry of Education at Nanjing, Lu Xun left Shaoxing in February of 1912 with few regrets.[16] He would follow the ministry northward to Beijing when the capital was shifted there a few months later.

Late in 1911 but before leaving his hometown, Lu Xun wrote his first short story, "Remembrances of the Past." Though written in the literary Chinese idiom, this story is modern in most respects and presents a view of reality consistent with that found in the twenty-five stories he would later write in the colloquial language between 1918 and 1925. But the fame enjoyed by Lu Xun's later colloquial stories has generally eclipsed the merits of this first literary experiment.

After "Remembrances of the Past," Lu Xun would not write another work of fiction until 1918, marking a literary hiatus that coincided with a dark period of political and cultural stagnation within the Chinese nation as a whole.

Not long after the Revolution, Sun Yat-sen, idealistic founder and first president of the republic, had ceded his position to Yuan Shikai (1859–1916). A high-ranking official and military man under the Manchu dynasty, Yuan had commanded enough military strength to complete and consolidate the overthrow of the old imperial regime. Recognizing the political reality that his power

---

15. Before the victory of the Chinese Republic, the two halves of Shaoxing, lying to the east and west of a line bisecting the city from north to south, had belonged to two different counties, Shanyin and Kuaiji. The school was named for these two counties.

16. Cai Yuanpei, then minister of education, made the offer to Lu Xun through his friend Xu Shoushang (see n. 8).

represented, Sun Yat-sen and the revolutionaries had yielded to him the presidency of their infant republic.

Through his autocratic administration, Yuan soon made it plain that he had little use for the democratic ideals held by the revolutionaries. They in turn were disenchanted with their president and in 1913 attempted to launch a "second revolution" from the provinces, hoping to overthrow him. They failed and Sun was forced to flee to Japan. Thereafter, President Yuan increasingly ignored the important principles upon which the republic had been founded and finally, in 1915, he declared himself to be emperor of a new dynasty. Disaffection in the provinces and his own death one year later closed the curtain on this farcical imperial revival. But the republic could only limp along toward warlordism and chaos thereafter.

In May of 1912 the new Ministry of Education moved to Beijing, where it was housed in what had been the premises of the old Imperial Board of Education. Indeed, some of the same personnel (under new republican titles) were carried over along with the buildings. With the vice-minister as their leader, this group of the old guard formed a powerful conservative faction against which the progressive new minister, Cai Yuanpei, only fought in vain. Like Sun, he too was quickly forced out of office. Thereafter the Ministry of Education settled down into a dull round of bureaucratic days.

But for Lu Xun, the year 1916 brought the brief diversion of an exciting family drama whose events would later provide material for his first story in the colloquial language, "Diary of a Madman." A certain maternal cousin of Lu Xun's arrived in the capital utterly convinced that he was pursued by deadly enemies. Once established in a hotel, he proceeded then to move around in it from one room to another, supposedly in an attempt to evade his persecutors. Eventually Lu Xun offered his cousin shelter in his own quarters. One morning, in a state of apparent panic, the cousin announced that he was going to be decapitated that very day, entrusting Lu Xun with a farewell letter addressed to his family. At this juncture Lu Xun packed his cousin off to a hospital, but when he showed no signs of improvement there was no choice but to arrange for someone to take him back home to Shaoxing.

Soon after Yuan Shikai's death in 1916, the new president of the republic, Li Yuanhong, was at loggerheads with the powerful northern warlord Duan Qirui (1867–1936). In the summer of 1917, President Li foolishly invited the military governor of Anhui Province, Zhang Xun (1867–1943), to proceed toward Beijing and support him against Duan. In the event, Governor Zhang was only too willing to respond. An ultraconservative man who, along with all his troops, had retained his traditional Manchu hairstyle, Zhang promptly marched into the capital and declared a restoration of the imperial monarchy. Duan Qirui then led a coalition of warlords against Zhang, defeated him, and forced Li Yuanhong to resign from the presidency. In his place a puppet president was installed. Eventually this whole sequence of events provided the background for Lu Xun's creation of the story "A Passing Storm."

At about this time, in August of 1917, Qian Xuantong began to come visiting. He urged Lu Xun to contribute a piece to *New Youth,* the journal then being published by another group of young intellectuals also attempting to spark a revolution in Chinese culture. Lu Xun's contribution to the magazine turned out to be "Diary of a Madman," the first truly modern short story—modern in content, structure, and language—in the Chinese literature of the period.

The story opens innocuously with a short introduction written in classical Chinese, explaining the origin of the diary entries that follow and assuring the reader that the madman author who penned them has now recovered. Proof of his recovery is claimed to lie in the fact that he has again taken his accustomed place within the official governing bureaucracy. The literary language of this introduction establishes a somber and impersonal tone, against which the colloquial language of the diary entries stand out in stark contrast. Through the fictional diarist Lu Xun delivers a withering attack on traditional Chinese society, portraying it as a cannibalistic feast with strong characters literally devouring weak ones while hypocritically cloaking their own barbarism in the high-sounding moralistic language of Confucianism. The ironic effects achieved by Lu Xun in this work made it not only the first short story of modern Chinese literature, but also one of the best.

With the exception of "Remembrances of the Past" (written in 1911), Lu Xun wrote all his short stories between 1918 and 1926. The first fourteen of them, collected under the title *Cheering from the Sidelines,* were completed over a five-year period between 1918 and 1922, while the eleven published in *Wondering Where to Turn* were all written within two years, during 1924 and 1925. Lu Xun was probably enabled to create these stories at this particular time because China was at last undergoing exactly that kind of revolution in culture that he and his brother had sought to encourage ten years before from Japan. Although various names have been used to refer to this Chinese cultural transformation, they are all misleading terms in one way or another. But since "May Fourth Movement" is the most commonly known of the historical epithets emerging from the period, we will adopt the term hereafter in reference to the events of this time.

Essentially, the developments leading up to the May Fourth Movement may be summarized as follows: after the abolition of the examination system, increasing numbers of Chinese youths received modern educations, both at home and abroad. As a result, the scope and audience of the mass print media widened, and these young people gradually became a force for change in China. The impetus to change was twofold. Imperialism from abroad threatened to end China's existence as a sovereign state, and feudalism at home in the form of traditional social patterns stifled innovation and freedom of choice among the young. After the establishment of the republic, the two evils were often perceived as symbiotically related—foreign imperial powers supported their favorite reactionaries in exchange for continued enjoyment of special privileges in China.

During the Versailles Peace Conference at the conclusion of World War I, news leaked out in China that Duan Qirui's warlord government in Beijing had agreed to let Japan take over Germany's "rights" in Shandong Province in exchange for Japanese military support that would enable Duan to put down his own competition at home. On May 4, 1919, students in Beijing staged a mass demonstration protesting the government's "sell-out" of the Chinese nation. Further demonstrations, student strikes, and boycotts of Japanese goods soon swept the major cities of China, until on June 28 Duan's government finally gave in to public pressure. Whatever Duan's original intentions may have been, the Chinese delegation in Versailles refused to sign the treaty. The students and their supporters had mounted a nationwide public opinion campaign against the government, and they had won.

This mass movement identified itself with, and gave fresh impetus to, the revolution in culture that had already begun in 1915 when a small group of capable young men began to publish a journal in Shanghai known as *New Youth.* Devoted to cultural, literary, and political themes, its material was written in literary Chinese in the same style as all serious journals of the time. Throughout Chinese history, the scholar-officials who governed the land and set the standards in matters of literary taste had considered colloquial Chinese, the language of everyday speech, appropriate only for popular novels. For any serious purpose—writing essays, history, letters, government documents—one had to write in the classical literary language, the language of the Confucian *Analects* and the *Mencius,* both written over two thousand years before. This was the language of serious books, a language one had to *see* written out in characters. Read aloud, it was not altogether intelligible—unless of course one quoted from one of the classics he had memorized as a youth preparing for examinations and a career in the civil service. Thus, it was nothing less than a bold and revolutionary step when, in 1918, these avant-garde young men began publishing *New Youth* in the colloquial language. Dismissing the *form* in which Chinese culture traditionally expressed itself, their attack on its *substance* was doubly effective.

Many of these young men were invited at about this time to join the faculty of Beijing University by Cai Yuanpei, the new and vigorous chancellor who had come to office in 1916 and had single-handedly transformed the university, changing it from an upper-crust school whose frivolous and wealthy students had once earned themselves the nickname "Brothel Brigade" into modern China's most prestigious institution of higher learning.

Lu Xun wished the *New Youth* group well. He had, however, become so disillusioned by the successive spectacles of a stillborn republic, two attempts at imperial restoration, and rampant warlordism that he could no longer approach the work of cultural transformation with the same high hopes he had held as a student in Japan ten years before. Within a few years, in his preface to *Cheering from the Sidelines,*[17] he would recall:

---

17. Published in 1923. As Wang Chi-chen first pointed out, the Chinese title *Nahan* suggests "cheering from the sidelines" in contrast to active participation. See Wang's "Lusin: A Chronological Record," *China Institute Bulletin,* vol. 3, no. 4 (January 1939).

> They were in the midst of publishing *New Youth* at the time. However, not only had no one come forward to approve of what they were doing, but no one had yet bothered to mount an opposition to it either. I knew that he [Qian Xuantong] must be feeling very lonely. Nonetheless, I gave this reply: "Suppose there were an iron room with no windows or doors, a room it would be virtually impossible to break out of. And suppose you had some people inside that room who were sound asleep. Before long they would all suffocate. In other words, they would slip peacefully from a deep slumber into oblivion, spared the anguish of being conscious of their impending doom. Now let's say that *you* came along and stirred up a big racket that awakened some of the lighter sleepers. In that case, they would go to a certain death fully conscious of what was going to happen to them. Would you say that you had done those people a favor?"
>
> "But since I'd awakened *some* of them, you can't say that they would have absolutely no hope of finding some way to break out."
>
> Yes, he had his point. Though I was convinced to my own satisfaction that it wouldn't be possible to break out, I still couldn't dismiss *hope* entirely, for hope belongs to the future. My conviction that such a thing would never happen wasn't sufficient grounds for entirely dismissing his hope that it *might*.

How seriously we are to take the studied negativity of Lu Xun's writing is a matter open to question. Ever concerned lest easy optimism soothe his readers into the same lethargy from which he sought to rouse them, Lu Xun remained rigorously pessimistic in his writing.

The period during which Lu Xun wrote his stories saw many changes in his private life. Ever since 1912, he had lived in the Shaoxing Club, a hostel that had been established by native Shaoxing men living in the capital.[18] In 1919, however, Lu Xun bought a house, traveled back to Shaoxing, sold the ancestral property there, and moved his family north to Beijing. The experiences of that trip provided material for one of Lu Xun's most beautiful and moving stories, "Hometown." The property he

18. There were many such hostels *(huiguan)* in Beijing, each established by men sharing common geographic origins, or sometimes a common occupation.

bought in the capital must have been fairly large, for in addition to Lu Xun himself, his wife, and mother, it also had to accommodate his two younger brothers, Zuoren and Jianren, as well as their wives and children.

In 1920—the year when the Ministry of Education declared the colloquial language to be the official medium of instruction throughout all of China—Lu Xun began to lecture on the history of Chinese fiction at Beijing University, in a course that eventually resulted in the first book-length study ever devoted to this subject.[19] Because women's emancipation contributed so much to the spirit of the May Fourth Movement, and was also so central a theme in Lu Xun's stories, we may also mention here that it was in the year 1920, too, that Beijing University first began to admit female students.

Two years later an intriguing foreigner, Vasily Eroshenko (1889–1952) arrived in Beijing. Born in the Ukraine, this blind Russian poet had lived in India, Burma, and Japan before coming to China.[20] In 1922 Cai Yuanpei invited him to Beijing University to lecture on Esperanto, a language in which he was something of an expert. But where would the university put him up? The solution, of course, was to put him at the Zhou family's house. Eroshenko knew no Chinese whatsoever but he spoke Japanese fairly well. What better place than the Zhou establishment, where Japanese was practically a second language. In fact, the pleasant stay with Lu Xun's family that was enjoyed by this Russian visitor is reflected in the stories "Some Rabbits and a Cat" and "A Comedy of Ducks."

But the family harmony that Lu Xun had hoped to enjoy did not last long, for he and Zuoren had a serious falling out—apparently because Lu Xun and Zuoren's wife could not get along together—bringing the situation to such a state that in 1923, accompanied by his wife and mother, Lu Xun finally moved out of the house.[21] It is difficult to establish in retrospect what was the exact nature of the quarrel, for neither brother ever discussed it in print. However,

---

19. *A Brief History of Chinese Fiction,* translated by Yang Hsien-yi and Gladys Yang (Peking: Foreign Languages Press, 1959).

20. Eroshenko had been deported from Japan in 1921 on suspicion of being an anarchist.

21. The new home that Lu Xun bought after moving out of the family quarters is now the site of the Lu Xun museum in Beijing.

the strain on their relationship did find its way into "Brothers," the only story where Lu Xun treats dreams as windows to the subconscious.

In his new and somewhat smaller quarters, the tempo of Lu Xun's writing increased, so that within two years he had completed the eleven stories collected in *Wondering Where to Turn:* he wrote four in 1924 and seven in 1925.

Beginning in 1925, personal and political events conspired to radicalize Lu Xun, to move him increasingly away from the indirect critique he could make through fiction writing to the open criticism of the political essay. A sinecure at the Ministry of Education, his literary research, creative writing, and part-time teaching posts—these had largely filled his life up to now. But from this point until his death in 1936 it would be student demonstrations, leftist organizations, occasional periods in hiding to avoid arrest, satirical essays written by the score, the support and encouragement of the leftist woodcut movement, and—yes—even love.

In 1906, as we have seen, Lu Xun had entered into an arranged marriage according to his mother's wishes. But while he had assumed financial responsibility for his first wife, he never loved her. And so far as we know there was no romance in his life whatsoever until 1925, when Xu Guangping, pretty, bright, and more than twenty years his junior, began to write to Lu Xun.[22] A Cantonese who had fled her home rather than submit to an arranged marriage, Xu Guangping was at this time a student at the Women's Normal College in the capital and had attended Lu Xun's classes there. Soon after initiating correspondence with her esteemed teacher, she became leader of a student movement organized to protest the Minister of Education's appointment of a conservative woman to the top position at her college. Lu Xun sided with the students and was temporarily dismissed from his post at the ministry. But this was a time of discontent outside the campus too: the people of Beijing were disappointed and disgruntled with the posture of the warlord government vis-à-vis the unreasonable demands of imperialistic foreign powers. In March of 1926, when a large group gathered before the Government House to protest

22. A record of their correspondence is preserved in *Letters From Two Places (Liang di shu),* published in 1933. An English translation is presently in preparation at Foreign Languages Press in Beijing.

the weak-kneed official attitude, police fired into the crowd, killing forty-seven and wounding one hundred and fifty people. One of Lu Xun's own students from the Normal College was among the dead. The vitriolic essays he wrote condemning the government for the atrocities committed on "this darkest day since the founding of the republic" caused Lu Xun's name to be placed on a list of fifty radicals who were marked for arrest. At first he went into hiding but then, toward the end of summer and accompanied by Xu Guangping, he fled Beijing.

She proceeded straight to a teaching post at the Women's Normal School in Canton while Lu Xun went on to assume a position at Amoy University that had been offered him by Lin Yutang, then dean of the College of Literature, who later would become internationally famous for his writings about China in English. Lu Xun was not happy at Amoy, in part because he shared little in common with the faculty there, a group of professors mostly Anglo-American in orientation. In part, however, we may assume that Lu Xun simply wanted to be reunited with Guangping. At any rate, he soon left Amoy to accept a position at Sun Yat-sen University in Canton.

While Lu Xun was teaching in Canton, Chiang Kai-shek's Nationalist Party adopted its policy of purging communists from its ranks, although they had been welcome as members since 1924. The subsequent bloodbath drove the vast majority of independent Chinese writers to the left, politicizing many who had previously taken only marginal interest in the state of society at large.[23] During the violence created by the purge, some of Lu Xun's own students were arrested and he was now powerless to help them.

In the fall of 1927, Lu Xun and Xu Guangping moved to Shanghai, where they lived as man and wife. Two years later they had a son, Haiying, Lu Xun's only child. Lu Xun would spend the last nine years of his life in modern China's most cosmopolitan, and most revolutionary, city. During these years he would devote his prodigious energies to cultivating younger writers, fostering the woodcut movement, translating, founding short-lived publishing ventures, lecturing, campaigning for the simplification of Chinese

---

23. The Nationalist Party had cooperated with the Communist Party since 1923 in forming a United Front against warlordism, but in 1927 it launched this brutal and bloody series of purges in a move to rid itself of all leftist influence. The purges were collectively known as the White Terror *(baise kongbu)*.

characters and their eventual replacement by an alphabetic writing system, and composing scores of the short, biting essays known as "miscellaneous writings" *(zawen).* Here in Shanghai Lu Xun would come to know communist activists and writers, would go underground himself to avoid possible arrest and execution, and would grow into the grand old man of China's leftist culture.

One after another, pulling them up from a seemingly inexhaustible source, Lu Xun hurled his daggerlike *zawen* at the Nationalist Party and all its rightist sympathizers. Terse, incisive, satirical in tone, and inimitably idiosyncratic, *zawen* flowed from his pen so rapidly and in such volume that they soon constituted the bulk of his creative work. Indeed, critics in the People's Republic of China have often valued Lu Xun's *zawen* over all his other writings, claiming they contributed more not only to literature but also to the Revolution. No contemporary of Lu Xun was able to match his achievement in this essay form, either in clarity of thought or brilliance of style. His *zawen* inspired a host of imitators, but none of them came even close to approximating the master's graceful yet deadly style. So popular were these politically charged pieces that writers in the communist base camps during the Anti-Japanese War (1937–45) attempted to use *zawen* "scalpels" to remove what they diagnosed as "malignant excrescences" within their own ranks. Finally Mao Zedong himself put an end to the practice, commenting that Lu Xun had employed the lethal *zawen* style only against his enemies.

The burgeoning of left-wing literature that followed in the wake of the terrifying purges of 1927 occasioned intense debate in China as to what leftist literature really should be. Lu Xun took part in these polemics and translated works of Soviet criticism, hoping to elevate the level of debate. The extent of his own leftward shift may be seen from the fact that in his inaugural address to the League of Left Wing Writers, an organization he helped found in 1930, Lu Xun suggested that the primary task of writers should be to serve the workers and the peasants. Given Lu Xun's view of Chinese society, this was a natural development in his thinking. But while he favored literature written in the *interests* of the workers and peasants, he scorned writers who pretended to know what workers or peasants actually *thought* and *felt.* Finally in 1931, observing that no contemporary left-wing writer actually came from peasant or worker stock, he said that the best works left-wing writers could reasonably hope to produce would be novels of "exposure," works depicting the revolt of petit bourgeois writers against their own class.

Throughout this period Lu Xun continued to argue against whatever he saw as illogical literary dogma, whether on the right or on the left. Against the rightists, he maintained that "human nature" in the abstract simply does not exist: in actual society one finds only *class* nature. Against the leftists, he pointed out that while it is true that all literature is propaganda, the reverse proposition does not hold—only *edifying* propaganda can be counted as literature. Understandably, Lu Xun was in his turn attacked from both the right and the left, but his own sympathies never wavered: he stood clearly on the left and maintained that anyone claiming to stand "in the middle" was a simply a rightist in disguise.

Since his earliest childhood Lu Xun had enjoyed reading illustrated books, and as he grew to adulthood he became exceptionally well informed about the history of woodcut printing in China. Little wonder, then, that he became an enthusiastic supporter of the Eighteen Society, formed in 1929, the eighteenth year of the republic. This was a group of revolutionary artists whose slogan was "out of the salon and into the streets." Lu Xun was drawn to their movement because woodcuts could readily be bent to political commentary, as Soviet and German artists had already demonstrated. In January of 1936, the last year of his life, Lu Xun wrote a preface to his own selection from the graphic art of Käthe Kollwitz, a German artist whose socialist and pacifist ideas he much admired. He commented that she had paid more attention to China than China had paid to her, for in 1931 she had been one of the signers to a letter of protest sent by the Progressive Writers and Artists of the World when the Nationalist Party secretly executed five young left-wing writers in Shanghai.

In literature and in art, then, Lu Xun consistently favored breaking down China's cultural walls so that she might look outward to the world—not to imitate, but to learn, and to share as well. As we have seen, he believed that China's cultural strengths shared the same cause as her weaknesses: her isolation from other major centers of world civilization, an isolation that had allowed China to develop independently, free from outside influence, but that also had deprived her of outside stimulation. Because of this belief, Lu Xun had been since early youth an ardent champion of translation and had himself become a prolific translator. In these final Shanghai years, too, he continually urged his fellow writers to bring more works of foreign literature over into Chinese, for translations, he argued, would make a greater contribution to the people than volumes of shoddy original work.

Four years after Lu Xun's death, Mao Zedong wrote of him:

> Lu Xun was a man of unyielding integrity free from all sycophancy or obsequiousness; this quality is invaluable among colonial and semicolonial peoples. Representing the great majority of the nation, Lu Xun breached and stormed the enemy citadel; on the cultural front he was the bravest and most correct, the finest, the most loyal and the most ardent national hero, a hero without parallel in our history.

Coming from Mao Zedong, such praise had the effect of virtual deification. Yet there is a certain irony in the fact that Lu Xun, a man who made a lifetime career of idol smashing, has himself become an idol over the years. In addition to the museums now devoted to him in China, there are photographs, posters, scrolls, and even hand-painted statues sold by the thousands.

Lu Xun responded to the dilemma posed by the massive onslaught of Western culture not by praising the glories of Chinese antiquity, nor by recommending wholesale westernization, but rather by helping China to look outward (through his translations) so that she might take her place in the modern world representing one civilization among many. He responded by attacking the old Confucian "man-eating" society at home (through his stories and *zawen*), a society so riven by inner conflicts that it could neither learn from the Western powers nor defend itself against their greed. During his earlier career he had already diagnosed China's illness, but he had no cure to offer. Later during the Shanghai years he took heart from the example of the Soviet Union and came to believe that communism would eventually bring about the cure: a classless society, one that would nurture the good in people rather than turning them into copies of Ah Q, the victimized and pathetic antihero of his longest and best-known work of fiction. At a time when his people were divided at home and despised abroad, it was the genius of Lu Xun that he could see himself as part of a world community of right-hearted people working for a better future. More than just a great writer, and without a trace of the sentimentality that often clings to those who preach the brotherhood of man, Lu Xun was one of our century's great internationalists.

The Stories

To characterize the twenty-five stories in *Cheering from the Sidelines* and *Wondering Where to Turn,* the term "classic" comes readily to mind. In the People's Republic of China, they have been read and reread; they are the subjects of seemingly endless commentary; and they have become the standard against which later works are measured. Varied in form, the stories draw on a mixture of influences, both Chinese and foreign, even while such influences do not provide, either singly or in combination, a simple explanation for these distinctive works. They are their own stories just as Lu Xun was his own man. Apart from their literary value, however, Lu Xun's *purpose* in writing each one of them was essentially the same as his larger purpose in turning from medicine to literature in the first place—he wanted to transform the Chinese psyche.

During his student days in Japan, Lu Xun and his lifelong friend Xu Shoushang often discussed three interrelated questions:

1. What is the nature of the ideal human being?
2. With respect to this ideal, what are the greatest deficiencies in the Chinese character?
3. What is the reason for these deficiencies?

With regard to the stories, their answer to the second question is most significant. They decided the most glaring deficiencies in the character of the Chinese people were (1) lack of love and compassion *(ai),* and (2) lack of honesty and integrity *(cheng).* This had come about, they concluded, because China had been twice occupied by foreigners: the Mongols who had established the Yuan dynasty (1279–1368) and the Manchus who established the Qing (1644–1911).

Close reading of the stories will show that by lack of honesty Lu Xun meant primarily the hypocrisy that arises when one either turns away from a painful reality or glosses over it with dishonest thinking until it is no longer recognizable for what it actually is.

Thus in "Soap" the middle-aged protagonist, whose Confucian upbringing has trained him to avert his eyes from all that is unseemly, cannot admit that the enthusiasm of his praise for the exemplary filial piety of an eighteen-year-old girl he encounters on the street stems more from his own repressed sexual desire than from admiration for her morality.

Lack of love and compassion is perhaps most poignantly documented in "Kong Yiji," where patrons at the *Prosperity for All* wineshop continue to taunt the failed old scholar even after both his legs have been crippled as punishment for stealing books and he is reduced to dragging himself about on his hands.

But if the Chinese people as a whole were deficient in love and in honesty, was Lu Xun exempt from the same charge? He himself provides an answer in an essay written in 1926: "It is quite true that I often dissect other people, but even more often—and more ruthlessly—I dissect myself."[24] The story "Brothers" is a case in point. Written two years after Lu Xun's split with Zhou Zuoren in 1923, it portrays the ostensibly selfless love of an elder brother for his younger brother in contrast to the specters of hostility that emerge at night in the elder brother's semiconscious dream awareness. Though we cannot be certain of the relationship between this story and Lu Xun's own personal life, it seems likely that in writing it he was indeed dissecting his own psyche, for from all testimony he had played just such a self-sacrificing role vis-à-vis Zhou Zuoren.

It is significant that almost half the stories are presented through a first-person narrator who usually, though not always, bears some resemblance to what we know of Lu Xun's personality. Indeed, Lu Xun was himself very much a part of the world he wrote about. He seldom analyzed it without also analyzing himself.

Still more complex are the "self-dissections" that take place in "Upstairs in a Wineshop" and "The Loner." In each of these stories, mirroring Lu Xun's own experiences, a young intellectual leaves a backwater childhood behind and receives a modern education that renders him politically and culturally sophisticated, so that he is no longer content with the status quo and longs for

24. "Postscript to *Tomb*" (Xie zai *Fen* houmian), in vol. 1 of *Lu Xun quanji* (Beijing: Renmin wenxue chubanshe, 1981), p. 284.

change. In the end, each of them fails, victimized by society and by the weaknesses in his own personality. Both stories are told by first-person narrators who, in the end, walk away from the failed protagonists with a sense of relief. Lu Xun shared many of the problems that weigh upon the protagonists of these two stories, but unlike them he chose hope instead of despair; like his first-person narrator, he walked away from the negativity represented by these two men. They stand for one side of the first-person narrator and one side of Lu Xun; they are what Lu Xun and his first-person narrators *might* have become. In real life, Lu Xun had a friend very much like the protagonists of these two stories in the person of Fan Ainong (1883–1912).

Since both these protagonists are partly based on Fan, let us pause for a closer look at this singular man. A native of Shaoxing, Fan was one of the student group that Xu Xilin had taken with him to Japan in 1905, to study and to make revolution. Though Lu Xun had accompanied the delegation that went to welcome Xu Xilin and his students on their arrival in Japan, he had not taken any special notice of Fan Ainong. It was not until two years later that Lu Xun really noticed him—and then it was with contempt. A student meeting had been called to discuss the execution of Qiu Jin in Shaoxing as well as the barbaric circumstances surrounding Xu Xilin's death.[25] Most of the students, Lu Xun included, favored sending a telegram of protest to the imperial government in Beijing. Fan Ainong, seeing no point in what he referred to as their "stinking telegram," opposed them. Since Fan had been a student of Xu Xilin's, Lu Xun was outraged at such apparent detachment. In the end the telegram was sent, and Lu Xun was not to see Fan Ainong again for four years.

Having lost both his parents as a boy, Fan had been brought up by his grandmother. Upon her death, the uncle who was left in charge of the family finances refused to continue supporting his studies in Japan. Fan was forced to return to China where, since he was known as a student of Xu Xilin's, the government watched him closely. After a stint teaching at the Shaoxing High School, he went off into the countryside and, like the protagonist of "Upstairs

---

25. Lu Xun describes this meeting in "Fan Ainong," the last of ten reminiscences written in 1926 and published as *Zhaohua xishi* (Dawn Blossoms Plucked at Dusk). The English translation is by Yang Hsien-yi and Gladys Yang (Beijing: Foreign Languages Press, 1976).

in a Wine Shop," eked out a living there as a private tutor. Whenever he felt demoralized, he would boat into Shaoxing[26] to visit the wineshops for some serious drinking. On one of these excursions in 1911 he ran into Lu Xun, who later remembered having been somewhat surprised by Fan's changed appearance—his hair had turned grey and his seedy clothing suggested poverty. But this time, at any rate, he and Fan hit it off well. Thereafter, whenever Fan came to town he would bypass the wineshop and make for Lu Xun's place, where the two would chat and drink late into the night, often saying such extravagant things while well into their cups that Lu Xun's mother would laugh to overhear them. Lu Xun and a friend across the table from him over wine—it was a scene that would be reflected in both "Upstairs in a Wine Shop" and "The Loner." This was, moreover, no ordinary friend but one who, like the protagonists of those two stories, reflected the negative side of Lu Xun's own personality, one who fleshed out the possibility of failure.

When revolutionary troops liberated Shaoxing in the wake of the Republican Revolution later that year, the new military governor, Wang Jinfa (1882–1915), made Lu Xun director of the Shan-Kuai Primary Level Normal School and Fan Ainong dean of studies. For a brief period Fan was a changed man; he cut down on his drinking and wholeheartedly devoted himself to his new job. Soon afterwards, however, Lu Xun left Shaoxing to join the new Ministry of Education in Nanjing, and the director who succeeded him, a stodgy Confucian moralist, made things so unpleasant for Fan Ainong that he was eventually forced out of his job.

An abrasive fellow who found it difficult to get along with anyone, Fan found it impossible to secure another post and was soon reduced to real poverty. He pinned his remaining hopes on Lu Xun's finding him some sort of position at the ministry and wrote several times begging him to do so. In his depression he drank more and more heavily, and finally either fell or leapt—since he was intoxicated at the time, it is not clear which—to his death from a boat while returning one evening from an opera.

While Fan may have been the victim of an unfortunate environ-

26. The countryside surrounding Shaoxing is crisscrossed by canals. In this area boating was and still is a common form of travel. A boating expedition to and from a local opera is described in loving detail in "Village Opera."

ment, he was no doubt also the victim of his own idiosyncracies. He seems to have been a man who could never quite fit in, no matter where he was. One likely reason is that although he lived in a society built around carefully and minutely prescribed social distinctions based on position in the family, class, education, bureaucratic status, age, wealth, and so on, Fan behaved as though the social hierarchy did not exist. He simply ignored it, as does the protagonist of "The Loner" early in that story. Moreover, even after the military governor made Fan dean of studies at the normal school, he continued to wear the same shabby costume he always had worn—in fact, Fan dressed like a peasant, right down to the conical felt hat so typical of Shaoxing farmers and boatmen.[27] It is likely that Lu Xun admired this quirk in Fan Ainong, though he himself was largely a conformist in the matter of clothing.

Fan and the military governor Wang Jinfa had both been among the students taken by Xu Xilin to Japan, but Fan can hardly have known Wang well enough to justify the familiarity of his behavior in Wang's office on one particular day when he addressed the governor as "old chum," rubbed his palm back and forth across the military man's shaved head, and bemusedly congratulated him for having risen to so high a position. Fan's utter unawareness of—or perhaps it was contempt for—the social pecking order must have fascinated Lu Xun, who had come to see hierarchy as one fundamental problem of Chinese society.

Lu Xun received news of Fan Ainong's death on July 19, 1912. Three days later, after attending a farewell banquet for Cai Yuanpei, who had now been forced out of office by the conservative faction at the Ministry of Education, Lu Xun wrote three poems lamenting his old friend Fan. The last one of them said:

> While storms rage across the land,
> memory's eye turns to Fan Ainong:
> the grey of hair, so sparse and thin,
> the whites of eyes turned in scorn
> from bootlickers scrambling for place.[28]

27. Such hats are still worn today, and they are also sold to tourists at the souvenir stand in the Shaoxing Hotel.

28. In the original text, this line contains a pun on the name of a man well known to Fan and Lu Xun for sycophantic flattery toward his superiors.

And yet the world has never liked a food
that leaves a bitter taste;
nor will it long abide a man
whose words and ways are straight.

Still, who would have thought that
just three months after our parting,
you'd leave forever this world
in which you never fit?

It seems very likely that for Lu Xun, Fan represented negativity and despair. The protagonists of "Upstairs in a Wineshop" and "The Loner" both serve a similar function in relation to the first-person narrators who, at the end of each story, finally turn away from the hopelessness represented by these characters to get on with the business of life. And what was Lu Xun's own attitude toward the *to-be or not-to-be* of existence? At the end of "Hometown"—a story that reflects Lu Xun's 1919 trip down to Shaoxing to sell the family property and move his wife and mother north to Beijing—the narrator, having experienced profound despair at the changes in people he had fondly pictured through the distorting lens of childhood memory, offers this definition of hope: "Hope isn't the kind of thing that you can say either exists or doesn't exist. It's like a path across the land—it's not there to begin with, but when lots of people go the same way, it comes into being." Love and honesty, too, are not waiting out there somewhere to be found, but rather come into existence when people practice them. Here and there in the stories, we occasionally find characters who bring them into being. In "An Unimportant Affair," for instance, a simple rickshaw man shows through his actions that integrity and compassion *do* exist, by simply creating them before the astonished eyes of the narrator.

The best known and best loved of all his works of fiction, "Ah Q—The Real Story," is perhaps also the most eloquent of all the stories in documenting what Lu Xun saw as a lack of love and honesty in Chinese society. The only one of his works to employ the diction and structure of traditional Chinese popular fiction, "Ah Q—The Real Story" is a long and rambling tale that first appeared in serial installments in a newspaper. By his own testimony, in the character of his vagabond, ne'er-do-well protagonist

Lu Xun attempted to sum up all the psychological weaknesses of the Chinese people, the most debilitating of which was the inability to face up to the here and now of reality.

Unable to cope with the present, Ah Q flees into fantasies of a past in which his ancestors *were* rich and powerful (conservative Chinese scholars of the period were boasting of the glories of ancient China while disdaining the Johnny-come-lately accomplishments of the West) or escapes into a future in which his unborn children *will* be. When temporal escape is not feasible, Ah Q rationalizes failure into success; the reader sees him suffer defeat after defeat, each of which is immediately transformed into an inner, psychological victory. Such was the impact of the story that "Ah Q-ism" and "psychological victory" became staple terms of everyday conversation in China, and these terms are still occasionally used even today.

Apart from this psychological emphasis, "Ah Q—The Real Story" has historical implications as well. Set against the background of the Republican Revolution of 1911, the story lays bare with a few deft strokes the fatal weakness of that revolution: it had been a movement of the privileged, by the privileged, and for the privileged. The common people had not been involved. Here, as in much of his literary corpus—especially the satirical political essays to which he devoted most of his creative energies during the last decade of his life—Lu Xun showed an unusual gift in his singular ability to see clearly and to articulate succinctly what others had only suspected or dimly perceived.

In the world through which Ah Q moves, we see a lack of honesty and integrity at every turn, but still more disturbing is the utter lack of love and compassion that the story reveals as it unveils the society of Wei Village. This is a world where the strong bully the weak and the weak fawn over the strong. Power, money, prestige, and position in the hierarchy—these are all-important; love and compassion count for nothing.

The sixth entry of Lu Xun's first colloquial story, "Diary of a Madman," reads:

> Pitch black out. Can't tell if it's day or night. The Zhao family's dog has started barking again.
>
> Savage as a lion, timid as a rabbit, crafty as a fox . . .

This passage provides a good example of Lu Xun's style. He demanded that his readers approach his work with an active attitude of participation, and this is especially true of the stories. He disdained the traditional Chinese concept of fiction, which allowed the work only a limited role as a form of entertainment, a diversion the passive reader might use to while away the time. Within the context of "Diary of a Madman," Lu Xun expects the reader to perceive that entry six ("Pitch black out . . .") has articulated a basic truth about the world the madman inhabits. That world is a hierarchical nightmare where strong individuals bully the weak with the fierceness of a lion, while the weak victims fawn over the strong with the timidity of a rabbit. And when two people are unsure—on first meeting perhaps—of their relative positions in the lion-rabbit order of things, they behave with the craftiness of foxes until they are.

In his emphasis on the hierarchical nature of Chinese society, it is likely that Lu Xun was strongly influenced by Zhang Taiyan.[29] Zhang started from the assumption that the Chinese people needed a religion to promote their morality and to inspire their own faith in themselves. Whatever its other excellences, Confucianism could not serve this function because it was inextricably linked with status and privilege. Buddhism, on the other hand, was more egalitarian and had potential to unite people of high and low station in Chinese society. Unlike Confucianism, Buddhism was in its very spirit incompatible with class distinctions and should therefore prove attractive not only to the masses but also to intellectuals.

Lu Xun never accepted the proposition that Buddhism could save China. Nonetheless, Zhang Taiyan, through his criticism of the hierarchical nature of Confucianism, and because of the importance he attached to including the common people in any solution to China's many woes, exerted an influence on Lu Xun. During his period of relative hibernation in Beijing, between 1912 and 1918, Lu Xun made his own study of Buddhism and there is little doubt that his understanding of Chinese society was influenced by it. If we can speak at all of heroes and heroines in his stories, they are invariably individuals who represent the groups in Chinese society for whom Buddhism had the greatest appeal: women of all classes and the common people.

---

29. The summary of Zhang's thought that follows is based on Michael Gasster's *Chinese Intellectuals and the Revolution of 1911* (Seattle & London: University of Washington Press, 1969), pp. 198–200.

The Translations

Translating Lu Xun is difficult, for like Gogol—whom he so much admired—Lu Xun was a stylist. That is, we remember not only what he said, but also how he said it. His narrative voice is as distinctive as his thought. The Russian critic Kornei Chukovsky has described Gogol's style in words that apply equally to that of Lu Xun:

> Gogol's style is characterized first and foremost by startling verbal colors brought to such a dazzling shine that one delights in every line as a gift. And though you may know the entire text by heart, it is impossible to get used to its sustained revolt against the dull banality of predictably stereotyped speech and fixed, moribund forms.[30]

Is it possible, then, to translate a style as idiosyncratic as either Gogol's or Lu Xun's? This question is not easily answered. Chukovsky, playing the role of prosecuting attorney, criticizes a translation of *The Inspector General* that was published in the United States by Bernard Guilbert Guerney:

> Mr. Guerney was honor bound to reflect all this revolt against dead blandscript in the language of his translation, because this is precisely where the essence of wonder-working Gogolian stylistics lies. Not to reproduce this essence means not to give foreign readers the slightest notion of what Gogol is about. What Russian when he speaks of *The Inspector General* does not delightedly recall his favorite Gogolisms, without which *The Inspector General* is not *The Inspector General* to him? There is good reason why immediately after the appearance of *The Inspector General* all his quotable expressions and words were immediately taken into the everyday language by progressive young people of the time.[31]

Having leveled these charges, Chukovsky, who presents this discussion of the translator's art in the style of a courtroom trial, then turns about to play the role of defense attorney, pointing out the near-impossibility of bringing a style across from one language into another:

---

30. Kornei Chukovsky, *A High Art,* trans. Lauren G. Leighton (Knoxville: University of Tennessee Press, 1984), p. 122.

31. Chukovsky, pp. 122–23.

> So it is pointless for the prosecutor to attack Bernard Guilbert Guerney . . . with such unseemly fervor and to see in . . . blandscript something so serious as sabotage. It is impossible to bring people to trial because they are not magicians and cannot perform miracles![32]

Blandscript or an attempt at style? It is a difficult choice. I have opted for the attempt to suggest something of Lu Xun's style in English, for more than any other modern Chinese author, Lu Xun is inseparable from his style. I have tried to recreate the experience of reading Lu Xun in Chinese, often asking myself the question, "How would he have said this if his native language had been American English?"

One of the hallmarks of Lu Xun's style involves the contrast between the classical or literary language *(wenyan)* and the colloquial *(baihua)*. To be sure, his stories are written in the colloquial language, but it is a highly stylized colloquial, studded with words, phrases, and whole quotations from the classics.[33] This makes for a style that is particularly suited to the intention of the stories in that Lu Xun almost invariably quotes the classical language in a satirical vein, so as to disparage the tradition that language represents. Since in English we do not have ready access to a classical register, such contrasts are difficult to reflect in translation.[34] Throughout my translations I attempt to suggest these contrasts in a variety of ways: by using an inflated style; by italicizing certain words and phrases; by rhyming certain lines that were not rhymed in the original text; or by using some combination of these devices.[35]

By risking looseness in translation, I hope I have remained faithful to Lu Xun's texts. I have translated as I think Lu Xun might have written had his language been American English rather than Chinese. Chinese and English are very different languages and

---

32. Chukovsky, p. 130.

33. When I first looked through Lu Xun's letters, I was surprised to find that he could on occasion—in responding to the letter of a high school student, for example—write in a flat, purely colloquial and undistinguished style.

34. At an international conference on Lu Xun and his legacy held at Asilomar, California, in the summer of 1981, I touched on this problem in a question posed to Irene Eber of the Hebrew University of Jerusalem. Since Hebrew does encompass both a classical and a colloquial register, she happily reported that the same problem does not complicate the task of translating Lu Xun's stories into that language.

35. For example, the entire opening paragraph of "Diary of a Madman" is italicized and phrased in a stilted idiom.

being *too* true to one (except in the bloodless prose that one sometimes encounters in social science writing) can mean being false to the other.

In translating the stories, too, I constantly ran into the problem of selecting a tense, a problem that points up one characteristic of Lu Xun's style as well as a certain peculiarity of the Chinese language. As a language, Chinese concerns itself much more with the sequence and logic of events than it does with the exact time *when* those events occurred. In Chinese it is of course entirely possible to be precise in the matter of tense, but the point is—and this makes for numerous possible literary renderings—that one does not have to be so. This is one of the reasons it is virtually impossible to translate a Chinese poem into English: so many of them are cut free from time. They come to life and happen *while* you read them. Translate such a poem into English, add whatever inflections you deem appropriate, and though the translated poem may still reflect something of its original beauty, it will invariably lose the timelessness it had in Chinese. Similarly, many of Lu Xun's stories are written in a prose so sparsely supplied with the usual tense markers that their style approaches poetry.

I was particularly struck by the problem of establishing a tense in the course of editing my own translations. It baffled me to find that some seemed so different from the originals. I compared my own work with other translations and found that they also failed to reflect the *kind* of experience I enjoyed when reading the stories in Chinese. Finally it dawned on me that when I was reading the original text, I did not feel that what I was reading was happening in the past. This seemed to be especially true of the story "Medicine." So I then tried recasting the entire translation in the present tense and, though the result seemed forced in one or two places, on the whole it conveyed a more accurate reflection of the original Chinese than my initial translation had done. Aside from "Medicine," I have also recast "The Eternal Lamp" and "A Warning to the People" in the present tense. But the fact remains that in Chinese an artist like Lu Xun can fine-tune his tenses by suggestive degrees. Since in English we have only an off-on switch, there is no ideal solution to the problem.

All the stories in this book have been ably translated before.[36]

---

36. So far as I know, the only one for which I can claim a "first" is my translation of "Brothers," which first appeared in the inaugural issue of *Renditions* in 1973.

The first translation to be widely known in the United States was Wang Chi-chen's *Ah Q And Others* (1941), which included a critical introduction and eleven stories. Wang rendered the stories into a smooth and fluent American English. Next came the magnificent four-volume *Selected Works of Lu Hsun* by Yang Hsien-yi and Gladys Yang of the Beijing Foreign Languages Press (1956–1960), the first attempt at a systematic introduction to Lu Xun in English. The first volume contains eighteen stories along with a generous sampling of Lu Xun's prose poems and reminiscences, while the final three volumes consist entirely of the daggerlike *zawen,* essays on political and cultural themes for which he was justly famous. More recently the Yangs have also published a complete translation of the stories in two volumes, entitled *Call to Arms* and *Wondering* (both 1981).[37] Since the Yangs translate into a British English, however, I am entitled to the modest claim of being the first to translate all of Lu Xun's stories into the American branch of the language.

In supplying notes to the stories I have, if anything, erred on the side of abundance: a translator should provide enough documentation to ensure that the reader can achieve roughly the same understanding—or misunderstanding—of the text that he has himself. Furthermore, he should seek to win as wide an audience for the translation as possible, expanding the circle of readers beyond that group who will read the story in any case because they already are familiar with Chinese history and culture. Thus, although some of my notes may appear superfluous to some readers, I trust there will be others who find them useful.

37. It was my privilege to meet the Yangs while attending the centennial celebration of Lu Xun's birth in the summer of 1981. During the second of my two weeks in China, Mrs. Yang accompanied a group of foreign guests on a visit to Lu Xun's hometown. *Call to Arms* is the Yangs' translation of *Nahan,* the title I translate as *Cheering from the Sidelines.*

A NOTE ON PRONUNCIATION

The introduction and translations are larded with names of Chinese people, places, and things. The *pinyin* system of spelling Chinese has been used throughout. Some Chinese words are easily pronounced, others are not. This note is primarily intended to help with the latter. Although not alphabetic, the arrangement of names possesses some modicum of logic. In the course of this note, I often mention the Yale system of romanization because, while it is not as accurate as *pinyin,* it is sometimes easier for speakers of English to pronounce.

Abbreviations

MBA may be (roughly) approximated
CW Chinese word
EW English word
RW rhymes with
SL sounds like

Any word in quotation marks following either RW or SL is assumed to be English. For example, *mang* RW *gong* means that the Chinese word "mang" rhymes with the English word "gong."

Cai Yuanpei
INTRODUCTION

Let us begin with Cai Yuanpei. The *ai* in *Cai* RW *high.* Easy enough. The *c* sound, however, does not exist in English. *Cai* MBA by saying, *It's I,* and then dropping the initial *I.* (The Yale system spells this sound *tsai.*)

As with all Chinese names, the family name appears first, the given name second. *Yuan* MBA by saying *You Anne* rapidly enough to elide the two words; *pei* SL *pay.*

Yuan Shikai
PREFACE

Yuan as in the preceding entry. *Shi* MBA by saying EW *her* and then putting an *s* in front, *sher*—now take the vowel out and you will

	have something like CW *Shi.* (Yale spells it *Shr.*) *Kai* RW *sky.*
Master Yangsheng REMEMBRANCE	*Yang* RW *gong; sheng* RW *sung.*

While we are on names, how does one know where to break a given name into its typical two syllables? For the most part, this will be obvious; if it is not, remember that all Mandarin syllables end in a vowel, diphthong, *n, ng,* or—rarely—an *r.* Sometimes when the break is not apparent, *pinyin* indicates it with an apostrophe. Let us take some examples.

Hong'er HOMETOWN	The *Hong* in *Hong'er* is a sound which is rare in English, but easy to make. The *o* SL the *oo* of EW *hoot.* Substitute *ng* for the *t* in *hoot* and you will have something like CW *hong.* Perhaps some readers will remember the famous Soong sisters and their brother, T. V. Soong. *Hong* RW their surname (spelled *Song* in *pinyin* / *Sung* in Yale). The *er* is easy enough —SL the American pronunciation of EW *are.*
Kong Yiji KONG YIJI	While we are on the Chinese *ong* sound, it would be well to deal with this protagonist of the story by the same name. The *Kong* is very close to EW *coot,* with an *ng* substituted for the final *t.* The *Yi* SL the *e* in EW *she;* the *ji* SL *gee* as in *gee whiz!* Now back to the apostrophe.
Xiu'er SOAP	The *Xiu* presents us with the strange-looking initial *x.* For the purposes of rough approximation the English *s* sound will do. The *iu* part MBA by saying *yo* in EW *yo-yo.* Put an *s* before the *yo,* and you have something similar to CW *xiu.*

Quite a few *x* initials occur in the introduction and translations, both in names of real people: Xu Guangping, Xu Qinwen, Xu

Shoushang, Xu Xilin; and in names of fictional characters: Xia Yu, Sister Xianglin, and Xuecheng. Let us examine a few of the more difficult ones.

Xu Qinwen
HAPPY FAMILY

We do not have the *u* of *Xu* in English, although EW *you* will give a very rough approximation. Thus, *Xu* is like *see you* said rapidly enough to drop the *ee* from *see*. *Qinwen* MBA by saying EWS *chin one*.

Xu Guangping
INTRODUCTION

Lu Xun's second wife was also surnamed *Xu*. The *Guang* of her given name MBA by saying CW *wang* (RW *gong*) and then tacking a *g* on the front: *gwang*. (And the Yale system would spell it so.) CW *ping* SL *ping* in EW *ping-pong*.

Xu Shoushang
PREFACE

Shou SL *show; shang* RW *gong*.

Sister Xianglin
NEW YEAR'S

Xi in *Xiang* MBA by EW *see;* the *ang* of *Xiang* RW *gong; lin* SL *lean*.

huixiang dou
MEDICINE

Hui MBA by saying EW *way* and then putting an *h* in front of it; *xiang* as in the preceding entry; *dou* SL *doe*.

Kangxi
NEW YEAR'S

Kang RW *gong; xi* MBA by EW *see*.

mantou
MEDICINE

Man MBA by saying EW *man* (the *an,* however, is as close to EW *on* as it is to the *an* of EW *man*); *tou* SL *toe*.

Fan Ainong
INTRODUCTION

Fan MBA by saying EW *fan* (as in the preceding entry, however, the *an* sound is also close to EW *on*); *Ai* SL *I;* for *nong* drop the *se* from EW *noose* and replace with *ng*. (Yale spells it *nung*.)

Xuecheng SOAP	The *Xue* is a bit tricky. Say EW *yeah* (yes), then put a *w* between the *y* and *eah* and say *yweah*. This is roughly equivalent to the *ue* in CW *Xue*. Now put an *s* up front, say *syweah*, and you have something like CW *Xue*. CW *cheng* RW *sung*.
Lu Xun	While still on the *x* sound, let us take up the pen name of the author, Lu Xun (his real name was Zhou Shuren—*Zhou* SL *Joe; Shu* SL *shoe;* and *ren* SL *wren*). The *Lu* RW *do* and the *Xun* SL *see you* said rapidly, dropping the *ee* in *see* and then tacking an *n* on the end. (Yale spells this *syun*.)
Zhao'er SOAP	The *zh* SL the *j* in EW *jowl;* the *ao* RW the *ow* in EW *how*. (*Pinyin* would spell EW *how* as hao.) For *er* see the entry on *Xiu'er* above.
Zhuang Qiguang ETERNAL LAMP	First say *wang* for the *uang* (the *u*, after all, represents a *w* sound) so as to rhyme with EW *bong*, then put a *j* in front of it (for the *zh*) and you will end up with something like CW *Zhuang*. *Qi* is like the *chee* in EW *cheer; guang* should pose no problem, just put a *g* in front of the same *uang* sound that occurs in CW *Zhuang* and you will have something like CW *guang*. (Yale spells this one *gwang*.)
zha HOMETOWN	The name of this animal is quite easy. RW *pa* or *ma; zh* SL *j*. (Yale spells it *ja*.)
Zhang Xun INTRODUCTION	Again the *ang* RW *gong;* the *zh* SL *j*, giving us something which SL the surname of the American author Erica Jong. For *Xun*, see *Lu Xun* above.

Zhang Peijun
BROTHERS

Zhang as above; *Pei* SL *pay,* and *jun* MBA by saying EW *June.*

Zhao Sichen
Zhao Baiyan
AH Q

See *Zhao'er* above for *Zhao* and *Siming* below for *si.* The *ch* of CW *chen* SL the *ch* of EW *church; chen* RW *ton. Bai* SL *buy,* and *yan* SL *yen.*

Zhejiang

This is Lu Xun's native province. The *Zhe* SL the *uh* of the English expression *uh-huh* with an English *j* tacked on front: *juh; jiang* SL the *gee* of the English expression *gee whiz!* with the *ong* of EW *gong* tacked on the end *(gee-ong)* and said quickly as a single syllable.

Zijun
MOURNING

Zi is a bit tricky; it MBA by saying the *ds* in EW *suds* or *buds* (the result sounds like *dz,* the spelling Yale uses); EW *June* will give you a very rough, but acceptable, version of CW *jun.*

Juansheng
MOURNING

For Juansheng, the name of Zijun's lover, go all the way back to the pronunciation of Cai Yuanpei's name at the beginning of this note. Follow the directions for *yuan* and then put a *j* in front to make CW *Juan* (Yale spells *jywan*); the second syllable, *sheng,* RW *sung.*

Siming
SOAP

The *Si* in *Siming* is not pronounced like the English *sigh,* but very roughly like the *su* of EW *suds;* if you can make the *u* sound like a English *z,* you will be even closer (Yale spells it *sz*); *ming* rhymes with EW *sing.*

Zhou Zuoren
INTRODUCTION

The name of Lu Xun's younger brother appears quite often in the introduction and notes to the stories. The *Zhou* can be approximated, as noted above, by simply saying EW *Joe.* (The same name as China's famous premier, Zhou Enlai.) *Zuoren* presents some difficulties. The *z* is the familiar *ds* of EW *buds* while the *uo* MBA by saying EW *awe* and then tacking a *w* on front—*wawe*. Now say *ds-wawe* and you will have something like CW *Zuo; ren* SL *wren.*

Zhou Jianren
INTRODUCTION

This was the youngest of the three Zhou brothers. *Jian* MBA by saying EW *jenny* and then dropping the *y*. Note that all three brothers have *ren* as the last syllable of the given name. This serves as a generational marker.

Fang Xuanchuo
DRAGONBOAT

Fang RW *gong. Xuan* MBA by saying *See you, Anne* fast enough to fuse the words into a single syllable; *chuo* consists of the same *uo* encountered in Zhou Zuoren's name above (pronounced *wawe*—EW *awe* with a *w* tacked on the front) with the *ch* in EW *church* put in front of it: *chwawe.*

Kuoting
ETERNAL LAMP

The *uo* in *Kuo* MBA by saying *wawe* as in the previous entry; tack a *k* on the front and you have *kwawe,* which roughly approximates the sound of CW *Kuo. Ting* RW *sing.*

Qian Xuantong
INTRODUCTION

Qian SL *yen* with a *ch* as in EW *cheer* tacked on the front: *chyen; Xuan* as in the entry for Fang Xuanchuo above; *tong* MBA by saying EW *toot* while substituting an *ng* for the final *t.*

Qiu Jin
INTRODUCTION

For *Qiu* say the *chee* of EW *cheer* and then add the *o* of EW *go; Jin* SL *gin.*

Lü Weifu
UPSTAIRS

The *Lü* may be approximated by putting an *l* in front of EW *you.* Note this is not the same sound as the *Lu* in Lu Xun. The pronunciation of Weifu is obvious.

He

The surname He appears in a number of the stories. It is not pronounced like the English third person pronoun. The *e* comes from deep in the throat so that CW *He* sounds like EW *huh* in *Huh, what's that you said?*

He Goubao
REMEMBRANCE

Gou SL *go; bao* RW *how.*

Yaozong
REMEMBRANCE

Yao RW *how; zong* is difficult. Say the *ds* of EW *suds* then tack an *ong* on it. (The pronunciation of *ong* is explained in the Kong Yiji entry above.)

Seventh Sister Zou
AH Q

For the *Zou,* say the *ds* in EW *suds* and then tack EW *owe* onto it: *dsowe.*

Mother Liu
NEW YEAR'S

Liu is included because it is so often mispronounced. It does not SL EWS *Lee* (surname) and *you* said together, but more like EW *Leo* said as a single syllable.

Runtu
HOMETOWN

Going back to "Hometown" for a moment, let us take up one of the most difficult names. The *tu* in *Runtu* presents no problem. Say EW *two* and you will be close enough. For the *Run,* say EW *wood,* then replace the *d* with an *n.* Put an *r* in front of that and you will have something like CW *Run.* It is not an easy sound to make.

Wei Lianshu
LONER

Here is an easy one. *Wei* is just like EW *way. Shu* is just like the shoe that you wear. For *Lian,* take the English name *Lee* and tack EW *yen* on the end of it; now say the two words fast enough to elide them into a single syllable and you will have something like CW *Lian; shu* sounds just like *shoe* (footwear).

Gao Erchu VENERABLE	*Gao* RW *how. Er* is like the American-English pronunciation of *are; chu* is like EW *chew.*
Aigu DIVORCE	*Ai* SL *I; gu* SL *goo.*

For more accurate pronunciations than any of those given above, go to a good textbook on learning Mandarin or to a Chinese friend.

Diary of a Madman
and Other Stories

Remembrances of the Past

There was a large *tong* tree outside the gate of my childhood home. It must have stood more than thirty feet tall. Once a year clusters of nuts would cover it like stars spread across an evening sky, and the neighborhood children would invariably try to knock them down with pebbles. The missiles that were wide of their mark would continue in flight and occasionally would come through the open window of our family study and land on my desk, whereupon our family tutor, Master Baldy, would run outside and give the young miscreants a good scolding.

The leaves were almost a full foot in diameter but in the heat of a summer's sun they would knot up into tiny little fists. And then when the night air settled in, the fists would revive, open up, and stretch out like hands. At about the same time Old Wang, the family gatekeeper, would draw water from our well and damp down the ground to dissipate the residual heat of the summer day. Sometimes he would grab his pipe and a dilapidated stool to go off and swap stories with old Amah Li. When the moon had set and the only light to be seen was provided by the embers in Old Wang's pipe, you would still find the two of them sitting there trading tales. I remember once while Old Wang and Amah Li were out there enjoying the first cool of the evening, Master Baldy was just in the midst of having me do an exercise in poetic composition. He chose a two-word expression for which I was expected to provide an antithetical response. He picked the words *red blossom* and I came back with *green tong*. He waved my answer aside, saying I had violated the rules of poetic tonality. Then he ordered me to go back to my seat and do it over again. At the time I was only nine

---

The present translation is based on a copy of the original text that was published under the pen name Zhou Chuo in *The Short Story Magazine*, vol. 4, no. 1 (1913), obtained through the Photo-duplication Service of the Library of Congress. On the whole I have done an interpretive translation, drawing out certain implicit elements that a reader of the original text would have seen unaided by explication. The story has been translated into English once before by Feng Yu-sing as "Looking Back to the Past," which appeared in *T'ien Hsia Monthly*, vol. 6, no. 2 (February 1938): 148–59. Feng's translation omits some passages, the most important being the narrator's aside on the theory of evolution.

and had not the vaguest notion of what was meant by "poetic tonality," nor had he ever explained it to me. Nonetheless I went back to my seat and wracked my brains for a good long time without managing to come up with anything.

Very slowly, I stretched out my hand. I brought it down in a good hard slap against my thigh, as if I had just swatted a mosquito. I was hoping to make Master Baldy aware of the difficulties I was having in coming up with another answer, but he didn't pay the least bit of attention. After a long time he finally called out in that drawn out pedantic voice of his, "C-o-me . . . h-i-ther." I moved smartly forward "thither." He wrote out the two words *green grass.*

"*Red* and *flower* are both even tones," he said, "and must be balanced by *green,* which is an entering tone, and *grass,* which is a low one. Very well, that will do for today." Not waiting to be told twice, I made a dash for the door. Master Baldy raised his voice once again. "No bounding about!" I continued on out, refraining from anything that might resemble a "bound."

I went outside, but no longer dared to play under the *tong* tree. Previously I used to go there quite often and tug at Old Wang's knees, hoping to get him to tell me stories about the mountain people, but Baldy would invariably follow, screw up his face, and say, "What a boy! You oughtn't to waste your time in tom-foolery. If you've finished your supper, go back to your room and do your homework." If I didn't obey him instantly, then in class the next day he would be sure to whack me with a pointer and demand: "Why are you so good at making mischief and so poor at your studies?" Because it was so obvious that Master Baldy saw his classroom as a place for evening up old scores, I gradually began to dread going to school. If tomorrow wasn't Clear-and-Bright, or the Dragonboat Festival, or the Mid-Autumn Festival either, what did I have to look forward to?[1]

If only, early in the morning, I were to be taken ill and then got

---

1. The Clear-and-Bright Festival falls at about Eastertime. Generally the whole family makes an outing to the ancestral graveyard. Though the destination is not pleasant to think of, the trip is, and a boy might well look forward to it. The Dragonboat Festival falls on the fifth day of the fifth lunar month and involves, among other things, colorful dragonboat races on the river. The Mid-Autumn Festival celebrates the full moon of the eighth lunar month and is enthusiastically greeted by offering mooncakes to all one's friends, young and old alike.

well again in the afternoon, then I could have a good half-day's vacation. Better yet, why not let *Baldy* be taken ill? Or ideally, just let him die! If neither illness nor death overtook him, however, then there would be nothing for it but to go to school the next day and study *The Analects of Confucius*.

Sure enough, Baldy was there the very next morning, lecturing me on the *Analects* and wagging his head back and forth as he explained the meaning of each character. He was so nearsighted his lips almost touched the book, as if he were about to bite a few pieces out of it. People often accused me of being mischievous and liked to say that before I had finished half a chapter of my books, the pages were sure to be in a state of terrible disrepair. If they'd only known that all that huffing and puffing from Master Baldy's flaring nostrils did more damage to my books than I ever could have done! After the working-over he gave a text with his snorting, how could one *expect* the pages to be anything but raggedy? Of course the characters had become indecipherable—they had been "breathed" into indecipherability by old Baldy! No matter how mischievous I might have been, I would never have been able to mess up my book the way he did.

Master Baldy said, "Confucius said that by the time he was sixty, his *er* had become an obedient organ for the reception of truth—that's the *er* in *erduo* of our everyday language, meaning 'ear'—and that by the time he was seventy he could do whatever his heart desired without transgressing the bounds of morality."[2]

I didn't follow his explanations of the text because most of the words on the page were so obscured by the shadow of his nose that I couldn't make them out. The only thing I could see was a big bald head plunked down on top of the *Analects,* a head so polished and bright that I could see my face in it, though it did appear a little on the blurry side—not nearly so sharp and distinct as the reflection I got in the old pond out in the backyard.

As Baldy got into the swing of the text, he began to wobble his knees in rhythm with its cadences and nod his head in great sweeps

---

2. Master Baldy is discussing *Analects* 2.4. *The Analects of Confucius* is a record of the teachings of Confucius (551–479 B.C.), teachings of his disciples, and conversations between the master and his disciples. For over two millennia this text was the cornerstone of Confucianism, a work schoolboys had to know nearly verbatim in order to sit for the civil service examinations, which were not abolished until 1905. My translation of the passage roughly follows Legge.

of moral affirmation. He was having the time of his life. I on the other hand was growing very bored. To be sure, the reflection projected by his head was interesting enough to hold my attention, but after a while I tired of that too. How much longer could I take it?

Fortunately, at this very juncture, a strange voice was heard outside. "Master Yangsheng! Master Yangsheng!" It sounded as though it belonged to a man who had just witnessed a disaster and was sounding the call for help.

"Yaozong, my honored friend, is that you? Please come in!"[3] The Master stopped lecturing on the *Analects,* raised his head, and dipping and bowing as he went, made his way out to the gate, hands clasped respectfully before him in salutation.

At first I was hard put to understand why the Master should treat Yaozong with such deference. For although Yaozong belonged to the wealthy Jin family, our neighbors to the east, he always went around in threadbare clothing and worn out shoes. Since he lived on a meatless diet to save money, his face had become as yellow and swollen as an autumn eggplant. Even Old Wang did not go out of his way to be polite. "That fellow's only talent is hoarding money. But since he never parts with a penny of it, why should we servants go out of our way to show him respect?" Old Wang treated me very well, but was rather arrogant to our neighbor, although Yaozong never seemed to notice.

Actually, in intelligence Yaozong was no match for Old Wang. Whenever Yaozong listened to people telling stories, for example, although he was never able to catch the drift, he would nonetheless nod his head and say, "I see, I see!" Moreover, Amah Li once told me that from infancy to manhood, Yaozong had always been tethered so close to his parents that you would have thought he was their prisoner. Since he never got out of the house to meet people, he was a very clumsy conversationalist. If the talk turned to rice, then he would say something about rice, but he didn't know the difference between ordinary rice and the glutinous variety. If the topic was fish, then he would manage to say something about fish too, but he couldn't tell a bream from a carp.

Sometimes when he didn't understand, you would have to give

---

3. Lu Xun has given them satirical names: Yangsheng means "admirer of sagehood" and Yaozong means "a credit to his ancestors."

him several pages of the kind of commentary scholars do on the classics. In the commentary itself, however, there would be much that wouldn't get through to him, and you would have to provide a *sub*commentary. But even in the subcommentary there would still be ideas that would prove too much for him and in the end you would have to drop the whole thing without his having gotten any of it. Since that's the kind of man he was, nobody liked talking with him.

And yet, much to the amazement of Old Wang and the others, Master Baldy was very partial to him. In the privacy of my own mind, I too sought out the logic for this odd affection. I remembered that in the past Yaozong, having reached the ripe old age of twenty-one without having sired a son, had taken three pretty, secondary wives into his household. Just at this time, Baldy also began to repeat the saying *Three things do unfilial be / The worst is to lack posteritie*[4] and promptly invested thirty-one pieces of silver to buy a secondary wife. I concluded that Baldy treated Yaozong with such unusual courtesy because the latter was, by virtue of being two secondary wives up on him, so purely filial. Although Old Wang was wise in his own way, he was not, after all, so learned in classical morality as Master Baldy. No wonder he hadn't been able to fathom the depths of my teacher's wisdom in treating Yaozong with such deference. Even I had to wrack my brains for a good many days before coming up with an explanation for Baldy's strange partiality.

"Master Yangsheng, have you heard the news today?"

"News? What news?"

"The Long Hairs are coming!"

"Long Hairs? Haha, you must be joking."

What Yaozong meant by the Long Hairs was what Baldy called the "Hairy Rebels." Old Wang called them that too. They were the ones who had come around way back during the Taiping Rebellion.[5] Old Wang told me he'd been just thirty at the time, and since he was past seventy now, that would have been over forty years

---

4. The other two things were following parents' orders when such a course would sink them into unrighteousness and refusing to become an official when the parents are old and poor.

5. The most significant peasant uprising in Chinese history, the Taiping Rebellion (1851–64) was finally suppressed by the combined forces of the Manchu dynasty and imperialist powers.

before. Even a boy of nine like myself knew through simple arithmetic that there couldn't be Long Hairs around anymore.

"But I got the news from His Third Excellency over at He Market. He said they'd be here any day now."

"His Third Excellency? Then you got the news from no less a source than His Honor the Prefect. In that case it won't do not to be on our guard!" Old Baldy held His Third Excellency in even higher esteem than the sages of antiquity. Therefore, upon hearing this news, his face changed color and he began to pace around the desk.

"He said there were some eight hundred of them. I've already sent one of my servants back over to He Market to get the lay of the land and try to find out when the rebels will actually arrive."

"Eight hundred Long Hairs? How could *that* be? Maybe he means the Mount Dai bandits or the Red Turbans hereabouts."

Master Baldy's brain was in control again and even *he* realized there couldn't be Long Hairs around anymore. But what he didn't realize was that when Yaozong spoke, he lumped mountain bandits, ocean pirates, White Hats, and Red Turbans together as *Long Hairs,* just the same way he lumped carp and bream together as *fish.* And so when Master Baldy began making distinctions between Red Turbans and Long Hairs, it all passed right over Yaozong's head.

"We ought to have food prepared against their arrival. The reception hall in my home is only large enough to accommodate half of them, so I've made arrangements to use the Zhang Suiyang Temple to feast the other half.[6] Once they've had a good meal, they'll be in the mood to issue the usual rebel proclamation stating that they intend the populace no harm." Yaozong was pretty thick about most things, but at least his family had managed to inculcate in him the time-honored technique of feasting invading armies. Old Wang once told me about the time when Yaozong's father actually met up with the Long Hairs. He had only managed to escape by throwing himself on the ground and begging for his life. What was more, in token of his submission, he had knocked his head on the ground so many times that he raised a massive red

6. Zhang Xun died defending the city of Suiyang (in present-day Henan Province) against the An Lushan Rebellion during the Tang dynasty (618–907). A temple was erected in his honor.

lump on his forehead and ended up looking more like a goose than anything else. But at least the Long Hairs had not killed him.

Later on Yaozong's father had even set up a kitchen and gone into business as their cook, winning no small favor with the Long Hairs while turning a very handsome profit in the process. When the Long Hairs were finally defeated, he managed to dissociate himself from them and return to Wu Market. And then, little by little, he had managed to grow quite rich. So by comparison, Yaozong's plan of using one piddling meal to put these new invaders in a good mood was not nearly so farsighted as the stratagem his own father had employed.

"Throughout history, the fate of such enemies has always been short. Read *The "Outline and Mirror" Made Easy*[7] from one end to the other and how many instances do you find of such people ever succeeding? To be sure, there are isolated instances, but they are very rare. There's nothing wrong with feasting them, but Yaozong, my esteemed elder brother, see to it that you don't get *your* name linked up with theirs! Let the village headman arrange the matter of the feast."

"Just as you say! By the by, Master Yangsheng, could you write the two characters OBEDIENT SUBJECT on a poster to tack up on my gate?"

"Don't do anything like that just yet. One should never be rash about such things. If, after all, the rebels actually *do* arrive, there'll still be plenty of time for writing OBEDIENT SUBJECT posters to welcome them. Elder Brother Yaozong, there is something else you ought to bear *firmly* in mind: while it's true that one can't risk incurring the anger of such rebels, it is also true that one shouldn't get too close to them either. Way back when the Long Hair rebels came, on occasion even OBEDIENT SUBJECT posters didn't save the homes of the people who put them up. And then when the government armies returned to the area, the families who *had* put them up were in serious trouble. We had best wait until the rebels are on

---

7. Published by Wu Chengquan in 1711, this work *(Cangjian yizhilu)* was both an abridgment and temporal extension of two earlier works: *Comprehensive Mirror as an Aid to Governing (Zizhi tongjian)* by Sima Guang (1018–86), and a summary of this work drawn up later under the direction of the celebrated Song philosopher Zhu Xi (1130–1200), *Outline and Digest of the "Comprehensive Mirror" (Tongjian gangmu)*. The work mentioned here was essentially a chronology of Chinese history from the beginnings down to the end of the Ming dynasty (1368–1644).

the outskirts of Wu Market before taking up this business of posters. The only thing you ought to worry about now is seeing to it that your family finds a safe hiding place as quickly as possible, but don't make it too far away."

"You're perfectly right. I'll go over to the Zhang Suiyang Temple and tell the monks about our plans." Seeming to half-understand what he'd been told, Yaozong took his leave in a flurry of appreciation for Master Baldy's advice.

People used to say that my teacher, Master Baldy, was the wisest man in all Wu Market. They really had something there, for he could have lived in any age of chaos and come through it without a scratch. From the time when Pan Gu[8] created the universe on down through generation after generation of fighting and killing, through alternations of war and peace, through the waxing and waning of dynasties, Master Baldy's forebears had never laid down their lives to preserve a government, nor had they lost their lives by joining rebel causes. Their line had survived down to this very day so that Master Baldy might explain to mischievous students like myself the wisdom of Confucius, a man who had been able at the age of seventy to "do whatever his heart desired without transgressing the bounds of morality."

If you were to explain Baldy's talent for survival on the basis of the modern theory of evolution, then you might attribute his talent to racial heredity. But in retrospect, I believe this peculiar talent must have been gained solely from books. Otherwise how could you explain the fact that neither Old Wang, Amah Li, nor myself had inherited this kind of ability? None of us could have even distantly approximated the intellectual elegance he had shown in his advice to Yaozong.

After the latter had left, Baldy did not resume his explanation of the *Analects*. Looking somewhat distressed, he said that he was going back to his own home and dismissed me. In high spirits, I bounded out to the *tong* tree. Although the summer sun scorched my head as I ran about, I didn't mind in the least, for it occurred to me that this was the *only* time when the territory around the old tree was completely my own. Before long I saw my teacher hurry-

8. Pan Gu is usually pictured as a dwarf with two horns. He carries a hammer in one hand and a chisel in the other, symbolizing his role as creator of the universe. The job took him eighteen thousand years and when he had it all done, his body dissolved into the various parts of the world as we know it.

ing away with a big bundle of clothes under his arm. Normally he would go home only on the occasion of a special holiday or at the New Year's Festival. At such times he would invariably take along several volumes of a text on how to write those deadly eight-part essays that one had to compose when taking the civil service examinations.[9] But this time the entire set of the text remained sternly on his desk. He had taken with him only the shoes and clothing that had been stored in that broken-down trunk of his.

Looking around, I noticed there were more people on the road than ants on an anthill. They looked frightened and confused as they scurried this way and that. Most were carrying things, though a few were empty-handed. Old Wang said they were probably trying to get out before the rebels came. I noticed that among them there were quite a few people from He Market who were apparently fleeing to Wu Market. The residents of Wu Market, on the other hand, were obviously headed off toward He Market! Old Wang said he had been through this kind of thing before and there was no reason to worry just yet.

Amah Li had gone over to the Jin family compound to see what news she could get there. Now she came back and reported that the Jin family servants had not yet left to go back to their own homes. The only unusual thing she had noticed was a swarm of concubines gathering up their cosmetics, perfumes, silk fans, and sheer silk gowns, all of which they stuffed into their bamboo traveling cases. These secondary wives of the rich seemed to take being refugees with all the seriousness of going on a spring outing, and on a spring outing, of course, one simply couldn't do without lipstick and eyebrow pencil.

But I really didn't want to waste my time on the latest rumors about the Long Hairs. Instead I went off by myself and spent the afternoon catching flies, with which I baited ants to come out of their hills. Then I trampled them down and flooded the ruins in order to test the mettle of any "Yu the Great"[10] of the ant world who might still be down there. Before long I saw the sun suddenly

---

9. This was the *Baming shuchao* (1784), a work consisting of model essays for study by those learning to write the very formal eight-part essay required in the civil service examinations.

10. In ancient China, according to legend, there was a gigantic flood that destroyed virtually the entire country before Yu the Great finally brought it under control. The tomb of Yu the Great is located in Lu Xun's native Shaoxing.

drop behind the branches of the trees and heard Amah Li call me to dinner. I couldn't understand why the time had gone so quickly. Ordinarily at this time of day I would have been wracking my brains for an antithetical response to a pair of characters put to me by Master Baldy, and would have had to watch him make a face while he waited for my answer.

When the meal was over, Amah Li took me out into the courtyard. Old Wang had also come out to cool off. All of this was commonplace. What was not, was the group of local people gathered about Old Wang, mouths agape, looking as though some monster had just frightened them out of their wits. The beams of a beautiful moon highlighted the irregularity and discolorations of their exposed teeth so that one rather imagined a scattering of multicolored jade. Old Wang slowly smoked his pipe and paced his words to match.

"The gatekeeper here back then was Fifth Uncle Zhao. That guy was really thick. When the master of the house heard the Long Hairs were on the way, he ordered everyone to flee for his life. And guess what Zhao said? 'But if the Master leaves, then there won't be anyone here to look after things. I'll stay on so those ruffians don't take over the house.' "

"Aiya, how dumb can you get!" Amah Li suddenly cried out, hardly able to believe her ears yet glad for the chance to castigate a "former sage" like Fifth Uncle Zhao.

"And Old Lady Wu the cook didn't leave either. She must have been seventy-plus at the time. Holed up in the kitchen and wouldn't come out for dear life. For days on end she heard nothing but footsteps here and there and the howl of a dog off in the distance. It was enough to scare any man. Then even those sounds stopped. The kitchen felt so spooky she thought she was already in the world of the dead. Then one day, she heard the sound of marching men way, way off. By and by, she heard those same footsteps as they marched by outside the wall of the family compound.

"A little time went by. And then some more time went by. Suddenly dozens of Long Hairs burst into the kitchen. Knives in hand, they dragged Old Lady Wu outside. Their speech was so throaty it was more like a growl than anything else and she had trouble making it out. They seemed to be saying, 'Old woman! Where's your master? Hurry up and get us his money!'

"Old Lady Wu bowed and said, 'Great King, our Master has

run away. The old woman standing before you hasn't had a bite to eat in days and days and must now beg the Great King to give her some food. How could she have any money to present to His Majesty?'

"One of the Long Hairs laughed and said, 'If you really need something to eat, then we ought to feed you!' With a sudden movement he threw something round into Old Lady Wu's bosom. It was so matted with blood she had to squint before she could make out what it was—Fifth Uncle Zhao's head!"

"Aiya! Old Lady Wu must have dropped dead of fright!" Once again Amah Li interrupted this narration with a frightened cry. The listeners gathered around Old Wang were so astonished at this twist in the story that their eyes popped out even farther and their mouths gaped a bit wider.

"It happened something like this. Fifth Uncle Zhao staunchly refused to open up and even cursed the intruders. 'You ruffians only want to get in so you can loot the place!' Then the Long Hairs—"

Someone noticed that Baldy had just returned and asked, "Is there any news yet?" I thought I was in for it, but when I examined Baldy's expression I noticed to my surprise that his face seemed to have lost its usual sternness. And so I didn't follow my first inclination to skulk away. If only the Long Hairs would come again, I thought to myself, and toss Baldy's head into the arms of Amah Li, then I could spend every day flooding anthills and wouldn't have to study the *Analects* anymore!

"No, it's too early for news yet," Old Wang observed before continuing with his narration. "And then the Long Hairs smashed the door down. When Fifth Uncle Zhao came out and got a good look at the rebels, he was scared senseless. Then the Long Hairs—"

"Master Yangsheng! My servant has returned!" Yaozong shouted at the top of his voice as he entered our family compound.

"Well, how do things stand?" Baldy asked as he went forward to greet his friend, his nearsighted eyes stretched open wider than I had ever seen them before. Along with the others, I too made a beeline toward Yaozong to get the news.

"His Third Excellency said that the whole business about the Long Hairs is nothing more than a rumor. Turns out it was only a large group of refugees fleeing through He Market. By 'refugees'

His Excellency probably meant the kind of people who often come round to our homes begging for food." Yaozong, fearful lest the crowd not understand the word "refugee," used all the knowledge at his command to define it for them—barely enough to fill a single sentence.

"Haha! So it's only refugees!" scoffed Baldy as though making fun of his own previous stupidity in having been so upset. He began to chuckle at the very idea of "refugees," for that was not frightening at all. The crowd of local people that had gathered began to laugh too. It wasn't so much that they had understood what was going on; it was just that, having seen an important person like Master Baldy laugh, they felt it was their duty to join in.

After obtaining more accurate intelligence from His Third Excellency, the crowd dispersed in a lighthearted mood. Yaozong went back home too. The area under the *tong* tree was suddenly quiet. Only Old Wang and a few others were left. Baldy paced around for a long time and then announced that he was going home with the good news in order to reassure his own family. Saying he'd be back in the morning, he gathered up his volumes on how to write the eight-part essay and headed for the gate.

Just before leaving, he looked at me and said, "Since you haven't studied all day, how do you expect to have your text memorized well enough to recite it for me in the morning? Hurry up and get back to your books, and stop being so mischievous." Feeling more and more depressed, I fixed my eyes on the glow in Old Wang's pipe in order to avoid having to answer him.

Old Wang continued smoking. The flickering light in his pipe reminded me of an autumn firefly fallen into a pile of grass. Then I remembered how the summer before I had fallen into a pond of reeds while trying to catch one. Thinking about these things, I managed to put Baldy completely out of mind.

"Eh, how many times have I heard people say, 'The Long Hairs are coming'? When the Long Hairs really did come, it was terrifying. But what did it amount to, after all?" Old Wang stopped smoking and sat there slowly nodding his head in reminiscence.

"Old man, did you ever see the Long Hairs? What were they like?" asked Amah Li as soon as he paused.

"Were you ever a Long Hair yourself?" I asked hopefully. I thought that if the Long Hairs came, then surely Baldy would have to go. In that case, the Long Hairs must be the good guys. Continuing to follow this line of reasoning, I decided that since Old Wang was so nice to me, he must have been a Long Hair once himself.

"Haha! No, I wasn't. By the way, Amah Li, how old were you back then? I must have been twenty-something myself."

"I was only eleven when they came. My mother took me and ran away to Pingtian, so I never got a chance to see what they really looked like."

"I ended up at Mount Huang myself. Luckily, when the Long Hairs got to my village I happened to be away. My neighbor Fourth Niu and two of my cousins didn't get out in time and were taken prisoner. They dragged them out onto the Taiping Bridge and slit their throats. They were still alive when the Long Hairs threw them in the water. You know, that Fourth Niu was really something else! He could carry almost three hundred pounds of rice for a whole half mile! They don't make men like that anymore.

"Well anyway, by the time I got to Mount Huang, it was coming on to evening. The sun hadn't touched the tips of the tall trees on the ridge yet, but the ricefields at the foot of the mountains were already wrapped in dusk and a much richer green than they are during the day. When I got to the foot of the mountain I stopped to look back. Luckily nobody had followed me, and I felt somewhat safer.

"But then, looking ahead and not seeing a soul in sight, I felt so sad and lonely I didn't know what to do. After a bit I managed to pull myself together. Night began to close in around me and I felt even more isolated than before. Couldn't hear a human voice anywhere, but I did hear *JURP JURP . . . WOK WOK WOK*—"

"JURP JURP?" I was confused and the question escaped my lips without my knowing. Amah Li gripped my hand to signal me to be quiet, as though what I had in the back of my mind would bring calamity down upon her if I said it out loud.

"Only a frog. I heard some owls hooting too and that was really a weird sound. Say Amah Li, do you know that a lone tree in the darkness looks a lot like a man? Haha, but when you take a closer look, there's really nobody there. We were terrified of the Long Hairs when they first came, yet when they fell back in retreat and we villagers chased them with spades and hoes, then a hundred of them wouldn't dare to stand and fight ten of us. Later on, people took to fishing for treasures. Isn't that the way His Third Excellency from He Market got so rich?"

"What's 'fishing for treasures'?" I was confused again.

" 'Fishing for treasures'? Well, you see, whenever we villagers were right on the heels of a group of Long Hairs, they'd throw down whatever gold, silver, and precious stones they had to slow us down. They knew we'd all stop and scramble after stuff like that. I got a nice big pearl that way once myself. Must have been big as a marble, but I hardly had time to be surprised at my own good luck before Second Niu laid me low with a club and made off with it! Otherwise, though I'd never have gotten as wealthy as His Third Excellency, I'd probably be pretty comfortably off by now.

"He Goubau, His Third Excellency's father, got back to He Market at just about that same time. When he got home, he spotted a Long Hair who had tied his hair up into a big queue and was lying in wait inside a closet he'd broken into. Then he—"

"Oh-oh, it's raining. We'd better go to bed." Amah Li, seeing the rain, had decided to go in.

"No, no! Let's stay here!" I didn't feel at all like going in. I felt much as I did whenever I reached the end of a chapter in a novel. Just when the hero was in the most precarious situation, the novelist would close the chapter with the words: "If you want to find out what happened after this, then turn to the next chapter." I would usually not only turn to the next chapter, but read straight through the whole book as well. Amah Li was apparently not like me in this regard.

"Come on now, let's go in. If you get up late tomorrow Master Baldy will give you a good taste of his pointer."

As I put my head down on the pillow I heard the rain come down ever harder as it pelted the leaves of the plantain tree outside my window. I remember thinking how much it sounded like crabs crawling across the sand. And then, quite gradually, I didn't hear it anymore.

"Don't hit me, Master Baldy, I promise that I'll prepare my lesson next time . . ."

"Hey, what's going on here? Are you dreaming? With all that shouting of yours you scared me right out of my own nightmare. What are you dreaming about?" Amah Li came to my bed and patted me on the back several times.

"I'm okay. It was only a dream. Amah Li, what were *you* dreaming about?"

"I was dreaming about the Long Hairs! Tell you about it tomorrow. It's almost midnight. You'd better hurry up and get to sleep!"

WINTER 1911

CHEERING FROM THE SIDELINES

Preface

As a young man I had my share of dreams too. Later on I forgot most of them but saw nothing in the least regrettable about that. To be sure, reminiscence can afford us pleasure, but it can occasionally make us lonely too, and keep the threads of our spirits attached to still other periods of loneliness that have long since gone by. In that case, what point can there possibly be in reminiscing? The trouble is that I have not been able to forget everything, and the part I *haven't* been able to forget is the source of this volume, *Cheering from the Sidelines*.

There was a four-year stretch of my life when you would find me, almost on a daily basis, going into a pawnshop and then to an herb store. I've forgotten exactly how old I was at the time, but at any rate the herbalist's counter was just my height while the pawnbroker's was twice as tall as I was. I would hand clothing and jewelry up to the one twice my height, and having received the money along with the contemptuous looks of the proprietor, would then proceed to the counter that was my own size and buy herbs for my long-ailing father. Even after I got home with the medicine I still had my work cut out for me. You see, the doctor who prescribed for him was one of the best known in the area, and therefore the ingredients he required were often extra-special too: roots of reeds (only those gathered in winter would do), sugarcane (it had to have seen three frosts), mated crickets (only an original pair would do),[1] ardisia (it had to have seeded)—in other words, things that took a great deal of hunting. The upshot was that my father grew worse with every passing day and finally died.

I think anyone who tumbles from affluence into poverty will, on the way down, come to see the true face of the world. In retrospect, I see that my going to N and entering the K Academy was

The Preface was published separately in the Ten-day Literary Supplement column of the Beijing *Morning Post* on August 21, 1923. The collection *Cheering from the Sidelines* appeared in the same month.

1. If either one of the pair had ever had another mate, the couple would be morally tainted and thus lack medicinal power.

prompted by a desire to escape, to take a different path, to seek out a different kind of people.[2] Since there was no way to prevent my departure, Mother scraped eight dollars together for traveling expenses and told me to spend the money as I saw fit. She wept. Given the times, those tears were quite understandable too. Back then, the only proper path for a young man to follow was to study the classics and sit for the civil service examinations. Most folks thought that anyone engaged in what was known as "studying foreign things"[3] must be a down-and-outer at the end of his rope, with no choice but to sell his soul to the foreigners. Such a person was of course fair game for the most severe forms of ostracism and ridicule. And as if that weren't enough, my mother wouldn't get to see her son anymore either. But I couldn't let such considerations hold me back, and when all was said and done, I proceeded to N and entered the K Academy.

For the first time in my life I learned about the existence of such things as natural science, geography, history, drawing, and even calisthenics. Physiology was not taught, but we did get to see books such as *A New Exposition of Physiology* and *Chemistry and Hygiene.*[4]

Recalling the diagnoses and prescriptions given by my father's doctors and comparing them with this new knowledge, it gradually dawned on me that Chinese doctors were nothing more than quacks, whether intentional or unwitting. I began to conceive a great sympathy for all the sick people they had deceived, and for the relatives of those people as well. What was more, through reading translated histories, I had also come to know that by and large the modernization of Japan had had its beginnings in their study of Western medicine.

Such sophomoric bits and pieces of knowledge later caused me to register in a specialized school of medical studies, off in the

2. "N" is for Nanjing, "K" for Kiangnan (south China). Lu Xun entered the Kiangnan Naval Academy in 1898. The following year he transferred to the School of Mining and Railroads, which was attached to the Kiangnan Army Academy (also in Nanjing). Upon graduation in 1902 he was sent to study in Japan on a scholarship provided by the Manchu government.

3. The "things" were primarily foreign science and foreign languages.

4. These two works were translated into Chinese from English and published in 1851 and 1879 respectively.

countryside.[5] My dream was a beautiful one: after graduation, I'd go home and alleviate the suffering of all those unfortunates who had been victimized like my father. In the event of war, I'd become a surgeon in the military; and in any case, I would strengthen my countrymen's faith in modernization.

I don't know what progress has been made in the method of teaching microbiology nowadays, but back then slides were used to familiarize us with the forms of the various microorganisms. Occasionally, when one section of the course outline had been completed and there was still some time before the class period was over, the instructor would show slides of scenery or current events. The Russo-Japanese War [1904–5] was being fought at the time and, understandably, a good number of slides were devoted to the military situation. And so it was that I often had to become part of the fun as my classmates clapped and cheered. At the time, I hadn't seen any of my fellow Chinese in a long time, but one day some of them showed up in a slide. One, with his hands tied behind him, was in the middle of the picture; the others were gathered around him. Physically, they were as strong and healthy as anyone could ask, but their expressions revealed all too clearly that *spiritually* they were calloused and numb. According to the caption, the Chinese whose hands were bound had been spying on the Japanese military for the Russians. He was about to be decapitated as a "public example."[6] The other Chinese gathered around him had come to enjoy the spectacle.

Before that academic year was out I had already returned to Tokyo,[7] for after this experience I felt that the practice of medicine was nothing urgent to begin with, since no matter *how* healthy or strong the bodies of a weak-spirited citizenry might be, they'd still be fit for nothing better than to serve as victims or onlookers at such ridiculous spectacles. There was no need to fret about how many of them might die of illness. The most important thing to be

5. In Japan, where Lu Xun entered the Sendai Specialized School of Medical Studies.

6. The phrase *shizhong* in the original text (a Chinese and Japanese phrase) literally means "to show the masses." Before execution, criminals were paraded through the streets to "show the masses" what fate was in store for them if they committed similar crimes. This expression provides the title for the story "A Warning to the People"; the last chapter of "Ah Q—The Real Story" also depicts the same practice. Criminals are still paraded publicly as a deterrent to crime in China today.

7. In 1906.

done was to transform their *spirits,* and of course the best way to effect a spiritual transformation—or so I thought at the time—would be through literature and art.

All right then, I would promote a literary movement. There were droves of Chinese students in Tokyo studying everything from law, politics, physics, and chemistry on down to police administration and industrial planning, but not a single one was studying either literature or art. Even in such a cold and uncongenial atmosphere, however, I was fortunate enough to find a few like-minded comrades. We rounded up some other people who would be essential to our project and after some consultation, decided that the first order of business would be—what else?—to put out a magazine. The name of our publication was supposed to express the idea of "new life," but since most of us were somewhat classically inclined at the time, we called it *Renascence.*[8]

As the publication date of *Renascence* drew near, some of those who had agreed to contribute dropped out of sight. Hard on the heels of that, the capital we had counted on took off for parts unknown, leaving us with only three people[9] and no money. Since we had launched our venture against the tide of the times, of course we couldn't really complain all that much when it failed. Later on, even we three—each driven by the exigencies of his own individual fate—were no longer able to hang together and freely share our dreams for the future. Such was the end of our *Renascence,* which had actually never been born in the first place.

After that, I was assailed by a feeling of aimlessness, such as I had never known before. At first I was unable to identify the cause of this feeling, but later on I managed to think it out. When a man comes forward with an idea and others approve, that's enough to encourage him to go on; if they disapprove, that's enough to goad him into keeping up the struggle. But a *real* tragedy occurs when he cries out in the realm of the living and there's no response at all—no approval, and no opposition either. It was like finding myself

8. The distinction Lu Xun draws here is between classical or literary Chinese *(wenyan)* and the vernacular language *(baihua).* Although there is no "classical" English in exactly this sense, I have translated the title as "Renascence" to suggest the same distinction. This periodical *(Xin sheng)* is to be distinguished from *The Renaissance (Xin chao),* cited in n. 1 on p. 59.

9. The other two were Lu Xun's younger brother, Zhou Zuoren (1885–1966), and Xu Shoushang (1882–1948). A lifelong friend to the Zhou brothers, Xu was also a native of Shaoxing.

in the midst of a boundless and desolate plain where there were no reference points, nothing to lay one's hand to—an agonizing plight. At that point I began to realize that what I actually felt was loneliness, a loneliness that grew larger by the day and coiled round my soul like a giant poisonous snake.

And yet, though the experience brought me this gratuitous freight of sorrow, I didn't mind in the least, for it also forced me to examine myself, to see myself for what I really was. I recognized that I was *not* the kind of man who can heroically rally crowds to his side with the wave of an arm and the shout of a battle cry.

That feeling of loneliness, on the other hand, was far too painful to bear. I simply had to find some way of shaking it off. I tried everything I could find to drug my soul, to make myself sink back into the depths of my people, to retreat into the recesses of antiquity. In the following years, I personally experienced or was witness to things that carried an even greater freight of sorrow and loneliness, things I don't want to be reminded of, things whose very memory I would gladly have disappear into the earth together with my brain. And yet the drugging *was,* apparently, quite effective, for I no longer reacted to any of those things with the magnanimity and ardor of my youth.[10]

* * *

There is a three-room apartment in the S Club where, it is said, a woman once hanged herself from the locust tree in the court-

10. Among those "things" the abortive establishment of the new republic was no doubt foremost. Sun Yat-sen was sworn in as president of the Republic of China on January 1, 1912. Though he embodied the ideals of the young revolutionaries, Sun was forced in that same year to yield his office to Yuan Shikai, who had been a high-ranking military official under the Manchu dynasty. Sun had dedicated followers and ideals, but Yuan had troops and the outcome was never in doubt. Opposition to Yuan, however, mounted quickly and in 1913 Sun Yat-sen's Kuomintang (Nationalist Party) launched a punitive expedition against him. This "second revolution" failed and Sun fled to Japan. Thus the new republic was now firmly under the control of Yuan's military dictatorship.

In 1915 Yuan went so far as to declare himself emperor of a new dynasty. Disaffection in the provinces and his own death one year later put an end to his imperial ambitions but left the republic fragmented into several independent fiefdoms controlled by local warlords. During the summer of 1917 one of them, Zhang Xun, occupied Beijing. Both Zhang and his men still wore the queue as a token of allegiance to the now-defunct Manchu dynasty, and Zhang proclaimed its restoration. A coalition of other warlords, however, soon drove him out of the capital. They, in turn, forced the resignation of the president, Li Yuanhong, and replaced him with a puppet of their own.

yard.[11] Although by the time I arrived the tree had already grown so tall you couldn't reach the lowest branch, there was still no one staying there. For a period of several years I lived in those rooms, devoting whatever spare time I had to making copies of ancient inscriptions.[12] Very few guests came by to shake me from my lethargy and of course I encountered nothing in the inscriptions—no social problems, plans for reform, and so on—to pull me out of it either. And yet the span of my years was in fact silently slipping away. But that was exactly the way I wanted it.

On summer nights when there were lots of mosquitoes I would sit under the locust tree, cooling myself with a rush fan. When I looked up at the patches of blue black sky visible through cracks in the dense foliage, ice-cold caterpillars would often plop down on my neck. An old friend, Jin Xinyi,[13] would sometimes drop by for a chat. He would place his large briefcase on my rickety old table, throw off his long gown, and sit across from me. Because he was afraid of dogs, his heart would often still be pounding hard.[14]

On one such night he leafed through a volume of inscriptions I had collated and asked, "What's the point in copying these?"

"None."

"Then why do it?"

"No reason."

"I think you might write a little something."

---

11. The S Club, or Shaoxing Club, was a hostel in Beijing where Shaoxing hometowners could rent rooms and take their meals. There were many such clubs in the capital for people from various parts of China. Lu Xun, who was working in the Ministry of Education during this period, lived at the Shaoxing Club from May 1912 until November 1919.

12. According to Zhou Zuoren, Lu Xun took up this hobby in earnest in 1915, the year Yuan Shikai attempted to restore the former dynasty. Yuan's agents were everywhere, on the lookout for potential opposition. Having a time-consuming hobby (copying inscriptions, gambling, or even visiting prostitutes would do equally well) was an effective way of demonstrating that one was politically harmless.

13. A name used by Qian Xuantong (1887–1939). Like Lu Xun, Qian was a native of Zhejiang Province. He and Lu Xun had come to know each other well in Tokyo. A professor at Beijing University at the time of his visits to Lu Xun, Qian was a vigorous advocate of replacing classical Chinese with the vernacular language. Qian was a competent philologist and made many contributions to the standardization of pronunciations, the creation of a phonetic system to represent the sounds of Chinese in writing, and the simplification of the Chinese characters.

14. The gatekeeper at the S Club kept a dog.

I knew what he was getting at. They were in the midst of publishing *New Youth* at the time.[15] However, not only had no one come forward to approve of what they were doing, but no one had yet bothered to mount an opposition to it either. I knew that he must be feeling very lonely. Nonetheless, I gave this reply: "Suppose there were an iron room with no windows or doors, a room it would be virtually impossible to break out of. And suppose you had some people inside that room who were sound asleep. Before long they would all suffocate. In other words, they would slip peacefully from a deep slumber into oblivion, spared the anguish of being conscious of their impending doom. Now let's say that *you* came along and stirred up a big racket that awakened some of the lighter sleepers. In that case, they would go to a certain death fully conscious of what was going to happen to them. Would you say that you had done those people a favor?"

"But since I'd awakened *some* of them, you can't say that they would have absolutely no hope of finding some way to break out."

Yes, he had his point. Though I was convinced to my own satisfaction that it wouldn't be possible to break out, I still couldn't dismiss *hope* entirely, for hope belongs to the future. My conviction that such a thing would never happen wasn't sufficient grounds for entirely dismissing his hope that it *might*.

In the end, I did agree to write something for him. This was my first piece, "Diary of A Madman." Once started, I couldn't stop. And so I continued, from time to time, to do these short-story-like

---

15. Published monthly in Shanghai, *New Youth* was devoted to cultural, literary, and political themes. Between 1915 (when it was founded by Chen Duxiu) and 1921, it was the most influential publication associated with the New Culture movement. In 1918, the year of Qian's visits to Lu Xun, the magazine was placed under the rotating editorship of a six-man committee consisting of the founder Chen, Hu Shi, Qian Xuantong, Li Dazhao, Liu Bannong, and Shen Yinmo. Five of them were professors at Beijing University (usually abbreviated in Chinese as Beida, the *-da* being short for *daxue* or "university"), while Li Dazhao was a librarian there.

Cai Yuanpei (1888–1940), a respected elder to Lu Xun as well as his fellow hometownsman, became chancellor of Beida in 1916, following the death of Yuan Shikai, and remained in that position until 1926. Beida had previously been contemptuously referred to as the "Brothel Brigade," recalling one of the many nonacademic pursuits of its well-to-do students. Cai Yuanpei single-handedly transformed it into China's most prestigious center of higher learning and made it the fountainhead of the New Culture movement. Lu Xun's "they" most probably refers to Cai and the editors of *New Youth*.

pieces to satisfy the requests of my friends. As time wore on, I found I had accumulated more than ten of them.

For my part, I thought I had long since ceased being the kind of person who is bursting to share his message. And yet—perhaps because I had not yet succeeded in entirely purging my heart of the sorrow and loneliness I too had once experienced in bygone days —I couldn't resist cheering now and then from the sidelines so as to console those bold warriors still charging through the fields of loneliness, and to encourage them to ride on. As to whether the sound of my cheers was heroic, woebegone, detestable, or even downright ridiculous—I couldn't really be bothered about that. Since I *was* cheering, however, I had to obey the orders of the bold warriors still out on the field. Therefore it often happened that I did not balk at twisting things a bit on their command: in "Medicine" I have a wreath appear out of nowhere on Yu Er's grave, and in "Tomorrow" I don't go so far as to say that Sister Shan never did see her son in her dreams. At the time our frontline officers were in no mood to tolerate negativity. And for my own part, I had no desire to take the loneliness that still afflicted me and infect young people with it, young people who were still dreaming the same sweet dreams that I had dreamed when I was their age.

Since this was the way these stories came into being, the distance that lies between them and real art can readily be imagined. And yet to have the opportunity to gather them into a collection and have them graced with the title "stories" is an unexpected piece of good luck. Though such luck makes me uneasy, it is also gratifying to think that, for the time being at least, I still have readers.

And so I have gathered them together and handed them over to the printer. Finally, for the reasons set out above, I have entitled the collection *Cheering from the Sidelines*.

DECEMBER 3, 1922
LU XUN IN BEIJING

Diary of a Madman

There was once a pair of male siblings whose actual names I beg your indulgence to withhold. Suffice it to say that we three were boon companions during our school years. Subsequently, circumstances contrived to rend us asunder so that we were gradually bereft of knowledge regarding each other's activities.

Not too long ago, however, I chanced to hear that one of them had been hard afflicted with a dread disease. I obtained this intelligence at a time when I happened to be returning to my native haunts and, hence, made so bold as to detour somewhat from my normal course in order to visit them. I encountered but one of the siblings. He apprised me that it had been his younger brother who had suffered the dire illness. By now, however, he had long since become sound and fit again; in fact he had already repaired to other parts to await a substantive official appointment.[1]

The elder brother apologized for having needlessly put me to the inconvenience of this visitation, and concluding his disquisition with a hearty smile, showed me two volumes of diaries which, he assured me, would reveal the nature of his brother's disorder during those fearful days.

As to the lapsus calami *that occur in the course of the diaries, I have altered not a word. Nonetheless, I have changed all the names, despite the fact that their publication would be of no great consequence since they are all humble villagers unknown to the world at large.*

Recorded this 2nd day in the 7th year of the Republic.[2]

I

Moonlight's really nice tonight. Haven't seen it in over thirty years. Seeing it today, I feel like a new man. I know now that I've been completely out of things for the last three decades or more.

First published in *New Youth,* volume 4, no. 5 (May 1918). This was the first time Zhou Shuren used the pen name Lu Xun.

1. When there were too many officials for the number of offices to be filled, a man might well be appointed to an office that already had an incumbent. The new appointee would proceed to his post and wait until said office was vacated. Sometimes there would be a number of such appointees waiting their turns.

2. April 2, 1918. This introduction is written in classical Chinese, while the diary entries that follow are all in the colloquial language.

But I've still got to be *very* careful. Otherwise, how do you explain those dirty looks the Zhao family's dog gave me?

I've got good reason for my fears.

2

No moonlight at all tonight—something's not quite right. When I made my way out the front gate this morning—ever so carefully—there was something funny about the way the Venerable Old Zhao looked at me: seemed as though he was afraid of me and yet, at the same time, looked as though he had it in for me. There were seven or eight other people who had their heads together whispering about me. They were afraid I'd see them too! All up and down the the street people acted the same way. The meanest looking one of all spread his lips out wide and actually *smiled* at me! A shiver ran from the top of my head clear down to the tips of my toes, for I realized that meant they already had their henchmen well deployed, and were ready to strike.

But I wasn't going to let that intimidate *me*. I kept right on walking. There was a group of children up ahead and they were talking about me too. The expressions in their eyes were just like the Venerable Old Zhao's, and their faces were iron gray. I wondered what grudge the children had against me that they were acting this way too. I couldn't contain myself any longer and shouted, "Tell me, tell me!" But they just ran away.

Let's see now, what grudge can there be between me and the Venerable Old Zhao, or the people on the street for that matter? The only thing I can think of is that twenty years ago I trampled the account books kept by Mr. Antiquity, and he was hopping mad about it too. Though the Venerable Old Zhao doesn't know him, he must have gotten wind of it somehow. Probably decided to right the injustice I had done Mr. Antiquity by getting all those people on the street to gang up on me. But the children? Back then they hadn't even come into the world yet. Why should they have given me those funny looks today? Seemed as though they were afraid of me and yet, at the same time, looked as though they would like to do me some harm. That really frightens me. Bewilders me. Hurts me.

I have it! Their fathers and mothers have *taught* them to be like that!

3

I can never get to sleep at night. You really have to study something before you can understand it.

Take all those people: some have worn the cangue on the district magistrate's order, some have had their faces slapped by the gentry, some have had their wives ravished by *yamen* clerks,[3] some have had their dads and moms dunned to death by creditors; and yet, right at the time when all those terrible things were taking place, the expressions on their faces were never as frightened, or as savage, as the ones they wore yesterday.

Strangest of all was that woman on the street. She slapped her son and said: "Damn it all, you've got me so riled up I could take a good bite right out of your hide!" She was talking to him, but she was looking at me! I tried, but couldn't conceal a shudder of fright. That's when that ghastly crew of people, with their green faces and protruding fangs, began to roar with laughter. Old Fifth Chen ran up, took me firmly in tow, and dragged me away.

When we got back, the people at home all pretended not to know me. The expressions in their eyes were just like all the others too. After he got me into the study, Old Fifth Chen bolted the door from the outside—just the way you would pen up a chicken or a duck! That made figuring out what was at the bottom of it all harder than ever.

A few days back one of our tenant farmers came in from Wolf Cub Village to report a famine. Told my elder brother the villagers had all ganged up on a "bad" man and beaten him to death. Even gouged out his heart and liver. Fried them up and ate them to bolster their own courage! When I tried to horn in on the conversation, Elder Brother and the tenant farmer both gave me sinister looks. I realized for the first time today that the expression in their eyes was just the same as what I saw in those people on the street.

As I think of it now, a shiver's running from the top of my head clear down to the tips of my toes.

If they're capable of eating people, then who's to say they won't eat *me?*

---

3. The cangue was a split board, hinged at one end and locked at the other; holes were cut out to accommodate the prisoner's neck and wrists. *Yamen* was the term for local government offices. The petty clerks who worked in them were notorious for relying on their proximity to power in order to bully and abuse the common people.

Don't you see? That woman's words about "taking a good bite," and the laughter of that ghastly crew with their green faces and protruding fangs, and the words of our tenant farmer a few days back—it's perfectly clear to me now that all that talk and all that laughter were really a set of secret signals. Those words were poison! That laughter, a knife! Their teeth are bared and waiting—white and razor sharp! Those people are cannibals!

As I see it myself, though I'm not what you'd call an evil man, still, ever since I trampled the Antiquity family's account books, it's hard to say *what* they'll do. They seem to have something in mind, but I can't begin to guess what. What's more, as soon as they turn against someone, they'll *say* he's evil anyway. I can still remember how it was when Elder Brother was teaching me composition. No matter how good a man was, if I could find a few things wrong with him he would approvingly underline my words; on the other hand, if I made a few allowances for a bad man, he'd say I was "an extraordinary student, an absolute genius." When all is said and done, how can I possibly guess what people like *that* have in mind, especially when they're getting ready for a cannibals' feast?

You have to *really* go into something before you can understand it. I seemed to remember, though not too clearly, that from ancient times on people have often been eaten, and so I started leafing through a history book to look it up. There were no dates in this history, but scrawled this way and that across every page were the words BENEVOLENCE, RIGHTEOUSNESS, and MORALITY. Since I couldn't get to sleep anyway, I read that history very carefully for most of the night, and finally I began to make out what was written *between* the lines; the whole volume was filled with a single phrase: EAT PEOPLE!

The words written in the history book, the things the tenant farmer said—all of it began to stare at me with hideous eyes, began to snarl and growl at me from behind bared teeth!

Why sure, *I'm* a person too, and they want to eat *me!*

4

In the morning I sat in the study for a while, calm and collected. Old Fifth Chen brought in some food—vegetables and a steamed fish. The fish's eyes were white and hard. Its mouth was wide open, just like the mouths of those people who wanted to eat human flesh. After I'd taken a few bites, the meat felt so smooth and slippery in my mouth that I couldn't tell whether it was fish or human flesh. I vomited.

"Old Fifth," I said, "tell Elder Brother that it's absolutely stifling in here and that I'd like to take a walk in the garden." He left without answering, but sure enough, after a while the door opened. I didn't even budge—just sat there waiting to see what they'd do to me. I *knew* that they wouldn't be willing to set me loose.

Just as I expected! Elder Brother came in with an old man in tow and walked slowly toward me. There was a savage glint in the old man's eyes. He was afraid I'd see it and kept his head tilted toward the floor while stealing sidewise glances at me over the temples of his glasses. "You seem to be fine today," said Elder Brother.

"You bet!" I replied.

"I've asked Dr. He to come and examine your pulse today."

"He's welcome!" I said. But don't think for one moment that I didn't know the old geezer was an executioner in disguise! Taking my pulse was nothing but a ruse; he wanted to feel my flesh and decide if I was fat enough to butcher yet. He'd probably even get a share of the meat for his troubles. I wasn't a *bit* afraid. Even though I don't eat human flesh, I still have a lot more courage than those who do. I thrust both hands out to see how the old buzzard would make his move.[4] Sitting down, he closed his eyes and felt my pulse for a good long while. Then he froze. Just sat there without moving a muscle for another good long while. Finally he opened his spooky eyes and said: "Don't let your thoughts run away with you. Just convalesce in peace and quiet for a few days and you'll be all right."

Don't let my thoughts run away with me? Convalesce in peace and quiet? If I convalesce till I'm good and fat, they get more to eat, but what do *I* get out of it? How can I possibly be *all right?* What a bunch! All they think about is eating human flesh, and then they go sneaking around, thinking up every which way they can to camouflage their real intentions. They were comical enough to crack *anybody* up. I couldn't hold it in any longer and let out a good loud laugh. Now *that* really felt good. I knew in my heart of hearts that my laughter was *packed* with courage and righteousness. And do you know what? They were so completely subdued by it that the old man and my elder brother both went pale!

4. In Chinese medicine the pulse is taken at both wrists.

But the more *courage* I had, the more that made them want to eat me so that they could get a little of it for free. The old man walked out. Before he had taken many steps, he lowered his head and told Elder Brother, "To be eaten as soon as possible!" He nodded understandingly. So, Elder Brother, you're in it too! Although that discovery seemed unforeseen, it really wasn't, either. My own elder brother had thrown in with the very people who wanted to eat me!

My elder brother is a cannibal!

I'm brother to a cannibal.

Even though I'm to be the victim of cannibalism, I'm *brother* to a cannibal all the same!

5

During the past few days I've taken a step back in my thinking. Supposing that old man wasn't an executioner in disguise but really was a doctor—well, he'd still be a cannibal just the same. In *Medicinal . . . something or other* by Li Shizhen, the grandfather of the doctor's trade, it says quite clearly that human flesh can be eaten, so how can that old man say that *he's* not a cannibal too?[5]

And as for my own elder brother, I'm not being the least bit unfair to him. When he was explaining the classics to me, he said with his very own tongue that it was all right to *exchange children and eat them.* And then there was another time when he happened to start in on an evil man and said that not only should the man be killed, but his *flesh should be eaten* and *his skin used as a sleeping mat* as well.[6]

When our tenant farmer came in from Wolf Cub Village a few

5. *Taxonomy of Medicinal Herbs,* a gigantic work, was the most important pharmacopoeia in traditional China. Li Shizhen lived from 1518 to 1593.

6. Both italicized expressions are from the *Zuozhuan* (Zuo Commentary [to the *Spring and Autumn Annals*]), a historical work which dates from the third century B.C. In 448 B.C., an officer who was exhorting his own side not to surrender is recorded as having said, "When the army of Chu besieged the capital of Song [in 603 B.C.], the people exchanged their children and ate them, and used the bones for fuel; and still they would not submit to a covenant at the foot of their walls. For us who have sustained no great loss, to do so is to cast our state away" (Legge 5.817). It is also recorded that in 551 B.C. an officer boasting of his own prowess before his ruler, pointed to two men whom his ruler considered brave and said, "As to those two, they are like beasts, whose flesh I will eat, and then sleep upon their skins" (Legge 5.492).

days back and talked about eating a man's heart and liver, Elder Brother didn't seem to see anything out of the way in that either—just kept nodding his head. You can tell from that alone that his present way of thinking is every bit as malicious as it was when I was a child. If it's all right to exchange *children* and eat them, then *anyone* can be exchanged, anyone can be eaten. Back then I just took what he said as explanation of the classics and let it go at that, but now I realize that while he was explaining, the grease of human flesh was smeared all over his lips, and what's more, his mind was filled with plans for further cannibalism.

6

Pitch black out. Can't tell if it's day or night. The Zhao family's dog has started barking again.

Savage as a lion, timid as a rabbit, crafty as a fox . . .

7

I'm on to the way they operate. They'll never be willing to come straight out and kill me. Besides, they wouldn't dare. They'd be afraid of all the bad luck it might bring down on them if they did. And so, they've gotten everyone into cahoots with them and have set traps all over the place so that I'll do *myself* in. When I think back on the looks of those men and women on the streets a few days ago, coupled with the things my elder brother's been up to recently, I can figure out eight or nine tenths of it. From their point of view, the best thing of all would be for me to take off my belt, fasten it around a beam, and hang myself. They wouldn't be guilty of murder, and yet they'd still get everything they're after. Why, they'd be so beside themselves with joy, they'd sob with laughter. Or if they couldn't get me to do that, maybe they could torment me until I died of fright and worry. Even though I'd come out a bit leaner that way, they'd still nod their heads in approval.

Their kind only know how to eat dead meat. I remember reading in a book somewhere about something called the *hai-yi-na*. Its general appearance is said to be hideous, and the expression in its eyes particularly ugly and malicious. Often eats carrion, too. Even chews the bones to a pulp and swallows them down. Just thinking about it's enough to frighten a man.

The *hai-yi-na* is kin to the wolf.[7] The wolf's a relative of the dog, and just a few days ago the Zhao family dog gave me a funny look. It's easy to see that he's in on it too. How did that old man expect to fool *me* by staring at the floor?

My elder brother's the most pathetic of the whole lot. Since he's a human being too, how can he manage to be so totally without qualms, and what's more, even gang up with them to eat me? Could it be that he's been used to this sort of thing all along and sees nothing wrong with it? Or could it be that he's lost all conscience and just goes ahead and does it even though he knows it's wrong?

If I'm going to curse cannibals, I'll have to start with him. And if I'm going to *convert* cannibals, I'll have to start with him too.

8

Actually, by now even they should long since have understood the truth of this . . .

Someone came in. Couldn't have been more than twenty or so. I wasn't able to make out what he looked like too clearly, but he was all smiles. He nodded at me. His smile didn't look like the real thing either. And so I asked him, "Is this business of eating people right?"

He just kept right on smiling and said, "Except perhaps in a famine year, how could anyone get eaten?" I knew right off that he was one of them—one of those monsters who devour people!

At that point my own courage increased a hundredfold and I asked him, "Is it right?"

"Why are you talking about this kind of thing anyway? You really know how to . . . uh . . . how to pull a fellow's leg. Nice weather we're having."

"The weather *is* nice. There's a nice moon out, too, but I *still* want to know if it's right."

He seemed quite put out with me and began to mumble, "It's not—"

"Not right? Then how come they're still eating people?"

"No one's eating anyone."

---

7. Three Chinese characters are used here for phonetic value only—that is, *hai yi na* is a transliteration into Chinese of the English word "hyena."

"No one's *eating* anyone? They're eating people in Wolf Cub Village this very minute. And it's written in all the books, too, written in bright red blood!"

His expression changed and his face went gray like a slab of iron. His eyes started out from their sockets as he said, "Maybe they are, but it's always been that way, it's—"

"Just because it's always been that way, does that make it *right?*"

"I'm not going to discuss such things with you. If you insist on talking about that, then *you're* the one who's in the wrong!"

I leaped from my chair, opened my eyes, and looked around—but the fellow was nowhere to be seen. He was far younger than my elder brother, and yet he was actually one of them. It must be because his mom and dad taught him to be that way. And he's probably already passed it on to his own son. No wonder that even the children give me murderous looks.

9

They want to eat others and at the same time they're afraid that other people are going to eat them. That's why they're always watching each other with such suspicious looks in their eyes.

But all they'd have to do is give up that way of thinking, and then they could travel about, work, eat, and sleep in perfect security. Think how happy they'd feel! It's only a threshold, a pass. But what do they do instead? What is it that these fathers, sons, brothers, husbands, wives, friends, teachers, students, enemies, and even people who don't know each other *really* do? Why they all join together to hold each other back, and talk each other out of it!

That's it! They'd rather *die* than take that one little step.

10

I went to see Elder Brother bright and early. He was standing in the courtyard looking at the sky. I went up behind him so as to cut him off from the door back into the house. In the calmest and friendliest of tones, I said, "Elder Brother, there's something I'd like to tell you."

"Go right ahead." He immediately turned and nodded his head.

"It's only a few words, really, but it's hard to get them out.

Elder Brother, way back in the beginning, it's probably the case that primitive peoples *all* ate some human flesh. But later on, because their ways of thinking changed, some gave up the practice and tried their level best to improve themselves; they kept on changing until they became human beings, *real* human beings. But the others didn't; they just kept right on with their cannibalism and stayed at that primitive level.

"You have the same sort of thing with evolution in the animal world. Some reptiles, for instance, changed into fish, and then they evolved into birds, then into apes, and then into human beings.[8] But the others didn't want to improve themselves and just kept right on being reptiles down to this very day.

"Think how ashamed those primitive men who have remained cannibals must feel when they stand before *real* human beings. They must feel even more ashamed than reptiles do when confronted with their brethren who have evolved into apes.

"There's an old story from ancient times about Yi Ya boiling his son and serving him up to Jie Zhou. But if the truth be known, people have *always* practiced cannibalism, all the way from the time when Pan Gu separated heaven and earth down to Yi Ya's son, down to Xu Xilin, and on down to the man they killed in Wolf Cub Village.[9] And just last year when they executed a criminal in town, there was even someone with T.B. who dunked a steamed bread roll in his blood and then licked it off.[10]

---

8. Darwin's theory of evolution was immensely important to Chinese intellectuals during Lu Xun's lifetime and the common coin of much discourse.

9. An early philosophical text, *Guan Zi,* reports that the famous cook, Yi Ya, boiled his son and served him to his ruler, Duke Huan of Qi (685–643 B.C.), because the meat of a human infant was one of the few delicacies the duke had never tasted. Jie and Zhou were the last evil rulers of the Shang (1776–1122 B.C.) and Zhou (1122–221 B.C.) dynasties. The madman has mixed up some facts here.

Pan Gu (literally, Coiled-up Antiquity) was born out of an egg. As he stood up he separated heaven and earth. The world, as we know it, was formed from his body.

Xu Xilin (1873–1907) was from Lu Xun's hometown, Shaoxing. After studies in Japan he returned to China and served as head of the Anhui Police Academy. When a high Qing official, En Ming, participated in a graduation ceremony at the academy, Xu assassinated him, hoping that this spark would touch off the revolution. After the assassination, he and some of his students at the academy occupied the police armory and managed, for a while, to hold off En Ming's troops. When Xu was finally captured, En Ming's personal bodyguards dug out his heart and liver and ate them.

10. A similar incident is the basis for Lu Xun's story "Medicine." Human blood was believed to be a cure for tuberculosis.

"When they decided to eat me, by yourself, of course, you couldn't do much to prevent it, but why did you have to go and *join* them? Cannibals are capable of anything! If they're capable of eating me, then they're capable of eating *you* too! Even within their own group, they think nothing of devouring each other. And yet all they'd have to do is turn back—*change*—and then everything would be fine. Even though people may say, 'It's always been like this,' we can still do our best to improve. And we can start today!

"You're going to tell me it can't be done! Elder Brother, I think you're very likely to say that. When that tenant wanted to reduce his rent the day before yesterday, wasn't it you who said it couldn't be done?"

At first he just stood there with a cold smile, but then his eyes took on a murderous gleam. (I had exposed their innermost secrets.) His whole face had gone pale. Some people were standing outside the front gate. The Venerable Old Zhao and his dog were among them. Stealthily peering this way and that, they began to crowd through the open gate. Some I couldn't make out too well—their faces seemed covered with cloth. Some looked the same as ever—smiling green faces with protruding fangs. I could tell at a glance that they all belonged to the same gang, that they were all cannibals. But at the same time I also realized that they didn't all think the same way. Some thought *it's always been like this* and that they really should eat human flesh. Others knew they shouldn't but went right on doing it anyway, always on the lookout for fear someone might give them away. And since that's exactly what I had just done, I knew they must be furious. But they were all *smiling* at me—cold little smiles!

At this point Elder Brother suddenly took on an ugly look and barked, "Get out of here! All of you! What's so funny about a madman?"

Now I'm on to *another* of their tricks: not only are they unwilling to change, but they're already setting me up for their next cannibalistic feast by labeling me a "madman." That way, they'll be able to eat me without getting into the slightest trouble. Some people will even be grateful to them. Wasn't that the very trick used in the case that the tenant reported? Everybody ganged up on a "bad" man and ate him. It's the same old thing.

Old Fifth Chen came in and made straight for me, looking mad as could be. But he wasn't going to shut *me* up! I was going to tell that bunch of cannibals off, and no two ways about it!

"You can change! You can change from the bottom of your hearts! You ought to know that in the future they're not going to allow cannibalism in the world anymore. If you don't change, you're going to devour each other anyway. And even if a lot of you *are* left, a real human being's going to come along and eradicate the lot of you, just like a hunter getting rid of wolves—or reptiles!"

Old Fifth Chen chased them all out. I don't know where Elder Brother disappeared to. Old Fifth talked me into going back to my room.

It was pitch black inside. The beams and rafters started trembling overhead. They shook for a bit, and then they started getting bigger and bigger. They piled themselves up into a great heap on top of my body!

The weight was incredibly heavy and I couldn't even budge—they were trying to kill me! But I knew their weight was an illusion, and I struggled out from under them, my body bathed in sweat. I was still going to have my say. "Change this minute! Change from the bottom of your hearts! You ought to know that in the future they're not going to allow cannibals in the world anymore . . ."

II

The sun doesn't come out. The door doesn't open. It's two meals a day.

I picked up my chopsticks and that got me thinking about Elder Brother. I realized that the reason for my younger sister's death lay entirely with him. I can see her now—such a lovable and helpless little thing, only five at the time. Mother couldn't stop crying, but *he* urged her to stop, probably because he'd eaten sister's flesh himself and hearing mother cry over her like that shamed him! But if he's still capable of feeling shame, then maybe . . .

Younger Sister was eaten by Elder Brother. I have no way of knowing whether Mother knew about it or not.

I think she *did* know, but while she was crying she didn't say anything about it. She probably thought it was all right, too. I can remember once when I was four or five, I was sitting out in the courtyard taking in a cool breeze when Elder Brother told me that when parents are ill, a son, in order to be counted as a really good person, should slice off a piece of his own flesh, boil it, and let them eat it.[11] At the time Mother didn't come out and say there was anything wrong with that. But if it was all right to eat one piece, then there certainly wouldn't be anything wrong with her eating the whole body. And yet when I think back to the way she cried and cried that day, it's enough to break my heart. It's all strange—very, very strange.

12

Can't think about it anymore. I just realized today that I too have muddled around for a good many years in a place where they've been continually eating people for four thousand years. Younger Sister happened to die at just the time when Elder Brother was in charge of the house. Who's to say he didn't slip some of her meat into the food we ate?

Who's to say I didn't eat a few pieces of my younger sister's flesh without knowing it? And now it's my turn . . .

Although I wasn't aware of it in the beginning, now that I *know* I'm someone with four thousand years' experience of cannibalism behind me, how hard it is to look real human beings in the eye!

13

Maybe there are some children around who still haven't eaten human flesh.

Save the children . . .

APRIL 1918

11. In traditional literature stories about such gruesome acts of filial piety were not unusual.

Kong Yiji

The layout of wineshops in Lu Town is different from that in other places.

You usually have a large counter in the shape of a carpenter's square facing on the street. Behind the counter, hot water is always on the ready so that wine can be warmed at a moment's notice. When working people get off at lunch or supper, they'll head off to such places and lay down four coppers for a bowl of wine. (I'm talking about the way it was twenty-odd years ago; by now it's probably gone up to ten.) Leaning against the counter, they'll sip the hot wine and relax.

If a man's willing to part with another copper, he can even buy something to down the wine with—perhaps a saucer of bamboo shoots, or maybe some fennel-flavored beans. If he's got enough to lay down a dozen coppers or so, he can even get a meat dish. But most of the patrons at such places belong to the short-jacket crowd and aren't as rich as all that. It's only members of the long-gown crowd, the gentry, who can afford to saunter into the room next to the bar, order a main course, some wine to go with it, and then sit down and linger over their cups.

When I was twelve, I got a job as a waiter in the *Prosperity for All* over on the edge of town. The boss said I was too young and stupid-looking to wait on the long-gown crowd in the side room, but he *could* use me to help out behind the bar. Now the short-jacket crowd *was* easy to deal with, but even so there were quite a few of them who would run off at the mouth and stir up trouble there was no call for, just because they couldn't keep things straight in their own heads when they ordered.

So I'd ladle the yellow wine out from the big earthenware crock and into a pot, and they'd watch like hawks to make sure I didn't slip any water in. They never felt at ease until they'd seen the pot safely placed in the hot water. Under supervision like that, cutting the wine wasn't easy. And so it wasn't long before the boss decided I wasn't cut out for that job either. Luckily the person who'd got-

---

First published in *New Youth*, vol. 6, no. 4 (May 1919).

ten me the job had a lot of prestige, so the boss couldn't just up and fire me even if he'd wanted to. And so he made me into a specialist. From then on I would tend to nothing but the boring business of warming the wine.

From one end of the day to the other there I'd be, standing behind the bar. Though I performed my assigned task to the best of my ability, it was downright monotonous. And what with the stern face of the boss and the unfriendliness of the customers, I was never able to loosen up. The only time I *could* relax a bit, and even have a laugh or two, was when Kong Yiji came around. And that's why I still remember him even now.

Kong Yiji was the only customer in a long gown who drank his wine standing up. A big tall fellow with a scraggly grey beard, he had a face that was pale and wrinkled. And every so often, sandwiched in between those wrinkles, you'd see a scar or two. Kong wore a long gown just like the gentry, but it was so raggedy and dirty you'd swear it hadn't been patched or washed in at least ten years. When he talked, he always larded whatever he had to say with *lo, forsooth, verily, nay* and came out with a whole string of such phrases, things that you could half make out, and half couldn't.[1] Because his family name was Kong, people nicknamed him Yiji. They got the idea from the first six words of a copybook that was used in teaching children how to write characters: ABOVE—GREAT—MAN—KONG—YI—JI, a string of words whose meaning you could half make out, and half couldn't.[2]

One day he came to the wineshop and all the regulars, as usual, started to eyeball him and laugh. Somebody yelled, "Hey there, Kong Yiji, you've put a few new scars on that old face of yours!"

Without responding, Kong looked straight toward the bar and said: "Warm two bowls of wine and let me have a saucer of fennel beans." He set out nine coppers all in a row.

Someone else kept the fun going by shouting, "You must have been caught stealin' again!"

Kong Yiji opened his eyes wide in indignation and replied,

---

1. Primarily a written language, classical Chinese is not easily intelligible when spoken. Identifying himself with the scholar-gentry class that ruled China under the imperial system, Kong uses the bookish language of the classics in his everyday speech.

2. Copybooks were essentially lists of characters to be learned. Some of the words formed phrases, some didn't. The characters were outlined in red, and students would fill them in with their brushes.

"How dare you, without a shred of evidence, besmirch a man's good name and even—"

"What good name? Wasn't it the day before yesterday I saw you trussed up and beaten with my own eyes?"

Kong's face flushed red and the veins stood out on his temples as he began to defend himself. "The *purloining of volumes*, good sir, cannot be counted as theft. The *purloining of volumes* is, after all, something that falls well within the purview of the scholarly life. How can it be considered mere theft?" Tacked onto that was a whole string of words that were difficult to understand, things like *The gentleman doth stand firm in his poverty,*[3] and *verily* this and *forsooth* that. Everyone roared with laughter. The space within the shop and the space surrounding the shop swelled with joy.

From what I heard folks say when he wasn't around, it seemed that Kong really *had* studied the classics, but somehow or other had never managed to pass the civil service exams. Since he didn't know how to do anything else, he got poorer and poorer as the years rolled by. It finally came to the point where begging seemed the only out, but fortunately he could write a good hand and was able to keep his ricebowl full by copying books. The only trouble with that was that while he wasn't overly fond of work, he did like to drink. And so it wouldn't be too long before books, paper, writing brushes, and inkstone would all disappear—right along with the copyist.

After he'd pulled that a couple of times, nobody would hire him anymore. At that point, of course, Kong Yiji was really at the end of his rope and couldn't help but turn his hand to a little theft now and then. At our wineshop, though, he was a model customer, for he never let his tab pile up. To be sure, once in a while when he didn't have any ready cash, we'd have to put his name on the chalkboard, but he'd always pay us back before a month was out, and we'd erase it again.

After half a bowl of wine, the indignant red left Kong's face and his expression gradually returned to normal. But then someone else started in: "Kong Yiji, do you *really* know how to read and write?" Kong glanced sidewise at his interrogator with the disdainful air of one who is above getting into such a petty squabble. But

3. Quoted from *The Analects of Confucius* 15.1.3.

the man persisted. "How come you haven't managed to scrape up so much as half a *Budding Talent?*"[4]

There was an immediate change in Kong's expression. Now he looked totally crestfallen and his face was shrouded in grey. He kept on talking—more or less to himself—but every last bit of what he said was of the *lo-forsooth-verily-nay* variety that nobody could understand. At that point everyone roared with laughter, and the space within the shop and the space surrounding the shop swelled with joy.

At times like this, even I could join in the laughter without having the boss get after me. Besides, the boss himself would often pull Kong's leg just to get his customers into a good mood. Before too long, Kong Yiji would realize that it was impossible to carry on a conversation with the other patrons, and would be forced to turn to a mere lad like myself for companionship.

I remember one day he asked me, "Have you had any schooling?" I gave him something like a nod and then he said, "Since you've had some schooling, let me give you a little test. How do you write the character for 'fennel' in 'fennel-flavored beans'?"

"How does somebody who's not much more than a beggar have the right to test me?" I thought to myself and turned away, ignoring him as best I could.

Kong Yiji waited for a long time and then continued in earnest tones, "Don't know, do you? Well, I'll teach you. Remember it now, because later on when you're the manager, you'll have to write such characters on the checks."

It seemed to me I was a long way from ever becoming manager. Besides, my boss never wrote "fennel-flavored beans" on the checks anyway. I was amused, but running out of patience too. I answered in an offhand way meant to show that I didn't really care one way or the other. "Who needs you to teach me? Isn't it a grass radical on top with the character 'back,' like in the phrase 'back and forth,' on the bottom?"

Tapping two long fingernails against the counter and beaming with approval, Kong nodded and said, "Right, right! But there are four different ways of writing the bottom part. Do you know what

---

4. In ascending order the three civil service degrees were Budding Talent, Selectman, and Advanced Scholar.

they are?" Now I was really out of patience. I curled my lips in contempt and walked away. Kong Yiji had dipped his fingernails in the wine as he prepared to write all four of the different ways on the counter right then and there. But seeing that I wasn't the least bit interested, he let out another sigh and began to look depressed again.[5]

There were a couple of times when, hearing all the laughter, the neighborhood children came over and gathered round old Kong to get in on the fun. He'd give them some of his beans, one to a child. But when they were finished with what he'd given them, they would continue to stand around, eyes glued to the ones he still had left. Old Kong would become very flustered, stretch his fingers defensively over the saucer, bend down, and tell them, "I don't have too many left." Then he'd straighten up, wag his head from side to side as though intoning the classics and say: *"Few be my beans. Hath the gentleman many? Nay, he hath hardly any."*[6] At this point the children would scatter in gales of laughter.

Old Kong was a delight to have around, but when he wasn't there, we managed to get along just as well without him too.

One day, it must have been two or three days before the Mid-Autumn Festival, when the manager was making a leisurely check of his accounts, he took down the chalkboard and said with a start, "Kong Yiji's not been by in a long, long while—still owes us nineteen coppers, too!" Until he said that, I hadn't realized how long it had been since I had seen him.

One of the customers at the counter said, "How could he come? He's gone and gotten his legs broken."

"Huh?" said the manager.

"He was stealin' as usual. But this time he really slipped his leash. Went and stole from Ding the *Selectman*'s house. Now how are you gonna get away with stealin' a *Selectman*'s stuff?"

"What happened then?"

"What happened? Well, first off, he wrote a confession. Then

---

5. In the spirit of Kong's pedantry, the four ways of writing the character are (1) 回, (2) 囘, (3) 囬, and (4) 𡇒. The fourth is extremely rare.

6. This passage is from *Analects* 9.6.3. Hearing that he has been criticized for having practical skills (unlike the ideal gentleman who disdains practical things), Confucius explains that when he was young he lived in humble circumstances and thus had to acquire many practical abilities. He then asks rhetorically whether a gentleman has such abilities and answers that he does not. Kong's use of the quotation is bizarre but appropriate, because both he and the sage share the surname "Kong."

came the beatin'. They let him have it for a good part of the night and then they went and busted his legs on top of that."

"And then?"

"And then they went and busted his legs like I just said."

"Yeah, but what'd he do *after* he got his legs broke?"

"What'd he do? Who knows? Maybe he died."

The manager didn't ask any more questions, but went back to his accounts.

After the Mid-Autumn Festival the wind grew colder by the day.

Winter was near at hand. I stuck as close to the fire as I could, but even then I still needed to wear my padded jacket.

One afternoon when there wasn't a single customer in the shop, I was sitting behind the counter with my eyes closed when suddenly I heard, "Warm a bowl of wine." Although the voice was faint, it sounded quite familiar. But when I opened my eyes to look, there was no one there. I stood up and peered out over the counter. There, sitting at the bottom of the counter opposite the threshold, was Kong Yiji, his face so dark and worn I hardly recognized him. He was wearing a raggedy old jacket and his legs were crossed under him. Beneath his legs was a grass mat that was fastened by ropes to his shoulders. Catching sight of me, he said a second time, "Warm a bowl of wine."

The manager stuck his head out over the counter too. "Is that you, Kong Yiji? You still owe us nineteen coppers!"

Looking up in despair, Kong replied, "This time . . . why don't I pay you back *next* time? This time I've got ready cash. Make sure it's good wine."

As though nothing very unusual had happened, the manager smiled at Kong the way he always did and said, "So, Kong Yiji, you got caught stealin' again!"

This time Kong didn't try to put up any defense, but simply said, "Don't make fun of people!"

"Make fun of people? If you hadn't been stealin', how would your legs've gotten broke?"

"It was a fall . . . a fall . . ." The look in his eyes was a plea for the manager to drop the whole thing. By now several people had gathered round, and they all joined together with the manager in a good laugh.

I heated the wine and served it to him there by the door. He fished around inside his gown until he'd found four coppers. As he handed them to me, I noticed his palm was caked with mud. So he'd dragged himself there on his hands! Before long, he had finished his wine and then, amid the talk and laughter of the other customers, he laboriously hauled himself away on those same muddy hands.

Another long stretch of time passed without my seeing Kong Yiji. At the end of the year, the manager took down the chalkboard and said, "Kong Yiji still owes us nineteen coppers!" Around the Dragonboat Festival of the next year, the manager noticed yet another time: "Kong Yiji still owes us nineteen coppers!" But by the Mid-Autumn Festival of that year the manager said nothing. The New Year soon rolled around, but there was still no sign of Kong Yiji.[7]

I never saw him again—guess he really did die.

MARCH 1919

---

7. The Dragonboat Festival (the fifteenth of the fourth month, according to the lunar calendar) and the Mid-Autumn Festival (the fifteenth of the eighth month) were traditionally times for settling accounts, in addition to the lunar New Year.

Medicine

I

The second half of an autumn night. The moon is down and the sun has yet to rise, leaving nothing but the dark blue sky. Except for creatures that roam in the night, everything sleeps. Suddenly Big-bolt Hua sits up in bed. Striking a match, he lights a grease-coated oil lamp. The two rooms of the teahouse fill with a bluish light.

"Little-bolt's dad, are you going now?"[1] It's the voice of an older woman. From the little room behind the shop comes the sound of coughing.

"Mmm." Big-bolt listens, answers, buttons his clothes. He thrusts out his hand: "Better let me have it now."

Mother Hua fumbles around under the pillow, fishes out a bundle of money, and hands it to Big-bolt. He takes it, packs it into his pocket with trembling hands, and then pats it a few times. He lights a large paper-shaded lantern, blows out the oil lamp, and walks toward the little room behind the shop. There is a *shish shish* of bedclothes followed by a round of coughing. Big-bolt waits until the coughing has subsided and then calls out in low tones, "Little-bolt, there's no need to get up. The shop? Don't worry, your mom will take care of it." Big-bolt stands there listening until the boy is quiet; finally satisfied that his son has gone back to sleep, he leaves the room and walks out the front door.

The street is black and empty. He can see nothing clearly save for the grey road that lies before him. The light of the lantern shines upon his feet as they move forward one after the other. He comes across a few dogs on the way, but not one of them barks. Though the air is much colder than in the teashop, Big-bolt finds it refreshing. It is as though he were suddenly young again; as

First published in *New Youth*, vol. 6, no. 5 (May 1919).

1. "Little-bolt" is a childhood name signifying that the boy has been "bolted" fast to life. Thus the name acts as a charm against childhood accidents and diseases. His father is known as "Big-bolt" by the same logic we might use in referring to "Big Terror" when speaking about the father of a child nicknamed "Little Terror."

though he were gifted with magical powers; as though he now carried with him the ability to give even life itself. He lifts his feet unusually high and his steps are unaccustomedly long. The more he walks the more clearly he sees the road, and the lighter the sky becomes.

Single-mindedly going his way, Big-bolt is suddenly startled as he catches sight of another road in the distance that starkly crosses the one he is walking on, forming a T-shaped intersection with it. He retreats a few paces, finds his way to a closed store, slips in under the eaves, and takes up a position beside the door. After standing there for some time he begins to feel cold.

"Huh, an old man . . ."

"Seems happy enough . . ."

The voices startle him. As he opens his eyes to look, a couple of men walk past. One even turns his head and looks at him. Big-bolt cannot make out the face very well, but he does take note of the predatory gleam that flashes from the man's eyes. He has the look of someone who has long gone hungry and has just caught sight of food. Big-bolt glances at his lantern. It is already out. He pats his clothing. Bulging and hard, the money is still there. He raises his head and looks up and down the street. He sees strange looking people—two here, three there, two on this side, three on that—all pacing back and forth like so many demons. He looks hard, but can't find anything else that appears odd.

Before too long, he notices some soldiers moving about. Even in the distance, he can make out the white circles on the fronts and backs of their uniforms.[2] When they march past him on the way to the intersection, he sees that their uniforms are bordered with dark red. Now there is a chaotic flurry of footsteps, and in the twinkling of an eye a small crowd forms. The people who had been pacing back and forth in twos and threes suddenly flow together to form a small human tide that rushes toward the intersection. Just before reaching the head of the T, the tide breaks and forms a semicircle.

Big-bolt also looks toward the intersection but can see nothing except the backs of the crowd. Their necks are stretched out long,

---

2. The uniform of soldiers under the Manchu dynasty included two large round pieces of cloth (sewn to the front and back), on which the word for "soldier" or "brave" appeared.

like ducks whose heads have been grabbed and pulled upward by an invisible hand. All is silence. Then there is a slight sound, and then once more all is motion. There is a mass rumbling of feet as the crowd falls back again from the head of the T. They spill down the street past the place where Big-bolt is standing. He is almost bowled over in the crush.

"Hey there, give me the money with one hand and I'll deliver the goods into the other!" A man dressed entirely in black stands in front of Big-bolt. The beams from his eyes bore into Big-bolt like two knives, making him shrink to what seems half his original size. The man extends a large open palm. In the other hand he holds a bright red *mantou,*[3] its color drip-drip-dripping to the ground.

Big-bolt hurriedly gropes for the money. He trembles. He wants to give it to the man, but can't bring himself to touch the *mantou.* Losing patience, the man shouts, "What are you afraid of? Why don't you just go ahead and take it!" Big-bolt still hesitates. The man in black snatches the lantern from him and tears off the paper shade. He wraps the *mantou* in the shade, shoves it at Big-bolt with one hand, and takes the money with the other. Pinching the money, he turns and walks away mumbling to himself. "Old dummy . . ."

"Who are you gonna cure with that?" Big-bolt seems to hear someone ask, but he doesn't reply. His whole spirit is now concentrated on that package. He carries it as though it's the sole surviving male heir in a family that owes its precarious succession to the birth of a single male child in each of the previous ten generations. He puts everything else out of mind. He longs to take this package of new life, transplant it in his own home, and reap a crop of happiness. The sun comes out now, too. Before him it reveals a broad road that leads straight to his home; behind him it shines upon four faded gold characters marking the broken plaque at the intersection: OLD * * * PAVI ON * * * ROAD * * * INTER CTION.[4]

---

3. A large, steamed bread roll.

4. There is a street in Lu Xun's native Shaoxing called Pavilion Road. On a memorial arch at one intersection there is, in fact, a plaque that reads: OLD PAVILION ROAD INTERSECTION. Today a tall stone monument to Qiu Jin (1879?–1907) stands close by. She was an ardent revolutionary and younger cousin of Xu Xilin; see "Diary of a Madman," n. 9. Captured soon after the execution of her cousin in the wake of an aborted anti-Manchu coup, she was tried before a Manchu judge and decapitated at this intersection. See Introduction, pp. xvii–xviii and p. xviii, n. 13.

why tremble, why so scared? What's in package?

2

Big-bolt arrives home. The wooden flats that cover the front of the shop at night have long since been taken down. Row upon row, tea tables glimmer in the morning light. There are no customers. Little-bolt sits at a table in the back row eating. Large beads of sweat roll from his forehead. His thin jacket sticks to his spine. His shoulder blades protrude sharply from underneath, forming the character 八 on the back of the jacket.[5] Seeing this, Big-bolt cannot help but draw his eyebrows, relaxed just the moment before, into a tight frown. Eyes opened wide, her lips trembling, his wife comes out of the kitchen and rushes excitedly toward him.

"Did you get it?"

"Yes."

The couple go back into the kitchen for a brief discussion. Then Mother Hua leaves the shop, returning soon with a large lotus leaf —this she spreads out flat on a table. Big-bolt opens the paper shade of the lantern and uses this leaf to wrap the red *mantou* anew. Little-bolt has just finished eating. "Little-bolt, you just stay right where you are, don't come over here!" his mother orders in alarm.

Big-bolt adjusts the fire. He takes up the jade green package and the torn, red-splotched lantern shade and shoves all of it into the stove. A red-black flame shoots up and the teashop is permeated with a strange aroma.

"Smells good! Having a morning snack?" Hunchbacked Fifth Young Master has arrived. This is a man who spends all his days in the teashop, the first to arrive and last to leave. He sidles in behind a corner table facing the street. No one answers. "Frying up some rice?" Still no answer. Big-bolt hurries out and serves him tea. "Little-bolt, come in here," Mother Hua calls her son into the back room. A bench is placed in the middle of the floor. Little-bolt sits on it. His mother serves him something on a plate. It is round and jet black. "Eat it," she says gently. "It will make you well."

Little-bolt grasps the blackened object in both hands, looks at it as though he were holding onto his own life. He is taken by a strange feeling that no words will express. He slowly rolls his

5. 八 (read *ba*) is the Chinese character for "eight."

hands away from each other until the scorched crust cracks. A burst of steam issues forth and then disperses, revealing the two bready halves of the *mantou.* Before too long the whole thing is inside his stomach, and he has forgotten what it tasted like. There is nothing left but the empty plate before him. His father stands on one side, his mother on the other. They look at their son as though hoping to infuse one thing into his body and take out another. Little-bolt's heart leaps into his throat. There follows another bout of coughing.

"Sleep for a while and you'll be all better."

Following his mother's instructions, Little-bolt goes to sleep—coughing. Mother Hua waits until his breathing has smoothed out and then covers him lightly with a comforter that is composed entirely of patches, from one end to the other.

3

There are quite a few patrons in the shop now. Running back and forth from guest to guest with a large copper kettle in hand, Big-bolt is very busy. Dark lines circle both his eyes.

"Aren't you feeling well, Big-bolt? Are you sick?" asks one greybeard.

"No."

"No? I didn't think you could be—all smiles like that." The greybeard cancels the force of his initial observation.

"Old-bolt's busy, that's all. If it weren't for his son . . ." Before Hunchbacked Fifth Young Master has finished the sentence, a tough-looking man with a beefy face barges in. A large black shirt, buttons undone, hangs from his shoulders and is sloppily drawn together at the waist by a broad black sash. He no sooner sets foot in the door than he begins shouting at Big-bolt.

"Has he eaten it yet, Big-bolt? You're in luck, really in luck! If I wasn't the kind to keep right on top of things . . ." Big-bolt still has the kettle in one hand. He lets the other drop straight down to one side as a gesture of respect. Face wreathed in smiles, he stands and listens. Mother Hua comes out with tealeaves, a bowl, and even an olive. Though dark around the eyes, her face is beaming too. Big-bolt pours hot water over the leaves.

"A guaranteed cure! Completely different from anything else

you could possibly give him. Just think, you brought it home while it was still warm and he *ate* it while it was still warm." Beefy-face keeps talking at the top of his voice.

"Isn't that the truth! If it wasn't for your kind help, Big Uncle Kang . . ." Mother Hua is duly thankful.

"Guaranteed cure! Guaranteed! When you eat it while it's still warm like that, a *mantou* soaked in human blood is a guaranteed cure for any kind of T.B. there ever was."

At the mention of T.B. Mother Hua pales a bit. She seems somewhat put out with Big Uncle Kang, but covers it up with a bevy of smiles, mutters a few polite phrases, and walks away. Insensitive to her feelings, voice still cranked up to full blast, Big Uncle Kang keeps right on talking. Finally, with all his racket, he wakes up Little-bolt, who then accompanies his monologue with a round of coughing.

"So that's the way the land lies. Your Little-bolt's had a real stroke of good luck. With medicine like that, he'll be all better in no time at all. No wonder Big-bolt keeps going around smiling all the time." Even as he speaks, Greybeard walks over and stands in front of Big Uncle Kang. With lowered voice and in the most deferential of tones he says, "I hear the criminal you finished off today was one of the Xia boys.[6] Which one was it? What was it all about anyway, Big Uncle Kang?"

"Who *was* it? Mother Xia's son, who else? The young bastard!" Seeing that everyone has an ear cocked to what he's saying, Big Uncle Kang is unusually full of himself. His beefy cheeks and jowls bulge and his voice grows even louder. "Little punk didn't care about dyin', just didn't care about it, that's all! And you know, this time I didn't get diddley out of it, not even his clothes. The jailer Redeye Ah-yi got those. But if you wanna talk about people who *did* make out on the deal, Big-bolt here is number one on the lucky list. And right after him comes Third Master Xia. Without spending a single copper, that one ended up pocketing a reward of twenty-five ounces of snowy white silver."

Little-bolt slowly walks out of the inner room, his hands to his chest, coughing continually. He goes to the kitchen, gets a bowl of cold rice, warms it with boiling water, and sits down to eat.

---

6. Taken together, the two surnames Hua and Xia (the names of Big-bolt's family and the "criminal's" family) form an ancient designation for China.

Mother Hua follows and asks softly, "Are you any better, Little-bolt? Still hungry?"

"A guaranteed cure, guaranteed!" Big Uncle Kang gives Little-bolt a sidelong glance and then turns back to the group. "That Third Master Xia is right on his toes, you can believe me. If he hadn't turned the kid in, the whole Xia family would've been rounded up and executed, himself included! But now? Silver! You know, that little bastard was really too much—even tried to get the jailer to rebel against the emperor!"

"Aiya! Have you ever heard the likes of that?" A man in his twenties is filled with overweening righteous indignation.

"Well, it was like this. Redeye Ah-yi went to question him and find out whatever he could, but the Xia kid acts as though it's just a regular conversation and starts tellin' Redeye how the Great Manchu Empire belongs to all of us. Now stop and think for a second, does that sound like talk you'd expect out of a human being? Redeye knew right from the start there was no one in the kid's family except his old mother, but he never imagined he could be *that* poor—couldn't squeeze a single copper out of him. Now that means Ah-yi is pissed off to begin with, right? Then the Xia kid's gotta go rub salt in the wound by talkin' *that* kinda stuff. Well Ah-yi gave him a couple good ones right across the mouth!"

"When it comes to using a club or a fist, Elder Brother Ah-yi is a trained expert. I'll bet the Xia lad really knew he'd been hit." Over in the corner Hunchbacked Fifth Young Master comes to life.

"Gettin' hit didn't faze that punk one little bit. His only come-back was to say, 'Pitiful, pitiful.' "

"What's so 'pitiful' about hitting a young punk like him?" asks Greybeard.

With an expression of utter disdain, Big Uncle Kang looks at Greybeard and laughs coldly. "You didn't hear me right. The way the Xia kid had it was that Ah-yi was pitiful."

The eye movements of all those who hear this suddenly freeze, and there is a general lull in the conversation. Little-bolt has already finished his rice. Sweat oozes from every pore of his body and a steamy vapor rises from his head.

"*Ah-yi* was pitiful—crazy talk! That's just plain crazy talk!" says Greybeard as though he has just experienced a sudden enlightenment.

"Crazy talk, crazy talk," says the twenty-some-year-old as though the light has just dawned on him too.

In a flurry of laughter and conversation, the shop's customers liven up again. Taking advantage of the noisy confusion, Littlebolt now coughs to his heart's content. Big Uncle Kang walks over to him and slaps him on the shoulder. "A guaranteed cure! Littlebolt, you—you don't wanna cough like that! A guaranteed cure!"

"Crazy talk," says Hunchbacked Fifth Young Master, shaking his head.

4

The area by the city wall outside the West Gate was originally public land. Through it there winds a narrow path made by the countless steps of people taking shortcuts, a path that has now become a natural boundary. On the left lie the bodies of criminals who have either been executed or died in prison. Paupers are buried on the right. So many people have been brought here that the burial mounds on either side of the path now lie row upon row in great profusion like so many *mantou* set out for a rich man's birthday feast. The Clear-and-Bright Festival this year is so unseasonably cold that the willows have barely managed to sprout tiny buds half the size of rice grains.[7] Though the sun has not long been up, Mother Hua has already set out four plates of various foods and one bowl of rice before a burial mound to the right of the path. Having done with her weeping and having burned her paper money, she now sits blankly on the ground. She is apparently waiting for something, though she herself cannot say what. A light breeze springs up and fluffs her short hair which shows more white in it than there was at this time last year.

Another woman comes along the path. Like Mother Hua, her hair is also half-white and her clothes are tattered. She carries a round and battered red basket with a string of paper money draped over it. Every few steps she stops to rest. All of a sudden she notices Mother Hua sitting on the ground watching her. She hesitates. A look of shame crosses her pale face. Finally she braces

7. The Clear-and-Bright Festival, a traditional time for visiting graves, falls in early April.

herself, walks to a burial mound to the left of the path, and puts down the basket.

This burial mound is directly across from Little-bolt's, separated only by the narrow path. Mother Hua watches as the woman sets out four plates of various foods and one bowl of rice, watches as the woman weeps and burns the paper money.

"That burial mound holds a son, too," Mother Hua thinks to herself. The other woman paces to and fro, obviously reluctant to leave. She looks all around. Suddenly her hands and feet begin to tremble. She staggers back a few steps and stands there staring, wide-eyed.

Fearing that grief is about to deprive the woman of her senses, Mother Hua stands up, crosses the path, and gently addresses her. "Try not to take it so hard, old mother. Why don't we both go home now."

The other woman nods, but her eyes do not move from the spot on which they are fixed. Her voice is gentle, too, as she stammers, "Look . . . look there . . . what . . . what's that?"

Mother Hua looks in the direction the woman is pointing, to the burial mound in front of them. The grass does not yet entirely cover it, and here and there pieces of yellow earth show through, lending a very ugly appearance to the entire mound. As Mother Hua examines it closely, she too cannot help but be startled—a circle of red and white flowers surrounds the peak of the mound! Though age has already dimmed their eyes for a good many years, the two women see those red and white flowers quite clearly. There are just a few and they have been arranged into a wreath which, while not luxuriant, is neat and tidy.

Mother Hua hurriedly glances at her own son's mound as well as those around it—nothing but a few pale blue flowers that have proved hardy enough to withstand the cold. Deep in her heart Mother Hua is suddenly aware of a certain lack, an emptiness. It is a feeling she doesn't want to pursue.

Mother Xia advances a few steps and examines her son's mound more closely. "There are no roots to those flowers," she says to herself. "They couldn't have grown there. Who could have come? Children aren't going to come to a place like this to play, and our clansmen stopped coming a long time ago. How could those flowers possibly have gotten here?" She thinks and thinks.

Suddenly she bursts into tears and cries, "Yu, my son, they've convicted you unjustly.[8] You can't forget the wrong they've done you. It's still making you suffer. Is it *you* who put the flowers here to let me know what a terrible injustice they've done you?"

She looks all around but sees nothing except a crow perched on a leafless tree. "I know they've wronged you . . . Yu, my poor, poor baby, they've wronged you in every way. But Heaven knows the truth of it. Sooner or later they'll get what they deserve. You just close your eyes in peace . . . If you really *are* here and understand what I've just said, make that crow fly over and perch on your mound as a sign!"

The gentle breeze has long since died down, and stalk by stalk the withered grass stands erect like so many copper wires. The sound of Mother Xia's quaking voice grows fainter and fainter as it trembles in the air. Finally it disappears entirely. All around, everything is still as death. Standing amid the withered grass, the two women raise their faces and watch the crow. Head pulled in, it stands straight as a writing brush on the branch, looking as though it were made of cast iron.

Some time passes and the number of visitors to the graveyard gradually swells. Old and young, they appear and disappear among the mounds. Somehow or other, Mother Hua feels that she has been relieved of a great burden and begins to think of going home.

"Why don't we both go home now," she urges.

Mother Xia sighs. Listlessly she picks up the rice and food she had set out earlier. She hesitates a moment, but finally starts walking slowly away. As though talking to herself she says, "How could they possibly have gotten here?"

Before they have gone more than a few dozen paces, a loud *CAW* is heard behind them. Timorously they turn their heads and watch as the crow crouches, spreads its wings, and then, straight as an arrow, flies away into the distance.

APRIL 1919

---

8. For contemporary readers, Xia Yu, immediately suggested Qiu Jin (see n. 4 above). The surname Xia is also the word for "summer," while the surname Qiu also means "autumn"; further, the given names, Yu and Jin, both refer to jade.

Tomorrow

"Don't hear the loom—wonder what's up with the little guy." Raising a bowl of yellow wine with both hands, Rednose Everbow[1] curled his lips in the direction of the room next door as he spoke. Blueskin Ah-five[2] put down his own bowl and gave Everbow a mighty slap across the back.

"Yer . . . yer . . . gettin' . . . gettin' all lovey-dovey again." Ah-five's voice was loud and slurred.

Lu Town was a quiet out-of-the-way place that still preserved a few ancient customs, and so it was that even before the First Watch everyone had long since bolted the front door and gone to bed. Given the lateness of the hour, there were but two places where people would still be awake. One was the *Prosperity* wineshop,[3] where two drinking companions were happily riding the crest of their bacchanalian pleasures at the bar; the other was the room next door to the wineshop where Sister Shan was still up and about.[4] Since becoming a widow the year before last, Sister Shan had been completely dependent on the cloth she wove to support herself and her three-year-old son, and as a consequence she too was a late sleeper.

It was quite true that her loom had been silent for the past few days. However, since the wineshop and her room were the only two places where people were still up late at night, whenever the loom *was* to be heard Everbow and friend were the only ones to hear it. And when it wasn't to be heard, they were the only ones not to hear it.

After receiving the slap, Everbow took a long drink of wine and began to croon a lovesong, obviously enjoying himself immensely.

At precisely the same moment, seated on the edge of her bed,

First published in *The Renaissance (Xin chao)*, vol. 2, no. 1 (October 1919).

1. His name suggests that he is always clasping his hands before him, as in the traditional gentleman's greeting.

2. In south China the syllable *ah* is commonly prefixed to given names in a familiar-polite form of address. Calling him "Ah-five" indicates that he was fifth-born in his family.

3. The *Prosperity for All* also figures in "Kong Yiji" and "A Passing Storm."

4. "Sister" *(sao)* is a polite form of address for a married woman. In the original text she is addressed as Sister Shan-four because her *husband* was the fourth child born to the Shan family.

Sister Shan was cradling Bao'er in her arms. Her loom stood silent on the floor. The dim light of her lamp threw a garish light on the boy's fevered face, a face that had flushed purple and now showed ominous patches of black. Sister Shan went over her situation: she had drawn lots at the temple; she had made her vow; and she had given the boy his medicine.[5] "But what if the prescription *doesn't* work?" she asked herself. "Well, then the only thing will be to let He Xiaoxian have a look at him.[6] On the other hand, maybe Bao'er's got the kind of sickness that gets bad at night and lets up a little in the daytime. Maybe *tomorrow,* as soon as the sun comes out, his fever will go down and his breathing will smooth out. After all, that kind of thing often does happen with sick people."

Sister Shan was a coarse and uneducated woman who didn't understand what a frightening expression *on the other hand* can be. To be sure, thanks to this expression, many bad things have taken a turn for the better. But also thanks to this same phrase, a number of good things have been utterly ruined, too.

Summer nights were short. Not long after Everbow and friend had stumbled to the end of their song, it began to grow light in the east. The silver rays of dawn poked through the cracks in Sister Shan's window.

Waiting for dawn had been particularly difficult, and she felt it had been unusually slow in arriving. A year seemed to pass with every breath her Bao'er took. Now it had grown bright outside and the light of the sky continued to brighten until it overwhelmed the light of the lamp. Sister Shan was now able to make out the shape of Bao'er's nostrils as they rose and fell with every breath. Something was wrong—she knew it.

"Aiya!" A hushed cry escaped her lips. "What can I do?" she asked herself. "There's only one road left—let He Xiaoxian have a look at him." Though coarse and uneducated, she could also be decisive. She stood, went to the cupboard, and fished out all the money she had—through daily economies she'd managed to put aside three silver dollars and one hundred and eighty coppers.

5. To draw lots was to seek advance knowledge of what was in store for her son; to make a vow to the Buddha, or to a Bodhisattva, meant promising to perform some good deed when her prayers were answered.

6. The doctor in "Diary of a Madman" is also surnamed He. This doctor's given name, Xiaoxian, means something like "junior immortal," an appropriate name for a Daoist physician.

Cramming it all into her pocket, with Bao'er clasped against her breast, she locked the door and rushed straight to Dr. He's house.

Early though it was, there were already four patients ahead of her. She paid out four dimes and got a registration slip in return. Bao'er was fifth to see the doctor. Stretching out two fingers, He Xiao xian felt the child's pulse. With secret pleasure, Sister Shan noted that his fingernails were a good four inches long.[7] "Bao'er must be fated to live," she thought to herself. But even so, somehow or other she couldn't help being apprehensive, couldn't keep herself from asking in a faltering tone, "Sir—what's my Bao'er got?"

"There's a blockage in the central tract."[8]

"Is it serious? He . . ."

"First of all, let's give him these two prescriptions."

"He can't breathe right and both nostrils keep quivering too!"

"A case of fire overcoming metal . . ."[9] Having given her the benefit of that half sentence, He Xiaoxian majestically closed his eyes. Sister Shan was embarrassed to go on with her questioning. By this time, a man of thirty or so who was sitting across from Dr. He had already made out the prescription. Pointing to some words on the corner of the paper, he told Sister Shan, "This first part of the prescription, 'Life-preserving Pills for Infants,' is only available at the Jia family's *Philanthropic Drug Store."*

Sister Shan took the prescription and left. Although she was a coarse and uneducated woman, she knew that the He residence, the *Philanthropic,* and her own house formed a triangle. Naturally it would be more efficient to buy the medicine first and then go home. She rushed to the *Philanthropic* as fast as her legs would carry her. The clerk's long fingernails curled upwards as he slowly read the prescription and, just as slowly, wrapped the medicine. As she waited with Bao'er clasped against her breast, the child suddenly lifted his little head and yanked hard at a wisp of his own

7. Long fingernails were a sign of affluence and therefore a good omen.

8. According to the *Yellow Emperor's Classic of Internal Medicine (Huangdi neijing suwen),* trans. Ilza Veith (Berkeley: University of California Press, 1972), the alimentary system is divided into three tracts: upper (above the stomach), middle (the stomach), and lower (below the stomach).

9. Traditional medicine envisioned the body as composed of five elements: fire, water, wood, metal, and earth. In this system fire represented the heart; metal, the lungs.

hair that had fallen out of place. He had never before done such a thing and Sister Shan was riveted with fright.

The sun had been up for some time. Trying to carry the package of medicine together with the child in her arms, she felt Bao'er becoming heavier the longer she walked, and the more he twisted and turned, the longer the road became. At last she couldn't keep her legs under her any longer. She sat down to one side of the road on the steps of a mansion. But after resting a bit, she became conscious of the cold dampness of the clothing next to her skin. Only then did she realize that she was bathed in sweat.

Bao'er seemed to have gone to sleep. She got up again and started walking very slowly toward her house. It was all she could do to stay on her feet. Suddenly she heard someone say, "Let me tote him awhile." The voice sounded like Blueskin Ah-five. She raised her head and looked. Yes, there he was, following along sleepy-eyed beside her.

Though she had been hoping at that very moment that some General of the Heavenly Host would suddenly tumble out of the blue and come to her rescue, she hadn't wanted it to be Ah-five. Blueskin, on the other hand, was quite insistent on being her knight in shining armor. She declined his help as best she could. Finally, however, she granted him permission to carry the child.

Ah-five immediately thrust out his arms, shoving his right hand straight down so that it passed between Bao'er and his mother's breast. Sister Shan felt a flash of heat in her chest, a heat that immediately spread upward until it reddened both her face and the lobes of her ears.

Keeping about two and a half feet between them, they walked along side by side. Ah-five did some talking, but Sister Shan didn't respond to most of it. Before they had gone very far, he handed the child back to her. He said he had made a date with friends the previous day to go out for something to eat at exactly this time. Sister Shan took the child. Fortunately she wasn't far from home. Up ahead she caught sight of Ninth Auntie Wang from across the way sitting by the side of the road. The older woman called to her in the distance. "Sister Shan, how's the boy? Seen the doc?"

"I saw him—for what it was worth. Say, Ninth Auntie Wang, you've got a few years on you and have seen a thing or two. Why don't *you* take a look at him with those old experienced eyes of yours?"

"Well . . ."

"Okay?"

"Well . . ." Ninth Auntie Wang looked Bao'er all over. She nodded her head twice and then she shook her head twice.

By the time Bao'er had taken his medicine, it was already afternoon. Sister Shan studied him with care: his breathing seemed to have smoothed out considerably. But later that afternoon he suddenly opened his eyes and cried out, "Ma!" Then he closed them again and seemed to sleep. After he had been sleeping awhile, beads of perspiration began to form one by one on his forehead and on the tip of his nose. When, ever so lightly, she wiped them away, she noticed that they stuck to her hand like glue. Frantically she put her hand to his chest. She began to sob uncontrollably.

Bao'er's breathing progressed from smooth to nonexistent, and Sister Shan's voice, from a sob to a wail. By now two groups of people had formed: inside the house, it was Ninth Auntie Wang and Blueskin Ah-five; outside the door stood the manager of the *Prosperity* and Rednose Everbow. It was Ninth Auntie Wang who issued the order to burn paper money for the dead; and it was also she who borrowed—on the security of two benches and five pieces of clothing—two dollars for Sister Shan, so that she would be able to provide a meal for everyone who helped out with the funeral.

The first problem was the coffin. Sister Shan still had a pair of earrings and a gold-plated silver hairclasp. This was handed over as security to the manager of the *Prosperity,* who was then to buy a coffin half on credit and half with cash.

Volunteering his services, Blueskin Ah-five tried to stake a claim to part of the action too, but Ninth Auntie Wang would go no further than to allow him to serve as a pallbearer the next day. "Old bitch!" Ah-five cursed and continued to stand there, his lips curled up in resentment. The manager of the *Prosperity* went off and returned later that evening only to report that the coffin would have to be made to order, and wouldn't be done until well after midnight.

By the time the manager got back, the helpers had long since eaten. Since Lu Town still preserved some ancient customs, well before the First Watch everyone had already gone home and to bed. But Ah-five was still leaning against the counter at the *Prosperity* drinking his wine, and Everbow's voice could still be heard as he crooned a song.

Next door to them, weeping as she sat on the edge of the bed, was Sister Shan. Lying on the bed was Bao'er. And silently standing on the floor, a loom. After some time, the tears ended. Her eyes grew large as she looked around the room. She felt it was all very strange—everything that had happened was something that couldn't possibly have happened. Sister Shan went over it all again in her own heart. "It's only a dream. Every bit of it is a dream. I'll wake up in the morning and find myself safe and sound in my own bed, and Bao'er will be sleeping safe and sound at my side too. He'll wake up, call me 'Ma,' and bound outside to play just like a young tiger."

The sound of Everbow's singing had long since died away and the lamps in the *Prosperity* had been extinguished too. Still sitting there, Sister Shan did not believe any of it. The cock crowed; it began to grow light in the east; the silver rays of dawn penetrated the cracks of the window.

Gradually the steely dawn took on a deep red hue. Sunlight began to fall on the roof. Wide-eyed, Sister Shan continued to sit on the edge of the bed as though in a trance. The sound of knocking startled her out of it—she ran across the room and opened the door. Outside stood a man she didn't know, carrying something on his back. Ninth Auntie Wang was behind him.

She caught her breath. "They've brought the coffin." The coffin was not finally closed until late in the day because Sister Shan, unable to bring herself to part forever with Bao'er, stuck close to the coffin, gazing at her precious son through her tears. Ninth Auntie Wang finally lost patience, and pulled her aside long enough for those standing around to rush in and close the lid.

Sister Shan had done everything for her dead son a mother could do: on the previous day she had burned a string of paper money; this morning she had burned forty-nine scrolls of the *Incantation of Great Compassion;*[10] she had dressed him in brand new clothes; and she had placed his favorite toys at the side of his pillow—a clay doll, two little wooden bowls, and two small bottles of colored glass. Later on when Ninth Auntie Wang carefully reckoned the whole business on her fingers, she could not come up with a single thing that had not been properly attended to.

---

10. It was believed that chanting or burning this incantation would help the deceased to be reborn in paradise.

Blueskin Ah-five did not show up all day, and consequently the manager of the *Prosperity* had to hire two porters whom Sister Shan paid two hundred and ten coppers apiece. They carried the coffin to the potter's field, found a place for it, and covered it with a mound. Ninth Auntie Wang helped Sister Shan prepare a meal. Anyone who had so much as lifted a finger or said a comforting word was fed. And as the sun gradually took on the appearance it usually showed just before going down behind the mountains, just so, and without their being aware of it, did the people who had just eaten assume the expressions they usually showed just before going home. At long last, they had all gone.

Her head swimming, Sister Shan actually managed to rest for a while, and the rest seemed to calm her. But then she gradually became aware that her world was terribly changed. She had gone through something she had never before experienced, something that could not possibly have happened, but in fact actually had. The more she thought, the more bizarre it all appeared. Then she became conscious of something else that had changed—her room was too quiet.

She rose and lit a lamp, but that made the room even quieter than before. In a daze she walked to the door and bolted it. She went back and sat on the bed; her loom stood silently beside her. She pulled herself together, looked around, and felt even more miserable. She didn't know whether to sit, to stand, or what to do. Not only was the room too quiet, but it was also too large and the things in it, empty—much too empty. From all four sides, a room too large hemmed her in. From all four sides, objects too empty crowded in on her until she could hardly draw a breath. Now she realized that her Bao'er really was dead. She no longer wanted to look at the room. She blew out the light and lay on her bed. She wept. She thought back to the time when she had spun yarn on her loom with Bao'er sitting at her side eating fennel-flavored beans. She remembered how he had once stared at her for a long time with those small dark eyes and then had suddenly announced, "Ma, when papa was alive he sold won ton. When I grow up I'll sell won ton too—lots and lots of them. And I'll give all the money to you." At that time even the yarn she spun, each and every inch, seemed full of meaning, full of life. And now? Sister Shan really hadn't given any thought to now. (I said a long time back that she was a coarse and uneducated woman. What thoughts would she have been capable of?) She only felt that her room was somehow too quiet, too large, and too empty.

But although Sister Shan was a coarse and uneducated woman, she knew that the dead never return. She knew she would never see her Bao'er again. She sighed and said, almost as though to herself, "Bao'er, I think your spirit is probably still here. Please, please let me see you in my dreams, if only for a little while." She closed her eyes hoping to fall quickly asleep so that she might see her son. Her labored breathing penetrated the silence, penetrated the largeness, penetrated the emptiness, and enabled her to hear that emptiness all too clearly.

At long last, a groggy Sister Shan entered the land of sleep. And now the entire room was quite still. By this time, Rednose Everbow's song had long since been sung. He staggered out of the *Prosperity* and once more raised his voice to a shrill pitch and sang: *"My darling! How I pity you, all alone in this great world . . ."*

At that point, Blueskin Ah-five reached out and grabbed Everbow by the shoulder. Laughing and bumping into each other as they stumbled along, the two friends zigzagged down the road.

Sister Shan had gone to sleep. Everbow and friend had left. The *Prosperity* had bolted its door.

Lu Town was totally still. Only the dark night, intent on becoming tomorrow, still rushed through the silence. And hiding in the darkness, a few dogs barked.

JUNE 1920[11]

11. Lu Xun's diary indicates that "Tomorrow" was actually written sometime between the end of July and the beginning of August 1919.

An Unimportant Affair

In the twinkling of an eye, six years have passed since I left the countryside to come to the capital.[1] If I stop to add up all the so-called important affairs of state that I have either witnessed or heard about during that time, there have been quite a few at that. And yet, not one has left so much as a trace in my memory, and as for their influence on me, it has only been to increase my stock of bad temper. To tell the truth, these "important affairs of state" have merely taught me to despise people more and more with every passing day.

But there was one unimportant affair that did have meaning for me, that dragged me out of the morass of my own bad temper, and that I cannot forget even today.

It happened during the winter of the sixth year of the Republic.[2] A fierce north wind was just at its peak. Nonetheless, in order to make a living, I had no choice but to be out on the streets bright and early. There was hardly anyone around and it was only with the greatest of difficulty that I finally managed to hire a rickshaw. I ordered the puller to take me to S Gate.[3] Before long the north wind subsided. It had blown away every last speck of dust, leaving a spotlessly clean thoroughfare stretched out before us. The rickshaw man started making better time too. Then, just as we were entering S Gate, one of the shafts of his rig snagged a piece of clothing and dragged someone to the ground.

It was a woman. Her hair was grey, her clothes ragged. Darting

---

First published in the Expanded Anniversary Supplement of the Beijing *Morning Post,* December 1, 1919.

1. In 1912, the first year of the republic, Lu Xun went to Beijing to serve as a minor official in the Ministry of Education. Like most young intellectuals at the time, he held high hopes for the new republican government. Disillusionment quickly set in, however, as the military man Yuan Shikai virtually usurped the presidency. It soon became apparent that the new government was to be the tool of warlords and the wealthy. It was unable to check the constant encroachments on Chinese sovereignty made by Japan and other foreign powers. Internally, despite the democratic ideals that had inspired the Revolution, it did nothing to alter the traditional hierarchy of Chinese society or to improve the lot of the common people.

2. 1917.

3. According to Zhou Zuoren, the *S* stands for Xuanwu (the name of a gate in Beijing). At that time *s* was sometimes used to represent the sound now indicated by *x* in *pinyin.*

out from the side of the street, she had cut straight across the rickshaw's path. The puller had slowed so that she might cross safely, but her tattered jacket was unbuttoned and a breeze had caught it at the last moment, making it billow out so that it snagged on one of the shafts. Fortunately the puller had been slowing down at the time, or she would surely have been thrown head over heels and seriously injured.

There she lay stretched out on the ground. The puller stopped. I was certain that the old woman had not been hurt and—since no one had seen the whole thing in the first place—was rather put out by his making so much of it. He was only going to stir up trouble for himself. Besides, he would make me late. "It's nothing," I said, "just keep going." Paying no attention at all—perhaps he had not heard me—my puller put down the shafts of his rig. He gently raised the old woman to her feet and supported her under the arms. "Are you all right?"

"I'm hurt real bad."

I saw you go down with my own two eyes, I thought to myself, and it was slowly at that. How could you possibly have been hurt? Just a big act, that's all. What a contemptible old woman! And the puller had no call to get mixed up in this either—just making trouble for himself. Well, he's gotten himself into it, now let's see him get himself out of it!

When she answered, without the least hesitation and still supporting her under the arms, he began walking the old woman down the street, one step at a time. Curious to see where he thought he was going, I glanced up ahead—a police substation! Although the wind had died down, there was still no one standing guard outside. Helping the old woman along, the rickshaw man was quite obviously headed for the main gate of that police station![4]

At this point a strange feeling came over me. It was as if the rickshaw man's receding and dust-covered form had, in a flash, somehow been magnified. It grew larger and larger with every step he took, until finally I had to look up just to take it all in. What was more, that form gradually solidified into an oppressive weight that bore down upon me until it had squeezed out the pettiness that was hidden beneath my big fur coat.

---

4. Since the police at that time might readily abuse a mere rickshaw man, under normal circumstances the puller would have given the substation a wide berth.

At this point my spirits must have been somewhat numbed, for I just sat there not moving, not even really thinking. It was only when I saw a policeman emerge from the substation that I stepped down from the rickshaw. He walked up to me and said, "Better get another rig. He won't be able to pull you now."

Without thinking, I took a handful of coins out of my coat pocket and handed them to the policeman. "Please give him these."

By now the wind had died down completely. The streets were silent. I walked along, thinking as I went, and yet I was somehow reluctant to think about myself. Even setting aside for the moment the way I had behaved up to that point, what could I have had in mind when I gave the policeman that handful of coins for my puller? Had I been trying to reward him? Was I even fit to pass judgment on this rickshaw man? I could not answer my own questions.

I often think of that unimportant affair even today, and consequently I am often forced through the painful business of thinking about myself. For me, the momentous civil and military affairs of the past several years have long since become one with all that *Confucius says* and *the Poetry Classic states* kind of thing that I had to memorize as a youth—can't recall so much as half a line. And yet that one unimportant affair remains ever before my eyes, sometimes with even greater clarity than when it actually occurred, constantly making me ashamed, urging me to turn over a new leaf—and increasing my stock of courage and hope.

JULY 1920

The Story of Hair

On Sunday morning I tore the previous day's page from the calendar and glanced at the new one. Then I gave it a second look. "Hey, it's October tenth—so today's Double Ten![1] Funny, there's no notation here on the page!"

Mr. N,[2] a man of the next generation above mine, had just walked over to my place for a chat, and hearing me say this he observed in the most disgruntled of tones, "They're right! They don't bother to remember—so what? You *do* remember—so what?"

Now this Mr. N had a rather feisty disposition to begin with. He would often fly off the handle for no apparent reason and say things that revealed a profound naiveté about the ways of the world. At times like that I'd just let him ramble on without putting in a word until he finally got to the end of whatever it was he had to say, and that would be that.

"I really have to give them credit, the way they do up the Double Ten here in Beijing. A policeman comes to the door in the morning: 'Fly the flag,' he orders. 'Yes sir, fly the flag.' Then from every home you'll see a citizen of the realm halfheartedly emerge and put up a raggedy old piece of cloth. There it hangs until nightfall when somebody will take it in again and close the door. Here and there a family forgets and it'll fly right through till the next morning.[3]

"They've forgotten to mark the day there on the calendar, but then the day hasn't remembered them either! I can be counted among those who have forgotten to keep the day, too. When I do remember it, all the things that happened just before and after that *first* Double Ten well up in my mind until I don't know whether I'm coming or going.

First published in the Lamp of Learning supplement of the Shanghai periodical *China Times,* October 10, 1920.

1. Double Ten (October 10, the tenth day of the tenth month) marks the anniversary of the Republican Revolution of 1911.

2. Zhou Zuoren says that Mr. N is based on a certain Xia Huiqing, Lu Xun's superior at the Ministry of Education. A great deal of what Mr. N says is a direct reflection of Lu Xun's own experiences in relation to hair; see the Introduction.

3. According to Zhou Zuoren, Lu Xun himself once expressed the same sentiments in a similar way.

"The faces of so many old friends float before my eyes. Some of those youngsters worked themselves to the bone for a decade or more just to bring about that day, only to have their lives taken away by a bullet fired in the secret recesses of some jail. Some, having failed in assassination attempts, endured more than a month's cruel torture in prison before they died. And still others, holding the loftiest of ideals, just disappeared without a trace. We didn't even know where their corpses were.

"They lived out their whole lives in a society that gave them nothing but ridicule, abuse, and persecution, a society ever on the lookout for some way of doing them in. By now their grave mounds have long since flattened away from neglect and forgetfulness. I can't bring myself to celebrate things like that. Let's switch to a more pleasant topic."

A smile suddenly spread across N's face as he extended a hand and felt the back of his head. "The one thing I *do* really feel good about is that I've been able to walk the streets since that first Double Ten without having anyone laugh at me or curse me out," he said, raising his voice with a touch of enthusiasm.

"You've got to remember, old friend," he continued, "that hair has always been both the beloved friend and hated enemy of the Chinese people. Just think of how many of us down through the ages have gone through the cruelest and most pointless suffering just because of *hair!*

"The most ancient of our ancients don't seem to have taken hair all that seriously. You can tell that from the order in which they listed the corporal punishments. The thing they set most store by, of course, was the head and that's why Decapitation topped the list. Next in order of importance came the sex organs and therefore Castration and Removal of the Ovaries were set up as terrifying punishments too. But when you got down to Haircutting, you were at the very bottom of the list.[4] And yet if you think about it a little more closely, who knows how many people have been trampled underfoot for an entire lifetime precisely because they had received that lightest of light punishments!

"Whenever we used to talk of revolting against the Manchus,

---

4. In ascending order of harshness, the Five (Corporal) Punishments in ancient China were (1) tattooing the face, (2) cutting off the nose, (3) cutting off the feet, (4) castration or removal of the ovaries, and (5) decapitation. Though not included in this standard list, shaving of the head was also a traditional form of corporal punishment.

we'd always make a big thing of the *Ten Days at Yangzhou* and the *Butchering of Jiading*, but that was just a little trick we used.[5] To tell you the truth, the intensity of the resistance we Chinese put up against the Manchus at the time of the Republican Revolution had next to nothing to do with the atrocities committed by Manchus when they destroyed us as a nation and a people a few centuries back. If the truth be known, we were simply sick and tired of wearing those queues!

"Once the Manchus established their dynasty and had killed all those who wouldn't submit; once those officials, still loyal to the Ming, had all died off;[6] once we had all actually gotten used to wearing the queue, then along came Hong Xiuquan and Yang Xiuqin. My grandmother once told me that the common people were put in a real bind then: the ones who let their hair grow out were killed by the government troops, and the ones who still did their hair up in the queue were killed by the Long Hairs![7]

"I don't know how many Chinese have suffered pain, martyrdom, and destruction just because of something as utterly insignificant as hair." N gazed at the beams in the ceiling as though thinking of something else, and then continued, "Who would ever have thought that some day my turn to suffer because of hair would roll around too?

"When I went overseas to study I cut off my queue. There was no particular significance to my act—I simply did it because wearing the darned thing was so inconvenient. Much to my surprise, however, some of my fellow students who had coiled *their* queues up on top of their heads absolutely detested *me* because I had cut mine off! The government-appointed supervisor of studies in charge of us was hopping mad too. Said he was going to cut off my government scholarship and send me home. But before too many days were out, some students got hold of the supervisor himself and cut *his* queue off, after which he ran away to who-knows-

---

5. The italicized phrases refer to massacres of Chinese that were committed by the Manchus in the course of conquering China during the seventeenth century.

6. The Ming dynasty (1368–1644) preceded the Manchu (or Qing) dynasty (1644–1911).

7. Hong Xiuquan and Yang Xiuqin were leaders of the Taiping Rebellion (1850–64). The hairstyle that had been imposed upon Chinese men by the Manchus involved shaving the front part of the head while braiding the hair at the back into a queue. The Taipings undid their queues and let their hair grow long, and thus they were also known as "Long Hairs."

where. One of those in on the cutting was Zou Rong.[8] It was because of that very incident that Zou Rong had to go back to Shanghai, where he later died in West Jail—but I daresay by now you've long since forgotten all of that.

"A few years later, my own family's fortunes sank. I had to either find work or go hungry, and so I was forced to go back to China too. As soon as I arrived in Shanghai I bought an artificial queue. The going price at the time was two dollars. When I wore it back home, my mother didn't say anything, but whenever anyone else set eyes on me they'd immediately launch a close investigation of the damned thing. Once they had established that it was artificial, they would sneer and act as though I'd committed a capital offense. As a matter of fact, one of my relatives was even getting ready to report me to the authorities, but then he began to worry that the Revolutionary Party's insurrection might actually succeed and scrapped the idea.

"I decided that a policy of open honesty would be preferable to all this chicanery, and so I went whole hog—threw away the artificial queue and started wearing a Western suit. When I walked out on the street, however, I was still cursed and ridiculed. Some people would even follow along behind and call me 'Savage' or 'Fake Foreign Devil'! At that point I stopped wearing my Western suit and went back to a Chinese gown. Got cursed out more than ever![9]

"When I got to the end of my rope, I made a slight addition to my daily costume—a walking stick. From then on, I laid into my tormentors with that stick. Worked wonders. A few good doses of that and people stopped bothering me. But whenever I'd go someplace I hadn't been to before, I'd *still* get cursed out.

"But my success with that walking stick made me sick at heart. I often reflect on it even today. When I was studying in Japan, I once saw a newspaper article about a certain Dr. Honda who had just completed a trip through Malaysia and China. Someone asked him, 'Since you didn't know Chinese or Malay, how did you manage to get around?' He raised his walking stick up high and replied, 'This is *their* language—they all understand it quite

8. Zou Rong (1885–1905) was the author of an impassioned and influential anti-Manchu tract, *The Revolutionary Army,* written when he was only eighteen; its publication led to his imprisonment and he died in custody only a month before his sentence was up.

9. Much of this is autobiographical material; see the Introduction.

well!'[10] That article made me boil with indignation for quite a while afterward. Who would have thought back then that someday I would do the very same thing—and what's more, it turned out that those people who were cursing *me* all understood this language too.

"During the first year of Xuantong, I was supervisor of studies right here at the local high school.[11] My colleagues avoided me like the plague and the local officials watched me like a hawk. From one end of the day to the other, I was so isolated that I might as well have been holed up in an icehouse or standing on an execution ground. And if the facts be known, there was absolutely no reason for it—except that I didn't have a queue!

"Several students suddenly appeared in my office one day and announced, 'Teacher, we're going to cut off our queues.'

"I said, 'Absolutely not!'

"Then they asked, 'Is it better to have one or not?'

"I started to explain to them that while it's better *not* to have one, still—But they immediately interrupted, 'Then how do you get off telling *us* absolutely not?'

" 'Because cutting it off is just not worth the trouble.' They didn't say anything, just pulled long faces and walked out, but the upshot was that they all cut off their queues. Well, that caused one hell of an uproar, believe you me! Everywhere you went people were talking about it, but I just went about my business as though nothing had happened and let the queue-less come to class right along with the queue-ed.

"Trouble was, this queue-cutting fad proved contagious. On the third day six queues suddenly bit the dust over at the Normal School, and the six students were expelled that very night. Those kids were in a real pickle—couldn't stay at school and couldn't go home, just had to fend for themselves as best they could. It wasn't until a good month after the first Double Ten that the stigma of their 'crime' disappeared.

"And me? Same thing. Even when I went to Beijing in the winter

10. Zuoren says that a newspaper did in fact report this story and that it had incensed his elder brother.

11. Xuantong (1909–1911) was the final reign period of the Manchu dynasty, ended by the Republican Revolution. Lu Xun became dean of studies at the Shaoxing Academy in 1910. N's words undoubtedly reflect Lu Xun's own experiences around this time.

of that first year of the Republic, I still got cursed out a couple of times. Later on the people who had done the cursing had their own queues cut off by the police and I wasn't bothered anymore. But I didn't get to the countryside, so I can't tell you whether they were still cursing people there."

N seemed quite pleased with himself. Then suddenly his face assumed a solemn cast again as he said, "And now idealists like yourself are going around making noises about young women having the right to bob their hair, causing a lot of them a great deal of needless sorrow. And they have nothing whatsoever to gain from it anyway! Haven't there already been cases of girls not being admitted to school because they've bobbed their hair, and girls being expelled for the same reason?[12] Revolution?[13] Fine, but where are their weapons? Work their way through college? Sounds good, but where are the factories for them to work in? They'd be much better off to keep their hair the way it is, marry and pursue a career as someone's daughter-in-law. Their happiness lies in forgetting hair-bobbing and all that goes with it. If they continue to concern themselves with all this talk of equality and freedom, they'll be letting themselves in for a lifetime of suffering!

"I'd like to put to you idealists the same question that Artzybashev asks: 'You promise a golden age to these people's sons and grandsons, but what do you have to offer them here and now?'[14] As long as the Creator's whip doesn't fall hard across China's back she'll always stay the same, unwilling to budge a single hair on her body. Since you people don't have any poisonous fangs, why do you insist on sticking a 'poisonous snake' label on your foreheads, inviting any beggar to come along and beat you to death?"[15]

---

12. Zuoren states that incidents of this kind were common in Beijing in 1920 (the year this story was written). In fact, hair-bobbing by young girls was thought even more unforgivable than queue-cutting had been a decade earlier. For a man to cut his queue was a political act; but when a girl bobbed her hair, her act was interpreted as a direct violation of traditional morality. In effect she proclaimed herself a "loose woman."

13. The original text has "reform," but Zhou Zuoren claims that at this time his brother would have avoided writing the word "revolution" even though the context calls for it, in order to avoid offending the authorities.

14. Though not phrased in these exact words, this question is raised several times in chapter 9 of Mikhail Artzybashev's (1878–1927) midlength novel *Sheviriof*. See *Tales of the Revolution*, trans. Percy Pinkerton (New York: B. W. Huebsch, 1917).

15. According to Zhou Zuoren, this is a question that Lu Xun himself often posed in conversation.

The more N spoke, the further afield he went, but as soon as he noticed my expression and realized I really wasn't all that keen on hearing him out, he stopped, stood up, and got his hat.

"Going home?" I asked.

"Yes, it's going to rain pretty soon." Then in silence I saw him to the door.

He put on his hat and said, "Goodbye. Excuse me for disturbing you. Fortunately, tomorrow it won't be the Double Ten anymore and we can just forget the whole business."

OCTOBER 1920

A Passing Storm

The sun gradually gathered in its bright yellow rays from over the threshing ground down by the river. The parched leaves of the tallow trees along the bank had no sooner taken a deep breath of relief than several spotted-leg mosquitoes began buzzing back and forth beneath them. The smoke that had been rising from the chimneys of the peasant homes facing the water gradually began to thin out. Women and children appeared in doorways and sprinkled water on the threshing ground just outside. Small tables and low stools were carried out and set down on the dampened earth. Suppertime had arrived.

Using large plantain leaves for fans, the old folks and the men sat on the stools and chatted. Children darted lickety-split from place to place or squatted under the tallow trees playing toss-catch.[1] Women carried out raven-black dried vegetables along with rice of a rich pinecone brown. All around the threshing ground steam rose from the piping-hot food. Just then, a pleasure boat full of scholars passed by on the river. Catching sight of the idyllic scene while sipping their wine, these lions of literature lyrically proclaimed, "Not a care in the world, a true example of the pleasures of peasant life!"

The words of these literary lions, however, did not entirely tally with reality, but that was only because they had not heard what old Mrs. Ninepounder was saying. In high dudgeon, she rapped her fan sharply against the leg of her stool. "I've lived seventy-nine years and that's long enough, 'cause I don't *want* to live to see such sure signs that the family's goin' to pot. Be better off dead! About to eat any minute now and *you* have to see how many roasted beans you can stuff down your throat. What are you tryin' to do, eat us all out of house and home?"

First published in *New Youth,* vol. 8, no. 7 (September 1920).

1. Requiring nothing but pebbles, the game could be played by the poorest of children. Using only one hand, a player would toss five pebbles into the air, catching one before it hit the ground. Then he would toss that one up again, pick one up from the four remaining on the ground and catch the tossed one again before it fell to the ground. Then he would toss up the two he now held in his hand, pick up a third, and catch the two in the air before they reached the ground, and so on. A successful player would finish by tossing up all five, catching them on the back of his hand, tossing them up again, and making the final catch in his palm.

Clutching a handful of beans, her great-granddaughter, Sixpounder, was running full tilt toward the old lady. But hearing this, she abruptly shifted course, headed down toward the river, and hid behind a tallow tree. She stuck her fork-horned little head[2] out from behind the trunk and cursed, "Old Neverdie!"

Though Mrs. Ninepounder was indeed quite well advanced in years, her hearing was still fairly good. This time, however, she did not hear the little girl's words and went right on. "Each generation's worse than the last."[3]

There was a rather singular custom in this village: when babies were born, the mothers would use their birthweights as childhood names. Ever since the grand occasion of her fiftieth birthday, Mrs. Ninepounder had gradually become something of a kvetch.[4] She would often say that back in her youth, the weather wasn't as hot as it was now. The beans were not as hard either. In sum, there was something wrong with everything in the world today. What further evidence was needed than the undeniable fact that Sixpounder was three pounds lighter than her great-grandfather Ninepounder, and one pound lighter than her father, Sevenpounder? This constituted irrefutable proof of Mrs. Ninepounder's theory, and so she loudly voiced it once again: "Each generation's worse than the last!"

Her granddaughter-in-law Sister Sevenpounder[5] was just com-

---

2. Girls' hair was done up in twin tufts that forked upward like a pair of horns. Thus young girls were often referred to as "fork-heads" *(yatou)*.

3. Regarding this passage, Lu Xun's younger brother Zhou Zuoren has commented:

"The lions of literature passing by in a pleasure boat on the river . . . actually see things exactly the same way as Old Lady Ninepounder. The only difference is that, rather than looking to the past, they seek the ideal life in a far-off realm totally separated from themselves. The countryside provides excellent material for such a quest. In any case, however, it's just talk, for they'd never really consider moving there.

"Chinese poets are generally identified with a distinctive tradition: while carrying on their work as officials, their minds may be occupied by ambition, their sole concern being to climb ever higher in the bureaucracy. But in their poems, their hearts are always off in the mountains or woods and they heartily recommend the hermit's life. For instance, in his 'Memorial to the Prime Minister' the poet Han Yu (768–824) waxes enthusiastic over his role as official, but in his poem 'Mountain Stones' (a familiar work contained in *The Three Hundred Tang Poems*) we find him saying, 'Since human life consists of such simple things, one can always be happy in oneself; what need then to go through the world forever tense and subject to the whip of other people's desires?' All such literary lions belong to the same club as Old Lady Ninepounder. The difference between them is similar to the difference between poetry and prose: a poet may sing the glories of mountain and forest in verse while complaining in prose that 'things ain't what they used to be'."

4. *Bupingjia* (translated here as "kvetch") is a borrowing from Japanese *(fuheika)*.

5. "Sister" *(sao)* is a respectful term of address for married women.

ing up to the table with a basket of rice as the old woman spoke. Obviously irritated, Sister Sevenpounder tossed the basket down on the table. "There you go again, old woman. Now when Sixpounder was born, didn't she really weigh six pounds *plus* five ounces? Besides your family's scales are crooked to begin with. They weigh light. It would take eighteen ounces to make a pound on your scales! If you used honest sixteen-ounce scales, our Sixpounder would have weighed in at over six pounds. I'll bet Sevenpounder's dad and granddad too didn't really tip in at a full eight or nine either. You were probably usin' scales that read a pound for every fourteen ounces!"

"Each generation's worse than the last."

Before Sister Sevenpounder had a chance to respond, she suddenly caught sight of Sevenpounder as he rounded a corner coming out of a small alley. She turned toward him and bellowed. "What do you mean draggin' that dead-ass carcass of yours back here this late? Where the hell've you been? Here we are waitin' supper on you, and *you* don't give a damn!"

Although Sevenpounder lived in a country village, his family had early on showed promise of scaling the ladder of prestige: from his grandfather on down to himself, for three generations their hands had not touched the handle of a hoe. Like them, he too made his living by poling a passenger boat. He would make one trip a day, leaving Lu Village for town first thing in the morning and returning early in the evening. His occupation caused him to become something of a sophisticate: for instance, he could tell you such things as where the Thunder God had killed a Centipede Spirit, or where a virgin had given birth to a *yaksha*.[6]

As a matter of fact, he had already become something of a public figure among the villagers. Despite this sophistication, however, in the matter of not lighting lamps at suppertime during the summer, he still observed the peasant custom. Therefore he was in for a scolding if he got back too late.

As he came home on this particular evening, Sevenpounder walked rather slowly. In one hand he held a pipe that was over six feet long. Made of Consorts Xiang bamboo, it boasted an ivory mouthpiece and a small pewter bowl.[7] Head bowed, he sat down

---

6. In popular Buddhism *yakshas* are violent demons that devour human flesh.

7. Named for two sisters (the Xiang Consorts) who were given to the ancient emperor Shun as consorts in 2288 B.C. When Shun died, they wept so copiously over his grave that their tears splashed onto the bamboo growing there, creating a new speckled variety.

on one of the low stools. Taking advantage of the diversion afforded by her father's arrival, Sixpounder appeared out of nowhere and sat by his side. "Daddy!" she cried in welcome, but Sevenpounder did not respond.

"Every generation's worse that the last," observed Mrs. Ninepounder.

Sevenpounder slowly raised his head, sighed, and said, "The Emperor's on the Dragon Throne again."[8]

Sister Sevenpounder was momentarily thrown for a loss, but then the light suddenly dawned on her as she decided exactly what that must mean. "Couldn't be better. A general amnesty will be declared by the grace of the Emperor!"

Sevenpounder sighed again. "I don't have a queue."

"Does the Emperor want queues?"

"The Emperor wants queues."

"How do you know?" she asked anxiously, showing a trace of genuine alarm.

"Down at the *Prosperity*[9] everybody says he does."

At this point Sister Sevenpounder intuitively felt that something really was not quite as it should be, for the *Prosperity* was the local news center. Glancing at Sevenpounder's queue-less head she could not help but feel angry. She blamed him, she hated him, she resented him, and then, quite suddenly, she sank into despair.

Angrily she filled a bowl, thrust it down in front of him, and said, "Might as well hurry up and eat your rice. Think that pullin' a long face like that is gonna grow you a new one?"

* * *

As the sun gathered in the last of its rays, the river air silently recovered its coolness. The threshing ground was now a busy chorus of chopsticks and bowls. Every spine was beaded with sweat. Having finished her third bowl of rice, Sister Sevenpounder happened to look up. Her heart began to *thump thump* out of control, for through the tallow leaves she had caught sight of chubby

---

8. This story is set against the background of the short-lived attempt (during the summer of 1917) by General Zhang Xun to bring down the republic founded in 1912 and restore the Manchu dynasty. As a token of their loyalty to the Manchus, Zhang and his men wore queues; see the Introduction. Also cf. n. 19 below.

9. The same wineshop figures prominently in the setting of "Kong Yiji."

little Seventh Master Zhao[10] walking up from the single-plank bridge. What was more, he was wearing his long blue cotton gown.

Seventh Master Zhao was proprietor of the *Bountiful Brook,* a wineshop in a neighboring village. He was the only person of renown for more than ten miles around—and something of a "scholarshipologist" to boot.[11] Since he was a man of learning, he always had about him something of the nostalgic air of a minister of state left over from a previous dynasty. He was the proud possessor of ten odd volumes of the Jin Shengtan edition of *Romance of the Three Kingdoms* and could often be seen sitting in his shop going over it word by word.[12] Not only could he reel off the names of the Five Tiger Generals, but he even knew that Huang Zhong was also known as Hansheng and that Ma Chao was also known as Mengqi. After the Revolution, Seventh Master Zhao had coiled his queue on top of his head, making himself look something like a Daoist priest.[13] Afterward he would often sigh and say that if only Zhao Zilung[14] were still alive, the world would never have fallen into its present state of disorder. Being keen of eye, however, Sister Sevenpounder had long since noticed, even from a distance, that Seventh Master Zhao had now ceased to resemble a Daoist priest: the front half of his skull was shaved and shiny, while the jet black hair on the back had been gathered into a queue.

Sister Sevenpounder was now certain that the Emperor really had ascended the Dragon Throne, that people would have to have queues, and that Sevenpounder was indeed in mortal danger. She

10. "Master" *(ye)* was a respectful term of address for males. He was the seventh-born among the males of the Zhao extended family (including cousins).

11. A satirical barb directed at the popular fashion of making everyone an "-ologist" of some sort.

12. Jin Shengtan (1610?–61) was unusual in that he valued popular fiction and drama as highly as he did the Confucian classics; see John Ching-yu Wang, *Chin Sheng-t'an* (New York: Twayne Publishers, 1972). *Romance of the Three Kingdoms* is a popular folk novel set in the Three Kingdoms period (A.D. 220–65) that assumed its present form during the fourteenth century. An English translation was made by C. H. Brewitt-Taylor in 1929, now available in reprint from Tuttle (1959). A more recent abridged translation by Moss Roberts is available from Pantheon under the title *Three Kingdoms: China's Epic Drama.*

13. The Qing dynasty (1644–1911) was founded by a non-Chinese people, the Manchus, who forced their Chinese subjects to adopt a hairstyle whose most distinguishing mark was the queue. After the Revolution of 1911, those who were either still loyal to the Manchus or not entirely convinced the Revolution would succeed often adopted Seventh Master Zhao's stratagem; see n. 8.

14. Most fearsome of the Five Tiger Generals in *Romance of the Three Kingdoms.*

was especially sure of this latter point, for Seventh Master Zhao rarely wore this blue gown of his without good reason. In the last three years he had worn it only twice: once when Pockface Ah-four, with whom he was on the outs, became ill; and once when Old Master Lu, who once smashed up his wineshop, had died.

This time made the third. Without a doubt, something else had happened that was cause for celebration on his part but spelled utter disaster for his enemies. Sister Sevenpounder recalled with a twinge that once when her husband had gotten drunk two years back, he had called Seventh Master Zhao "a sorry sonofabitch." Thus, catching sight of Zhao just now, she had immediately realized the danger Sevenpounder was in, and her heart had begun to pound instinctively.

Right on course, Seventh Master came cruising in toward Sevenpounder. Wherever he passed, people stood in his wake, pointed toward their bowls with chopsticks, and said, "Please join us, Seventh Master."

Nodding his head and saying, "Please go on with your meal," he passed them all by and sailed straight on to Sevenpounder's table. Sevenpounder and family hastened to greet him. Seventh Master smiled and said, "Please go on eating." At the same time he carefully scrutinized their food and commented, "Smells really good. Heard the news?" Now he stood directly behind Sevenpounder, facing Sister Sevenpounder.

"The Emperor has ascended the Dragon Throne," Sevenpounder answered.

Keeping her eye on Seventh Master Zhao, Sister Sevenpounder put on her best smile. "Since the Emperor has ascended the Dragon Throne, when is he going to announce the general amnesty?" she asked cheerily.

"General amnesty? Yes, I suppose there's bound to be one eventually." Having conceded this, however, Seventh Master Zhao assumed a stern air and asked, "But where, pray tell, is your Sevenpounder's queue? It's much more important than you might think. Remember back in the time of the Long Hairs how people used to say, *'Keep your hair and lose your head or keep your head and lose your hair'?*"[15]

---

15. The Taiping Rebellion (1851–64) was led by anti-Manchu rebels who let their hair grow free and were therefore known as "Long Hairs."

Since neither Sevenpounder nor his wife had any book learning, they were unable to plumb the depths of this historical allusion. Nonetheless, they did feel that since a man of great learning like Seventh Master Zhao had said so, the situation must indeed be grave. Thus his words struck their ears with a resounding clang, as though the death sentence had just been pronounced. Husband and wife were both speechless.

"Each generation's worse than the last . . ." Feeling very down-at-the-mouth just at this moment, Old Lady Ninepounder took advantage of the silence to address Seventh Master. "The Long Hairs nowadays—all they know how to do is to go around snippin' people's queues off so they don't look like Buddhists, and don't look like Daoists either.[16] Would the *old* Long Hairs have acted like that? Never! I've lived seventy-nine years and that's enough. Why the old Long Hairs would wrap their heads in whole bolts of red satin. It would trail way, way down to their ankles. And the princes they had! They'd be all dressed up in yellow satins that hung way down—way, way down. Yellow satins . . . red satins . . . yellow satins . . . I've lived long enough . . . seventy-nine years . . ."

Sister Sevenpounder got up and, talking to herself as much as to anyone else, said, "What are we going to do? Young and old, we all depend on him for a livin'."

Seventh Master Zhao shook his head. "Won't make a bit of difference. The punishment for not having a queue is written down in a book, plain as can be. Doesn't make any difference *how* many people are in the family."

Now when Sister Sevenpounder heard that it was written down in a book somewhere, she gave up all hope. Gripped by fear, she suddenly turned to her husband again and pointed at the tip of his nose with her chopsticks. "This deadbeat got himself into it, now let's see him get himself out of it. Back when they first started the Rebellion,[17] I'm the one who told him not to pole his boat for a

---

16. A Buddhist monk would have the head shaven clean; a Daoist one would have let the hair grow long. But since the hairstyle imposed by the Manchus involved shaving only the forehead, once the queue was cut off, a man would resemble neither a completely bald Buddhist monk nor an entirely hirsute Daoist one.

17. In their own minds, the Revolutionaries were taking away *(ge)* the Manchus' mandate *(ming)* to rule. In Chinese this is the origin of the term "revolution" *(geming)*. In the minds of villagers like Sister Sevenpounder, however, the Revolutionaries were starting

while, and *certainly* not to go to town. But, come hell or high water, he was bound and determined to haul his dead ass into town. Well, he went and got his queue cut off for his trouble. Used to have a nice long shiny black queue. Now he's got himself fixed up so he doesn't look like a Buddhist monk *or* a Daoist priest either. Wasn't enough that he got himself into this fix, he had to go and drag us along with him! Dead-ass jailbird!"

When the villagers had seen Seventh Master Zhao coming, they had all rushed through their meals and now they were all gathered round Sevenpounder's family dinner table. Sevenpounder himself was well aware that he was the star attraction of this little show and that it would be unseemly to simply allow his wife to curse him out in front of all his neighbors without letting out a peep.

Sevenpounder raised his head and began to speak slowly. "It's easy enough for you to talk now, but at the time you—"

"Dead-ass jailbird!"

Of all the spectators, Sister Bayi was the most kindhearted. Holding her two-year-old posthumous son[18] in her arms, she stood right next to Sister Sevenpounder taking in all the excitement. At this point she felt that Sister Sevenpounder had gone too far, and stepped in to make peace. "Forget it, Sister Sevenpounder. None of us are gods who can look into the future. At the time didn't I hear Sister Sevenpounder herself say that not havin' a queue was no disgrace? Besides, the Big Old Master in the *yamen* hasn't said anything yet one way or the other—"

Long before the young widow had said her piece, Sister Sevenpounder's ears had flushed scarlet. She shifted her chopsticks from Sevenpounder's nose and directed them at Sister Bayi. "Aiya, what in the world do you mean? I still consider myself human, you know—would a human ever come out with gibberish like that? Why, at the time I . . . I cried for three whole days. Everybody saw me. Even this little devil, Sixpounder, cried too." Having just finished a big bowl of rice, little Sixpounder now thrust an empty

---

(zao) a rebellion *(fan)*. The Chinese term "rebellion" *(zaofan)* has very different connotations from "revolution," and would have been the term used at the Manchu court to refer to the 1911 Revolution. The word *fan* may also describe the "rebellious" behavior of children, or of any person who tries to break down the barriers imposed by the prevailing social order. In "Ah Q—The Real Story," Ah Q also understands the Republican Revolution as *zaofan*.

18. *Yifuzi,* a son born after the death of the father.

ricebowl toward her mother and clamored for a refill. She could not have caught her mother at a worse moment. Sister Sevenpounder raised her chopsticks and brought them squarely down between Sixpounder's fork-horns with a loud crack. Then she turned her attention back to Sister Bayi. "And who asked you to butt in anyway, you man-starved young widow!"

Clang! The empty ricebowl fell from Sixpounder's hand and struck the corner of a brick lying on the ground. The metal gave way, leaving a large crack. Stamping his feet in anger, Sevenpounder picked up the bowl. He squeezed the crack shut, and examined it. "Little fucker!" he shouted and sent his daughter flying with a well-aimed blow.

The little girl now lay on the ground bawling. Old Lady Ninepounder grabbed one of her hands and pulled Sixpounder to her feet while repeatedly observing, "One generation's worse than the last."

Sister Bayi lost her temper too and yelled, "Sister Sevenpounder, it's not fair for you and your old man to take it out on your kid!"

At the beginning Seventh Master Zhao had been just a smiling bystander, but as soon as Sister Bayi remarked that the "Big Old Master in the *yamen* hadn't said anything one way or the other," he began to wax a little wroth himself. Now he came around the side of the table and picked up where Sister Bayi's remark left off. "Who's got time to worry about taking it out on a kid? Soldiers will be arriving here any minute! There's something else you people ought to know. The defender of the throne this time is none other than General Zhang. And General Zhang is a descendant of the famous Yan general Zhang Fei.[19] He has an eighteen-foot spear and courage enough to take on ten thousand men! Who can stand up to a man like that?" He raised his two hands and held them apart, slightly cupped and parallel, as if they grasped an invisible eighteen-foot spear. He lunged toward Sister Bayi and demanded, "Can *you* stand up to him?"

---

19. Zhang Fei is a well-known hero in *Romance of the Three Kingdoms,* while General Zhang refers to Zhang Xun (1854–1923), a contemporary warlord who was originally an officer in the Manchu army. Because of their loyalist sentiments, Zhang Xun and his men had retained the queue even after the Republican Revolution. In the summer of 1917, General Zhang and his "pigtail army" briefly occupied Beijing and announced the restoration of the Manchu dynasty. He was opposed by other warlords who quickly suppressed the attempted revival. The present story reflects these events. Cf. n. 8 above.

Holding her child and still trembling with rage, Sister Bayi now shifted her gaze from Sister Sevenpounder to Seventh Master Zhao: his face was bathed in sweat, his eyes starting from their sockets, and as he lunged forward, his imaginary spear was aimed straight at her! Frightened out of her wits, Sister Bayi did not dare stay around to finish what she had to say. She turned and fled. Seventh Master Zhao followed in pursuit.

While blaming Sister Bayi for having butted in to begin with, the spectators cleared a path for both of them. A few men who had cut off their queues and had now started growing new ones quickly fell to the rear of the crowd lest Seventh Master catch sight of them. At this point, however, Seventh Master was not interested in conducting a queue survey. Having made his way through the crowd, he abruptly changed course and disappeared behind the tallow trees shouting, "Can any of *you* stand up to him?" Finally he stepped up on the single-plank bridge and haughtily strode away.

The villagers stood there speechless. They turned his question over in their own minds, and they all arrived at the same conclusion: they were indeed no match for Zhang Fei, and thus they also concluded that Sevenpounder was dead meat for sure. What was more, thinking back on things it occurred to them that since Sevenpounder was after all a man who had gone against the imperial law, he should not have acted so high and mighty in the past when he used to sit there and smoke his pipe as he told them all the news he had picked up in town. They even seemed a bit pleased to learn that he was a lawbreaker. They also seemed inclined to express their opinions about what had just transpired, but at the same time they felt that they had no opinions worth expressing.

In a chaos of buzzes, the evening mosquitoes bounced off bared chests and swarmed back to nesting places under the tallow trees. Slowly the villagers dispersed to their homes, bolted their doors, and went to sleep. Mumbling to herself, Sister Sevenpounder cleared the table, moved it and the stools back inside, bolted the door, and went to sleep too.

Sevenpounder carried the broken bowl to his door and sat down on the threshold to smoke. However, he was so upset tonight that he didn't even draw on the ivory mouthpiece, and the glow in the pewter bowl at the end of his six-foot bamboo pipe gradually died out. In his heart he simply felt that what he was facing had all the earmarks of a full-blown crisis. He tried to think of ways to avert it, to come up with a plan or two, but his thoughts were so vague and disconnected that he was unable to string them together into any coherent program of action. *Where's your queue, where's your queue? . . . A spear eighteen feet long . . . One generation's worse than the last! . . . The Emperor's ascended the Dragon Throne.* "I'll have to take the broken bowl to town and have it riveted." *Can you stand up to him? . . . Written down in a book, as plain as can be.* "Motherfuckers!"

* * *

As usual, early the next morning Sevenpounder poled his boat from Lu Village into town. He returned toward evening, carrying his six-foot pipe of Consorts Xiang bamboo along with a single ricebowl. At the supper table he told Old Lady Ninepounder that he'd had the bowl repaired in town. Because the crack was so large, it had taken sixteen copper rivets at three coppers a rivet. He had spent forty-eight coppers on it.

With great dissatisfaction Old Lady Ninepounder said, "One generation's worse than the last. I've lived long enough. Three coppers a rivet. Did rivets used to be so expensive? Rivets *used* to cost . . . I've lived seventy-nine years . . ."

Although Sevenpounder continued to go into town every day as he'd always done, the atmosphere at home was somewhat bleak and quiet. Rather than coming over to hear what news he had brought back, most of the villagers now avoided him. Sister Sevenpounder was also somewhat less than civil and often referred to him as "jailbird."

After about a week and a half, Sevenpounder came home from town one evening and found his wife in an unaccountably cheerful mood. "Happen to hear anything in town today?" she asked.

"Nothin' in particular."

"Is the Emperor on his Dragon Throne?"

"Nobody talked about it."

"And you didn't hear anything over at the *Prosperity* either?"

"Not there either."

"I think it's a sure thing he's *not* gonna take back the Dragon

Throne either. I walked past Seventh Master Zhao's place today. He was just sittin' there with his books again, the way he always used to. His queue was coiled right up on the top of his head, too. Wasn't wearin' his long robe either."

"You mean you think the Emperor's not gonna take the Throne after all?"

"I think not."

* * *

Today's Sevenpounder has once again become that Sevenpounder who is respected and treated well by wife and villagers. When summer comes, smiling and waving to each other, the villagers eat on the threshing ground in front of their own doors as they always have. Old Lady Ninepounder has long since celebrated the grand occasion of her eighth decade of longevity. She is still as dissatisfied and healthy as ever. Sixpounder's fork-horns have been transformed into a single large braid. Although her feet have recently been bound, she is still able to help her mother do some of the work and can be seen hobbling back and forth on the threshing ground, a ricebowl repaired with sixteen rivets in her hands.

OCTOBER 1920

Hometown

Braving the bone-cold weather, I was headed back to my hometown, a hometown from which I was separated by over six hundred miles and more than twenty years.

It was in the depth of winter and as I drew closer to the place where I'd grown up, the sky clouded over and a cold wind whistled into the cabin of my boat. Through a crack in the canopy, I peered out into the distance. Scattered across the distant horizon, towns and villages came into view under the vast and graying sky: they were drab, desolate, devoid of any semblance of life. I was assailed by a depression against which I was utterly powerless.

No! This was not the countryside I had recalled time and again for more than twenty years. The area *I* remembered was far, far more lovely. And yet, had you demanded that I summon its beauties from the recesses of memory or catalog its various excellences, no concrete image would have appeared in my mind's eye and I would have been unable to reply. My "hometown" was probably nothing more than what lay before me. "This is probably what it really *was* like," I told myself. "To be sure, there are no signs of progress, but then again it's probably not so depressing as I seem to feel at the moment either. Perhaps it's just that my attitude has changed, especially since I'm not coming back in a happy mood to begin with."

My sole purpose in coming back this time was to bid my home an everlasting farewell. The old family compound[1] in which members of our clan had lived for so many years had already been sold lock, stock, and barrel to people of another surname. The transaction was to be completed by the end of the year. In the short

---

First published in *New Youth,* vol. 9, no. 1 (May 1921).

1. Family compounds were large enough to afford living space to an extended family of several generations. In 1919 Lu Xun bought a house in Beijing and went back to Shaoxing to sell the family dwelling there and to bring his wife and mother back to the capital, where they would live in the newly acquired house along with Lu Xun's two younger brothers, Zhou Zuoren and Zhou Jianren, and their wives and children. Lu Xun, his wife, and mother would stay there until 1923, when they would move out in the wake of a quarrel between Lu Xun and Zhuo Zuoren. "Hometown," of course, reflects Lu Xun's 1919 experience in going back to Shaoxing to sell the family property.

interim before the New Year, we would have to take our final leave of those comfortable old rooms and move away from this familiar countryside to the strange and faraway place where I now earned my keep.

Early the next morning I stood before the gate of our family compound. Up on the tile roof, broken stalks of withered vines trembled in the wind and made plain the reason it had not been possible to keep those old rooms from changing hands. The pervading silence suggested that several branches of the family must have already moved out. By the time I made my way back to the rooms that our branch occupied, my mother had already come out to greet me. My eight-year-old nephew Hong'er darted out from behind her.

Though she was obviously happy to see me, I also read hints of melancholy in her face. She bade me sit down and rest, gave me some tea, but avoided any mention of the impending move. Hong'er, whom I had never seen before, stood off at a distance observing me.

At long last we broached the subject of moving. I said I had already rented a place for us and had even bought a few sticks of furniture. I explained that we would have to sell our household goods down here and then use that money to buy whatever else we might need up north. Mother readily assented. She already had our baggage pretty much gathered together and ready to go. On her own initiative, she had even sold the heavy furniture that couldn't readily be moved. She had not yet, however, been able to collect the money people owed her for it.

"As soon as you've rested a day or so, you can make the rounds of our relatives and then we'll be all set," she told me.

"Yes, Mother."

"And don't forget to see Runtu. He asks for you every time he comes by. Says he would really like to see you again. I told him around what day you'd be back, so he *could* show up most anytime."

Instantaneously, a marvelous scene flashed before my eyes: a round moon hanging against a blue black sky, beneath it a stretch of sandy ground planted with emerald green watermelons stretching as far as the eye could see, and standing in the midst of all those melons a twelve-year-old boy, a silver ring around his neck, a pitchfork in his hand. Suddenly and with all his might the boy stabs at a *zha,* but the crafty animal makes a lightning turn, runs back between his legs, and makes good its escape.[2]

The boy in that scene was Runtu.[3] Back when I first met him—it will soon be thirty years ago—I couldn't have been much more than ten myself. Since my father was still alive at the time, our family was still fairly well-to-do, and I was something of a "young gentleman." That particular year it was incumbent upon our branch of the clan to perform a certain sacrifice that rolled around, or so it was said, only once every thirty-odd years. Consequently it was to be an occasion of great solemnity.

During the first month, images of our ancestors would be displayed on the altar. The offerings set out before them would be lavish and the sacrificial utensils exquisite. With so many people participating, it would be necessary to guard against theft. However, we had only one "busy-monther" to help out and he already had more work than he could keep up with. And so he suggested that his son Runtu be brought in to keep an eye on the sacrificial vessels. (Down home, workers were divided into three categories: if they worked the whole year long for one family, they were "yearlongs"; if they worked by the day, they were "short-timers"; and if they tilled their own land but worked for a specific family just during the holidays or when rents were being collected, they were "busy-monthers.")

Since I had heard about Runtu for a long time, I was glad when father agreed. I knew he was about my own age. He'd been born in the *run* month and among the five elements he was lacking only in *tu,* so his father had called him Runtu.[4] Best of all, Runtu knew all about how to set snares and catch birds!

---

2. Lu Xun invents his own character for the word *zha* (the "animal radical" plus a phonetic element to suggest the sound). When he was later asked to give a closer identification of this animal, he said that it was probably a badger *(huan)* of some kind. Since the local dialect called it a *zha* he had made up a character to suit both the sound and meaning.

3. Mentioned in several of Lu Xun's writings, the character Runtu is based on an actual peasant who lived close to Shaoxing. Now deceased, his name was Zhang Yunshui. His son Zhang Changming is still alive and well, and his grandson Zhang Gui is employed at the Lu Xun Museum in Shaoxing.

4. *Run* is the name of the intercalary month. The lunar calendar required adjustment every so often—if nothing were done, snow might eventually have fallen in June. Thus, every few years an extra (intercalary) month was incorporated to make real time accord

From that time on I looked forward eagerly to the New Year, for I knew that when it came so would Runtu. It seemed that *this* year would never end. But the day did finally arrive when Mother summoned me to announce that Runtu had come and was now in the kitchen. I ran as fast as my legs would carry me.

He had a purplish round face and wore a little felt hat. You could tell that his father loved him very much, because around his neck he wore a large, shimmering silver ring. That meant that his father had feared he might die during childhood and had taken him before a statue of the Buddha where, in exchange for the protection of his son, he had promised to do something for the Buddha in return. It was then that they would have put that neckring on to show that Runtu was tied to life and protected by Buddha.

Runtu was shy with the adults around our house but wasn't at all timid with me, and would talk a blue streak whenever we were by ourselves. Before half the day was out, we had actually gotten to know each other quite well. I can't recall *what* we talked about —I only remember how excited and happy Runtu was. He told me that this was the first time he'd ever been to town and that he had already seen all sorts of strange and wondrous things he'd never even dreamed of before.

The next day, I wanted him to catch birds. "Can't right now. You have to have lots of snow. Out by the ocean where we live, I always wait till there's a good snowfall. Then I sweep a place nice and clean, take a little stick, and prop up a big, big bamboo basket. I sprinkle some grain underneath and tie a string to the bottom of the stick. Then I back way, way off and wait for the birds to come. One little tug and I've got them. A little bit of everything —bluebacks, hornchicks, paddychicks, pigeons . . ."

How I longed for snow!

"It's kind of cold now, but you oughta come out our way in the summer. Days, we could go out to the beach and collect shells— reds, blues, ghost-scarers, Guanyin hands.[5] Nights, when Dad

---

with the calendar. *Tu* is the "earth" element. Whenever a baby was born, a man or woman specialized in interpreting the five elements was called in to assess the balance of the elements in the child's constitution, for these were believed to determine its fate. One could compensate for any lack or imbalance that was discovered by giving the child an appropriate name.

5. "Ghost-scarers" were shells that the local children sometimes wore on bracelets to ward off evil spirits. "Guanyin hands" were starfish, so named because their many arms called to mind the arms of the Thousand-handed Guanyin (Goddess of Mercy).

and me go to guard the watermelon patch, you could go right along with us."

"Are you afraid people are going to steal your melons?"

"Nope. If somebody happens to be walkin' by and picks one 'cause he's thirsty, we don't take that as stealin'. What we're lookin' out for are badgers, porcupines, and *zha.* When the moon's out and you hear a *crunch crunch,* you know you've got a *zha* bitin' into a melon. You grab your pitchfork and . . ."

At the time I didn't know what sort of thing a *zha* was to begin with—still don't as a matter of fact—but somehow or other I felt it must look like some sort of little dog and be fierce as all get-out.

"Won't it bite you?"

"Well, you've got your pitchfork, right? You sneak up on him and when you've got him in sight, you let him have it. Are those little guys ever quick on their feet! They'll turn around and run right back between your legs if you don't watch 'em. They've got these coats all slippery-slick, like oil, and . . ."

I had never dreamed that the world was so full of so many new and marvelous things. Just to think that the seashore had all those wonderful colored shells to offer! And even watermelons had a danger-filled story behind them that I'd never suspected. All I'd known was that you buy them in fruit stores.

"Out there by the seashore just before the spring tides, you'll see a whole bunch of jumperfish hoppin' around all over the place. They've got these two little legs on 'em just like frogs and . . ."

Wow! Runtu's mind was an inexhaustible treasure-house of exotic things, things my everyday friends knew nothing about, for while Runtu was out there by the sea, they—like me—had nothing to look out on but the square patch of sky that was visible above the high walls of a family courtyard.

Unfortunately the first month of the New Year came to an end and Runtu had to go home. I wailed. He cried too. Then he hid in our kitchen and refused to come out. In the end, however, his father took him away. Later on he sent me a package of shells by way of his father, and some beautiful bird feathers too. And I also sent him some things a few times after that, but I never saw him again.

Now, when my mother said that Runtu might drop by, memories of my boyhood suddenly came alive again as though illumined by a brilliant flash of lightning. For a fraction of a second, I even seemed to recapture that beautiful homeland I thought I had lost. "Great!" I said. "How . . . how's he doing these days?"

"Now? Well, things aren't going at all well for him." Mother turned and looked outside as she answered. "*Those* people are back again. Pretend they're looking at the furniture and then make off with whatever they can get hold of. I'd better go out and keep an eye on them."

Mother got up and went out. I could hear the voices of several women outside the door. I motioned to Hong'er to come over and chat with me. I asked him if he knew how to write yet and if he was looking forward to our trip.

"Will we get to ride a train?"

"Yes."

"A boat, too?"

"First we take the boat and then . . ."

"Would you look at him now! He's even got a beard!" A strange, shrill voice suddenly sliced through the air.

Startled, I quickly raised my head and saw a woman of fifty or so standing before me. Her cheekbones protruded and her lips were thin. Wearing a pair of trousers (she hadn't tied a skirt over them), hands on her hips, legs wide apart, she stood balanced on a pitiful little pair of bound feet, looking for all the world like a pair of compasses out of someone's drafting kit.

"Don't recognize me, huh? I used to hold you in my arms when you were just a kid!"

I was even more at a loss. Fortunately my mother came back in at this juncture and said, "He's been away a good many years and he's forgotten everything." Then she turned to me. "But you really ought to remember her. She's Second Sister Yang. You know, the woman who lived kitty-corner to our place and ran the beancurd shop."

Now I remembered. When I was a child there had been a Second Sister Yang sitting from one end of the day to the other in the beancurd shop diagonally across from us. People called her the "Beancurd Beauty."

Back then she used to powder her face, and her cheekbones weren't so high, nor were her lips so thin. What was more, since she had always been seated, I had never before seen this "compasses" pose of hers. Back then people used to say that she was the reason the shop did such a surprisingly good business. No doubt because of my tender age, I must have been immune to the alchemy of her charms, for I had forgotten her completely. Thus, "Compasses" was more than a little put out with me. She looked at me with utter disdain and the kind of smile that one might wear upon discovering a Frenchman who had never heard of Napoleon or an American who didn't know who Washington was.

Her laugh was cold. "Forgot, huh? Case of the higher you go, the snootier you—"

"How could I ever be like that . . . why I . . ." Completely flustered, I stood up.

"Well in that case, Elder Brother Xun, I'll put it right up front. You're rich now and it's not all that easy to move big, heavy stuff anyway, so why not let me take all this rickety old furniture off your hands. Poor folks like us can still get a lotta use out of it."

"I'm not rich at all. I have to sell this furniture just to—"

"Come off it. I know you're a big official—a Daotai, they say.[6] And you're gonna stand there and tell me you're not rich? You've got three concubines and an eight-man sedan chair team to carry you around wherever you wanna go. Not rich? Hah! You can't put anything over on me!"

I knew it would make no difference no matter what I said, so I held my peace and simply stood there.

"Yup, it's true all right. The more money they get, the less they'll turn loose. And the less they turn loose, the more they get!" Compasses angrily turned her back to me and slowly walked away, issuing a steady stream of chatter as she went. On her way out, she picked up a pair of my mother's gloves and shoved them into the waistband of her trousers.

During the next few days clansmen and relatives who lived nearby came around to pay visits. I met these social obligations as best I could, stealing time from them whenever possible to finish packing.

One very cold afternoon just after lunch I was sitting and drinking tea when I heard someone come in from the outside. When I turned around to look I couldn't help but start with surprise. I scrambled to my feet and rushed over to welcome him.

---

6. Although the republic had been established a half dozen years or so earlier, Second Sister Yang still refers to him with an official title that was employed during the late Manchu dynasty.

It was Runtu. Although I recognized him right off, he was not at all the Runtu who lived in my memory. He seemed twice as tall now. The round and ruddy face of yesteryear had already turned pale and grey, and it was etched with deep wrinkles. The rims of his eyes were swollen and red just like his father's. I knew that most farmers who worked close to the sea got that way because of the wind. He was wearing a battered old felt hat, and his cotton clothes were so thin that he was shivering. His hands held a paper package along with his pipe. They were not the smooth and nimble hands that I remembered. Now they were rough, clumsy, and as cracked as pine bark.

I was beside myself with enthusiasm, but didn't know how to begin and simply said, "Brother Runtu, you've come . . ."

There was so much I wanted to say. There were so many words waiting to gush out one after the other like pearls on a string: hornchicks, jumperfish, Guanyin hands, *zha*—but at the same time I was aware of something damming them up inside me, so that they simply swirled around in my brain without a single one coming out.

As he stood there his expression was a mixture of happiness and melancholy. His lips began to move, but not a single word came out. Finally he assumed a very respectful attitude and addressed me in a loud clear voice: "Master!"

I shuddered as I realized what a wretched, thick wall now stood between us. I too was at a loss for words. He turned around and said, "Shuisheng, kowtow to the Master." He grabbed a child who up to this point had been hiding behind him and hauled him around front. This boy was Runtu—twenty years ago, although somewhat paler and thinner than his father had been. The only real difference was that Shuisheng had no silver neckring. "This is my fifth. Hasn't been out and around much, so he's pretty shy."

Mother and Hong'er must have heard us talking because they came down from upstairs.

"Old Missus. I got your letter a long time back. You don't know how happy I was to hear the Master was comin' home," said Runtu.

"Hey, what in the world's come over you that you're so formal. You two used to call each other 'Brother.' Just call him 'Brother Xun' the way you used to."

"Ah, the Old Missus is really too . . . What kind of manners would that be? We were just kids then. We didn't know any better." While Runtu was talking, he was also trying to get Shuisheng to bow to my mother, but the boy was very embarrassed and stuck like glue to his father's back.

"Is that Shuisheng, your fifth?" Mother asked. "To him, we're all strangers. No wonder he's so shy. Why not let him and Hong'er go out together and play."

When Hong'er heard that, he immediately ran over and greeted the boy. Shuisheng wasn't the least bit shy with him, and apparently feeling very much at ease, went outside with my nephew to play. Mother asked Runtu to have a seat. He hesitated for a bit but finally sat down and leaned his long pipe against the table. He handed the paper package across to me and said, "We don't have much of anything in the winter, but these dried peas are ones I sunned myself. Please accept them, Master . . ."

I asked how he was doing. He shook his head.

"Things are pretty rough. Even my sixth is old enough to help out now, but still with all the fightin' and people wantin' money of you every place you turn—you can never be sure how much—and what with all the bad harvests, we just never seem to have enough to eat. When you *do* take whatever crop you've got and head off to market, you've gotta pay a whole bunch of taxes before you ever get there. Ends up so you don't even get back what you've put into it. But if you *don't* take it to market, it's just gonna rot in the field anyway . . ."

He stopped talking but continued to shake his head. There was no movement in any of the wrinkles that life had etched upon him and one would have thought that his face was carved from stone. He probably felt all the pain, but could not find the words to express it. He sat in silence for a while and then picked up his pipe and began to smoke.

Through further questioning, Mother learned that he still had much to do at home and would have to leave tomorrow. She also found out that he'd gone without lunch and told him to go into the kitchen and make himself a little something.

After he went out, Mother and I both sighed at his plight: too many children, famine, harsh taxes, soldiers, bandits, officials, gentryfolk—everything had plagued until he'd become the lifeless wooden figure we saw today. Mother said that we ought to see to it that he got as much of what we weren't going to take with us as possible. So we told him to take whatever he wanted.

He selected a few things that very afternoon—two long tables, an incense burner, some candlesticks, and a set of scales. He also asked for the ashes from our kitchen stove. (We cooked with rice stalks, and the ashes would provide good fertilizer for the sandy soil out his way.) He gathered everything together and said he would come for it in a boat the day we moved out.

We chatted a bit more that night, but none of it amounted to anything. Early the next morning he took Shuisheng and headed back on home.

Nine days later the time for our departure finally arrived. Runtu came early in the morning. Shuisheng wasn't with him this time, but he'd brought along a five-year-old girl to keep an eye on the boat. We were so busy that we had no time to chat. Several other people came by, some to see us off, others to get things, and still others to get things *and* to see us off. By the time we boarded the boat that afternoon, the old house had been swept clean of old and used things of every imaginable size and description.

As we proceeded upriver, the twilight-green mountains on either bank took on deeper hues and joined together in a single blue-green mass as they fled away into the distance behind the stern. Hong'er and I leaned against the window and watched the dimming landscape. Suddenly he asked, "Uncle, when are we coming back?"

"Coming back? What are you doing thinking about coming back before we've even left?"

"But Shuisheng invited me to go have some fun at his place." Engrossed by thoughts of his new friend, Hong'er opened his large black eyes even wider in fascination.

Mother and I weren't immune to nostalgia ourselves, and began talking about Runtu again. She told me that ever since she'd started packing, Second Sister Yang—the Beancurd Beauty—had never let a single day pass without coming by. Just the day before yesterday she had retrieved a dozen or so plates from the pile of rice-stalk ashes. After questioning my mother, Second Sister Yang concluded that they must have been hidden there by Runtu so that he could make off with them when he came for the other stuff.

Having made this discovery, she apparently felt that she'd rendered us a rewardable service, for she picked up the dog-crazer without so much as a by-your-leave and took off with it just as fast as her legs would carry her. (The dog-crazer was a device we used back home in raising chickens. It consisted of a wooden bowl covered with a lattice-like arrangement wide enough for the chickens to poke their heads through, but too narrow for the dogs, who could only stand around "crazed" with frustration while the chickens ate.) Mother said she had never imagined that Second Sister Yang could develop such speed on those little feet of hers.

My hometown receded ever farther into the distance and the familiar landscapes of the surrounding countryside gradually disappeared too. Strange to say, there was not a shred of regret in my heart. I only felt that there was a high and invisible wall all around me that isolated me from my fellow human beings, a wall that was squeezing the breath out of my body. That usually comforting image of a little hero with silver neckring standing in the middle of a melon patch was now blurred out of focus and stirred nothing in me but a feeling of melancholy.

Mother and Hong'er had both gone to sleep.

As I lay there and listened to the gentle slapping of water against the hull, I knew that Runtu and I were going on separate roads. "Even though we're irrevocably cut off from each other," I thought, "didn't Hong'er start to miss Shuisheng when we had barely set out? I hope they'll never live like my generation with everyone cut off from everyone else. And yet, just to keep that from happening, I wouldn't want them to have this vagabond life of mine, any more than I'd want them to have Runtu's barren one. Still less would I want them to muddle through the hedonistic lives other people lead. There ought to be a *new* life for them, a life that none of us has ever known."

As my thoughts turned toward hope, a feeling of anxiety suddenly possessed me. When Runtu took the censer and candlesticks, I had laughed at him behind his back. "Can't let go of that superstitious idol-worship of his for a single minute!" But what was this thing called "hope" if not an idol that *I* had fashioned with my own hands. The things he hoped for were immediate, while what I wanted was somewhere far off in the murky distance—that was the only difference.

As I lay there half asleep, an emerald green plot of land by the sea appeared before my eyes. In the deep blue sky above it hung a moon, full and golden. "Hope isn't the kind of thing that you can say either exists or doesn't exist," I thought to myself. "It's like a path across the land—it's not there to begin with, but when lots of people go the same way, it comes into being."

JANUARY 1921

Ah Q—The Real Story

Chapter I
An Introduction

For at least a couple of years now, I've had it in the back of my mind to do a biography of Ah Q, but whenever it's come right down to it, I've always had second thoughts. Goes to show I'm not the kind of writer who *Forgeth words of immortalitie / For generations yet to be.*[1] Besides, if you're going to get your words to last all that long, they've got to be about someone worth remembering all that long in the first place. Then the man gets remembered because of the words, and the words because of the man. And then after a while people gradually lose track of which one's remembered because of which. Knowing all of this, why did I finally settle on the likes of Ah Q for a biography? Guess the devil made me do it.

No sooner did I take up my writing brush to begin this very *un*immortal work of mine than I ran into a horrendous host of difficulties.

One. The question of a title. What *kind* of biography was it to be? As Confucius once said, *"Be the title not just so / Then the words refuse to flow."*[2] You really *do* have to be pretty darned careful about titles. But there are so many! Why, just for biographies alone there are enough titles hanging around to make your

---

First published in weekly, sometimes biweekly, installments under the pen name Ba Ren in the literary supplement to the Beijing *Morning Post* from December 4, 1921, to February 12, 1922. In 1921 the *Morning Post* began to publish a humorous weekly column entitled "Cheerful Anecdotes." Editorial responsibility was placed in the hands of Sun Fuyuan (1894–1966), a native of Shaoxing, who had once been Lu Xun's student there. Thus it was only natural that he should press his former teacher for a contribution. After reading the first installment, however, Sun decided that "Ah Q" was inappropriate for the humor column and moved it to "New Literature" instead. Though the author used a new pen name, he gave his readers hints—we shall point one out below—that "Ah Q . . . " was written by the same writer they knew as Lu Xun.

1. The *Zuo Zhuan,* a historical work dating from the third or fourth century B.C., lists three immortal accomplishments of the virtuous man: establishing virtue, establishing civil or military merit, and establishing words.

2. *The Analects of Confucius* 13.3.

head swim: *narrative biography, autobiography, private biography, public biography, supplementary biography, family biography, biographical sketch.* Trouble is—not one of them fits.

Narrative biography? That's the kind done for well-heeled people rich enough to make it into the official histories, and Ah Q certainly wouldn't be at home in that crowd. *Autobiography?* But I'm not Ah Q. *Public biography?* Okay then, where's the *private* one? Or, why not just make this one the *private* one? But then *private biography* is the term they use for accounts of Daoist monks who live forever, and Ah Q doesn't fit in with that crew either. *Supplementary biography?* But then there'd have to be a *basic biography* for this to be supplementary *to,* and the president of our republic has yet to order the National Historical Institute to do the basic one. Still and all, that didn't stop Charles Dickens. You won't find any section entitled "Narrative Biographies of Gamblers" in the standard English histories, but he went right ahead and called one of his works *Alternate Biographies of Gamblers* just the same, even though there were no standard ones for them to be alternate to.[3] Well, a literary giant like Dickens might get away with something like that, but I certainly wouldn't be able to pull it off.

How about *family biography?* Yes, but I'm not part of his family, nor has any of his descendants come by to commission me to do it. *Abbreviated biography* won't work either because there's no full one around. When you come right down to it, what I'm writing here is going to be the only standard biography of Ah Q you'll find anywhere. Of course I don't dare forget my place and call it that, for the style is "vulgar" and the language I've cast it in is not the language of the classics but rather the "vile vernacular of mere rickshaw boys and peddlers."[4] And so in the end I've taken my title

3. Lu Xun, as he himself recognized a few years later, is mistaken here. *Alternate Biographies of Gamblers (Botu biezhuan)* is the Chinese title of Sir Arthur Conan Doyle's *Rodney Stone.*

4. A sarcastic reference to Lin Shu (1852–1924). A prolific and respected translator of foreign fiction, Lin always wrote in the literary language. As an implacable enemy of the vernacular movement, in 1919 he wrote an open letter to the liberal chancellor of Beijing University, Cai Yuanpei (1876–1940), accusing him of utterly destroying Confucian morality. At one point he indignantly penned, "only real scholarship and real morality can survive and command respect. If all the old classical books were discarded and replaced by the vernacular, then all the rickshaw boys and peddlers in Beijing and Tianjin could be regarded as professors because their vernacular is more grammatical and correct than the Fujian and Guangzhou dialects." Lin Shu was himself a native of Fujian. See Chow Tse-tsung, *The May Fourth Movement* (Stanford: Stanford University Press, 1967), p. 69.

from a phrase that's popular among the storytellers, those lowly souls who have always been beyond the pale of the Three Doctrines and Nine Schools.[5] Storytellers often end a long digression with the cliché, "Enough of this idle chatter, let's get back to the *real story.*" That's where I got my title from. And if "real story" in this context gets mixed up with the "real story" in that book left to us by the ancients, *The Real Story of Calligraphy*—well, sorry, I just don't have the time to worry about all that.[6]

Two. The standard format for biographies requires that you begin with something like: "So-and-so, whose courtesy name was this-or-that, was a native of such-and-such." The trouble is I don't know what Ah Q's family name was. There was once a day when it *seemed* to be Zhao, but then the very next morning it wasn't all that clear anymore. That was the day Old Master Zhao's son passed the *Budding Talent* exam.

With a *clang-clang* of gongs and all the usual pomp, the good news arrived in the village. As luck would have it, Ah Q had just downed a bowl of wine or two. Soon as he heard the news, he danced for joy and told everyone what a great honor this was to him *personally* because he belonged to the same clan as Old Master Zhao. As a matter of fact, the way Ah Q had it worked out, he even came out three notches above the *Budding Talent* in the clan's generational pecking order! The people who were standing around when Ah Q announced this actually began to treat him with more respect too.

Who could have foreseen that the very next day the local sheriff would order Ah Q to hightail it on out to the Zhaos' place? As soon as Old Master Zhao clapped eyes on Ah Q, the old fellow's face flushed scarlet. "Ah Q, you miserable bastard," he bellowed, "did you say you're a clansman of mine?"

Ah Q didn't let out a peep. The more the old man looked at him, the madder he got. He bore in a few steps closer: "How dare

---

5. The three doctrines are Confucianism, Buddhism, and Daoism. The nine schools are (1) Confucian, (2) Daoist, (3) Yin-yang, (4) Legalist, (5) School of Names, (6) Mohist, (7) Alliances and Strategies, (8) Miscellaneous Writers, and (9) Agriculturalist.

6. A Qing dynasty (1644–1911) work by Feng Wu. The Chinese expression translated as "real story" *(zheng zhuan)* may be alternately read as *zheng chuan,* meaning "orthodox transmission." Thus the title of Feng Wu's work might be more accurately translated as *Passing on the Correct Way of Doing Calligraphy.*

you talk such rubbish? How could *I* possibly have a clansman like *you?*"

Still not a peep. Just as Ah Q was about to beat a hasty retreat, Old Master Zhao bolted forward and slapped him across the face. "How could *you* be named Zhao? How could you even *deserve* to be named Zhao?"

Instead of offering any argument to prove that he was an honest-to-goodness Zhao, Ah Q simply retreated on out through the gate, putting his hand to his cheek as he went. The sheriff escorted him and gave him another good bawling out once they were outside. Only after Ah Q had greased that notable's palm with two hundred coppers was he free of him. Everybody who heard about this agreed that Ah Q had been too reckless, that he had gone *looking* for a beating, for more than likely he wasn't named Zhao in the first place. And supposing he was? What with Master Zhao living right there in the area, he shouldn't have been dumb enough to say so. After that, nobody ever mentioned Ah Q's family background again. And so—to make a long story short—I have no idea what his family name was.

Three. I don't know how to write his *given* name either. While he was alive everybody called him Ah-QUEI,[7] but after he died, even the man on the street never thought of mentioning his name again. Much less did any scholar-official take it into his head to *inscribe it on bamboo and silk for generations yet to be.*[8] And so it is that I lead the way in facing up to a linguistic crisis: should the QUEI be written with the character meaning "laurel" or with the one meaning "high rank"?

If Ah Q had used the character meaning "moon pavilion" as his courtesy name, or if he had been born in the eighth lunar month, then his given name would certainly be written with the QUEI meaning "laurel."[9] But he didn't *have* a courtesy name. Or if he

7. The "Ah" of Ah Q is a common prefix for given names especially in south China, and is always written with the same Chinese character. Here Lu Xun spells out the "quei" in roman letters, claiming he does not know which Chinese character (there are many homophones) it should be. This makes for a jarring effect in a Chinese text; I have attempted to convey this by using capital letters. The current *pinyin* spelling of this syllable would actually be *gui.*

8. The *locus classicus* for this phrase is a work of the third century B.C. entitled *Historical Anecdotes of Mr. Lü (Lü shi chun qiu).*

9. The eighth lunar month is also known as the Laurel Month.

did, nobody knew it. If only at some point in his career he had sent out invitations soliciting eulogies on the grand occasion of his fiftieth or sixtieth birthday, the way scholar-officials do, then I could check "laurel" against those. But since Ah Q never sent out any such invitations, it would be downright dogmatic of me to insist on "laurel."

Again, if he'd had an elder or younger brother named Ah Fu, written with the *fu* that means "riches," then Ah Q's QUEI would certainly be written with the character meaning "high rank" so as to balance it. But Ah Q was a loner, and so I've got no evidence in favor of the word meaning "high rank" either. I have even less of a case for any of the other relatively obscure characters pronounced "QUEI." I once tried asking Old Master Zhao's son, his nibs the *Budding Talent.*[10] You can imagine my surprise when I ended up drawing a blank from someone as learned and cultivated as Mister *Budding Talent* himself. But the upshot of what little he *did* have to say was that there was no longer any way of telling what character "QUEI" should be, because ever since Chen Duxiu[11] had put out that radical magazine *New Youth* and advocated scrapping the Chinese characters altogether in favor of spelling with a foreign alphabet, our "national heritage" had sunk into utter oblivion.

The only thing I hadn't tried was writing to a certain friend back home. And so I got off a letter to him asking him to look up Ah Q's police record. Didn't get a reply for eight months. When it did come, my friend said he hadn't been able to find any name that sounded even remotely like Ah-QUEI. I still don't know if that was really the case or whether he just hadn't bothered to look it up in the first place. At any rate, I was at a dead end.

I'm afraid the Chinese phonetic symbols[12] aren't all that popular yet, and so I've had to resort to a foreign word to represent the

---

10. Here the original text calls him *maocai* rather than the more usual *xiucai,* which I have elsewhere translated as *Budding Talent.* Both terms suggest a budding or blossoming *(xiu)* talent *(cai). "Maocai"* was used at one point during the Han Dynasty (206 B.C.–A.D. 220) to avoid the given name of an emperor, Liu Xiu.

11. Chen Duxiu (1879–1942) began to publish *Youth Magazine (Qingnian zazhi)* in 1915; its title was changed to *New Youth (Xin Qingnian)* the following year. Beginning in 1918 this influential organ of the New Culture movement was published entirely in the vernacular language. Chen was also one of the founders of the Chinese Communist Party.

12. A set of symbols that was widely used before 1949 to represent the pronunciation of Chinese characters. Though they stood for phonetic sounds, the symbols themselves had been derived from Chinese characters and thus appeared less "foreign" than the ABC's.

second character in my hero's given name. According to the popular English way of spelling Chinese it would be QUEI, or just "Q" for short.[13] Now I'll grant you this comes perilously close to blindly following *New Youth*—and I am terribly sorry about that —but when even a wise and learned *Budding Talent* doesn't know what character to use, what can you expect from the likes of me?

Four. The question of his native place. If his family name were definitely Zhao then I could follow the custom, so popular in present-day biographical writing, of naming the ancient district from whence his family hailed. That way, basing myself on the standard reference, *The Hundred Surnames and Their Places of Origin,* I could assert with confidence that our Ah Q *doth a Tianshui man of Longxi be.*[14] Trouble is, since it's somewhat doubtful that Zhao was his family name in the first place, how can I assert with any degree of certainty *where* his family came from? Granted, he lived mostly in Wei Village, but he often spent time in other places too. And so if I wrote that Ah Q *doth a Tianshui man of Longxi be,* I'd be downright guilty of violating the hallowed principles of historiography.

There's one thing I do pride myself on: when you take the "Q" away from "Ah Q," you've still got an "Ah" there, and I'm positive I haven't mixed that character up with any other. I could show that one off to anybody, no matter how learned.[15] As to the rest, well, that's beyond the scope of a man of shallow scholarship like myself. I can only hope that the disciples of Mr. Hu Shi,[16] who describes himself as having a "weakness for historical research

---

13. According to Zhou Zuoren, Lu Xun was intrigued by the letter Q because it resembled a man's head with a queue at the back.

14. *The Hundred Surnames* was a school primer in which common Chinese family names were grouped together into twenty-five rhyming lines of four characters each. The edition mentioned here also had a commentary that gave the name of the ancient administrative district where each family was thought to have originated. Tianshui is a city in present-day Shaanxi Province.

15. Since "Ah" is such a common prefix in given names, this is somewhat like saying, "I may have gotten the 'Smith,' 'Smithe,' or 'Smythe' wrong, but I'm certain I've spelled the 'John' right."

16. A frequent target of Lu Xun's satire, Hu Shi (1891–1962) was the earliest and most influential advocate of abolishing classical Chinese altogether and replacing it with the vernacular language. Though Lu Xun agreed with this position, he objected to Hu Shi's preference for scholarship over political activism at a time when China was under the control of warlords, compradors, and imperialists. Hu Shi had described himself complacently, using the quoted phrase.

coupled with an addiction to textual criticism," will be able to ferret out new clues at some time in the future. But by that time I'm afraid my "Ah Q—The Real Story" will have long since passed out of existence.

What I've written up to here may be taken as a preface.

Chapter 2
A Brief Account of His Victories

Not only is there a certain vagueness surrounding Ah Q's given name, family name, and place of origin, but there is also a great deal of uncertainty regarding his "official resumé."[17] Since the people in Wei Village were only interested in Ah Q for his labor—or to serve as the butt of their jokes—they had never paid any attention to what "positions" he had held in the past. Nor did Ah Q himself ever throw any light on his background, except when in the course of a squabble he would occasionally glower at someone and say, "We used to be much richer than you! Who the hell do you think you are anyway?"

Having no family, Ah Q lived at the local Land-and-Grain Temple, and having no fixed occupation, he did odd jobs. When there was wheat to be harvested, he harvested it; when there was rice to be hulled, he did that; and if there was a boat to be poled, he'd turn his hand to that too. When a job lasted a bit longer than the usual, he might temporarily put up at the home of his employer, but once the work was done, he'd move out.

When the busy season came, to be sure, people's minds would turn to Ah Q, but what they would think about was his ability to work and not the particulars of his "resumé." Once the busy season was over they would have forgotten his very *existence,* not to mention the details of his past career. There was only a single instance when anyone had ever praised him, and that was when an old man had said, "That Ah Q's *some* worker!" Bare-chested at the time and standing right in front of the old man, Ah Q looked so scrawny and worn-out that one couldn't tell whether the old fellow had really meant it or was simply making fun of him. Nonetheless, Ah Q had been pleased as punch.

---

17. *Xingzhuang,* translated here as "resumé," actually refers to the posthumous account of a deceased official's career put together by his relatives.

Since he thought so well of *himself,* Ah Q considered the other villagers simply beneath his notice. He went so far with this that he even looked down his nose at the village's two *Young Literati.*[18] He didn't realize, of course, that up there in the rarefied world of scholar-officialdom *those whom one doth Young Literati name* can darn well get to be *those whom one must Budding Talents proclaim*—if you don't keep an eye on them. That's why Old Master Qian and Old Master Zhao were so all-fired respected in the village: they were daddies to those two *Young Literati*—and rich to boot. Ah Q, however, was less than impressed. "My son's gonna be a lot richer." On top of that, Ah Q had been to town a couple of times and that made him even more full of himself. Yet he could be contemptuous of townsfolk too. For instance, Wei Villagers called a seat made from a three-foot plank a *longbench* and so did Ah Q, but the townsfolk called it a *stickbench.* "That's not right, that's flatass dumb!" he thought to himself. And how about fish? When frying bigheads, Wei Villagers would toss chopped scallions into the pan, but the townsfolk always used *shredded* ones. "That's not right, that's flatass stupid!" he thought to himself. "On the other hand, I gotta remember that next to me, Wei Villagers are just a bunch of hicks. They've never even *seen* how bigheads are fried in town."

So Ah Q used to be rich, had seen a thing or two, and was "some" worker—in sum, he came very close to being the perfect man. Unfortunately, however, he had a few physical shortcomings, the most annoying of which was an assortment of shiny scars that had been left on his scalp by an attack of scabies. Despite the undeniable fact that those scars had the good fortune to be attached to Ah Q's body, strange to say, he didn't seem to think them particularly worth bragging about. And so it was that he shunned the word "scabies" and any other word sounding even remotely like it.

He later expanded the scope of this taboo until it included words like "bright" and "shiny" and—still later—even "lamp" and "candle." Whether it was intentional or not, if anyone should violate this taboo, Ah Q would seethe with anger until every last one of his scabies scars would flush its deepest red. Then he would size

18. *Wentong,* translated here as "literati," referred specifically to young men in preparation for the *Budding Talent* examination.

up his opponent: if it happened to be someone who stuttered so badly that he couldn't get the second word out after the first, Ah Q would curse him up one side and down the other; if it was someone so puny and weak that he could hardly stand, Ah Q would start a fight. And yet, strange to tell, in all such encounters Ah Q somehow still managed to come out the loser more often than not. After some time, he modified his plan of battle and for the most part simply gave his opponent a dirty look.

Who would have expected that after Ah Q adopted his policy of dirtylookism, the Wei Village idlers would take even greater pleasure in taunting him? As soon as they set eyes on him, they would draw back in feigned surprise and say, "Hey, it's getting lighter out!"

As usual, Ah Q would start to go into a slow boil.

"Oh, so that's it, there's a kerosene lamp here—no wonder!" They weren't about to be intimidated by any dirty look from the likes of Ah Q.

Since a dirty look didn't seem to do it, he would try a snappy comeback: "Why you guys don't even deserve to gaze on . . ." At this point it usually seemed as if those whatchamacallits up there on his head had been transformed into grand and glorious *Scars de Scabie,* not at all to be confused with the ordinary variety. But as I have said before, our Ah Q was a man of keen insight, and therefore he would realize immediately that he was on the verge of violating his own taboo and would catch himself up in midsentence.

Not content to let it go at that, the Wei Village idlers would keep right on baiting him until it all ended up in a fight anyway. From a purely formal point of view, Ah Q would be defeated: he would be grabbed by his discolored queue, and would have his head given four or five resounding thumps against a wall. Then the idlers would walk away, fully satisfied and fully victorious. Ah Q would stand there for a bit and then think to himself, "It's just as though I'd been beaten up by my own sons! What's the world coming to, anyway, when sons . . ." At this point Ah Q too would walk away, fully satisfied and fully victorious.[19]

---

19. Contemporary readers saw Ah Q as representing China in miniature: continually humiliated by the imperialist powers, China had gained "psychological victories" by boasting about the superiority of her ancient civilization.

From a purely formal point of view, Ah Q would be defeated: he would be grabbed by his discolored queue, and would have his head given four or five resounding thumps against a wall.

Later on Ah Q took to saying out loud the various things he thought to himself. And so it was that before long every Ah-Q-baiter in the village was onto his schemes for winning psychological victories. From then on, whenever Ah Q's discolored queue was grabbed, his tormentor would steal a march on him as well: "Ah Q, this isn't a son beatin' up on his old man, it's a human being beatin' up on an *animal!* Let's hear *you* say it now, 'A human being beatin' up on an animal'!"

Holding fast to the base of his queue with both hands, Ah Q would cock his head to one side and rejoin: "Beatin' up on a *bug,* does that make you happy? Now give a guy a break, huh?"

But even though he was only a "bug," the idlers still wouldn't let him off the hook. In the time-honored fashion, they would seek out the nearest wall and give his head four or five resounding thumps before walking away, fully satisfied and fully victorious—and convinced that *this* time they had done him in once and for all. But before ten seconds were out, Ah Q would also walk away, fully satisfied and fully victorious, for he was convinced that of all the "self-putdown artists" this old world has seen, he was number one. Take away "self-putdown artist" and what did you have left? *Number one*—that's what! What was a *Metropolitan Graduate?*[20] *Number one*—that's all. "Who the hell do these jerks think they are anyway!" Having subdued his foes with such ingenious strategems, Ah Q would go happily off to the wineshop and down a few bowls. He would banter with some, squabble with others, and then on the crest of fresh victories, would make his way happily back to the Land-and-Grain Temple, put his head down on his pillow, and go to sleep.

If he happened to have money, he'd go and play a round of *Pickaside.*[21] As people crowded around the gambling stand, Ah Q would sandwich his way in among them, his face bathed in sweat. Of all the voices his would be the loudest.

"Four hundred on *Green Dragon!*"

"Oh-kay, off with the cover and let's see which side has turned up!" His face bathed in sweat, the stakeholder would take off the

---

20. "Metropolitan Graduate" was a title given to the examinee who had, in effect, the highest "pass" of all those who had competed for the *Advanced Scholar* degree.

21. The *Pickaside* stakeholder would set up a square gambling stand with four sides arranged as below.

cover. "*Heaven's Gate* gets the money! *In-the-Corner* splits even! Nobody on *White Tiger* or *Through-the-Hall!* Pass Ah Q's dough over here!"

"One hundred on *Through-the-Hall*—make it a hundred and fifty!"

In the midst of the stakeholder's incantations, Ah Q's money

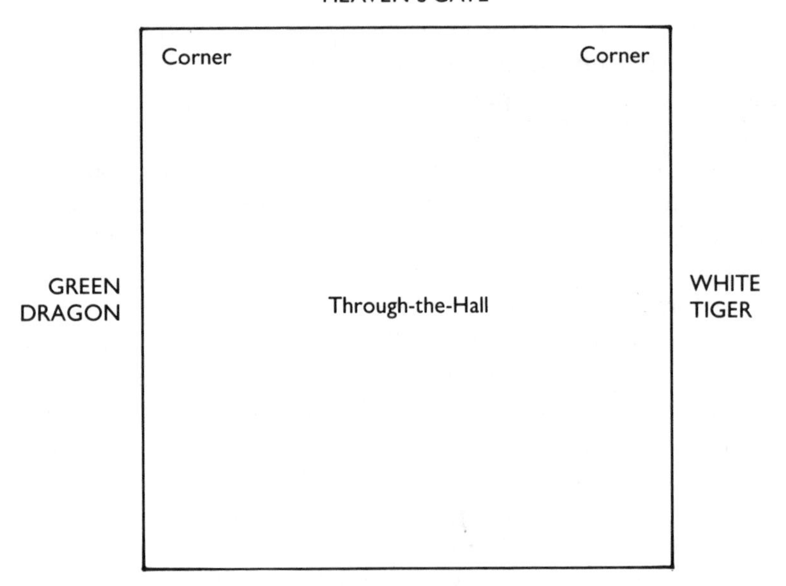

A small, rectangular brass plate (one side painted white, the other black) was inserted into a four-sided brass box. The box was covered and shaken so that the plate turned about within. The four sides of the box bore names corresponding to the four sides of the stand. When the lid was taken off, whichever name the white side of the brass plate faced was the winner. A bet placed on any of the three playing sides brought a threefold return if that side won.

There were two ways of hedging one's bets (at the risk of reducing potential winnings): (1) A player could bet on one of the corners across from the stakeholder. He might, for example, place a bet on the *Green Dragon / Heaven's Gate* corner. If *White Tiger* or the *Stakeholder's Side* won, he lost; if *Heaven's Gate* won, he doubled his money. If *Green Dragon* won, his bet would be returned to him. (2) He could bet *Through-the-Hall,* connecting opposite sides. For example, he might bet on *Green Dragon* "though the hall" to *White Tiger.* If *Heaven's Gate* or the *Stakeholder's Side* won, he lost his money; but if *Green Dragon* won, he doubled it. And if *White Tiger* won, his bet would be returned.

Stakeholders had two ways of hedging their bets when the game started to go against the house. A confederate in the crowd might (1) start a ruckus, enabling the croupier to fold up his tent and steal away, or (2) pose as an official, break up the "illegal" game, and confiscate both gaming equipment and money.

would gradually make its way into the pockets of other people whose faces, like his own, were also bathed in sweat. Finally Ah Q would have to squeeze his way back through the crowd and stand on the sidelines, now reduced to becoming excited or disappointed on someone else's behalf. He would continue to watch until the game broke up and then reluctantly make his way back to the Land-and-Grain Temple. Next day, with swollen eyes, Ah Q would go to work.

It is true, however, that losing can sometimes be a blessing in disguise, for once when Ah Q *did* actually win, he came very close to losing.

It was on a night when Wei Village was holding a festival of thanksgiving to the gods. As usual, a religious opera was performed. As usual again, a number of gambling stands were set up close to the stage. So as far as Ah Q was concerned, the orchestra's crashing cymbals and pounding drums might just as well have been miles away, for he heard nothing but the singsong chant of the stakeholder. Ah Q won! He won again! And then again he won some more! Copper pennies turned into silver dollars, and the dollars piled up into a tall stack. Ah Q was beside himself. "Two dollars on *Heaven's Gate!*"

He never found out who started the fight or why, but at any rate he suddenly found himself buried under a pandemonium of curses, blows, and kicks. No sooner had he struggled to his feet than he discovered that the gambling stand was gone, and the people who had been surrounding it were nowhere to be seen. His body seemed to hurt in a couple of spots, as though he too had taken a few punches and kicks. One or two people looked at him in surprise. Looking somewhat lost, he made his way back to the Land-and-Grain Temple. After collecting himself a bit, he realized that his pile of silver dollars had disappeared. Since most people who set up gambling stands at festivals like this didn't come from the village themselves, there was no possible way of ever finding out what actually had happened.

What a bright and glittering pile of dollars that had been, too. And now they were gone. Gone! He tried to write the whole thing off by telling himself that he'd been robbed by his own sons, but somehow or other he still felt disappointed and depressed. Then he considered dismissing it by calling himself a bug, but somehow or other that left him feeling just as depressed and disappointed as ever. For the first time in Ah Q's life, he tasted something like the real bitterness of defeat.

But then, in the twinkling of an eye, he transformed that defeat into victory! He raised his right hand and, one after the other, gave himself two sharp slaps across the mouth. His face burned with a prickly pain. After those slaps, however, he began to feel at peace with himself. It was as though Ah Q had done the slapping and the person he had slapped was some *other* Ah Q. And before too long it actually seemed as though he had slapped someone else altogether—though he had to admit that his own face still stung a bit. Complacent and content, Ah Q now lay down—victorious.

He slept.

Chapter 3
A Brief Account of His Victories (cont.)

Although Ah Q was indeed often victorious, it wasn't until he had been graced with a slap across the mouth from Old Master Zhao—for his temerity in laying claim to the Zhao family name—that he finally became famous.

That day, after he had greased the sheriff's palm to the tune of two hundred coppers, Ah Q went home and lay down fuming with anger. But before very long, he began to think, "What's the world coming to when a son strikes his own father?" And then his thoughts turned another corner as he considered the great prestige that Old Master Zhao enjoyed in the village. Gradually Ah Q began feeling quite pleased with himself that such a prestigious man was now his son. He got up and headed off to the wineshop, singing the strains of *The Young Widow Visits Her Husband's Grave* as he went.[22] At this juncture, Ah Q truly felt that Old Master Zhao really *was* a cut above everyone else.

Strange to tell, after the slapping incident everyone did in fact seem to treat Ah Q with unusual respect. The way Ah Q saw it, this was probably because he was Old Master Zhao's father. But if the truth be known, that wasn't it at all. Instead it was the result of a Wei Village precedent that ran something like this: if Ah-seven slugged Ah-eight, or if Li-four clobbered Zhang-three, no one

22. A Shaoxing opera that was popular at the time this story was written.

thought anything of it.[23] But if such an incident was connected to some eminent personage like his nibs Old Master Zhao, then it would be permanently recorded on the lips of the people. And after that, because the man who had done the striking was already famous, the man who had been hit would ride to renown on his coattails.

It goes without saying, of course, that everyone laid the blame for the incident on Ah Q. Now, here one might be tempted to ask, *"Pray tell wherein lieth the why and the wherefore of that?"* Simple. His nibs Old Master Zhao *couldn't* be wrong! But if Ah Q *was* the one at fault, then why should everyone treat him with such respect? Well, that's a tough one. A rough answer might go something like this: though it's true that Ah Q got slapped for claiming to be a clansman of Old Master Zhao, who's to say that there might not be some truth to it? On the off chance that there was, it would still be prudent to treat Ah Q with respect. Or perhaps it may have been related to the example of the Sacrificial Ox in the Confucian Temple. Although the ox is just as much a domestic animal as the pig or sheep, Confucian scholars would not dare commit the blasphemy of eating its meat once the spirit of Confucius had set his chopsticks to it during the sacrifice. And in point of fact, for several years after the slapping incident things went swimmingly for Ah Q.

In the spring of one year, a pleasantly inebriated Ah Q was walking down the street when he chanced upon Bearded Wang. Chest bared, Wang sat in the sunlight at the base of a wall, picking lice out of his jacket. Ah Q suddenly became aware of an itching sensation on his own body too. Now this Bearded Wang was not only bearded, but boasted a set of scabies scars as well, and so everyone else called him *Scabby* Bearded Wang. Ah Q, on the other hand, edited out the "scabby" but disdained the man completely nonetheless. It wasn't that Ah Q saw anything all that unusual in being scabby, but that beard of Wang's was going just a bit too far—what an eyesore! But now Ah Q sat down right next to him. Had it been any other villager, he wouldn't have been so bold, but what did he have to fear from the likes of Bearded

23. These are, of course, Chinese equivalents for such expressions as Tom, Dick, and Harry; or John Smith and Jane Doe.

Ah Q sat down right next to him. Had it been any other villager, he wouldn't have been so bold, but what did he have to fear from the likes of Bearded Wang? As a matter of fact, he was doing Bearded Wang an honor by being willing to sit down with him in the first place.

Wang? As a matter of fact, he was doing Bearded Wang an honor by being willing to sit down with him in the first place.

Ah Q peeled off his raggedy old jacket and turned it inside out. But a prolonged search yielded—perhaps because the jacket had recently been washed, or perhaps because Ah Q didn't look carefully enough—only three or four lice. He looked over and saw that Bearded Wang was picking them out one after the other and sometimes even two or three at a time. What's more, those lice kept going *pow pow pow,* as loud as you please, when Bearded Wang popped them between his teeth.

At first Ah Q felt merely disappointed, but after a while he began to resent the downright injustice of it all—to think that even the low-life likes of Bearded Wang could come up with all those nice lice while he, on the other hand, could find only a paltry few. Why it was nothing short of a social disgrace! How he longed to find a couple of good big ones. But he simply couldn't. It was all he could do to come up with even one *medium* louse. He angrily thrust that one between his teeth and bit down with all his might—only a piddling little *pop,* nothing to compare with Bearded Wang's loud and lusty *pows.* Now every last scabies scar on Ah Q's head flushed scarlet. He hurled his jacket to the ground and spat with disgust. "Hairy beast!"

"Who are you cursin' out, you mangy dog?" Bearded Wang raised his eyes and gave Ah Q a contemptuous glance.

Although people had treated Ah Q a bit more respectfully of late, making him more full of himself than ever, still he was always cautious in the presence of the Wei Village idlers, all of whom would just as soon fight as have breakfast. In fact this was the first time he had dared to put on such a martial display before one of them. Did this hairy-faced beast actually have the gall to use intemperate language within Ah Q's hearing?

"If the shoe fits!" Ah Q got up and put his hands on his waist.

"Are your bones itchin' for a good trouncin'?" Bearded Wang stood up and threw his jacket across his shoulders.

Thinking that Bearded Wang was getting ready to make a run for it, Ah Q sprang forward and threw a punch. But before his fist had reached its mark, Bearded Wang grabbed it and gave it such a yank that Ah Q went stumbling forward completely off balance. At the same time, with his free hand, Bearded Wang grabbed Ah

Q's queue, twisted it fast, and prepared to drag him over to the wall and smack his head against it in the time-honored fashion.

"His fists need never be swung, for the gentleman useth his tongue," quoted Ah Q, head cocked to one side.

It would appear, however, that Bearded Wang was no gentleman, for ignoring this classical lore, he slammed Ah Q's head against the wall five times in succession, and then gave him a good hard shove that sent Ah Q staggering away, fighting to regain his balance. Thoroughly satisfied then, Bearded Wang strode away.[24]

In Ah Q's memory, this could probably be reckoned as the first real disgrace of an entire lifetime, for Bearded Wang—flawed by a beard growing rampant all over his face—had always been the object of Ah Q's taunts, and had certainly never before made light of Ah Q, much less dared to lay hands on him. Thus the event that had just transpired was something totally unexpected. Could it possibly be true, as people were saying in town, that the emperor had put an end to the civil service examinations and did not need *Budding Talents* anymore? Could it be that the Zhao family's prestige had consequently declined and that people now felt free to look down on Ah Q as a result?[25]

Thrown for a loss, Ah Q just stood there.

Out of the distance, someone else was coming toward him—another enemy had arrived. This too was one of the people whom Ah Q most detested, the son of Old Master Qian. Some time back, this lad had gone off to town and attended one of those new fangled academies where they taught foreign things along with Chinese subjects. After that, somehow or other, he'd sailed off to Japan. By the time he came back half a year later he was walking stiff-legged, just the way foreigners do, and his queue was gone! That was enough to send his mother into a good dozen fits of wailing and his dear wife had thrice tried to drown herself in the well. Later on his mother went around saying: "Some hoodlums got him

24. Some contemporary readers drew an analogy between this encounter and the Sino-Japanese War of 1894. China had been accustomed to looking down on Japan as a cultural stepchild and was rudely surprised when a modernized Japan defeated her quite handily.

25. In one of the most drastic moves of modern Chinese history, the Manchu government announced the abolition of the civil service examinations in 1905. The examination system had existed in some form ever since 136 B.C. All through that long period, knowledge of the classics had provided virtually the only access to the Confucian ladder of success. Now that ladder was gone.

drunk and cut it off. He could have been an important official, but now we can't make any plans until it grows back again." Ah Q, however, did not buy a word of it and made a point of calling him "fake foreign devil" or "foreign sellout," cursing him under his breath the moment he set eyes on him.

But the thing that Ah Q, in the tradition of all the doughty heroes of yore, did *shunneth full well and righteously repel* was that fake queue. To have a queue and sink so low as to let it be a *fake* one was clear proof that the man had lost all claim to humanity, and since that wife of his hadn't taken a fourth dive into the well, she obviously couldn't be a good woman either.

This Fake Foreign Devil came closer.

"Baldy! Jackass!" Now, previously Ah Q had always said that kind of thing under his breath, but today after his defeat at the hands of Bearded Wang, he was seething with fury and hungry for revenge. Lightly, yet quite audibly, the words escaped his lips before even *he* knew they were out.

To Ah Q's surprise, "Baldy" started moving directly toward him, a yellow-lacquered cane—what Ah Q called a *wailing stick*—in his hand.[26] In that split second Ah Q realized he was probably in for a drubbing. Pulling his head down between his shoulders, he braced himself for the worst. *WHACK!* Sure enough, there was the right sound, and it felt as though a blow had landed on his head, too. Ah Q pointed to a child nearby and offered defensively, "I was talking about *him!*"

WHACK! WHACK-WHACK!

In Ah Q's memory, this could probably be reckoned as the *second* real disgrace of an entire lifetime. Fortunately, however, by the time the whacking sounds had subsided, he had begun to feel somewhat relaxed. It was rather as if he'd just completed some pressing task that had to be done. What was more, "forgetfulness" —that priceless medicine handed down to us by our ancestors— began to take its effect too. He headed away toward the wineshop and by the time he drew near the door he had long since begun to feel quite happy again.

---

26. Young foreign gentlemen of the time often carried canes, and young Chinese who had studied abroad often emulated them even after returning home. The "wailing stick" *(kusang bang)* had been traditionally carried by filial sons in funeral processions; the idea it represented was that the son was so overwhelmed with grief he would have been otherwise unable to walk.

Ah Q realized he was probably in for a drubbing. Pulling his head down between his shoulders, he braced himself for the worst.

But walking straight toward him was a young Buddhist nun from the Convent of Silent Cultivation. Even in ordinary times, Ah Q would always have spit whenever he ran across a nun and now, having just been humiliated, he had all the more reason. At this point he began to think back over his day and once again began itching for revenge. He walked straight toward her and spat on the ground.

"Aaaaaaawk . . . tuh!"

Doing her best to ignore him, the young nun lowered her head and kept on her way. Ah Q fell in step beside her. Suddenly he reached over and fondled the skin of her shaved head. "Hey Baldy, better hurry on back—your monk's waitin' for ya," he said with an inane smile.

"What's gotten into you? Get your filthy paws off me!" Her face flushing scarlet, the nun hurried onward.

The patrons of the wineshop roared with laughter. Seeing that his meritorious service to the court had gained such great favor with these tippling nobles, Ah Q felt his spirits soar ever higher. "If the monk can fondle you, then why can't I?" He pinched her cheek between his thumb and forefinger.

Once again the patrons of the wineshop roared with laughter, and Ah Q was even more elated. Then, so as to fully satisfy these courtly connoisseurs of his martial performance, he gave the nun's cheek a final pinch before letting her go.

Because of this encounter with the nun, Ah Q had long since forgotten Bearded Wang and the Fake Foreign Devil as well. It was as if he'd avenged himself for all the bad luck he'd had that day. Strange to tell, his whole body seemed to feel relaxed, too, even more relaxed than after the echoes of the Fake Foreign Devil's *WHACK! WHACK-WHACK!* had died away. Walking on air, Ah Q seemed ready to take off and soar away at any minute.

"May you never have a son, Ah Q!" He heard the sound of the nun's sobbing voice in the distance.

"Hah, hah, hah!" One hundred percent elated, Ah Q laughed.

"Hah, hah!" Ninety percent elated, the patrons of the wineshop laughed too.

Chapter 4
The Tragedy of Love

It has long been noted that some conquerors prefer enemies as fierce as tigers and brave as eagles, for only then can they savor the true joy of victory. If, on the other hand, their foes are as tame as sheep or timid as chickens, then they find no pleasure in their triumph.

Then too, you have the conqueror who overcomes all opposition, sees his enemies die or surrender, and finally reports his victory back to the throne: *"In fear and trembling, thy servant draws his breath, who, in addressing you, deserveth only death."*[27] Such a conqueror has no enemies, no rivals, and no friends—he has nothing left except himself, standing there in utter isolation at the very apex of his triumph, lonely and forlorn. At such a time the hero experiences not the joy of victory, but rather its poignant melancholy.

Rest assured, dear reader, that our Ah Q was not so feckless as any of the above. No, he was *always* full of himself. Perhaps we have here yet another proof that the spiritual civilization of China is superior to any other on the face of the earth.

Why just look at him! Tripping along on air like that, he might well soar skyward and fly away at any moment!

And yet there was something about this *particular* victory that made Ah Q feel somehow—different. After tripping along on air for quite some time, he finally floated back to the Land-and-Grain Temple. Now ordinarily at this point he would have flopped down and begun to snore. Who would have thought that tonight he wouldn't even be able to get his eyes shut? There was something very strange—he could feel it—going on in the index finger and thumb of one hand. Could it be that there was something soft and smooth on that young nun's face that had somehow rubbed off on them? Or could it be that he had somehow rubbed his finger and thumb smooth on her face?

"May you never have a son, Ah Q!"

---

27. "Deserving only death" in that he has taken the liberty of addressing the throne directly. This stock phrase is an example of the exaggerated politeness that was the norm in framing memorials to the emperor.

There was something very strange—he could feel it—going on in the index finger and thumb of one hand.

The nun's curse echoed in his ears again and set Ah Q to thinking, "That's right, oughta have a woman! If I die with no son, who's gonna sacrifice a bowl of rice now and then for my ghost to eat? Yeah, gotta get me a woman!"

Now bear in mind, gentle reader, *Of three things which do unfilial be / The worst is to lack posteritie.*[28] And then too, if you also remember how the classics tell of the exemplary concern of Ziwen, in those days of yore, lest *the ghosts of the Ruo'ao clan go hungry, woman and man*—a great human tragedy, indeed!—then you'll see right off quick that Ah Q's thinking was, as a matter of fact, thoroughly in accord with the sagacious morality of our classical tradition.[29] Unfortunately, however, after his thoughts started galloping off in this direction, Ah Q *completely lacked the art to rein in his unbridled heart.*[30]

"Woman, woman!" Ah Q thought to himself.

And then Ah Q thought to himself again, ". . . if the monk can fondle you . . . woman . . . woman!"

There is no way of telling when it was that Ah Q finally began to snore that night. What is certain, however, is that from that time forward his index finger and thumb always had a certain smooth feel to them, and so it was that from that time forward, too, he was always walking on air. "Woman!!!" Ah Q thought to himself.

From this instance alone, you can see what baleful creatures women be. Now by rights most Chinese men could have become saints or sages a long time back—trouble is, they were all done in by women. The Shang dynasty [1766–1122 B.C.] was brought down by the enticing Da Ji, and the captivating Bao Si destroyed the Zhou [1122–221 B.C.].[31] As for the Qin dynasty [221–206

28. The other two are following parents' orders when one knows that such a course will sink them into unrighteousness and refusing to become an official when one's parents are old and poor.

29. The story of Ruo'ao Ziwen is recorded under the fourth year of Duke Xuan (604 B.C.) in the historical classic *Zuo Zhuan;* see n. 1 above. Observing the inauspicious countenance of his younger brother's baby son, Ziwen exhorted the father to kill the boy lest he bring down destruction on the entire clan. The father did not heed his elder brother's advice, and when the boy grew up he fulfilled his uncle's prophesy, so that, with no posterity to sacrifice to them, *the ghosts of the Ruo'ao clan* did in fact end up going hungry.

30. Based on a passage in the Bi Ming chapter of the *History Classic.*

31. The women mentioned here were concubines to the last rulers of their respective dynastic periods. According to the paternalistic views of traditional Chinese historiography, they beguiled their royal consorts into debauchery and ruin.

B.C.], though we can't find any clear statement as to exactly what happened, we probably wouldn't be one hundred percent wrong if we assumed that a female had put that one on the skids, too. And we know for an undeniable fact that it was because of the singsong girl Diao Chan that Dong Zhuo [d. A.D. 192] was killed.[32]

Now our Ah Q started out as an upright man too. Though we don't know if this was because he had been shown the way by some enlightened teacher, we do know that he rigorously observed *the great barrier that should be 'twixt the he and the she* and was well endowed with a sense of moral uprightness that made him despise heretical behavior such as that of the young nun or the Fake Foreign Devil.[33] Ah Q's philosophy ran like this: Any nun is bound to be secretly shacked up with a monk. If a woman is out walking on the street, she's certainly trying to seduce a man or two. If a man and woman are talking to each other, they're sure to be arranging a tryst. He often employed his dirtylookism to punish such miscreants. Occasionally he would voice a loud comment to show that *he* knew what a couple was "really up to," no matter how innocent their behavior might seem on the surface. And occasionally—if the place was isolated—he'd throw a pebble at them from behind.

Who could possibly have foreseen that just as he was approaching the age when, like Confucius, he should have "stood firm,"[34] Ah Q would be so subverted by a young Buddhist nun that he would go around walking on air. Now according to the tenets of Confucian morality, the kinds of feelings engendered by airwalking are *not* the kinds of feelings one should have in the first place. So we can readily see what utterly despicable creatures females really are. If the young nun's face had not been so smooth, Ah Q would not have fallen, or had there been a veil between her face and his fingers, things would never have gone so far either. As a

---

32. During the decline of the Han (206 B.C.–A.D. 220), Wang Yun (a minister of the dynasty) presented the singsong girl Diao Chan to a subordinate of Dong Zhuo (a contemporary warlord). Later the crafty Wang spirited the girl away and presented her to Dong Zhuo himself. He then told the subordinate that Dong had taken her by force. As Wang had anticipated, the subordinate then assassinated the much-despised minister.

33. According to the puritanical ethics of traditional Confucian morality, any contact between an unrelated man and woman was potentially, if not actually, immoral. A popular proverb decreed that "a man and woman, unless related, should not touch hands when giving or receiving things" *(nan nü shoushou buqin)*.

34. In a well-known passage of the *Analects* Confucius says, "At thirty, I stood firm."

matter of fact, five or six years back he'd even pinched a girl's thigh once while watching an opera, but in that case her trousers had separated his fingers from her skin, so that the experience had not been enough to set him airwalking afterwards. In the case of the young nun, however, things had been entirely different. Goes to show you what a detestable and heretical doctrine Buddhism really is, too.

"Woman!" thought Ah Q.

He constantly kept an eye out for women who were "trying to seduce a man or two," but none of them so much as smiled at him. Whenever a woman talked with him, Ah Q kept a close ear to everything that was said but still he heard nothing that was even vaguely related to "having an affair." Why of course! That's partly what made women so rotten in the first place—the hypocrites all *pretended* to be straight!

After supper one evening, Ah Q sat in Old Master Zhao's kitchen having a leisurely smoke on his pipe. He had just put in a full day of hulling rice. If it had been at anyone else's place, he would have gone right home after supper, but here the situation was somewhat different. Ordinarily the Zhao family ate quite early, for it was an established item of family protocol that no one was allowed to waste good money lighting a lamp. People simply went straight to bed after supper. There were, however, certain exceptions to the rule: Old Master Zhao's young hopeful had been permitted to burn the midnight oil while preparing for his *Budding Talent* exam, and Ah Q was allowed to hull rice by lamplight whenever he came to help out during the busy season. Indeed, that's why he could not afford to sit and dawdle over his pipe like this.

Having finished the dishes, Amah Wu, the one and only maid in Old Master Zhao's household, sat down on the *longbench* next to Ah Q and began to chat. "The Old Missus hasn't eaten a thing for days now. It's all because the Old Master's going to buy a concubine."

"Woman . . . Amah Wu . . . this nice young widow," Ah Q thought to himself.

"Our Young Missus is going to have a baby in August and . . ."

"WOMAN," thought Ah Q to himself. He put down his pipe and stood up.

". . . the Young Missus says . . ." Amah Wu prattled on.

Now Ah Q moved directly in front of her and knelt at her feet. "Sleep with me! Sleep with me!"

For a brief instant you could have heard a pin drop.

"AIYA!!!" Amah Wu had been stunned speechless at first. And then quite suddenly, she had begun to tremble, and then she had let out that big aiya-scream. Now she bolted for the door and ran outside, screaming as she went. It sounded as if she was crying, too.

Ah Q found himself kneeling before a blank wall. He too was stunned for a moment. Placing his hands on the *longbench,* he slowly dragged himself to his feet, barely conscious that he'd probably gotten himself into some kind of mess. Heart pounding, he hastily thrust his pipe into his belt and made ready to go back to his hulling when *BONG!* a good solid blow landed on his head. He turned and saw the young *Budding Talent* standing before him, a heavy staff in hand.

"Rebellious wretch, why you . . ."

The heavy pole clove the air again. Ah Q grabbed the top of his head with both hands. *WHACK!* The blow landed on his knuckles and hurt more than a little. As he burst through the kitchen door, he seemed to feel yet another hard blow land on his back.

"Turtle's egg!" the *Budding Talent* cursed from behind.[35]

Ah Q ran to the hulling shed as fast as his legs would carry him. He stood there alone. Pain lingered in his fingers, and the expression "turtle's egg" in his mind, for that was one locution that the countryfolk of Wei Village never used. Only rich people who rubbed noses with officials said fancy things like that, and thus it made a deep impression on Ah Q and gave him quite a fright to boot. By now, all those "woman" thoughts had left him. What was more, having taken a good cursing and beating, he felt as though he had actually accomplished something, gotten it over and done with. And so before long, without a care in the world, Ah Q set himself to hulling rice again. He worked up a sweat and paused to strip down.

While taking off his shirt, Ah Q heard a loud commotion somewhere outside. Now Ah Q had never liked anything better than a bit of excitement, and so without a second thought he headed off

---

35. Cuckolds were called turtles, and thus "turtle's egg" comes close to "S.O.B." in English.

in the direction of the noise. Little by little, the sounds led him to the inner courtyard outside Old Master Zhao's rooms. Although it was dusk, Ah Q was able to make out several of the people: Old Master Zhao's wife—the one who hadn't eaten for two days in a row—Seventh Sister Zou from next door, and two honest-to-goodness Zhao clansmen, Zhao Baiyan and Zhao Sichen.

The Young Missus was leading Amah Wu out of the servants' quarters. "Come on outside. Don't hole up in your room and brood like that."

"Everyone knows what a virtuous woman you are. Don't go looking on the short side of things, no matter what!" said Seventh Sister Zou from the sidelines.[36]

Amah Wu went right on with her wailing. She sandwiched in some words too, but they weren't all that easy to make out. "Now that's interesting," thought Ah Q. "Wonder what kind of tricks this Young Widow's been up to anyway?" He moved in closer and stood next to Zhao Sichen to find out what was going on.

Suddenly Ah Q caught sight of the *Budding Talent* bearing down on him. What's more, there was a large bamboo pole in his hands. As Ah Q looked at the pole, it suddenly occurred to him that he had recently been whacked with just such a pole, and that the commotion in progress somehow or other seemed to have something to do with him personally. Ah Q turned, intending to hightail it back to the hulling shed, but found himself cut off by the pole. He backtracked, went the other way, and made it safely out the rear gate. Before long he was back inside the Land-and-Grain Temple.

After Ah Q had sat there for a while, his skin started to break out in goosebumps—he was cold. Though it was spring, the nights were still quite chilly and it was certainly no time to be going around bare-chested. Now he remembered, he had left his cotton jacket back at the Zhaos'place. Fear of the *Budding Talent*'s bamboo pole, however, kept him from going to get the jacket. At this impasse, the sheriff entered.

"You motherfucker, Ah Q! Even tryin' to make out with the Zhao servants. You're a rebel, pure and simple! You've screwed up my sleep too, mother!" On and on in this vein, the sheriff gave Ah Q a good tongue-lashing, and there was, of course, no reasonable

36. Seventh Sister Zou is afraid Amah Wu will commit suicide.

"You motherfucker, Ah Q! Even tryin' to make out with the Zhao servants. You're a rebel, pure and simple! You've screwed up my sleep too, mother!"

defense that Ah Q could offer. Toward the end of this harangue, the sheriff demanded a four dollar tip (twice the usual amount because he had been forced to come out at night). Since Ah Q had no ready cash, the sheriff took his old felt hat as security. Then he laid down the law:

(1) Ah Q was to take a pair of candles (one catty apiece) along with a packet of incense to the Zhao residence and apologize.

(2) The Zhao family was to hire Daoist priests to exorcise the ghosts of people who had hanged themselves—cost to be borne by Ah Q.

(3) Henceforth Ah Q was never to darken the Zhao family's door again.

(4) Should anything at all *ever* befall Amah Wu, Ah Q would be held responsible.

(5) Ah Q would not be allowed to ask the Zhao family for his back wages or his jacket.

Ah Q, of course, agreed to all these conditions—trouble was he didn't have the money to make good on them. Fortunately, since it was already spring, he didn't need his cotton quilt all that much anymore, and so he hocked it for two thousand coppers so as to fulfill the five conditions.

After a bare-chested Ah Q had kowtowed his apology to the Zhaos, he even had a few coppers left over. But instead of redeeming his felt hat, he simply bought some wine and drank them up. The Zhao family didn't actually light the candles or burn the incense he had bought either, but since the Old Missus could make good use of them when she worshipped Buddha, they kept them all the same. The best part of Ah Q's raggedy old jacket went into making diapers for the baby born to the Young Missus in August. The rest of it was converted into liners for Amah Wu's shoes.

Chapter 5
The Problem of Livelihood

Having complied with the five conditions laid down by the sheriff, Ah Q went back to the Land-and-Grain Temple just as he always did. But after the sun went down that night, he gradually became aware that something was not quite right in this world of his. He wracked his brains for a good long while and then finally figured it out: the reason for his not-quite-right feeling probably had some-

Fortunately, since it was already spring, he didn't need his cotton quilt that much anymore, and so he hocked it for two thousand coppers so as to fulfill the five conditions.

thing to do with his being bare-chested. Remembering that he still had a tattered old winter jacket, he threw that across his shoulders and lay down. When he opened his eyes again, the rays of the rising sun were already falling on top of the west wall. He sat up straight and declared, "Shit!"

After rising, he went out and wandered around the streets just as he always did. Although this time it wasn't any physical discomfort that bothered him—as had his bare-chested state the previous night—once again Ah Q began to feel that there was something not quite right in this world of his, for it seemed that from this day forward all the women of Wei Village began turning shy on him. As soon as they saw Ah Q approaching, they'd scurry into their houses. Even Seventh Sister Zou, who was fast approaching fifty, scurried inside like all the others and called her eleven-year-old daughter inside after her. Ah Q was puzzled. "The bitches have started actin' like high-class young ladies all of a sudden—sluts!" But it wasn't until several days later that this not-quite-right feeling took on a critical intensity. First off, the wineshop wouldn't extend him any more credit. In the second place, the old man who took care of the temple started running off at the mouth with the obvious intention of running him off. In the third place, it had been quite some time—though he couldn't remember exactly how long—since anyone had asked Ah Q to do any odd jobs. No credit at the wineshop? He could deal with that. And so what if the caretaker did try to run him off? He could handle that one too. But if no one gave him any work to do, his stomach would be empty in short order and that would truly constitute an extraordinarily "shitty" state of affairs.

At the end of his rope, he went to hunt up the people who used to hire him to see what was going on. Of course the one place he couldn't go was to the Zhaos' house, because he'd been enjoined never to darken their door again. But it turned out that even at his former employers' places the situation had changed radically too. Everywhere he went, a man would walk out looking quite put out at his intrusion and shoo him away like a beggar. "We don't have anything for you. Now scram!"

At this point Ah Q was more confused than ever. "Always used to be that these folks couldn't do without me," he thought to himself. "Doesn't make any sense that they just don't have any more work all of a sudden. There's gotta be more to this than meets the eye." Only after carefully asking around did he discover that *now* whenever people had any work, they all went to a certain Young Don.[37] Now in Ah Q's eyes, this Young D was a miserable little critter, all skinny and weak as could be. Why he was even lower than Bearded Wang! Who would ever have dreamt that a young nobody like that would actually do him out of his ricebowl?

In light of all the above, Ah Q's present fury was not to be compared with any of his ordinary rages. As he walked along, seething with resentment, Ah Q suddenly raised a fist and belted out a line of local opera: "*My mace of steel I grasp full tight / And with it I shall now thee smite!*"[38]

A few days later he finally came across Young D in front of the short stretch of wall that protected the Qian family compound from prying eyes. As the saying goes, "*When met by chance, foe spots foe at one fell glance.*" Ah Q immediately moved in on Young D and the latter stopped dead in his tracks.

"Animal!" shouted Ah Q, giving him his dirtiest look as spittle shot from the corners of his mouth.

"I'm a bug—does that make you happy?" responded Young D.

Such modesty only served to intensify Ah Q's ire. Since he had no steel mace handy, however, he was forced to join battle barehanded. He reached out and grabbed Young D by the queue. Young D defended himself by holding tight to the root of his own queue with one hand while grabbing Ah Q's with the other. In like fashion, Ah Q used *his* free hand to protect himself by holding fast, too, to the root of his own queue. The old Ah Q had never considered Young D's martial skills to be worthy of mention, but the new Ah Q hadn't had anything to eat recently and by now yielded nothing to Young D in miserable-little-critterliness himself. It was an even match. As Young D and Ah Q bent toward each other, four hands grasped two heads. The blue shadow that was cast by the two men on the Qian family's whitewashed wall was shaped like a rainbow, a rainbow that froze and then remained motionless for a good half hour.

---

37. In the original text, "Don" is printed in English. In a letter to the editor of *Theatre,* Lu Xun wrote that the Chinese word he had in mind was *tong* (this word, meaning "alike, identical," sounds something like "don" in Lu Xun's native dialect). The idea behind this is that when Young D grows up, he will turn out just like Ah Q.

38. A line from a local Shaoxing opera, *Battle of the Dragon and Tiger Generals,* which recreates an epic battle fought by Zhao Guangyin, founder of the Song dynasty (960–1269).

A few days later he finally came across Young D in front of the short stretch of wall that protected the Qian family compound from prying eyes. As the saying goes, "When met by chance, foe spots foe at one fell glance."

"Okay now, okay!" said some of the people who had gathered round to watch—they were probably trying to break up the fight. "All right now, *all right!*" said some others. One couldn't tell whether they were simply expressing admiration or were urging the combatants to show greater animation. But whatever the case, neither Ah Q nor Young D was paying any attention to the crowd.

When Ah Q advanced three steps, Young D retreated three steps and they both stood still. When Young D advanced three steps, Ah Q retreated three steps and they both stood still. After approximately half an hour of this—it's really hard to tell because there were very few clocks in Wei Village that struck the hours, so maybe it was only twenty minutes—both their heads were steaming and their faces were bathed in sweat. Finally Ah Q's hands released their hold; at precisely the same moment Young D's hands released their hold, too. Simultaneously the two men straightened up; simultaneously they backed away from each other and elbowed their separate ways out through the ring of spectators.

"Let that be a lesson, you fucker!" said Ah Q, turning his head back to Young D.

"Let that be a lesson, you fucker!" said Young D, turning his head back to Ah Q.

So it would seem that there was no victory or defeat in the epic battle that was mounted by these two renowned warriors, nor is it known whether the spectators were satisfied with the show. At any rate, Ah Q came out of it in the same fix he had been in before —no one came to offer him work.

One day when it was quite warm and a gentle breeze was just bringing the first hint of summer into the village, quite incongruously Ah Q started to feel cold. This he could put up with. The first order of business was that hungry stomach of his. His cotton quilt, felt hat, and cotton shirt had long since disappeared, and after that he'd even sold his padded-cotton winter jacket. Now he was left with nothing but a pair of pants—he couldn't part with those no matter what—and a raggedy unlined jacket. He might have been able to *give* that away for somebody to make shoe soles with, but he certainly wouldn't be able to turn a profit on it.

For quite some time now he had fantasized about *finding* some money on the street someplace, but so far he hadn't seen any lying around. Okay then, why not find some money right here in this dilapidated room of his at the Land-and-Grain Temple? Eagerly he

When Ah Q advanced three steps, Young D retreated three steps and they both stood still.

searched his quarters over. His room was empty, so empty that he could see at a glance there was nothing to be found in it. At this point, Ah Q decided to go out and scare up something to eat.

Although his intention in going out was to "scare up something to eat," yet when he saw the familiar wineshop, the familiar steamed breadrolls, strange to tell, he walked right on by. Not only did he fail to stop, but what's more, he didn't even want the bread or wine. That's not what he was really looking for. Then, exactly what was it that he *was* looking for? Even Ah Q himself couldn't have told you.

Now Wei Village wasn't very large to begin with, and before too long Ah Q had walked clear through the place. Then he came to a sea of rice paddies covered with fresh green sprouts and extending as far as the eye could see. It was animated here and there by bobbing dots of black—peasants working in the fields. But Ah Q did not take time to stop and savor the rustic charm of such a scene; he kept right on walking, for he knew instinctively that all of that was far removed from his basic concern of "scaring up something to eat." Finally he came to the walls of the Convent of Silent Cultivation.

The whitewashed walls rose abruptly out of the green sea surrounding them. The low earthen wall behind the convent enclosed a vegetable garden. Ah Q hesitated for a moment, but looking around and seeing no one in sight, he grabbed the blackhair vines that covered the wall and started to climb.[39] Everyplace he managed to get a toehold, the dirt of the wall crumbled and *whooshed* down through the leaves while the trembling of his feet rustled the vines. Availing himself of a nearby mulberry limb, he finally made it over the wall and jumped down into the garden. There was a profusion of things growing there but there didn't seem to be any wine or steamed breadrolls handy, or anything else you could readily sink your teeth into. There was a copse of bamboo over by the western wall with lots of sprouts growing below. As luck would have it, though, none of them were steamed and ready to eat. There was also some rape, but it had long since gone to seed. There was some mustard, too, but it was about to flower, and the little cabbages were also long past ripe.

---

39. "Blackhair" refers to *Polygonum multiforum,* known popularly in Chinese as *heshouwu:* so powerful in its rejuvenative function that it turned a certain Mr. He's head *(shou)* of hair black *(wu)* overnight.

Feeling every bit as wronged as a Young Literatus who had just failed the civil service examinations, Ah Q slowly walked through a gate into the rear courtyard. He was suddenly greeted by an extraordinarily pleasant surprise, for what met his eyes could be nothing else but a turnip patch. He squatted down and started pulling them up when suddenly a very round head thrust itself out of a door and then shrank back as quickly as it had emerged. Now *that* could be nothing else but a young Buddhist nun. Ah Q thought young Buddhist nuns were worthless to begin with and was not about to be intimidated by the likes of them, but still, men of the world have always appreciated the wisdom of "playing it safe," and so he stripped the leaves from four turnips without further delay and hastily stuffed them into the front of his shirt. By that time, the old abbess herself had already come out.

"Buddha preserve us, what do you think you're doing climbing into our garden to steal turnips, Ah Q? Aiya! Such a sin! Buddha preserve us!"

"When did *I* ever climb into *your* garden to steal turnips?" Ah Q asked, walking away but keeping an eye on the nun too.

"Just now . . . aren't those . . ." The old nun pointed to his bulging shirt.

"Oh, you think these are yours, huh? Can you call 'em by name and make 'em come to you? Why you don't even—"

Before he could finish, a black dog was lunging toward him and Ah Q broke into a run. The dog had been at the front gate but somehow or other had come around to the back. It was right on Ah Q's heels and about to grab his leg when, as luck would have it, a turnip dropped out of his shirt, startling the animal long enough to give Ah Q time to climb the mulberry tree and vault over the wall. Outside, both Ah Q and turnips went spilling all over the ground; inside, the black dog kept barking at the mulberry tree while the old abbess continued to invoke the name of Buddha.

Afraid lest the abbess might let the dog out after him, Ah Q quickly gathered up the turnips and hurried on his way. He picked up a few pebbles at the side of the road just in case, but since the black dog did not reappear, he finally threw them away and began eating the turnips as he walked along. "Not gonna find anything to eat around here," he thought to himself. "I could always go to town." By the time he had finished the third turnip, he was already quite firm in his decision to head for town.

Chapter 6
From Dynastic Revival to the Fading Days of Empire

It was just past the Mid-Autumn Festival that year when Wei Village caught sight of Ah Q again.[40] "Ah Q's back." All who heard the news were surprised and forthwith rolled back their minds to ponder: "Wonder where he went?" The last few times he went to town, Ah Q had been bursting with news when he got back and had wasted no time telling everyone about his trip. But this time—nary a word. No one had even noticed that he was gone, although it is possible he may have told the old man who looked after the Land-and-Grain Temple that he was going. According to old established Wei Village precedent, however, going to town was no big thing unless it was Old Master Zhao or Old Master Qian who did the going. Even a trip to town by the Fake Foreign Devil was nothing to get worked up about, much less a trip by the likes of Ah Q. Thus the old caretaker at the temple hadn't bothered to spread word of our hero's departure for town, and consequently the inhabitants of Wei Village had been ignorant of the event.

The circumstances of his return this time were rather different too—to tell the truth, they were downright odd. The sky was almost black when Ah Q appeared, all sleepy-eyed, at the door of the wineshop. He shuffled up to the counter, extended a hand from his waist, and threw down a whole fistful of silver and copper coins. "Hard cash! Bring on the wine!" He was sporting a brand new unlined jacket and a money pouch weighed his belt down into an arc. According to old established Wei Village precedent, should one chance to meet a presentable personage with anything about him that caught the eye, then *Come what may, sweet courtesie / Should be the order of the day.* Now there was no mistaking that it really *was* Ah Q they were dealing with, but *this* Ah Q was entirely different from the raggedy-jacket Ah Q they were accustomed to, and thus they treated him with deference. This was an instance of what the ancients had in mind when they advised: *After an absence of even three days / A scholar-official rates a fresh gaze.*[41]

---

40. The Mid-Autumn Festival falls on the fifteenth day of the eighth lunar month.

41. Who could tell what examinations had been passed, what fresh honors attained in the interim?

Thus, from the manager to the waiters, and from patrons on down to mere passers-by, everyone quite naturally assumed a respectful, albeit inquisitive, air. *Behold how yon manager doth begin, with a nod to which he now appendeth some words:* "Hey, it's Ah Q! You're back!"

"I'm back."

"Looks like you've done pretty well for yourself. Let's see, you were at . . . uh . . . at . . ."

"Went to town."

This momentous item of intelligence had blanketed all of Wei Village by the very next day.

Everyone wanted to hear the saga of Ah Q's "dynastic restoration" to his present ready-cash and new-lined-jacket level of affluence. In the wineshop, in the teashop, and under the eaves of the temple, bit by bit people ferreted out the details. And as a consequence of all this, Ah Q was treated with new respect.

The way Ah Q told it, he had been working for an Old Master in town—a *Selectman,* no less. All who heard this chapter and verse looked impressed. This *Selectman*'s last name was Bai, but since he was the only *Selectman* in the whole town, there was no reason to use it. Whenever a *Selectman* was spoken of, it would have had to be Bai. This was true not only in the town but also in every place within a hundred miles around. It was as if people actually thought this man's family name was *Selectman,* and his given name, Old Master. To have been employed in the residence of such a man was, of course, impressive enough. But according to what Ah Q further revealed, he had not deemed it appropriate to remain in Bai's employ, for he considered the Old Master *Selectman* a bit too "fuckin' " this and a mite too "fuckin' " that. All who heard this sighed, but they were secretly pleased as well. They sighed because Ah Q had thrown away such a good job, but they were secretly pleased because they felt he hadn't deserved it to begin with.

The way Ah Q told it, the main reason for his return to Wei Village was his general dissatisfaction with the townsfolk. They called a *longbench* a *stickbench* and used shredded leeks—yes, *shredded*—when frying fish. And as if that weren't enough, he'd recently discovered an even greater shortcoming among them: when the women walked, their fannies didn't have much wiggle. Despite all that, however, here and there one did find things in

Everyone wanted to hear the saga of Ah Q's "dynastic restoration" to his present ready-cash and new-lined-jacket level of affluence.

town worthy of admiration. For instance, when it came to gambling, the Wei Village bumpkins couldn't manage anything better than a simple game played with thirty-two bamboo counters. Here only the Fake Foreign Devil knew how to play Ma John, but in town every little shitkicker on the block knew it up one side and down the other.[42] If the Fake Foreign Devil ever fell into the clutches of one of those little bastards, it'd be like some two-for-a-nickel ghost coming up against the King of Hell! All who heard this chapter and verse took on an embarrassed air.[43]

"Have you ever seen a de-capi-tation?" Ah Q asked. "Wow! Is that ever somethin' to see! Killin' the revolutionaries—yup, that's a real sight!" He shook his head with such appreciative enthusiasm that spittle flew from his mouth and landed on the face of Zhao Sichen, seated directly opposite him. All who heard this chapter and verse assumed an air of solemnity. Once more Ah Q looked all around and surveyed his audience. Listening with rapt attention, Bearded Wang had stretched out his neck, the better to hear Ah Q's rendition. Suddenly Ah Q raised his right arm, took aim at the nape of Bearded Wang's neck, clove the air with his hand, and shouted, "*ZAP!*"

Fairly jumping out of his skin with fright, Bearded Wang jerked his head in as quick as lightning. All who heard this chapter and verse of Ah Q's story took on a frightened—albeit appreciative—air. For several days afterward, Bearded Wang wandered around in a daze, no longer daring even to come near to Ah Q. And the others who had listened to Ah Q that day were similarly wary.

Although I dare not make so bold as to say that at this point Ah Q's standing in the eyes of the Wei Villagers was actually higher than that of Old Master Zhao, still if I were to characterize it as almost equivalent, I should probably not be guilty of any great linguistic lapse.

This being the case, it was not long before the great name of Ah Q was bruited about in the boudoirs of Wei Village for a second time. Actually only the Qians and Zhaos lived in households large enough to boast "boudoirs." Nine out of ten families had only ordinary bedrooms at best. But be they boudoirs or bedrooms,

---

42. In the original text, Ah Q hears *majiang* (the game of mahjong) as two other characters, pronounced the same way but with a completely different meaning.

43. Presumably, embarrassed at the provincialism of their own village.

women's quarters are women's quarters and it was something of a miracle that Ah Q's name should ever be heard in such precincts at all. Yet it seemed that of late, whenever the village women met, conversation would invariably turn to Ah Q. How about that blue silk skirt Seventh Sister Zou had bought of him! Secondhand, to be sure, but for ninety cents who could complain? And what about the red calico shirt Zhao Baiyan's mother had bought—seven-tenths new and it had only cost her three strings of cash, at ninety-two to the string.[44] (One authority states that it was actually Zhao Sichen's mother. Pending further research, however, this identification can only be regarded as tentative.)[45]

And now all the women's eyes throughout the village were hanging out: they all wanted to see Ah Q. In the market for a silk skirt? See Ah Q. Need a calico shirt? Go look up Ah Q. Not only did they no longer avoid him, but occasionally they would even hunt him down. "Any more silk skirts, Ah Q? No? How about calico then? You've gotta have some calico ones left." News of all this excitement eventually made its way from the shallows of ordinary village bedrooms into the depths of the Zhao and Qian boudoirs, carried thence by Seventh Sister Zou, who in an excess of smug satisfaction had taken the blue skirt and shown it off to Mrs. Zhao. That lady had, in her turn, told Old Master Zhao about Seventh Sister's purchase in terms of highest approbation. That gentleman, in his turn, had discussed it with Young Master Zhao, his *Budding Talent* son, at a dinner-table conclave that very evening, opining that there was something suspicious about Ah Q. "We had better be a bit more careful about locking our windows and doors at night. Wonder what kind of stuff he has left? We might be able to get some real bargains."

At just that time, Mrs. Zhao happened to be in the market for a good sleeveless fur jacket—if the price was right. That did it. The clan conclave approved a resolution that called for one of their number to prevail upon the good offices of Seventh Sister Zou to

---

44. Supposedly, a string of cash consisted of one hundred round coins with square holes through the middle. The string was threaded through the holes, and its two ends tied together so as to form a loop. However, such strings seldom carried a full hundred coins.

45. Lu Xun is having fun at the expense of contemporary Chinese scholars who, returning from sojourns in foreign universities, attempted to apply Western academic methodology to every problem and seemed to value research over action; cf. Lu Xun's remark about Hu Shi in the introduction to this story (chap. 1).

seek out Ah Q on that very night. Furthermore, in order that the resolution might be carried out, an exception to family protocol was also passed: an oil lamp would be lit after sunset.

The lamp burned and burned, but Ah Q was nowhere to be seen. The entire Zhao household was thrown out of kilter. Forever yawning, some faulted Ah Q's fly-by-night character, while others blamed Seventh Sister Zou for lack of diligence. Mrs. Zhao was of the opinion that Ah Q was afraid to come because of the restrictions imposed on him by the sheriff back in the spring. Old Master Zhao, on the other hand, believed that this wouldn't have made any difference because "*I* am the one who sent for him." In the end, it was Old Master Zhao who proved best at predicting the ways of the world, for Seventh Sister finally arrived with Ah Q in tow.

"He kept telling me . . . he didn't have anything left, but I told . . . I told him to come and tell you that to your face. He even said . . . even said . . ." Still trying to catch her breath, Seventh Sister Zou wheezed heavily.

"Old Master!" Ah Q hailed, stopping dead in his tracks under the eaves and smiling a smile that didn't look like a smile.

"Ah Q, I hear that you prospered while you were away," offered Old Master Zhao, who strode forward in greeting, his eyes busy with a head-to-toe inventory of Ah Q. "Glad to hear it, very glad. Now . . . uh . . . I hear you have a few secondhand items for sale. Why not bring over whatever you've got and let us have a look. The only reason I'm interested is that I just happen to be in the market for—"

"I've already told Seventh Sister Zou, stuff's all gone."

"Gone?" The plaintive note slipped out before Old Master Zhao had time to catch it. "How could they all go so quickly?"

"It was only some stuff a buddy of mine let me have. Wasn't much to begin with. Sold some to—"

"Surely you must have something left."

"All I've got now is a door curtain."

"All right then, bring *that* over," said Mrs. Zhao excitedly.

"In that case, we'll see you again tomorrow," said Old Master Zhao without much enthusiasm. "Ah Q, whenever you have anything from now on, be sure to bring it to our place first."

"We would certainly offer you better prices than anyone else around," added the *Budding Talent.* Mrs. *Budding Talent* stole a furtive glance at Ah Q to see if her husband's words had had any effect.

"I need a sleeveless fur jacket!" Mrs. Zhao came right out with it.

Although Ah Q had promised to do as they said, he sauntered out in such a lackadaisical way that it was hard to tell if he really meant it. This whole business proved a great disappointment to Old Master Zhao. In fact he was so vexed that he stopped yawning. The *Budding Talent* was quite put out with Ah Q as well. "Have to keep a sharp eye on that turtle's egg. Maybe we ought to have the sheriff drive him out of town and be done with it."

Old Master Zhao, however, did not see things the same way and opined that such a course would only serve to turn Ah Q into a lifelong enemy. Besides, people in that line of work were likely to bear out the truth of the saying *The hawk is always a pest, but never 'round its own nest,* and hence there was no need for concern around Wei Village. "As long as we keep a little more alert nights, we should be all right." The beneficiary of this "courtyard guidance" promptly decided that his father couldn't be more correct and immediately tabled the resolution calling for exile.[46] Furthermore, he enjoined Seventh Sister Zou to refrain from telling anyone that such a possibility had even been entertained. The following day Seventh Sister Zou took the blue silk skirt she had bought from Ah Q and dyed it black. Then, far and wide, she broadcast all the Zhaos' suspicions regarding Ah Q—though she did not, in good faith, touch on that particular chapter and verse having to do with the *Budding Talent*'s suggestion about exile. Nonetheless, what she did say proved quite damaging to Ah Q.

First off, the sheriff hunted him down and made off with the door curtain, steadfastly refusing to return it despite Ah Q's protestation that Mrs. Zhao was anxious to see it. Worse yet, the sheriff even tried to press Ah Q into making a monthly "filial donation."[47] Second, there was a sudden transformation in the form of respect that Wei Villagers showed Ah Q. The expressions they wore now announced that although they still weren't about to take any liberties with him, they would just as soon give him a

46. "Courtyard guidance" alludes to Confucius' education of his own son; see *The Analects of Confucius* 16.13.

47. Many Chinese expressions acknowledge the superior status of another person by referring to him as father, or even grandfather. Protection money that was extorted by gangsters (or as in this case, hush money extorted by the sheriff) could thus be spoken of as a sum of money offered out of filial respect.

wide berth. These expressions were by no means identical to the ones they had worn earlier when guarding against a surprise "*ZAP!*" either. No, there was now an element of the attitude that Confucius recommended one should take with regard to ghosts and spirits: "*Respectful you may be, but keep some distance 'twixt them and thee.*"

Only the village roustabouts had the temerity to get close to Ah Q. They moved in and subjected him to an unrelenting barrage of questions, hoping to find out exactly what he'd been up to in town. For his part, Ah Q didn't hold anything back either. On the contrary, he related his urban experiences with a real touch of pride. It was now they learned that, in the brief course of his criminal career, Ah Q's role had been little more than that of an extra. He had neither *scaled walls* nor had he *tunneled through barriers* the way real burglars are supposed to do. In fact, he had merely waited outside to receive the stolen goods as they were passed to him from inside. One night, just after the head of the gang had handed him a sack of stuff and headed back for more, Ah Q heard a great commotion break out on the inside. He had immediately taken to his heels, climbed over the city wall, and fled back to Wei Village, no longer possessing the nerve to continue in his new calling.[48]

Strange to say, these revelations had a remarkably adverse effect on Ah Q. The Wei Villagers' *respectful-be* attitude had been sustained by fear, pure and simple. Who would ever have guessed that in point of fact Ah Q was nothing more than a burglar who no longer dared to burgle? It was truly a case of *He whose years bring nought of fame / To our respect can lay no claim.*[49]

Chapter 7
Revolution

On the Fourteenth Day of the Ninth Month of the Third Year of the Xuantong Reign—in other words, on the day Ah Q sold his money pouch to Zhao Baiyan—on the Fourth Stroke of the Third

48. The gates of the city wall would have been locked for the night.

49. The reference is to *Analects* 9.22. "The Master said: Those who are born after us merit our respect. How do we know that in the future they will not be equal to what we are now? If, on the other hand, by the age of forty or fifty a man has done nothing to make his name known in the world, then such a common lout merits not our respect."

Watch,[50] a large black-canopied boat tied up at the Zhao family wharf. Since it had been poled in during the middle of the night, the villagers were sound asleep and unaware of its arrival. When they left their homes before dawn next morning, however, quite a few of them caught sight of it. After some quick nosing around, they discovered it belonged to none other than Old Master *Selectman.*

That boat carried a cargo of unrest into Wei Village. Well before noon, everyone had heard about it and was quite worried. The Zhaos, of course, were secretive as to the boat's real mission, but out on the street word had it that the Revolutionary Party was about to occupy the town and that Old Master *Selectman* had come out to Wei Village to hole up until things blew over. The sole dissenting opinion was offered by Seventh Sister Zou. The way she told it, the boat only carried a few battered old trunks that Old Master *Selectman* wanted to store at the Zhaos' place, but Old Master Zhao had refused and the trunks had been sent back to town. If you stopped to think about it, she probably had something there, for despite their both being members of the educated scholar-official class, *Budding Talent* Zhao and Old Master *Selectman* had never hit it off very well and it would seem unlikely that there could be any "brothers-in-adversity" relationship between them. What was more, since Seventh Sister Zou was a *neighbor* of the Zhaos, her view of things ought to be closer to the mark. And so people decided that, more likely than not, Seventh Sister Zou had the right of it.

Nevertheless rumors continued to fly. One of them went like this: although, to be sure, Old Master *Selectman* had probably not come in person, he *had* sent along a lengthy letter in which, after many a twist and turn through the maze of kith and kin, he had established himself as at least a "kissin' cousin" to the Zhaos. After reading the said letter, Old Master Zhao had given that possibility a quick roll around his brain and concluded that such a relationship could certainly do him no harm. He had therefore kept the battered old trunks, which were at this very moment stuffed under his wife's bed. And as to the Revolutionary Party, there were those

50. Xuantong was the reign title of the last Qing emperor. The lunar date given here corresponds to November 4, 1911, the day Lu Xun's own hometown was "liberated." The time given is about midnight.

who held that it had occupied the town that very night, every soldier wearing a white helmet—obviously in mourning for the Emperor Chong Zhen.[51]

Ah Q's ear had long since been exposed to the expression "Revolutionary Party." What was more, only this year he had seen members of that same party being executed. His idea of the whole thing—though he wouldn't have been able to tell you exactly how he came by it—had always been that "revolutionaries" were troublemakers, hell-bent on turning the world upside down, and that meant giving Ah Q a hard time personally. Hence his own attitude toward such mischief makers had been one of *antipathy most intense* and *abhorrence most immense*. But who could ever have guessed that Old Master *Selectman*—respected and feared as he was for miles and miles around—would be utterly terrified by this Revolutionary Party? It was a sweet thought and it made Ah Q lean their way. Furthermore, with all the "cocksuckin' villagers" running around like chickens with their heads cut off, how could Ah Q help but be pleased?

"Why *not* be a revolutionary?" he asked himself. "There's a whole bunch of fuckers I'd like to revolution clear out of this world and into the next, the sorry bastards! I just might throw in with that Revolution Party myself!"

Ah Q had been a bit hard up lately and that probably helped put him out of sorts to begin with. On top of that, he'd had two bowls of wine on an empty stomach that very afternoon. He thought as he walked; and he walked as he thought. And then he began to walk an inch or so above the ground. Thoughts and wine had suddenly transformed his single person into an entire revolutionary army! Everyone in Wei Village was now his prisoner. Everyone! He was soon so full of himself he could no longer contain it.

"On with the rebellion!" shouted Ah Q.

The Wei Villagers watched him with a look that bordered on a look of terror, a look that made Ah Q feel as comfortable as a man drinking melted snow in the middle of June. Now he was full to

51. White was the traditional color of mourning. Chong Zhen was the last Ming emperor before the Manchu invasion that established the Qing dynasty (1644–1912). Many peasant rebel groups that tried to overthrow the Manchus did so under the slogan "Destroy the Qing, restore the Ming." So it is natural for the Wei Villagers to assume that the Revolutionary Party, which has just established a new republic, is just one more of these restorationist groups.

"On with the rebellion!"

the point of overflowing. "Whatever Ah Q wants, Ah Q gets! Whatever *woman* Ah Q wants, Ah Q gets!" he shouted happily and then began to sing.

> *"Da-da dum-dum!*
> *In my cups, would that I had ne'er . . .*
> *Da-da dum-dum!*
> *. . . taken the head of my brother-in-arms,*
> *Brother Zheng.*
> *Would that I had ne'er . . .*
> *Ah . . . ah-ah . . . ah . . .*
> *Da-da dum-dum, da dum-ya-dum!*
> *My mace of steel I grasp full tight,*
> *And with it I shall now thee smite . . .*

Two Zhaos were standing at the front gate of their family compound discussing the implications of the revolution with two honest-to-goodness relatives. Head held jauntily aloft, Ah Q cruised on past without deigning to notice them.

"Da-da . . ."

"Q, my friend," hailed Old Master Zhao somewhat diffidently.

"Dum-dum!" Never dreaming that his own name could possibly be linked with "friend," it did not occur to Ah Q that these words had anything to do with him, and so he kept right on singing: *"Da-dum . . . dum-ya-dum . . . dum!"*

"Old friend, Q!"

"Would that I had ne'er—"

"AH Q!" The *Budding Talent* was forced to shout out the name they usually used on him.

Ah Q stopped dead in his tracks, cocked his head to one side, and inquired, "What?"

"Q, my friend. Now . . . uh . . ." Old Gentleman Zhao seemed at a loss for words. "Uh . . . you've gotten rich, huh?"

"Rich? You betcha! From here on out, whatever Ah Q wants, Ah Q gets!"

"Ah Q . . . I mean, Elder Brother Q. Poor folks like us won't be in any trouble, will they?" Zhao Baiyan asked anxiously in an attempt to determine which way the revolutionary winds were blowing.

"Poor, my foot! You sure as hell have a lot more dough than I

Ah Q stopped dead in his tracks, cocked his head to one side, and inquired, "What?"

do." Ah Q turned and walked away, bringing all conversation to a disappointing halt.

Old Master Zhao and son went back inside and discussed everything that had transpired until it was time to light—or time not to light—their lamps. Zhao Baiyan went back home, undid his moneybelt, and ordered his wife to hide it at the bottom of the family trunk.

Walking on air, Ah Q continued floating hither and yon for quite a while so that by the time he got back to the Land-and-Grain Temple, he was thoroughly sober. Tonight even the caretaker turned affable and invited him in for tea. Ah Q asked him for two crackers, and after finishing them, even managed to hit him up for a four-ounce candle and candlestick. Alone in his little room at last, luxuriating, Ah Q lit the candle and lay down. He was indescribably happy.

The flames shimmered and danced as if it were New Year's Eve, and Ah Q's thoughts began to do some high stepping too. "Throw in with the troublemakers? Yeah, that would be fun. I can see it now. A bunch of those Revolution Party guys'll come by the temple here, all decked out in white armor and white helmets, wearin' sabers too! They'll come marchin' right in and shout: 'Let's go, Ah Q, come with us!' And I'll go with them too! Steel maces, bombs, foreign rifles, spears, knives—they'll have it all. Then those cocksuckin' villagers will find out how pitiful they really are. I can see 'em kneelin' on the ground and beggin' me to spare 'em. Fat chance! Young D and Old Master Zhao'll be the first to go. I'll get the *Budding Talent* too, and then I'll do in the Fake Foreign Devil. Wonder if I should let any of 'em live? Well by rights I suppose I could spare Bearded Wang—but no, I'm not gonna.

"And think of all the stuff I'll get, too. March right into their houses and rip open their trunks—gold, silver, foreign money, foreign calico shirts! For starters I'll take that Ningbo bed the *Budding Talent*'s wife has and move it over here to the temple. The Qians' tables and chairs will do just fine, thank you—maybe I'll take some from the Zhaos, too. Won't even have to lift a finger. Get Young D to do all the heavy work. Better step lively too, if he doesn't want a good belt or two.

"Let's see. Zhao Sichen's sister is a real dog, and there's not much point in talkin' about Seventh Sister Zou's daughter for a couple of years yet. Fake Foreign Devil's wife is willin' to sleep with a husband that's got no queue—she can't be any damn good!

If only *Budding Talent*'s old lady didn't have that mole on her eyelid. Haven't seen Amah Wu in a while, wonder where she is? But then she's got those big-ass feet."

Before he had time to arrange all the pieces just right, Ah Q was already snoring. The four-ounce candle had burned down less than half an inch and its bright rays shone warm and red on his open mouth. And then all of a sudden he screamed, raised his head, and looked around in panic. Finally his gaze came to rest on the four-ounce candle. He put his head back down and went to sleep.

Ah Q didn't get out of bed until quite late the next day. He went out on the street and did a quick survey—everything was exactly as it had always been. His stomach was exactly as it had always been too—empty. He thought about what he should do next but failed to come up with anything. And then suddenly he seemed to have hit on something, for his body gradually began to move. Thinking more with his feet than with anything else, Ah Q finally arrived at the Convent of Silent Cultivation.

It was every bit as quiet as he remembered it from the previous spring. He knocked on the gate. A dog began to bark inside. Ah Q hastily picked out a large piece of brick and approached the gate again. He began knocking with the brick, much harder than before, but it was not until many a pockmark had appeared on the surface of the big black gate that he heard someone coming out.

Ah Q immediately secured a better hold on the brick, spread his feet wide, and prepared to do battle with the dog. The gate opened no more than a crack, however, and no guardian canine burst forth. Peeking in through that crack, Ah Q saw nothing but an elderly nun.

"What are *you* doing here again?" she asked in alarm.

"There's been a revolution, haven't you heard?"

"Revolution? Haven't we had just about enough revolution for one day?"

"Huh?" Ah Q was puzzled.

"Don't you know? The revolutionists have already been here."

"*What* revolutionists?" Ah Q was more puzzled than ever.

"The *Budding Talent* and Fake Foreign Devil!"

Ah Q was stunned by the news. The elderly nun, sensing his loss of momentum, quickly shut the gate. By the time he realized what had happened, the gate was locked tighter than a drum. Ah Q pounded on it once again, but this time there was no response.

It had all happened that very morning. Always right on top of things, *Budding Talent* Zhao learned that the revolutionaries had taken the town during the night. He responded by coiling his queue up on top of his head and heading out bright and early to pay his respects to the Fake Foreign Devil, a man with whom he had never been on good terms heretofore. However, since this was "a time for people from all walks of life to unite in national renewal,"[52] they now hit it off just fine, quickly became the comradeliest of comrades-in-arms, and joined together to undertake the task of revolution.

But where to begin? After wracking their brains at great length, they finally remembered that there was a "Long Live the Emperor" tablet over at the Convent of Silent Cultivation. They righteously decided that this tablet would have to go, and set out forthwith for the convent. Giving the two a good piece of her mind, the elderly nun had tried to stop them. Thereupon, taking her as a symbol of the entire Manchu establishment, they gave her a sound thrashing. After they left, the old nun had collected herself enough to survey the damage. The objectionable tablet, of course, lay shattered on the ground. She also discovered that an extremely valuable antique censer that had stood before a statue of the Bodhisattva Guanyin[53] was nowhere to be seen.

It was only much later that day that Ah Q found out about all this. He was more than a little sorry that he had been asleep during the foray and was also quite put out that they hadn't come to get him. He backed up another step in his thoughts and wondered: "Do you suppose they don't know I've already thrown in with the Revolution Party?"

Chapter 8
Request to Revolt Denied

The Wei Villagers felt more reassured with every passing day. The word from town was that although the Revolutionary Party had indeed taken over, it hadn't made any changes to speak of. His honor the county magistrate was still the same man, though they

52. This slogan *(xian yü wei xin)* is quoted from the *History Classic* and was widely popular around the beginning of the republic.

53. The Goddess of Mercy, better known to Western readers by her Japanese name, Kannon.

called him something else now. Old Master *Selectman* had also acquired some sort of new label (the Wei Villagers couldn't keep track of all these new revolutionary titles). And the same old lieutenant was in charge of the soldiers, too.[54]

The only worrisome thing about this whole business was that some bad elements had slipped into the Revolutionary Party and started lopping queues off the day after they arrived in town. The boatman from over in the next village, Sevenpounder, had fallen into their clutches and had been so transformed that he no longer looked even human.[55] The incident occasioned but little anxiety among the Wei Villagers, however, because few of them ever ventured into town in the the first place, and the one or two who were thinking of making the trek immediately changed their plans. Why risk ending up like Sevenpounder if you didn't have to? At first, Ah Q had considered going into town to look up some old friends, but on hearing of Sevenpounder's tragic fate, he too had no choice but to cancel his trip.

And yet you couldn't say that the revolution hadn't triggered any reforms in Wei Village, either. Within a few days after the revolutionaries took the town, for instance, the number of people with queues coiled up on top of their heads gradually began to increase. As I have reported earlier, it was his nibs the *Budding Talent* who led the way; next came Zhao Sichen and Zhao Baiyan; and after that Ah Q also joined the parade. During the summer, of course, it was not uncommon for people in Wei Village to coil their queues up on top of their heads, or even to do them up in knots. But this was late autumn, not summer. And so, from the point of view of those who did the coiling, one cannot maintain that this "autumn practice of summer etiquette" demonstrated anything less than a magnificent decisiveness worthy of the doughtiest heroes. And once that's granted, one cannot say that the revolution didn't trigger any reforms in Wei Village either.

When Zhao Sichen came walking down the street with the back of his head scandalously bared, people would look at him and then warn each other: "Look out, here comes a revolutionary!"

---

54. As Lu Xun saw it, the 1911 Republican Revolution had done nothing to alter the basic power structure of Chinese society.

55. A reference to the protagonist of "A Passing Storm" (published under the pen name, Lu Xun) and another clue to the identity of Ba Ren, the pseudonym under which Lu Xun first published the present story.

When Ah Q heard of this, he was quite envious. Although Ah Q had long since gotten wind of the momentous news about the *Budding Talent*'s coiling his queue up, the idea that *he* might do the same had never crossed his mind. It was only when he saw Zhao Sichen do it that Ah Q gave a thought to imitating this new fashion. Having resolved to put that thought into practice, and using a chopstick for hairpin, Ah Q coiled up his queue too. After some hesitation, he even got up the nerve to go out on the street looking like that.

People actually did give him a second look, but they didn't warn each other about a revolutionary coming. At first, Ah Q merely felt displeased, but later on he began to resent the injustice of it all. He got so worked up that he began flying off the handle at the least provocation. In point of fact, however, he wasn't any worse off now than he had been before he revolted. People were passably polite to him and the stores didn't insist on cash every time he bought anything, yet somehow or other Ah Q felt that this whole revolution business was a big disappointment. Since there really *had* been a revolution, there ought to be more to it than just this.

Later on he ran into Young D. That was the straw that broke the camel's back—Young D had coiled up his queue too! What was more, he'd had the gall to use a chopstick! Never in his wildest dreams had Ah Q expected that someone the likes of Young D would have the nerve to join in on the queue-coiling and he was simply not going to have it! Just who the hell did Young D think he was anyway? Ah Q felt like seizing him on the spot, breaking that chopstick, putting that queue back down, and slapping him across the mouth a few times as punishment for forgetting his place. In the end, however, Ah Q let him off with a contemptuous *"Aaaaaaawk . . . tuh!"* accompanied by a dirty look.

During these parlous times, the Fake Foreign Devil was the only one who ventured into town. *Budding Talent* Zhao had briefly considered going in to visit Old Master *Selectman* in order to cash in on the goodwill the Zhaos had earned by hiding the *Selectman*'s trunks. But the *Budding Talent* was also mindful of the risk he would bring to bear on his queue and decided against it. Instead, he wrote a yellow-umbrella letter[56] and prevailed upon the Fake

56. Yellow umbrellas had been a distinctive part of the emperor's regalia. In a "yellow-umbrella letter" the Chinese characters were so arranged that the middle vertical line (the text was written from top to bottom, starting at the right-hand side of the page) was much

Foreign Devil to take it into town and show it around in the right places, so that he might gain entry to the Revolutionary Party. When the Fake Foreign Devil returned, he promptly relieved the *Budding Talent* of four dollars, in exchange for which the latter received a Silver Peach to pin onto his lapel. That peach bowled the villagers over. Everyone said it was the symbol of the "Persimmon Oil Party"[57] and worth at least an Imperial Academy Button.[58] Old Master Zhao's prestige soared to even greater heights than it had reached when his son won the *Budding Talent*. The upshot was that Old Master Zhao began lording it over everyone again and even started getting uppity with Ah Q.

Ah Q, in turn, felt he wasn't getting a square deal. He was left out of things at every turn. But as soon as he heard about the Silver Peach business, he realized why this was so. If you're going to revolt, just *saying* so isn't enough. And coiling your queue won't cut it either. The first order of business is to get in touch with the revolutionaries.

Now Ah Q had known only two revolutionaries in his entire life. The one in town had gotten his head *ZAPPED!* off a good while back. The other one was the Fake Foreign Devil. That settled it. Like it or not, Ah Q would have to get in touch with him.

The front gate at the Qians' stood wide open. Ah Q skulked inside and was somewhat startled by the sight that greeted him. There in the middle of the courtyard stood the Fake Foreign Devil, decked out from stem to stern in solid black—foreign clothes, it looked like—and sporting a Silver Peach too! His hand grasped the cane from whose instruction Ah Q had so often profited in the past. His queue, grown out to a good foot and a half by now, was

---

longer than those on either side, in a form suggesting the stem of the umbrella, while the lines of characters to the right and left (lines of varying lengths) suggested the umbrella covering. To send such a letter expressed profound respect on the part of the sender. It is ironic here that a letter whose form calls to mind the old imperial court is sent to the Revolutionary Party, presumably a petition for membership.

57. Unfamiliar with the concept of "freedom" *(ziyou)*, the villagers hear the name of the party in question as "persimmon oil" *(shiyou)*.

58. Qing dynasty officials wore buttons on their their ceremonial hats. Oval in shape, the buttons varied in color according to the rank of the wearer. An Imperial Academy Button was the most prestigious. After passing the first two levels of the civil service examinations *(Budding Talent* and *Selectman)*, a candidate receiving a "high pass" on the third exam *(Advanced Scholar)* might then sit for an additional examination over which the emperor himself presided. A "pass" on this one entitled the candidate to join the Imperial Academy and to wear the corresponding button.

all undone. The freed hair cascaded down over his shoulders, making him look for all the world like some kind of Daoist Immortal. Standing just opposite this apparition, at straight-arrow attention, were Zhao Baiyan and a trio of Wei Villagers. Making a great show of deference, they hung on the Fake Foreign Devil's every word.

Quietly Ah Q made his way in, taking up a position behind Zhao Baiyan. He wanted to say something to the black-garbed star of the show but couldn't figure out what to call him. "Fake Foreign Devil" obviously wouldn't do. "Foreigner" was no better. And "Revolutionary" didn't quite do it either. Maybe he just ought to call him *Mr.* Foreigner.

"Mr. Foreigner" hadn't even noticed Ah Q. Eyes rolled skyward, he was just now hitting his stride: "I'm an impatient sort myself, and so whenever I met him, I'd always say, 'Brother Hong, let's get on with it.' But he would reply, '*Mais non, mon ami!*'—that's a foreign expression for 'no.'[59] If he hadn't kept 'no-ing' me like that, the revolution would have come off a long time ago, but it goes to show you how carefully he proceeds in everything. He's tried to get me to take a post up there in Hubei I don't know how many times, but I've never agreed. After all, who wants a post in some insignificant county seat?"

"Ahem . . . Mr. . . ." Ah Q took advantage of a momentary pause in the Fake Foreign Devil's monologue to say his piece. It had taken all the courage he could muster, and then some, to even open his mouth.

But for some reason or other his intended form of address, "Mr. Foreigner," stuck in his throat.

"Out with it! What is it?"

"I . . . I . . ."

"Get out of here!"

"I want to throw in with . . ."

"Beat it!" Mr. Foreigner raised his *wailing stick* ominously high.

Then Zhao Baiyan and the village idlers began to bark at him

59. "Brother Hong" is a pretentious reference to Li Yuanhong (1864–1928), the Qing commander who reluctantly took charge of the revolutionary government in Hubei (at the behest of his own troops) following the 1911 Wuchang uprising. Subsequently he served twice as president of the republic. The italicized French expression in the translation appears as English "No!" in the original Chinese text.

"Beat it!" Mr. Foreigner raised his wailing stick *ominously high.*

too. "The gentleman has told you to beat it. That should be enough!"

Letting his feet do the thinking, Ah Q escaped through the gate, one hand shielding his head. To his surprise, however, Mr. Foreigner didn't bother to come after him. Nonetheless Ah Q hightailed it some sixty paces or so before gradually slowing down to a walk. He was heartbroken. If Mr. Foreigner wouldn't give him permission to revolt, he was done for. Never again could he look forward to having men in white helmets and white armor come by and ask him to join up. The idlers back there at Mr. Foreigner's place would waste no time in spreading word of what had just taken place, and Ah Q would become a laughingstock to the likes of Young D and Bearded Wang. That was bad enough. But the worst of it was that all his ambitions, hopes, and plans for the future had been wiped out at a single stroke.

In his entire life, Ah Q had never before experienced such a feeling of utter aimlessness. He felt that even coiling up his queue was pointless and briefly considered letting it down again just to get even. In the end, however, he didn't. With no particular goal in mind, Ah Q loafed around until nightfall. Then he put two bowls of wine on his tab and promptly drank them down. Gradually his spirits began to rise and glimpses of white helmets and white armor began to flicker across his brain once again.

One night, as had become his habit of late, Ah Q dawdled around in the wineshop till closing time and then started to trudge on back to the temple. *BIFF BANG BAM BOOM*—an odd kind of racket. Didn't sound like firecrackers either. Always a lover of excitement, Ah Q liked nothing better than minding everyone else's business. So he made a beeline through the darkness to the source of the noise. Hearing some footsteps, he stopped and cocked his head, the better to listen. A man hurtled past him in full retreat from something or other. Ah Q reversed his own course and fell in beside him. When he made a turn, Ah Q made a turn. When he stopped, Ah Q also stopped. Seeing there was no one behind them, Ah Q took a closer look—Young D!

"What's goin' on?" Ah Q felt left out again.

"The Zhaos . . . the Zhaos . . . got robbed!" Young D tried to catch his breath. The news made Ah Q's heart *thump thump* all the faster. Having caught his breath, Young D continued to make his escape under the eaves of the houses and so, at first, did Ah Q. Having had some experience in "this line of work," however, Ah Q was the bolder of the two and finally headed back up the street to see what was really going on. He stopped and watched while a steady line of white helmets and white jackets came out of the Zhaos' place—with trunks, furniture, even the stylish Ningbo bed that belonged to the *Budding Talent*'s old lady. He wanted to get closer for a better look, but his feet simply wouldn't move.

Wei Village lay very quiet in the darkness, as quiet as it might have lain during the reign of Fu Xi.[60] Ah Q stood and watched until he was tired of watching, but there was still no end in sight. A steady stream of people went back and forth moving things out, so many things that Ah Q could scarcely believe his eyes. He decided against getting any closer and headed back to the temple.

It was pitch black in the Land-and-Grain Temple. Closing the main gate behind him, Ah Q groped his way back into his room. He lay there for a long time before he was finally able to collect his thoughts enough to assess his own situation. Quite clearly the white-helmet white-armor people had arrived, but also just as clearly, they had not invited him to join them. And so no matter how much loot they made off with at the Zhaos' place, he didn't stand to get any share of it. "It's all because that Fake Foreign Devil wouldn't let me revolt, otherwise I'd sure as hell have gotten some of that stuff." The more he thought, the madder he got, until at last he could contain himself no longer. "Won't let me revolt, huh? You're the only one allowed to revolt, fuckin' Fake Foreign Devil! Okay, go right ahead and revolt to your heart's content. Revolt's a crime you can get your head chopped off for. Just watch and see if I don't turn your ass in! I'll just sit back and watch 'em haul you into town and lop off your head! They'll do in your whole family—*ZAP! ZAP! ZAP!*"

Chapter 9
The Grand Reunion

After the burglary at Old Master Zhao's the villagers were, for the most part, quite pleased—and frightened too; Ah Q was, for the most part, quite pleased—and frightened as well. Four days later he was arrested in the middle of the night and hauled off to town.

As luck would have it, there was no moon that night and taking

60. Legendary ruler of high antiquity under whose idyllic reign China prospered in peace and tranquility.

Expectantly, they set up a machine gun opposite the temple gate. Ah Q, however, failed to come roaring out on cue.

full advantage of the darkness, one squad of soldiers, one squad of militia, and five detectives slipped into the village to surround the Land-and-Grain Temple. Expectantly, they set up a machine gun opposite the temple gate. Ah Q, however, failed to come roaring out on cue. They waited and waited, but there was nary a peep within the temple compound. Unable to stand the suspense, the lieutenant persuaded two of his bravos—for a reward of twenty strings of cash, one full thousand to the string—to scale the temple wall. Once inside they let their cohorts in through the gate, and together they all thundered onward to Ah Q's room and took him captive there. When they had dragged him out to the machine gun emplacement, he was beginning to wake up.

And by the time they entered the town with Ah Q in tow, it was already high noon. He watched himself supported under the arms and escorted into a rundown *yamen*[61] where, after five or six shifts in direction, he was finally shoved into a cell. A big barred door slammed shut at his heels as he stumbled inside. The other three sides of the cell were bare walls. Upon closer inspection he discovered two other men over in one corner.

Although somewhat upset, Ah Q was not particularly dissatisfied with his present accommodations, for his own room back at the temple was certainly no more elegantly appointed than this cell. The other two men, it turned out, were country people like himself, and it wasn't too long before he had struck up a conversation with them. One said he was there because Old Master *Selectman* was dunning him for rents owed by his dead grandfather. The other had no idea why he had been arrested. When they asked Ah Q what he was in for, he replied without the slightest hesitation: "Cause I wanna revolt."

During the second half of the day, the big barred door opened once again. Ah Q was hauled out and taken to the courtroom. Up front an old man, head shaved clean, sat on a dais. Ah Q thought he must be some kind of monk at first, but then he noticed a line of soldiers standing below the old fellow and many long-gowned gentry types on either side of him as well. Some of these long-gowns had their heads shaved clean just like the old geezer, but one had hair that was a good foot and a half long and fanned out all over his shoulders just like the Fake Foreign Devil's. Every

61. The seat of a local government.

When they asked Ah Q what he was in for, he replied without the slightest hesitation: "Cause I wanna revolt."

mother's son of them looked mean and ugly. What was more, they nailed Ah Q with dirty looks. At this juncture, it occurred to Ah Q that there must be something more to the bald old geezer than met the eye. Ah Q's knees instantly loosened of their own accord and he sank to a kneeling position.

"Stand! Stand while addressing this court! No kneeling!" barked the long-gowned types virtually in unison.

Ah Q appeared to understand, but didn't seem able to stay on his feet. As if of its own accord, his body collapsed into a squat and then, capitalizing on the momentum already built up, continued right on down into a full-fledged kneel.

"A born slave!" observed the long-gowned types with contempt, but they didn't try to get him to stand up again either.

"Why not come right out and confess it all now, and spare yourself a lot of needless suffering later on. We know exactly what happened anyway." The bald-headed old man's gaze never left Ah Q's face. His voice was kindly—calm and clear. "Just fess up and we'll let you go."

"Confess!" bellowed the long-gowns.

"Well, to tell the truth . . . I was gonna . . . gonna come and throw—"[62]

"Then why *didn't* you come?" asked the old man in the sweetest of tones.

"Fake Foreign Devil wouldn't let me!"

"Nonsense! Too late to talk about that now anyway. Where are your confederates?"

"My what?"

"The bunch that burglarized the Zhaos' place with you?"

"Those guys didn't even come by to get me! Carted all that stuff off for themselves!" Ah Q waxed indignant at the very thought of it.

"Where did they cart it off to? If you tell, I can let you walk out of here." The old man's voice was more mellifluous than ever.

"How should I know? They didn't come by to get me!"

At this juncture the old man gave a wink, and Ah Q was once again shoved through the big barred door.

The next morning he was hauled out a second time. The court-

62. Ah Q is about to say "throw in with the Revolutionaries." The judge, however, thinks he is going to say "throw in the towel" or surrender *(touxiang).*"

room was exactly as it had been yesterday—the bald-headed old man sitting on the dais while Ah Q knelt on the floor before him. "Do you have anything to say to this court?" asked the old man, voice dripping with compassion.

Ah Q thought for a bit. He didn't, and said no.

Then one of the long-gowns presented him with a sheet of paper and a writing brush. When the said personage thrust the brush into the prisoner's hand, Ah Q was so terrified that it was almost a case of *the heavenly part of the soul took to wing, and the earthly part to heel,* for this was the first time in his whole life that any relationship had ever been established between his hand and a writing brush. Just as he was wondering how you were supposed to hold the thing, the long-gown pointed to a place on the paper and told him to sign.

Ah Q's fingers tightened around the brush. In a voice that echoed with fear and shame he confessed: "Don't . . . don't know how to write."

"In that case we'll go easy on you. Just draw a circle."

Ah Q tried to compose himself enough to make the circle, but the hand that held the brush refused to stop trembling. The long-gowns carefully spread the paper out flat on the floor before him. Ah Q leaned forward over it, and marshaling all the strength and concentration at his command, approached the task at hand. Dreadfully concerned lest someone laugh at him, he was determined to make that circle a nice round one, but that damned brush lay heavy in his hand and turned out to be disobedient as well. Tremble after tremble, he traced the circle around and was on the point of closing it up when suddenly the brush shrugged off to one side, producing something that looked more like a watermelon seed than a circle.

Just as Ah Q was starting to feel conscience stricken at not being able to make a nice round circle, one of the long-gowns, not seeming to mind in the least, made off with both brush and paper.

The second time Ah Q was shoved into the cell, it didn't seem to bother him much at all, for he had come to the conclusion that in this old world of ours there must be times when a man is supposed to get hauled in and out of cells, and times when he's supposed to draw circles on a sheet of paper too. "It would take a real jackass to draw a nice *round* circle anyway," he told himself and then promptly fell asleep.

. . . he was determined to make that circle a nice round one . . .

Old Master *Selectman,* on the other hand, didn't get a single wink that whole night, for he'd had a good go-round with the lieutenant during the day. The *Selectman* had maintained that the first order of business was recovery of the stolen property, but the lieutenant had insisted that the most important thing was to make a public example of Ah Q. The lieutenant, who had only recently stopped giving a hoot *what* Old Master *Selectman* thought, had slammed his fist hard on the table and quoted: "*Make an example of only one / And a hundred crimes will go undone.* Put yourself in my shoes. I've been a lieutenant in the Revolutionary Party for less than three weeks and we've already had a dozen cases of burglary. Not a single one solved, either. Now what kind of face does that give me? When I finally do figure one out, you have to come along and start acting like some old fuddy-duddy scholar. Well I won't have it! *I'm* the one in charge of this case!" But Old Master *Selectman* held his ground. He even threatened to resign his new position as deputy in the Revolutionary Government if the lieutenant didn't do his best to recover the stolen property. "Be my guest!" had been the lieutenant's only response. And so it was that Old Master *Selectman* didn't get a single wink that whole night. We can thank our lucky stars, however, that he did not actually resign the next day.

The third time Ah Q was hauled out through the big barred door was on the morrow of the entire night during which Old Master *Selectman* didn't get a single wink.

Ah Q entered the courtroom once again. Just as before, the bald-headed old man sat on the dais while Ah Q knelt on the floor before him.

"Do you have anything more to tell the court?" asked the old man in kindly tones.

Ah Q thought for a bit. He didn't, and said no.

And then all of a sudden some of the long-gowned and short-gowned types put a white cotton vest on him, a vest with words written all over it.[63]

Now a very queasy feeling came over Ah Q, for such an outfit was like unto the *mourning clothes* that people wore when their parents died—and mourning clothes were definitely unlucky.[64]

---

63. The words give details of his crimes.
64. White, not black, is the color of mourning.

Hands tied behind him, Ah Q was hauled out through the front gate of the *yamen* and lifted up onto an open cart. Two men in short jackets seated themselves on either side of him. The cart lurched into motion.

Ah Q saw that there were some militiamen and a squad of soldiers marching in front of the cart. The soldiers were shouldering foreign rifles. Mouths agape, spectators lined both sides of the road. He couldn't see, of course, whatever it was that was bringing up the rear. Suddenly it dawned on him. It couldn't be anything else—this was an execution!

Ah Q panicked. Everything went black. There was a loud ringing in his ears and he slipped to the edge of unconsciousness. But rather than falling in, he stayed there teetering on the brink. Remaining in this state, he was by turns terror-stricken and perfectly at ease. As his mind flickered on and off, Ah Q concluded that in this old world of ours there must be times when a man is supposed to get hauled away and have his head chopped off.

He recognized their route of march. He was puzzled—why weren't they headed to the execution ground? Ah Q didn't realize that he was first being paraded through the streets as "a warning to the people." But even if he had known, it would have made no difference. He would simply have concluded that in this old world of ours there must be times when a man is supposed to be paraded through the streets as a warning to the people. Then he solved the puzzle—yes, he was in fact headed toward the execution ground, but they were taking the long way around.

There was no longer even the slightest doubt. He was going to be beheaded—*ZAP!* In a daze, he turned his head first to one side and then the other. Everywhere he looked people were following along behind him just like ants. Then he just so happened to catch sight of Amah Wu standing in the midst of a group over by the roadside. Because she had been working in town, he had not been able to pay his respects to her in a long, long time.

Ah Q was suddenly gripped by shame at his own lack of pluck—all this time and he still hadn't sung a single line of opera.[65] Thoughts began to swirl around like a cyclone in his brain. *The Young Widow Visits Her Husband's Grave* was not stirring

65. Defiant lines quoted from popular heroic operas are the stuff of melodramatic execution scenes.

enough. *"Would that I had not . . ."* from *Battle of the Dragon and Tiger Generals* did not have any real wallop either. Better stick to that old reliable: *"My mace of steel I grasp full tight / And with it I shall now thee smite!"* Having made his selection and suiting gesture to word, he started to raise his hand, but it wouldn't go up. Then he remembered—it was tied behind him. Couldn't sing that one either.

"Twenty years from now . . ." Ah Q shouted the first half of the sentence, a sentence he had never used before, one he had never been taught but which he seemed to have mastered on his own nonetheless.[66]

"Bravo! Bravo!" Shouts rose from the crowd like the howls of so many wolves.

The cart continued relentlessly forward. Amid all the cheering, Ah Q turned and looked at Amah Wu once again. It was apparent, however, that she had not even noticed him, for she was lost in contemplation of the novel-looking foreign rifles the soldiers were carrying. So he turned back and looked again at the people who had just cheered.

Once again thoughts began to swirl around like a cyclone in his brain. He was taken back to a time four years earlier when he had encountered a hungry wolf at the foot of a mountain. It had stalked him with persistent tenacity, neither closing in nor dropping back by so much as half a step, patiently awaiting its chance to tear into his flesh. Ah Q had been terrified and it was only because he happened to be carrying a small hatchet at the time that he had mustered the courage to make it back to Wei Village. He had never forgotten that wolf's eyes—ferocious and timid at the same time and glowing like two fiendish flames that might, at any moment, burn through his body from afar.[67]

But now he saw eyes that were even more terrible, eyes such as he had never seen before. Sharp and dull at the same time, these eyes had already devoured his words and now sought to tear into something beyond mere flesh and bone. Neither closing in nor

66. To show contempt for authority and indifference to death, condemned criminals would often shout just before execution, "Twenty years from now I'll come back as big and bad as ever." The idea, based on the Buddhist doctrine of rebirth, was that the criminal's spirit would enter a fetus lodged inside a pregnant mother's womb at the moment of his death.

67. Cf. the sixth entry in "Diary of a Madman."

And then they all merged into a single set of fangs that ripped and tore at Ah Q's soul.

"Help . . ."

dropping back by so much as half a step, they stalked him with persistent tenacity. And then they all merged into a single set of fangs that ripped and tore at Ah Q's soul.

"Help . . ."

But before Ah Q could get it out, everything went black before his eyes, there was a loud ringing in his ears, and he felt his entire being crumble like so much dust.

As for the impact of his death, the greatest was on Old Master *Selectman,* for he was thus unable to recover any of the stolen property. Hence his entire family took to wailing. Next came the Zhao family. Some Revolutionaries cut the *Budding Talent*'s queue off when he went into town to report the burglary. On top of that, they forced him to tip them twenty strings of cash for their services. Thus the entire Zhao family took to wailing, too.

As to public opinion, the inhabitants of Wei Village were unanimous. Everyone agreed that Ah Q had indeed been an evil man, the clear proof of which could be found in the fact that he had in truth been executed. If he hadn't been bad, then how could he have gone and gotten himself executed?

Public opinion in town was something less than favorable too. Most townsfolk were disappointed—a shooting had not proved nearly so much fun as a good old-fashioned beheading. Worse yet, in his role as condemned criminal Ah Q had given a miserable performance—paraded through the streets all that time and not a single line of opera! They had followed him in vain.

DECEMBER 1921

Dragonboat Festival

Fang Xuanchuo[1] had recently grown so fond of saying "There's not much difference" that the expression seemed to have established permanent residence on the tip of his tongue. It wasn't simply something he said, either. It was an entire way of thinking that had rooted itself firmly within his brain. In the beginning he used to just say, "It's all the same thing anyway," but then he had come to feel he wasn't *entirely* on safe ground with that one and had emended it to "There's not much difference," a phrase he had employed ever since.

Since his discovery of this all-too-ordinary linguistic gem, things that had in the past stirred his deepest emotions continued to occur, but he no longer felt them as keenly, for now he had his new way of thinking to comfort him. For instance, in the past he would seethe whenever he saw elders lording it over the young, but now his mind would take a different tack and he would think, "Later on, when these youngsters have children and grandchildren of their own, they'll probably put on airs too." Presto—he was no longer troubled by any sense of injustice! In the past, too, he would fume whenever he saw a soldier abusing a rickshaw puller; but now it didn't bother him in the least. "Put the puller in the soldier's place and he'd probably do the same thing." On such occasions, Fang would sometimes suspect that he was only deceiving himself in fashioning such excuse-studded routes of escape, that he no longer had the courage to stand up against the ills of society, and that he had come dangerously close to being one *who loses*

First published in the Shanghai periodical *The Short Story Magazine*, vol. 13, no. 9 (September 1922). The festival itself falls on the fifth day of the fifth lunar month (around June) and roughly corresponds to the summer solstice. The important customs associated with this celebration are throwing ricecakes into the river to feed the soul of the fourth-century B.C. patriot and poet Qu Yuan (the festival is also known as Poets' Day); competing in dragonboat races on the river; and (most importantly for the present story) repaying debts. The Mid-Autumn Festival (the fifteenth of the eighth lunar month) is the other traditional period during the year for wiping the financial slate clean.

1. Zhou Zuoren says that Fang reflects Lu Xun. Indeed, the surname Fang was once applied to Lu Xun by friends who compared him to a character of that name in the eighteenth-century novel *The Scholars (Rulin waishi)*.

sight of what is wrong and what is right.[2] Such suspicions made him feel that he had better change while the changing was good. And yet, in spite of everything, this new way of thinking became more deeply rooted in him with every passing day.

The first time he gave public expression to his *not-much-difference-ism* was in the course of a lecture he delivered at the College of the Highest Good.[3] In the midst of expounding on antiquity he announced, "People in modern times are not very different from the ancients." He had gone on to note that *Though in customs they may drift apart / All men share one nature at the start.*[4] Jumping off from there, he had managed to work his way around to the more contemporary problem of the hostility existing between students and officials. It was at this point that he first gave public utterance to his new *-ism:* "In society nowadays, it's quite fashionable to castigate officials, and students are particularly merciless in this regard. Yet officials are by no means some separate species especially ordained by Heaven. Officials are, after all, cut from the same cloth as ordinary people. What's more, there are quite a few officials walking around today who started out as modern students just like yourselves. And yet what difference is there between these new officials and the old-fashioned kind? *Exchange their places / And they'll wear the same faces.*[5] When a modern *student* becomes a modern *official,* you won't see any great difference between him and any other official: he'll think the same things, he'll say the same things, and he'll *do* the same things. He'll even carry himself in the same way. Let's turn it around and look at the various enterprises launched by students themselves. Isn't it true that many such projects have come to naught because even students haven't been able to steer entirely clear of corruption? *There's not much difference.* And yet it's precisely *because* there's not much difference that it behooves us to be concerned over the fate of China!"

There were twenty-odd students scattered through the lecture

---

2. A phrase from the Gongsun Chou chapter of the *Mencius:* "No more a part of humankind is he who loses sight of what is wrong and what is right."

3. A play on "Realm of the Highest Good" *(shou shan zhi qu),* a traditional epithet for Beijing. Lu Xun was interested by the possibly satirical implications of the phrase, and also used it at the beginning of "A Warning to the People."

4. A phrase from the Yang Huo chapter of *The Analects of Confucius.*

5. A phrase from part 2 of the Li Lou chapter of the *Mencius.*

hall. Fearing, perhaps, that what he said was true, some of them appeared depressed. Probably thinking that he had sullied the sacred name of youth, others seemed indignant. And there were even a few who snickered, no doubt convinced that he was only fashioning excuses for *himself:* after all, it was true that besides his teaching, Fang Xuanchuo was concurrently serving as an official.[6]

But if the truth be known, they were all wide of the mark. He was simply giving vent to a new resentment he had begun to feel of late, one reflecting his belief that people ought to stay in their proper places and mind their own business. Whether out of laziness or pure uselessness—he couldn't have told you which—Fang had always seen himself as a man above any sort of political action, a man who scrupulously kept to his own place and minded his own business. So long as his position as an official in the ministry was not in actual jeopardy, his department chief there could malign him as a "neurotic" to his heart's content and Fang would not let out a peep. What was more, the educational authorities could slide right on past the Dragonboat Festival without paying him a cent and—provided the ministry continued to issue his official salary—Fang would not utter so much as a whisper of complaint.

When the other professors banded together to demand their back pay, he criticized them behind their backs for lacking discretion and stirring up a needless fuss. It wasn't until he heard his fellow officials openly ridiculing professors that his sense of injustice was aroused, albeit ever so slightly. But then his brain went off on a different tack and it occurred to him that perhaps he felt that way only because he was strapped for cash at the moment and, what was more, was the only one among his colleagues who was concurrently employed as a professor. Thus, having satisfactorily explained his own discomfort to himself, he ceased to feel it.

Fang hadn't joined the group formed by his fellow professors when they voted to strike. Nonetheless, when they stopped meeting their classes, so did he. He felt no *real* hostility toward the government however, until it announced its "no-class no-pay" policy, for that came very close to treating the faculty like so many monkeys before whom one dangled bananas. And it wasn't until a

6. When this story was written in 1922 Lu Xun, like his protagonist, was concurrently serving as an official in the Ministry of Education and a professor at Beijing University.

noted educationalist[7] opined that "it's tacky for a professor to go around with a book in one hand and a begging-bowl in the other" that he began to openly express dissatisfaction to his wife.

The day he heard the "tacky" remark, he looked down the dinner table at her. "Hey! How is it that you've only prepared two dishes tonight?"

Since neither of them had received a modern education, his wife had no "school name" or elegant nickname, and thus he had no fashionable term of address to use with her. In accordance with old and established precedents, of course, he could simply have called her "Wife," but he didn't want to appear *too* far behind the times, and so he had invented the title "Hey!" His wife had not even so much as a *hey* to use on him, but according to the common usage of their household, whenever she spoke with her face set in his direction, he knew that whatever issued forth from that face was intended for him.

"The fifteen percent of last month's salary they gave you is all gone. I had to buy the rice yesterday on credit, and you've no idea what I had to go through to get it, either." She was standing next to the dinner table, face set in his direction.

"See! And then they have the gall to say that it's "tacky" of professors to demand their salary. You have to eat, and to eat you have to have food, and to *get* that food, you have to have money—those idiots don't even understand something as simple as that."

"Exactly! If you don't have money, how are you going to buy your rice, and if you don't have your rice, how are you going to—"

He tightened his cheeks as though genuinely irked that *there wasn't much difference* between her response and the opinion he himself had just expressed, making her appear to be nothing more than his own echo. He turned his face aside. According to the common usage of their household, this constituted an official announcement that their discussion was concluded.

One cold and windy day the faculty braved the rain to mount a demonstration that was to underscore their demands. On the surface of it, the only tangible result of this demonstration was that

---

7. A remark like this was in fact made by the then minister of education, Fan Yuanlian (1875–1927). During his career, Fan served three times as minister: June 1912–January 1913, succeeding Cai Yuanpei; June 1916–June 1917; and August 1920–May 1921. It was in March of 1921 that Beijing professors went on strike for back salary.

government troops beat the professors bloody on a soggy stretch of ground in front of the New China Gate.[8] And yet something did come of it after all, for the authorities actually did issue the professors a small part of the salary they had coming. And thus, without lifting a finger, Fang Xuanchuo was able to get his hands on some money and pay off a few debts. Even at that he still owed a considerable sum, for his salary as an official was in arrears as well.

At this point, even their eminences the *honest and incorruptible officials of the realm* gradually began to feel that it might be a good idea for them to press for *their* back pay too, a circumstance that made Fang much more sympathetic to the actions of his fellow faculty members. And so it was that even though he was not present at the meeting where the faculty resolved to continue the strike, he was only too glad to abide by their decision.

A few days prior to that, however, the Student Alliance had formally presented a petition to the government that suggested the following: "Let there be no back salary issued to the professors until they actually begin attending their classes." Although the petition had no effect, the wording reminded Fang of the government's own position during the previous strike: "Only professors who actually go to class will be paid." *There's not much difference* —the phrase appeared before his mind's eye again. What was more, it lingered there with no signs of fading. And so it was that once again, in the course of a lecture, Fang gave public expression to his *not-much-difference-ism.*

With this new evidence in hand, we can readily appreciate that while it might be fair to charge that Fang's *-ism* was tainted by personal interest, it would be entirely unjust to simply dismiss it as a defensive ploy he had adopted in order to rationalize the fact that he was an official as well as a professor. No, the function his *-ism* served lay in a slightly different direction. For whenever he launched into his *not-much-difference-ism,* he would also haul in other themes of a far grander nature—"the fate of China" and the like. If he wasn't careful (and he usually wasn't) he would begin to see himself as a righteous warrior genuinely concerned about the fate

8. These details reflect an actual incident that occurred in front of the presidential palace (Xu Shichang was president) on June 3, 1921. The following day President Xu issued a statement to the effect that the faculty had brought the beating on themselves by demonstrating there in the first place. In the end, the government came up with some money and classes were resumed.

of the entire nation—such is the extent to which people sometimes suffer from a lack of self-knowledge.

Not long after that, another *not-much-different* thing happened. At first it had only been those pestiferous professors whose pleas the government had rigorously ignored. Now it began to favor petty officials with the same treatment. They weren't paid, and they weren't paid, until finally they were so hard pressed that not a few of these well-behaved servants of the state, the very ones who had looked down their noses at the professors, were themselves transformed into doughty generals at a mass meeting that was called to press their own demands for pay. Now the local daily began to print articles in which the *officials* came in for their share of scorn and mockery too. Fang Xuanchuo was not in the least surprised, nor did he particularly mind, for from the vantage point of his *not-much-difference-ism* he knew that the newsmen only did this because *they* were still drawing their salaries. On the off chance that the government should withdraw its publications subsidy, or the paper's own fat-cat backers should withdraw theirs, then the newsmen would probably take to holding mass meetings themselves.

Since he had already expressed his sympathy for the faculty's demands, it was only natural that he should approve those of his fellow officials. When they actually went to present those demands, however, he remained safely ensconced in his office at the *yamen.* And if people thought he did so because he considered himself too "good" to take part in such activities, well, that would just have to be their mistake. His own explanation was that although others had occasionally come to dun him for money that he had borrowed, he had never—not since the day he was born—gone to dun anyone else for money that *he* had loaned out. Thus it was something that he was, as he said, "not very good at."

Furthermore, he had a positive dread of having to go see people in positions of financial power. Granted, when such men fell from their lofty perches and were piously padding about in Buddhist serenity with copies of the Mahayana *Awakening of Faith* in their hands, they would of course be *full gentle, meek, and mild;* but so long as they were secure in their positions, they wore expressions that would have done credit to the King of Hell and treated people like dirt. You could tell what they were thinking: "We've got the power of life and death over two-for-a-nickel paupers like you!"

And that's why he neither wanted nor dared to go see them. There were times when even Fang himself felt that he had adopted this attitude because he *did* in fact think himself too good to have to do certain things. What was more, he often suspected that he might have adopted it because he was too useless to do anything else.

By borrowing a bit here and a bit there, people managed to squeak by from one holiday to the next. But compared to the way he'd had it before, Fang was really hard up. And for that reason, the one servant that he employed, along with the shopkeepers, and even *Mrs.* Fang for that matter, gradually turned more and more disrespectful. All you had to do was look at Mrs. Fang's failure of late to cheerily echo his every opinion, her increasing tendency to come out with her own ideas, her general brusqueness with him, and you could pretty well tell the lay of the land. When he came back from the office just before noon the day before the Dragonboat Festival, she shoved a stack of bills under his nose the moment he came in the door, something she had never done before.

"Altogether, it's going to take a hundred and eighty dollars just to cover expenses. Did you get paid?"

"Hmph! I'm going to quit that job tomorrow. The government *has* issued the checks, but the representatives who were elected at the mass meeting won't give them out. At first they said they wouldn't give checks to anyone who hadn't physically accompanied them when they went to present the demands. Then they decided they could give out checks to people in that category *if* they appeared before them, hat in hand, and begged for their money! With nothing more than those measly checks in their hands, they've already started wearing expressions that would do credit to the King of Hell! Well, I don't *want* their money! I don't even want to be an *official* anymore! Trying to humiliate a man like that—"

Startled by this rare display of righteous indignation, Mrs. Fang quieted down for a moment. Then she looked him square in the eye and said, "I think you might as well go and ask for your check then. What difference does it make anyway?"

"I will *not* go to them on bended knee! This is an official salary we're talking about, not some sort of reward. By rights it should be *sent* to me from the Accounting Office."

"And what if they *don't* send it to you? I didn't bring it up last night, but the children say the school's been after them more than once for their tuition, told them that if we put off paying any longer—"

"Totally ridiculous! The father of the family puts in a good day's work at a government office and teaches classes to boot, but nobody gives *him* any money. Yet when his children go and crack a book or two, *he's* expected to cough up cash on demand!"

She could see that he was in no mood to be constrained by mere logic. From the looks of things, he was about to cast her in the role of school principal and then take all his frustrations out on her. It wasn't worth it. She decided to say nothing more.

Husband and wife ate their lunch in silence. After pondering things for a while, Fang went off in a huff.

In recent years, his pattern was never to come home so much as a minute before midnight on the day before a festival or New Year's Day. Fishing cash up from the depths of his pockets, he would walk in and address his wife. "Hey, I've got it!" Then looking rather pleased with himself, he would hand over a stack of crisp new China-Communications bills.[9] But today, the day before the Dragonboat Festival, he broke this pattern and quite unexpectedly came home before seven. Thinking that he actually *had* quit his job, Mrs. Fang was quite alarmed. She peeked at him out of the corner of her eye—nothing in his expression indicated that he'd had any particularly bad luck.

"Back so early? What's up?" she asked, looking him straight in the eye.

"They didn't have time to get our pay out and so I didn't get any. Since the banks are already closed, we'll have to wait until the eighth."

"Will you have to go in person?" she asked apprehensively.

"No, they've dropped all that. I hear it's going to be sent out by the Accounting Office as usual, but the banks are going to take a three-day holiday, so I'll have to wait until the morning of the eighth." He sat down, stared at the floor, sipped some tea, and slowly continued. "Fortunately, there's no problem at the *yamen* either.[10] Pretty definite that we'll get *some* money by the eighth

9. Money issued jointly by the Bank of China and the Bank of Communications, both government banks.

10. A *yamen* is a local government office.

. . . Going around trying to borrow from relatives and friends that you don't have too much to do with in the first place is unpleasant. Anyway, after lunch I braced myself and went over to see Jin Yongsheng. After we'd been talking for a while, he praised me for not physically accompanying the others to present the demands and also for not being willing to go pick up the check in person. Said I was very high-minded and had behaved as a man should. But when he discovered that I wanted to borrow fifty dollars to tide me over, every last bit of skin on that face of his that was capable of wrinkling, did. You'd have thought I'd just shoved a handful of salt in his mouth. He began going on about how he hadn't been able to collect his rents and was losing money at his business. And then he told me there was really nothing *all* that bad about going to the representatives and asking them for my check anyway! Got rid of me so fast I could hardly believe it!"

"On a holiday like this with everyone trying to straighten out his own finances, you can't expect people to want to lend anything out," said Mrs. Fang flatly, refusing to share in her husband's indignation. Fang Xuanchuo realized that there really *was* nothing strange in Jin Yongsheng's behavior at that, and lowered his head. After all he had never been close to the man to begin with.

Fang rolled his mind back to what had happened last New Year's. Someone from his hometown had come to borrow ten dollars. At the time Fang had a *yamen* salary-voucher right in his pocket, but because he was afraid the man might not repay him, he put on the most helpless expression he could muster and said that he hadn't been able to get any of his own salary, either at the *yamen* or at school. Saying that he had "the heart but not the cash," he had sent the man away empty-handed. Although Fang could not have seen, of course, the kind of expression he himself must have worn at the time, as he thought about it now, he felt very sheepish. His lips moved ever so slightly and he shook his head.

Before long, however, an inspiration bathed his brain with its light: he ordered their servant to go out and buy a bottle of *White Lotus* on credit. He knew the wineseller would be hoping that his customers would clear up their tabs the next day and would, in all likelihood, not dare to refuse him, for if he did he ran the risk of bringing down such bad luck on himself that none of his customers would pay back so much as half a cent tomorrow, and it would serve him right too!

Fang succeeded in obtaining his *White Lotus*. After two cups his pale face turned red, and by the time he'd finished his supper, he was feeling thoroughly mellow. He lit a king-sized *Hatamen,* picked up a copy of *Experiments*[11] from the table, went over to the bed, lay down, made himself comfortable, and prepared to read it.

Mrs. Fang followed behind him, stood directly in front of the bed, looked him straight in the eye, and demanded: "How am I supposed to handle the shopkeepers when they come around tomorrow?"

"Shopkeepers? Tell them to come back sometime during the afternoon on the eighth."

"They're not going to believe anything like that. There's no way they'll go along with it."

"And why *shouldn't* they go along with it? They can go check for themselves. No one in the *yamen* got any money. Everybody's got to wait until the eighth!" Ensconced inside the mosquito net, Fang lounged on the bed. He extended his index finger, which then described a small semicircle through the air. His wife's eyes followed it until it came down and opened the cover of *Experiments.* Seeing that he was in such an unreasonable mood, she had no choice but to revert to silence.

At long last she thought of another tack. "The way I see it, we simply can't go on like this. One way or another we've *got* to think of some way to get ourselves clear. How about doing a little work of . . . of some *other* kind?"

"*What* other kind? *'For martial things he hath no knack / Civilian skills doth he also lack.'* What else *can* I do?"

"Didn't you send some things off to a Shanghai publisher?"

"Shanghai publisher? Hah! They pay by the word and they don't count the blank spaces either. Go over to the desk and look at the colloquial language poetry I've done. See how many blank spaces there are on every page—probably wouldn't bring in more than three dollars for the lot. Besides, I haven't heard anything from Shanghai for half a year now. *Distant water won't put out a*

11. Written by Hu Shi (1891–1962), this influential work was a pioneering attempt, or experiment, at writing Chinese poetry in the colloquial language.

nearby fire. Who's got time to sit around and wait for them anyway?"

"Well then, maybe you could try one of the local newspapers—"

"Local *newspapers?* Even the one with the largest circulation—and it would be taking advantage of my relationship with a former student who happens to be an editor there, at that—I'd still only get a few dollars.[12] Even if I worked from morning till night, how could I possibly support us on what I'd make writing? Beside I don't have all that much to write about anyway."

"Then what do you propose to do after Dragonboat?"

"After Dragonboat? Well, I'll go right along being an official, same as always. Look, when the shopkeepers dun you for money tomorrow, all you have to do is tell them to come back the afternoon of the eighth."

He went back to his *Experiments* but Mrs. Fang, fearful lest she lose her opportunity to speak, stammered, "I think . . . I think that after the holiday, we'd really be better off to . . . we'd really do just as well to . . . to buy a lottery ticket."

"What absolute *nonsense!* To think that you'd come up with such an *uneducated* . . ."

Suddenly Fang thought back to something that had happened that afternoon right after Jin Yongsheng had given him the brush-off. Feeling frustrated and disappointed, he had been walking past the *Sweetfield Emporium* when an advertising board set up at the entrance happened to catch his eye. The characters were large and bold: FIRST PRIZE TEN THOUSAND DOLLARS. His heart had skipped a beat and his pace had slackened as well. But then, remembering that he had only sixty cents left in his wallet, he had with a great show of courage and determination marched right on past.

Noting the change in his expression, Mrs. Fang attributed it to his being furious with her for being so "uneducated," and immediately walked away without finishing her sentence. Nor did her husband finish his. Rather, he stretched out on the bed and began to recite aloud from *Experiments.*

JUNE 1922

---

12. Zhou Zuoren has said that this detail reflects the real-life relationship between Lu Xun and his former student Sun Fuyuan, who was an editor at the Beijing *Morning Post;* see the first note to "Ah Q—The Real Story."

The White Light

Though he had left home quite early in the morning, it was already afternoon when Chen Shicheng came back from looking through the list of successful candidates in the district examination.

As soon as he'd set eyes on the list that morning, he had started looking for his own name. There were a good many Chens at that, and each one leaped into his eyes as though intent upon getting there before the others. Not one, however, was followed by "Shicheng." Again, and with great care, he searched through circle after circle of names on the twelve pages of the list, but even when the last of the candidates who had come to see the list finally drifted away, he still had not found it. There he stood before the short stretch of wall on which the pages were posted—alone.

Though the breeze that brushed through his short and greying hair was chilly, the early winter sun felt warm on his body. Yet its rays seemed to make him a bit faint too, for his face grew paler by the minute and a strange light began to glimmer in his red and swollen eyes. Chen had long since ceased to actually *see* the list posted up there on the wall. Now he was merely conscious of so many black circles floating and drifting about before him.[1]

Having obtained his Budding-Talent, *he went on to take the provincial examination, and then just kept right on climbing up. Not only did the gentryfolk use every last trick in the book to marry off their daughters to him, but even ordinary people treated him with all the respect and deference reserved for the gods, while bitterly regretting their former disdain, their stupidity.*

He rounded up all the people who rented rooms in his dilapidated family compound—people with surnames different from his own—and drove them out. Actually there was no need to speak of "driving," for they all had the good sense to move out of their own accord. He remodeled the entire compound, and in order to advertise his new status, set up the traditional flagpole before the main gate and put up the customary plaque as well. If he decided to pur-

---

First published in the Shanghai periodical *Eastern Miscellany,* vol. 19, no. 13 (July 1922).

1. The names of successful candidates were written on each page of the announcement so as to form a circle.

sue the disinterested career of an honest and upright scholar-official, he might take a post in the capital. Or perhaps he would seek out some lucrative provincial position and . . .

Like a candy pagoda that has gotten wet, the future—ordinarily so neatly arranged in his mind—suddenly collapsed yet another time, leaving behind nothing but a pile of sugary debris. Feeling as though his very being had similarly disintegrated, Chen wheeled his body around and no longer conscious of his own physical acts, headed off in a daze toward the road leading back to the family compound.

No sooner had he reached the gate of his home than seven children cranked up their voices and began reciting their texts. The sound startled him. It was as though a great jade chime had been struck right next to his ear. Chen looked up and saw the backs of seven black heads swaying back and forth before his eyes. Queues dangling, the heads filled the room. Sandwiched in among them, large black circles joined the dance. He sat down. The expressions on the youngsters' faces as they came up to turn in their homework revealed their contempt.

After a moment's hesitation, Chen told them in despondent tones, "You might as well go home." Helter-skelter they gathered things into their schoolbags, tucked them under their arms, and disappeared like a puff of smoke.

A chaos of black heads and black circles continued to dance before his eyes. In utter disarray at first, they began to cluster together in an orderly pattern. Then little by little they diminished in number and began to fade away.

"All washed up again!"

Chen leaped from his chair with a start. Quite clearly the words had come from nearby, but when he turned around he found no one there. Once again it was as though someone had struck a jade chime next to his ear. But now the words were coming out of his own mouth. "All washed up again!"

Abruptly, he raised one hand, crooked his fingers, and began counting. "Eleven . . . thirteen . . . throw in this year and it's sixteen times. And to think that in all those times not a single examiner knew a good essay when he saw one. They have eyes, but . . . A pitiful state of affairs when you come to think of it!" Chen could not keep himself from giggling at the ineptitude of the examiners, but his amusement rapidly turned to indignation.

He quickly yanked some copies of examination essays and examination poems out from under his book-satchel and headed outside. No sooner had he set foot in the doorway to the courtyard than he was immobilized by several pairs of flashing eyes—even the chickens were laughing at him! Try as he might, Chen could not calm his pounding heart and was reduced to shrinking back into the room.

He sat down again. The gleam in his eyes was extraordinarily bright as he stared at the blurred and indistinct objects spread out before him—it was his own future that lay there like a collapsed sugar pagoda, a future that had expanded and grown until at last it had cut off every other road he might have taken.

The smoke from the stoves of the other families who lived in the Chen compound had dissipated into the evening air. Bowls and chopsticks had long since been washed and put away. Chen Shicheng, however, had still not started to prepare his own supper. These non-Chen people who rented rooms in his family homestead had long been familiar with their landlord's habits: whenever an examination year rolled around and that strange glimmer appeared in his eyes after the list was posted, they knew their best course was to close their doors early and mind their own business. The sounds of their voices gradually died away. One after another their lamps were extinguished. Now the only light that was left came from the moon, which was slowly rising into the chilly night. The sky turned a dark blue, making it look like a large expanse of open water. Here and there clouds drifted by as if some unseen hand were tracing a chalk wash through a sea of ink.

And then the moon began to focus its icy beams on Chen. It hung there like a freshly polished steel mirror. And then, mysteriously, this mirror-moon began to shine right *through* him, imprinting its shadow on his body as it penetrated.

Chen began to pace back and forth in the courtyard. His eyes were clear and serene, his entire being pervaded with calm. With no warning, however, his serenity was suddenly shattered by a low, urgent voice right next to his ear: *"Left turn, right turn . . ."* It all came back to him! In the past, back in the days when the compound was not the threadbare affair that it was today and summer was at its peak, he and his grandmother had been used to coming nightly to this same courtyard to enjoy the cool air. No more than a lad of ten at the time, he would lie on a bamboo couch while Grandmother sat nearby and spun out wonder-filled tales. She told him she had once heard *her* grandmother tell how wealthy their ancestors had been. Why this very compound had once been the heart of the Chen holdings! What was more, those same ancestors had buried an enormous quantity of silver here, a fortune that some lucky descendant of the clan was eventually bound to find. Although it had not yet been unearthed, its location was said to be contained in a riddle:

Right turn, left turn,
Forward and back,
Gold and silver,
Sack after sack.

Even in ordinary times, Chen would often try to unlock the meaning of these words. But unfortunately he would no sooner have them decoded than he would immediately perceive a flaw in his reasoning. There had been one time, however, when he was sure—beyond the shadow of any reasonable doubt—that he had it: the treasure was buried under the rooms that were rented out to the Tang family. But before he was able to work up the nerve to go over there and actually start digging, he perceived the flaw in that solution too. The scars left around his own room by previous excavations offered mute testimony to the various states of shock that had followed in the wake of past examination failures. The mere sight of them was always enough to embarrass him.

But tonight was different. The steely light of the moon enveloped Chen Shicheng and gently counseled him. He hesitated a moment at first but then, faced with the undeniable evidence of the moon, and what was more, given its eerie urging, he could not help but turn his gaze once again toward his room. Yes! Rocking back and forth like a round white fan, a light had begun to glow inside!

"So it *is* here after all!" With leonine strides, Chen entered his room. But once inside, he no longer saw any traces of the light—nothing but a desolate old room hiding a few rickety bookcases in its shadows. Dejected, he stood there and slowly focused his eyes: quite distinctly, and even larger than before, the white light appeared again! More intense than the fires of hell, yet lighter than a morning mist, there it was right under the desk by the east wall!

Like a lion, he sprang to the door and felt around behind it for the hoe. His hand bumped against something in the shadows and without really knowing why, he was a bit frightened. Hastily, he lit a lamp—nothing but the hoe, leaning against the wall in its accustomed place.

Chen moved the desk aside, and without stopping to take a break, one after the other he pried four large flagstones up out of the ground. He crouched down for a closer look—the soil was the same brownish yellow he had encountered on previous digs. Rolling up his sleeves, he scraped it away, revealing the darker earth that lay beneath. With extreme care and proceeding as silently as possible, he took up the hoe and dug down into the darkness, stroke after stroke. Despite all his precautions, however, the deep silent night refused to be his conspirator and, with complete indifference to his feelings, broadcast the heavy metallic sound of his hoe as it struck the earth.

The hole was already over two feet deep, but there was still no sign of anything like the mouth of a crock that might contain silver. Just as his patience was wearing thin, the blade of the hoe struck something hard that sent shock waves coursing through the handle and stunned his wrists. He quickly threw down the handle and felt around in the earth. His hoe had struck a large square tile. With single-minded concentration Chen dug the earth away from the tile and flipped it over. Underneath, he found nothing but more of the same dark earth. He loosened up quite a bit of it with his bare hands, but it seemed to go on forever. And then, all of a sudden, he came upon still another hard object. It was small and round, probably an old corroded coin. Other than that—nothing but crumbled pottery shards.

He felt drained. Nonetheless, bathed in sweat, he gave himself completely over to a frantic clawing of the earth. Already dangling by a thread, his heart now jumped as his hands encountered yet another strange object. It seemed to be shaped like a horseshoe and crumbled a bit when touched. With single-minded concentration, Chen dug away the earth around it. Gingerly he picked it up and brought it near to the lamp for closer inspection. It was spotted and discolored, something like a rotting bone. Here and there teeth could be distinguished. Just as Chen began to realize that this was in fact a human jawbone, it began to tremble and to wriggle in his hands. Worse yet, it broke into a hideous grin: *"All washed up again!"*

As a chill of terror coursed through his body, Chen let go of the bone. It floated gently back into its hole. Making a hasty escape back into the courtyard, Chen stole a sidelong glance in the direction of his room. But the brilliance of the lamplight and the jeering smile of the jawbone so frightened him that he dared not look in that direction for very long.

Taking shelter in the shadows under the eaves some distance away, he felt somewhat safer. In the midst of this calm, however, he suddenly heard the voice again. It was next to his ear and the words were whispered. The tone was conspiratorial: *"It is not here . . . go to the mountains . . ."*

Chen Shihcheng seemed to remember having overheard someone say something similar on the street that day. Even before he had heard the whispered voice out, the truth suddenly dawned on him. Immediately, he raised his face toward the sky. Off in the distance the moon had already disappeared behind Highpeak West. Standing black and erect against the sky, Highpeak West looked like one of those wooden tablets high officials carried to court when summoned by the emperor. From behind it, a shimmering white light flooded out in all directions. Though miles and miles away, the mountain seemed to stand right before his eyes.

What was more, the light seemed to be just in front of him too. "Why, of course! I must go to the mountains," he thought decisively as he rushed outside. A series of doors and gates, opening one after the other, was heard throughout the Chen family compound. And then all was silence. Forming large and constantly shifting patterns of light and shadow, the lamp continued to illumine the empty room and the hole. Finally, after a series of sputters, the patterns grew ever smaller and disappeared altogether as the remaining oil was consumed.

"Open the gate!" An anguished voice, compounded of hope and fear, called out just inside the West Gate of the town wall. Its timorous tones floated like gossamer in the dawn air.

At noon the following day, someone spotted a corpse in the Wanliu Lake, five miles outside the town's West Gate, and immediately spread the word. The news eventually reached the ears of the local sheriff, who in turn had a peasant go fish it out of the water. The body proved to be that of a male somewhat over fifty: "pale complexion, middle stature, beardless," and without a stitch of clothing. There were those who said it was Chen Shicheng, but none of his neighbors was willing to take the time to go and make a positive identification. Nor did any relatives come forward to claim the corpse either.

After the district coroner's examination, the sheriff had the corpse hauled off and buried, and that was that. As to the cause of death, that of course posed no problem, for stripping a corpse was a common occurrence to begin with and certainly insufficient grounds for suspecting foul play. What was more, the coroner proved that the male in question had been alive when he fell into the lake. There was riverbottom mud embedded under every fingernail, clear evidence that he had fought for his life after falling in.[2]

JUNE 1922

2. Chen Shicheng was modeled on one of Lu Xun's granduncles, Zhou Zijing. Like the protagonist of "The White Light," Zijing repeatedly failed the civil service examinations. At last the examiners told him that his compositions were so disjointed they never wanted to see him again.

A lonely old widower, Zijing seems to have done very little around the Zhou household except for tutoring some of the boys in the classics. For a brief period, Lu Xun studied composition and the *Mencius* with him.

There was, in fact, a rumor in the Zhou family that a great treasure was buried somewhere on their property. The key to its location was contained in a riddle: *A single pull away from the well / And one straight line from the eaves will tell.* One day after Zijing's latest failure at the examinations, a tipsy old servant bungled into the room where he was holding class and started going on about a white light that had appeared close to Zijing's bed. Zijing immediately dismissed his students, called in stonemasons, and undertook an excavation. He found no treasure, but severely wrenched his back in the process.

After that, he deteriorated mentally. Then one day he walked out to the middle of a bridge, cursing and striking himself as he went. He seated himself on some kerosene-soaked paper he had prepared beforehand, lit it, stabbed himself repeatedly with a pair of scissors, and then leaped into the river shouting, "The old ox is drowning!" He apparently saw himself as a faithful old ox who had labored many years on behalf of family and country without receiving the appreciation he felt was his due from either one. He was still alive when some neighbors fished him out, but he died a day or so later. Lu Xun also drew on the figure of Zijing in creating Ah Q.

Some Rabbits and a Cat

During the summer Third Missus, who lives in the rear courtyard, bought her children a pair of white bunnies.[1] You could tell they hadn't been separated from their mother very long, for though belonging to a different species, even a human being like myself could discern that they were still naive and trusting. And yet, when they erected their long pink ears and twitched their nostrils, their eyes could take on an apprehensive and suspicious look too. After all, this new environment was probably somewhat strange to them, and they didn't feel as secure as they had felt back home.

If you waited for a temple fair and went out and bargained for a pair of small animals like that, at most each would have cost you no more than, say, two strings of cash. Third Missus, however, had sent a servant out to buy them at a regular store where they had cost her one dollar each.

The children, of course, were delighted and chattered excitedly as they gathered round in a circle to get a look at the tiny creatures. The adults came out and gathered around to watch too. Even the little dog called "S" came running up, barged in, took a few sniffs, started to sneeze, and then backed off again. Third Missus slapped him on the head and scolded, "Now you listen to me S, you are *not* going to be allowed to bite those bunnies!" S actually did walk away and never bothered the rabbits again.

Third Missus kept them mostly penned up in the little yard out behind the back window. From what I heard, this was because they had shown a disposition to tear at the wallpaper and gnaw on furniture legs when she kept them indoors. There was a wild mulberry in the yard and when the berries fell, the bunnies would absolutely gorge themselves, refusing even to look at the spinach that had been bought for them. When crows and magpies tried to come down for a share of the berries, the bunnies arched their backs, extended their powerful hind legs, and *whoosh!* shot

---

First published in the Literary Supplement section of the Beijing *Morning Post,* October 10, 1922.

1. Third Missus would be the spouse of the third eldest male living in the family compound. This probably reflects the wife of Zhou Jianren, youngest of the three Zhou brothers—Shuren (Lu Xun), Zuoren, and Jianren.

straight up in the air like twin spirals of dry snow whirling up into a winter sky. The crows and magpies were immediately scared off, and after a few more doses of the same medicine, didn't even dare come close.

Third Missus said she wasn't really all that worried about the crows and magpies in the first place, for the worst they could do was steal a bit of the bunnies' food. What we *really* had to guard against was that obnoxious big black cat who often perched atop the low courtyard wall, watching them with savage eyes. Fortunately, however, S and the cat were natural enemies, so perhaps nothing would go amiss after all. The children would often scoop the bunnies up from the ground and hold them. The bunnies, for their part, were quite friendly and willing to be held. Ears up and noses twitching, they would remain docile in encircling hands, but if those hands relaxed long enough to provide an escape route, they would immediately slip through and scamper away.

After things had gone on like this for several months, the pair, now full-grown, suddenly began digging a burrow one day. They accomplished this with amazing efficiency. Clawing their way in with their forepaws and kicking the dirt out with their hind ones, they'd succeeded in excavating a good-sized hole before the day was half over. We all wondered what was up, until it was noticed, on closer inspection, that one rabbit's belly was considerably larger than that of the other. The pair spent most of the next day busily carrying straw and leaves into the burrow.

Everyone was quite happy and said we'd soon have more baby bunnies to play with. At this juncture, Third Missus issued a stern injunction to the children against picking up the rabbits. My mother was very pleased at their fecundity and even said that after the new litter was weaned, she planned on asking for one or two to raise outside her own window.

From then on the pair kept to the confines of the burrow they'd fashioned for themselves, occasionally venturing forth to get a little something to eat. Then they disappeared entirely. We didn't know whether it was because they'd stored so much they didn't need to come out any more, or whether they'd simply stopped eating. After another ten days or so, Third Missus told me that they had reappeared. She assumed the litter had been born and had perished, for although there were many teats visible on the female, there was no indication that she ever went into the burrow to nurse her young. As Third Missus spoke, she seemed rather put out with them, though of course there was nothing she could do.

One balmy day when there was no breeze and not a single leaf was stirring on any of the trees, all of a sudden I heard some people laughing over next to Third Missus' place. When I got to where the sound was coming from, I found several people leaning out her back window and watching something outside—a little bunny bounding about in the yard, a bunny that was much smaller than its parents had been when Third Missus first bought them. And yet, firing its hind legs out behind it, it was already able to bound high into the air. The children all competed to be the first to tell me they'd seen still another little one poking its head out the opening of the burrow for a look around, but that it had immediately shrunk back inside—presumably a younger sibling of the one that was in the yard.

The latter began gathering bits of grass, but its parents for some reason would not tolerate such behavior, for they kept pulling the grass out of its mouth, albeit without eating any of it themselves. The children laughed loudly at this, and so startled the young bunny that it scampered over to the hole and started burrowing in. The adult pair followed. One of them, placing forepaws on the youngster's spine, helped push it on through. Once they were all inside, one of the parents loosened some of the clay around the opening and used it to seal the entrance. After this, the little courtyard was more lively than ever, and people could often be seen at Third Missus' back window, peeking out at the rabbits.

And then, old and young alike, the rabbits all disappeared again. Third Missus began worrying that the big black cat had done them in. Since we were having a cloudy spell at the time, I maintained that it had nothing to do with the cat, but was simply a function of the chilly weather. I was convinced that they were all holed up in there to keep warm. When the sun came out again, so would they.

But when the sun did come out again, the rabbits were nowhere to be seen. At this point everyone forgot about them. Third Missus, however, continued to think of them, for she was the one who had gone to the burrow every day to feed them their spinach. One day she went into the small yard outside her back window and discovered *another* hole at the base of the wall. When she inspected the entrance of the old burrow she detected faint pawprints, prints that looked far too large to have been made by either of the adult rabbits.

Her mind turned uneasily to the big black cat who so often sat atop the low wall. At this point she had no choice but to screw up her courage and initiate an excavation of her own. She got a hoe and dug straight down into the burrow. Although she had her doubts, she still hoped against hope that she would be surprised and find live rabbits down there. When she reached the bottom, however, all she found was some bunny fur matted into a pile of rotten straw—straw that had probably been spread there when the female was about to give birth to her litter. Apart from such faint reminders the burrow was desolate. There was not the slightest trace of that snow-white bunny who had frolicked in the courtyard not so long ago, or of the younger sibling who had once peeked outside but never ventured forth.

A combination of anger and disappointment, coupled with a feeling of emptiness, so worked upon Third Missus that she had no choice but to go on and excavate the *new* hole at the foot of the wall as well. She had no sooner started to dig than the two large white rabbits wriggled out of the hole. Third Missus, thinking they had simply moved house, was very happy. She continued digging and when she reached the bottom, came upon a fresh mattress of grass and fur. Sleeping on top of it, bodies all flesh-pink, were seven tiny bunnies. Taking a closer look, she discovered that their eyes were still closed.

Now it all began to fall into place. She realized that the first pair of bunnies had in fact met exactly the fate she had feared. As a precaution against future danger, she took all seven new bunnies and put them into a wooden box which she then moved into her own room. She even shoved the mother into the box and forced her to nurse her young.

From then on, Third Missus not only detested the black cat but was also more than a little put out with the parent rabbits. As she saw it, there must have been more bunnies in that first litter than just those who had been done in by the cat, for a rabbit litter would certainly have had more than two in it.

As Third Missus pieced it together, since the mother hadn't nursed them evenly, those bunnies in the first litter who had not been aggressive enough to get a teat probably had died long before the cat got the two we had all seen. She may well have had something there because out of the seven in this new litter, two were quite skinny and weak. For this reason, whenever she had time to spare, Third Missus would get the mother rabbit and put the seven bunnies to her teats, one after the other, not allowing any one to get more milk than another.

My mother told me that she had never heard of, much less seen, such a fussy way of raising rabbits in her entire life. She even thought that Third Missus ought to be included in *You Won't Find Another.*[2]

The family of white rabbits was thriving more than ever and everyone was happy again. And yet after that, somehow or other, I always felt lonely. I would sit by the light of my lamp in the middle of the night and muse over how those two tiny lives had long since been lost, lost at some unknown time without anyone—man or spirit—having been conscious of the loss.

In the book of life, those two bunnies had not left the slightest hint that they had ever existed. Even S had not signaled their passing with so much as a bark.

I remembered how I had once gotten up early in the morning when I was living at the S Club[3] and had seen a chaotic pile of pigeon feathers under a big locust tree, obviously the leftovers from some hawk's feast. The janitor swept it all up the same morning without leaving a trace. No one would ever have guessed that a life had been snuffed out right there under that very tree.

I recalled too how once when I passed Fourth Gate West, a little dog caught my eye. It had been run over by a horsecart and was breathing out its last. When I passed again later on that day, there was nothing—the carcass had been cleared away and the pedestrians jostling past each other as they hurried along their way would never have guessed that a life had recently been cut off right there by the gate.

I also remembered how once on a summer's night I heard the long drawn-out buzz of a fly outside my window, trapped in a spider's web and crying out as the spider tore into its flesh. Yet I

---

2. *You Won't Find Another (Wushuang pu),* by Jin Guliang of the Manchu dynasty, was a collection of forty paintings of famous and unusual people from the Han dynasty (206 B.C.–A.D. 220) down to the Song (960–1279).

3. A hostel for fellow provincials living in the capital. Lu Xun lived in the Shaoxing Club in Beijing during the early years of the republic. The *S* here (the roman letter appears in the Chinese text as well) stands for Shaoxing, Lu Xun's hometown.

wasn't really all that bothered by the sound myself, and other people hadn't even noticed it.

If one can call the Creator to accounts, then I think he ought to be faulted for being too prodigal in the creation of life and too prodigal in its destruction.

Yeow!—A pair of cats fighting again outside my window.

"Xun'er, is that you mistreating the cats again?"

"No, they're laying into each other. Why in the world would *I* hit them?"

My mother had long been put out with me for the way I mistreated cats. She probably asked because she suspected that I was avenging those two bunnies in some particularly cruel way. Besides, within the family, I had a reputation for being a mortal enemy of the feline world. I had been known to do them real violence in the past, and even under ordinary circumstances I would take a swipe at them whenever I had the chance—especially when they were mating. But the reason I struck them wasn't at all because they were mating, but rather because they made so much infernal noise about it that I couldn't sleep. Copulation is no justification for all that yelling and screaming.

As I saw it, since the black cat had killed the bunnies, any act on my part now would constitute *provoked* aggression. I felt that my mother was really far too kind and forgiving, and that's why I had answered her in such an ambiguous—almost contentious—fashion.

The Creator is really too reckless. I shall have to oppose him, although perhaps I shall really be helping him.

"That black cat is not going to strut and swagger on top of that wall for much longer," I promised myself decisively. Without premeditation on my part, my glance fell on a bottle of potassium cyanide that was stored inside the bookcase.

OCTOBER 1922

A Comedy of Ducks

Not long after the blind Russian poet Eroshenko brought his balalaika to Beijing, he complained to me, "It's quiet here, *too* quiet, might as well be living in the middle of a desert!"[1]

What he said was probably true, but I didn't feel that way myself. *Stay too long in a room filled with orchids and you no longer notice their fragrance.*[2] I must have lived in Beijing too long, for I no longer noticed its quiet. To me, it was a very lively place indeed. And yet what I called "lively" may have been precisely what he meant by "quiet."

However, I had a bone of my own to pick with this city: Beijing didn't have anything you could call a spring or an autumn. Longtime Beijingers countered that there had been a change in the climate, that in days gone by springs and autumns were not so mild and warm as they were now. Maybe. But as I saw it, there just *wasn't* any spring or autumn to begin with. The end of winter was tacked onto the beginning of summer, and as soon as summer was past, winter started right in all over again.

First published in the Shanghai periodical *The Ladies' Journal (Funü zazhi)*, vol. 8, no. 12 (December 1922).

1. Blind from the age of four as the result of measles, Vasily Eroshenko (1889–1952) compensated for his handicap by developing his linguistic abilities to their fullest potential: he became at once a singer, poet, linguist, and teller of children's tales (some of which Lu Xun translated into Chinese). Before coming to China, he had lived in India, Burma, and Japan. In 1929 he was deported from Japan on suspicion of anarchism and went to Shanghai, where he met Cai Yuanpei (1868–1940), then chancellor of Beijing University. Cai invited him to come to the capital in 1922 to teach Esperanto. Vasily was proficient in (and a strong advocate of) this one-world language. He also knew English and Japanese but unfortunately no Chinese. Cai, therefore, was faced with the problem of finding an appropriate place to put him up. He called on the Zhous: Zhou Shuren (Lu Xun), Zhou Zuoren (his younger brother), and Zhou Jianren (youngest of the three brothers). At the time, the brothers occupied a family compound in common. The wives of the two younger brothers were Japanese (a pair of sisters) and hence Japanese was spoken around the compound as much as Chinese, making this a convenient place for the Russian visitor to stay. In addition to the Esperanto course, Eroshenko also gave a series of lectures (in Esperanto, with simultaneous Chinese translation by Zhou Zuoren) on modern Russian literature. Eroshenko stayed in Beijing off and on until the spring of 1923. Zuoren has suggested that Beijing may have proved dull to the Russian poet because of the language barrier.

2. The *locus classicus* for the common saying quoted here is in Book Six of *The Family Sayings of Confucius (Kongzi jiayu)*.

One day, during one of those junctures between the end of winter and the beginning of summer, I had some free time in the evening and went to call on Eroshenko.

Ever since coming to Beijing, he had lived with Zhongmi's family.[3] At this hour everyone over there was fast asleep and the whole world seemed wrapped in silence. He was alone, reclining on his bed. Beneath the long golden hair falling across his forehead, the corners of his high-set eyebrows were ever so slightly drawn. He was recalling one of the places he had visited in his travels—Burma, a summer's night in Burma.

"On a night like this in Burma," he said, "there is music everywhere. Inside the houses, out in the grasses, and in the trees, the insects sing and chirp with every imaginable kind of sound. What's more, those various calls often blend together into something like a symphony—it's really quite marvelous. And from time to time, sandwiched in among all those sounds, there'll be the *hiss-hiss* of a snake harmonizing perfectly with all the insect calls . . ."

He went off into a deep reverie, as though trying to recapture that scene somewhere in the depths of his memory.

What was I to say? I certainly had never heard such wonderful harmonies in Beijing and no matter how patriotic I was, there was simply nothing I could say in her defense, for although Eroshenko saw nothing, his ears were anything but deaf.

"You don't even hear frogs in Beijing," he said with another disappointed sigh.

"Hold on there. I'll have you know we *do* hear frogs croaking!" That last sigh of his had emboldened me to dispute him. "In the summer, after a heavy rain, you'll hear plenty of frogs. They live in drainage sluices, and Beijing has drainage sluices everywhere you go."

"Oh . . ."

* * *

A few days later my words were confirmed: Eroshenko bought a dozen tadpoles to raise in the small pool in the courtyard outside his window. Zhongmi had originally dug it as a lotus pond,

3. Another name for Zhou Zuoren, second of the brothers.

although I never saw it produce so much as half a bloom. It was about two by three feet and proved an ideal place for raising tadpoles. They would swim through the water in large formations and Eroshenko would often stroll over to visit with them. One day the children told him, "Mr. Airy-send-go, your tadpoles are sprouting legs."

He smiled happily. "Ah ha!"

Raising a crop of musicians in the lotus pond was but one of his activities. A great advocate of self-sufficiency, he often said that women ought to raise domestic animals and that men should grow vegetables. And thus it was that whenever he talked to a close friend, he would try to talk him into planting a few cabbages in his yard. And he had already exhorted Zhongmi's wife to raise bees, chickens, pigs, cows, and even camels.

Sure enough, it wasn't long before several chicks could be seen scampering through the courtyard at Zhongmi's place, pecking about until they had utterly devoured the ground cover that had carpeted the yard. It's probable that all this came about as the result of Eroshenko's repeated exhortations.

Later on, a peasant who sold chicks began to drop by, and quite often too, for Zhongmi's wife could always be counted on to buy a few—chicks easily fall victim to gorging or the colic, and she soon found that keeping them alive through a normal lifespan was no mean task. One of the chicks she lost became the protagonist of the only short story Eroshenko wrote while he was in Beijing, "A Chick's Tragedy."[4] One morning the peasant showed up not with chicks, but ducklings. Zhongmi's wife wasn't interested. *Queep-queep*. Eroshenko ran out too. They put one of the tiny creatures in his hands. *Queep-queep*. The poet found them quite lovable and simply couldn't resist. He took four at eighty cash per duckling.

And to tell the truth, they really were lovable. Soft yellow down covered their bodies, and as soon as you put them down, they'd jostle themselves into a little flock and waddle away, chattering back and forth as they went. Everyone agreed they were quite nice

4. Eroshenko wrote this story in Japanese in June 1922. Lu Xun translated it into Chinese, and it was published in the October 1 issue of *The Ladies' Journal (Funü zazhi)*. The story concerns a chick who prefers to play with ducks, and finally drowns in a pool while trying to swim like them.

and decided we ought to buy some fish for them the very next day. Eroshenko immediately volunteered, "I ought to pay for the fish too."

But by then it was time for him to go teach his class and we all went our separate ways.[5] A bit later when Zhongmi's wife came out with some cold rice to tide them over until we could go get the fish, she heard a splashing sound in the distance. She ran over to see what it was and found the four ducklings bathing in the lotus pond. What was more, they were turning somersaults and eating something or other. By the time she got them out, they had turned the whole pond muddy. When the water finally cleared, all you could see was a few scraggly lotus roots and not a trace of the leg-sprouting tadpoles.

"Mr. Airy-send-go, they're all gone. The frog babies are all gone!" reported the youngest of the children excitedly when Eroshenko came back toward evening.

"What, the tadpoles?"

Zhongmi's wife also came out and told him how the ducklings had eaten the tadpoles.

"Oh, no!"

* * *

By the time the ducklings had lost their baby down, Eroshenko had begun to yearn desperately for his "Mother Russia" and hurried off in the direction of Chita.[6]

When the croaking of frogs was to be heard once again from all sides, the ducklings had already grown to maturity—two white ones and two spotted. Now they didn't *queep-queep* anymore, but rather *quack-quacked* quite lustily, and the lotus pond was no longer large enough to accommodate their paddling about. Fortunately, however, Zhomgmi had a low-lying courtyard that readily flooded whenever it rained, making it a place where they could swim about, poke their heads down into the water, and strike their wings against its surface to their hearts' content.

Now we are again at the juncture between the end of summer

---

5. This was his class on Russian literature. Using brailled lecture notes, he spoke in Esperanto.

6. In southeastern Siberia.

and the beginning of winter. We have had no news at all of Eroshenko and have no idea where he is.[7]

Although he is gone, four ducks are still quacking away for all they are worth in the midst of this "lonely desert."

OCTOBER 1922

7. Eroshenko had gone off to attend an Esperanto conference in Finland. He returned to China the month after Lu Xun's story was written and would remain until the following spring. Lu Xun did not know this at the time and therefore wrote this piece (with its title chosen to balance that of Eroshenko's story) as a farewell reminiscence to his Russian friend.

Village Opera

As I count back, I realize I've only seen Chinese opera twice in the past twenty years. And during the first decade of this period I didn't see any, having neither the inclination nor the opportunity.[1] The two times that I *did* go both fell during the second ten years. I didn't see anything in it on either occasion and simply walked out.

My initial exposure was during the first year of the Republic, when I first arrived in Beijing.[2] A friend said, "Beijing Opera is the best there is. Why not go and broaden your horizons a bit?"

"Seeing an opera *is* fun," I thought, "and seeing a Beijing one ought to be a real eye-opener." On the crest of this enthusiasm, off I went with him to some theatre or other. By the time we got there the opera was already under way. I heard the *clang-clang-clang* of the orchestra's cymbals long before we ever reached the entrance.

We squeezed our way through the door. Dazzling patches of red and green flashed back and forth on the stage. I looked around: clumps of heads everywhere. When I had collected myself a bit and had time for a more thorough survey, I made out that there actually *were* a few empty places in the middle of the row next to us. When I squeezed my way in and was about to sit down, however, someone started talking at me. Because my ears were already ringing with all that *clang-clang-clang,* I had to concentrate to make out what he was saying. "Taken!"

We retreated to the back of the house where an usher with a shiny queue led us off to one side of the theatre and pointed out two places that *weren't* taken. Our "places" appeared to be nothing more than vacant spots on a long bench. The single board that formed the top of that bench was scarcely wide enough to support

---

First published in the Shanghai periodical *The Short Story Magazine,* vol. 13, no. 12 (December 1922).

1. Since this story was written in 1922, the first decade would have been from 1902 to 1912. During most of that time (1902–1909) Lu Xun was a student in Japan, where he would in fact have had little opportunity to see Chinese opera.

2. This would have been 1912. In real life Lu Xun was invited by Cai Yuanpei (1868–1940) to Nanjing, to join the republic's newly established Ministry of Education in January of that year. Then when the provisional government moved to Beijing in April, Lu Xun followed. He was to remain in the capital until 1926.

three-quarters of my upper leg, while it towered above the floor by something more than *twice* the length of my lower leg! Now in the first place, I lacked the courage requisite for the ascent. On top of that, though, my brain began associating *bench* and *instrument of torture.* Gripped with terror, I fled the theatre.

After I had gone some distance, I suddenly became conscious of my friend's voice. "What in the world's gotten into you anyway?" I turned, looked, and realized I had dragged him out in my wake. In the most bewildered of tones, he asked, "Why did you just keep on walking like that? Didn't even answer when I called to you!"

"Sorry, but my ears were so deafened with all that *boom-boom* of the drums and *clang-clang* of the cymbals. I didn't even hear you!"

Whenever I thought back on it later, this experience struck me as bordering on the bizarre: that opera must have been singularly bad—the only other explanation would be that I had somehow become "unfitted" for existence in front of stages.[3]

I've forgotten what year it was when I went the second time, but at any rate it was the year when a benefit performance was staged for the relief of flood victims in Hubei and when Tan Xinpei was still alive.[4] You made your flood relief contribution by buying a two-dollar ticket which entitled you to see an opera performed at the *Foremost.* Many of the performers were stars and one of them was Tan Xinpei himself. I bought a ticket—mostly to get the person who was taking up the collection off my back—and thought that would be the end of it. But then a certain busybody got into the act and explained to me the absolute metaphysical necessity of my going to see Tan Xinpei. Well, the upshot of it all was that I forgot my *boom-boom clang-clang* disaster of a few years before and actually ended up going to the *Foremost.* To be perfectly honest, the fact that I had bought that precious ticket at a highly inflated price, and would feel uncomfortable if I didn't use it, had a lot to do with my going, too. I asked around and found out that Tan Xinpei wouldn't come on until fairly late in the evening. I knew that the *Foremost* was a modern theatre where you didn't

---

3. Darwin's theory of evolution, as popularized by T. H. Huxley's *Evolution and Ethics,* was well known in China at the time Lu Xun wrote, primarily through Yan Fu's translation, *Tianyan lun,* published earlier in 1898.

4. Tan Xinpei (1847–1917) was famous for his interpretation of "old man" *(laosheng)* operatic roles.

have to fight for seats, and so felt perfectly safe in putting off my departure for the theatre until nine o'clock. I never dreamed it would be just as packed as ever, and that it would be difficult to find even standing room. It was all I could do to squeeze my way into the crowd at the back. On stage in the distance I saw an old woman with two burning paper-twists thrust in her mouth and a devil-soldier standing by her side. After wracking my brains a bit, I concluded that she must be Mulian's mother, for a monk had just come on as well.[5]

But I still didn't know which star was singing the part. Standing to one side of me was one chubby representative of the gentry who had been squeezed down to half his original girth by the press of the crowd. I asked him. He glanced at me with utter disdain. "Gong Yunfu!"[6] Ashamed of my rustic lack of sophistication and embarrassed by my previously cavalier attitude toward the opera, I felt the blood rush to my cheeks. At the same time my brain issued a solemn injunction against asking any further questions.

I saw ingenues sing. I saw coquettes sing. I saw old men sing. I saw who-knows-what-they-were sing. I saw the entire troupe engage in gymnastic battles. I saw smaller groups of two locked in combat. I watched from nine until ten, ten until eleven, eleven until eleven thirty, eleven thirty until twelve—but still no Tan Xinpei. In my entire life, I'd never before shown such patience in waiting for anything. It was a patience all the more remarkable when you consider that I had to put up with that chubby representative of the gentry at my side panting for breath all the while. Up on the stage, reds and greens swayed and rocked while the *boom-boom* of the drums and the *clang-clang* of cymbals continued to assault my ears. On top of all that, it was already midnight. Everything conspired and pushed me to the verge of a sudden enlightenment: I was not "fitted" to exist in such an environment.

Mechanically I twisted my body around and threw all my strength into working my way back through the crowd. I could

---

5. *Mulian Saves His Mother (Mulian jiu mu)* is one of the most popular of all Chinese operas. It portrays the story of how the pious Mulian, a disciple of Buddha, goes to Hell to rescue his mother, who has been sent there for the sins of covetousness and greed. Such a plot, of course, cleverly reconciles Buddhist teachings with the traditional Chinese concern for filial piety.

6. A contemporary Beijing actor, famous for his "old woman" *(laodan)* operatic roles.

feel the space I had occupied filling in as fast as I vacated it, no doubt a function of the elasticity of my chubby gentry-friend's body, which immediately fattened out to fill whatever space was made available to it. And since my original place was now occupied, I had no choice but to press onward, shove after shove, until I finally made it out through the main entrance.

Up and down the street, there were hardly any pedestrians, though there were a few cars waiting for the audience to come out. A group of perhaps a dozen or so people clumped themselves together at the main entrance, their heads raised high as they read the program posted there. There was another group just standing around not looking at anything. "Probably waiting to gawk at the women who come out after the opera is over," I thought to myself. Getting back out into the crisp night air was nothing short of invigorating. I can't recall having ever before encountered such refreshing air in Beijing.

That was the night I bade adieu to Beijing Opera. Never again did I give it so much as a second thought. Afterward, even when by chance I would walk past an opera house, I always felt that we had absolutely nothing in common, for spiritually we were at opposite poles.

A few days back I came across a Japanese book on Chinese opera. Unfortunately I can recall neither title nor author. But I was struck by one chapter that said something to the effect that Chinese opera involves so much banging, shouting, and jumping about that it makes a spectator's head swim, and that it is therefore unsuitable for performance within the confines of a theatre, although it does have its own peculiar charm when viewed from a distance out-of-doors. I thought the author had hit upon the exact words to express my own feelings, for I really can remember once having seen a very, very good opera out-of-doors. That was an experience that perhaps made my two bouts with the opera in Beijing suffer by comparison. (Unfortunately I've completely forgotten the title of that Japanese book.)

That particular "once" when I did see a very good opera out-of-doors already belongs to the distant days of yore, for I couldn't have been more than ten or so at the time.

Back then it was the custom in Lu Town for married women—so long as they were not yet in charge of the household affairs of the family they'd married into—to go back and spend the summers with their parents.[7] Although my father's mother was still hale and hearty, Mom had already taken over a considerable share of the household management. Thus she couldn't afford a very long summer visit to her own home—a few days after Clear-and-Bright was all she could manage.[8]

Every year when she went back to Grandma's for her abbreviated visit, I was allowed to accompany her. Grandma Lu lived in a village called Flatbridge, an out-of-the-way little place on a riverbank close to the sea. Other than the family who operated the village's one store, the rest of the fewer than thirty families who lived there were all farmers or fishermen. That village was my paradise: not only was I treated as a privileged character, but—better yet—while I was there, I wasn't forced to read all that *Percolate, percolate doth the rill / Distant, distant lieth the hill* stuff.[9]

I had quite a few young friends to play with. Since I was a guest from far away, their parents let them cut down on work hours so that they could join me. In such a small place the guest of one family was, in effect, the guest of the entire village. Though the children were all just about my age, in the generational pecking order they ran all the way from uncle clear up to great-grandfather, for everyone in the village had my mother's maiden name Lu, and thus we were all related. But more than that, we were all friends, so that even if we did get into a squabble and someone took a poke at "great-grandfather," none of the villagers, young or old, would have thought of the term "generational insubordination," a term they wouldn't have recognized even if they had seen it, since ninety-nine out of a hundred of them didn't know how to read in the first place.

For the most part, we'd begin our days digging up worms for shrimping. Sticking them onto tiny hooks we made of copper wire, we'd get down on our bellies, lean over the edge of the riverbank, and try our luck. Shrimp are the dumb-dumbs of the water-

---

7. The maiden surname of Lu Xun's mother was Lu. That he chose it as part of his pen name is one mark of the intensity of his attachment to her.

8. Clear-and-Bright is a springtime festival. Traditionally it is a time for visiting and tidying up the family graves. Lu Xun's father was a rather withdrawn person, addicted to both opium and alcohol, a circumstance that no doubt added to the number of things for which his mother had to be responsible.

9. Quotation from the *Poetry Classic,* whose archaic language was a headache for young students, however attractive it may sound to English-speaking readers of translations by Waley, Pound, and others.

world: they'll grab a hook with their feelers, and feed it right into their own mouths without the slightest hesitation. And so before long we'd have filled a good-sized bowl which, as a rule, I'd get to take home with me. Next on the agenda would be grazing the draft animals. Now yellow oxen and water buffalo—perhaps because they've ascended so high up on the evolutionary scale—like to take advantage of strangers, and they actually had the gall to bully me. So I didn't dare get up too close, but would follow along behind at a respectful distance, stopping in my tracks whenever they did. At times like that, my young friends, making no allowance whatsoever for my ability to read *Percolate, percolate doth the rill,* would start laughing at me.

Of the various things I looked forward to doing while at Flatbridge, number one on the list was going to Zhao Village—it was a tad larger than Flatbridge and only about two miles away—to see the opera. Since Flatbridge was too small to afford its own opera, it contributed money to Zhao Village every year and the opera presented was considered the joint production of both villages. Back then it didn't occur to me to wonder why they put on an opera at that particular time every year. As I think back on it now, it was probably because the opera was, in effect, a spring invocation to the gods—a religious opera.

I remember one year when I was ten or eleven and the longed-for day of the opera finally arrived. Unfortunately and unexpectedly, when we tried to get a boat that morning we found that virtually all of the ones that were for rent had already left. The only ones left were either too large or too small. To be sure, Flatbridge did have a passenger boat that made a daily run to town on workdays, but it was a very large craft and it would have made no sense to hire it just for ourselves. There were a few other boats around, but they were so tiny that they didn't suit our purpose either. My maternal grandmother was thoroughly upset that no one in the household had had the foresight to reserve something suitable earlier, and prattled on about it at great length. Mother comforted her by saying that back in Lu Town we had much better operas than any you were likely to find in a small village anyway and, since we saw several Lu Town operas every year, that it would be no great tragedy if I didn't get to see this one. I, on the other hand, was on the verge of tears. Mother exhorted me every which way she could, not to make a scene for fear of making Granny angry.

Nor would she give me permission to go with someone else, because that might make Granny worry.

In sum, my day was absolutely ruined. By afternoon all my young friends were gone and the opera (I was sure of it) had already begun. In my mind's eye, I saw them all gathered round the stands that would have been set up close to the open-air stage. They were buying bowl after bowl of delicious beancurd soup. I could even hear the gongs and drums.

I didn't go shrimping that day. Didn't eat much either. After supper even Granny caught on to the mood I was in and said that I had every right to be unhappy. She said it was unconscionable of them not to have come by for me and that it was certainly no way to treat a guest.

After supper, the youngsters who had been to see the opera before gathered round and began to discuss it with great relish. Seeing that I was the only one who didn't say anything, they sighed and expressed their sympathy. And then as though a light had suddenly dawned on him, Shuangxi—one of the brightest of the group—suggested, "If it's a boat that's needed, how about Eighth Gramps's passenger boat? Isn't it back now?" And then the light dawned on the dozen or so other children too. They picked up the ball and said that as long as they were taking Eighth Gramps's big passenger boat, then we could *all* go! I was beside myself.

Granny, however, worried that since the village kids were all so young, they couldn't really be depended upon to take care of me properly. On top of that, Mother said it wouldn't be reasonable to ask any of the adults to give up a whole night's sleep to chaperone us, because they all had to be up and out in the fields at the crack of dawn. Again, it was Shuangxi who found a way through the impasse. In loud, authoritative tones he proclaimed, "I'll personally guarantee his safety. It's a big boat to begin with and besides, Brother Xun is not the kind of kid who runs all over the place. The rest of us are all at home on the water anyway."

Wasn't that the truth! Every one of them was a strong swimmer, and one or two were real aquatic champs. By now he had apparently won over Granny and Mother, for offering no rebuttal, they both smiled. We kids immediately burst out the door.

My heavy heart suddenly lightened. Now I was so full of myself that my body seemed to have ballooned out into something indescribably large. As soon as I stepped through the door, I caught sight of a white-canopied passenger boat moored just under the flat bridge for which the village was named. Everybody jumped aboard. Shuangxi took up the pole at the bow and Ah-fa manned the one at the stern. The younger children all kept me company on seats in the middle cabin while the older boys congregated at the stern. By the time Mother came down with a final injunction to be careful, we had already untied and pushed off.

The boat banged its bow into the side of the stone abutment, retreated a bit, moved forward again, and then emerged from under the bridge. At this point two oars were put into place. Each was manned by a pair of boys and each pair was relieved every third of a mile or so. Their talking, laughing, and shouting were accompanied by the rhythmic *slap-slap* of water against the bow. Keeping to the middle of the flowing river, the boat flew straight toward Zhao Village. Beanfields of emerald green flashed by on our right and left.

Blended in with the mists, the fresh fragrance of beans and the scent of floating river grasses swept gently across our faces. Moonlight shone softly through the haze. At a fair distance on either side, like dancing animals cast of iron, the rising-falling ridges of dull dark hills converged on a point far to our stern and galloped toward it. But it was still too slow for me. By the time the oars had changed hands four times, gradually and indistinctly something began to appear way off in the distance. Zhao Village? I seemed to hear singing and made out what could have been torches set out to light the stage, but then again they could have been fishing fires too.[10]

That new sound was probably a flute. Its subtle melody stilled my mind and made me lose all sense of self until I began to feel that, just like its notes, I would simply disperse through the night air, so thick with the fragrance of beans and floating river grasses.

The fires drew closer. Yes, they were fishing fires. Now I realized that what I had seen off in the distance just a few moments before was not Zhao Village, but rather a stand of pines off the bow. I had been on an outing there last year and remembered having seen a broken stone horse lying on the ground as well as a stone goat crouching in the grass. Once past the woods, the boat turned into a small inlet and Zhao Village was truly before us.

---

10. Fires set to attract fish at night.

First to catch the eye were the hazy, moonlit outlines of a temporary stage erected on the empty strand between the village and the river. We were still so far away that it was difficult to distinguish the boundary between stage and sky as you looked through the river mists. Given the way they blended one into the other, I suspected for a moment that one of those traditional paintings depicting the abode of the Daoist Immortals had suddenly come to life. Now the boat began to move faster. Dressed in flashing reds and greens, actors began coming into focus. The area where the river flowed past the stage was swathed in black—boat canopies of waterborne playgoers.

"No empty spaces close to the stage, we'll have to watch from a distance," said Ah-fa.

The boat slowed down and soon we were there. You could see that there really was no way of getting close in. We had no choice but to put down our poles and moor at a spot even farther from the stage than the god shed that stood facing it.[11] Actually it didn't matter that there was no empty space among the black-canopied private craft, for our white-canopied passenger boat had no yen to mix with such august company in the first place.

While the boat was being hastily moored, I looked at the stage and saw a man with a long spear holding off a throng of bare-chested men. He was done up in blackface and four flags protruded from his back.[12] Shuangxi said that it was Iron Head, an acrobat famous for his old *sheng* roles.[13] This man could turn eighty-four somersaults in a row! Shuangxi had counted them himself, earlier that very day.

Hearing this, we all crowded up to the bow to watch the fighting. Our famous acrobat didn't do a single somersault, but some of the bare-chested actors did. They even made their exits with a concluding flurry of head-over-heels leaps. Next a young *dan* came on, her voice squeaking like a rusty hinge. "Since there's not

11. A temporary mat shed erected as a sort of grandstand, from which the gods were supposed to enjoy the performance presented on their behalf and where sacrifices might be offered to them. According to Lu Xun's brother Zuoren, the gods were represented here by wooden name tablets, and these would include tablets for the gods of land, grain, fire, wealth, and disease.

12. According to the code of color symbolism in Chinese opera, black stands for loyalty. The flags represent the number of units under a military officer's command.

13. The names of the stock operatic roles are: *sheng* 'male', *dan* 'female', *jing* 'painted face role', and *chou* 'clown'. There are many subdivisions within each category.

much steam in the small crowd he's got tonight," explained Shuangxi, "the old *sheng* acrobat has run out of steam too. Who'd want to put himself out for an empty house anyway?" I thought he really had something there, for the area in front of the stage had thinned out considerably. After all, the farmers did have to get up and go out into the fields the next morning and couldn't very well afford to be night owls. The few people left scattered about on the open stretch of ground before the stage were mostly idlers from this and the neighboring villages. The rich families in the black-canopied boats were still there, of course, but they weren't that interested in the opera to begin with. They had poled in and moored close to the stage in large part to enjoy the cakes, cookies, fruit, and watermelon seeds they'd brought along. Shuangxi could, in good faith, describe it as an "empty house."

But to tell the truth, I wasn't at all interested in seeing the old *sheng* turn his somersaults in the first place. What I *really* wanted to see was the Snake Spirit who would come out all wrapped in white cloth, hands high over his head, holding something that looked like a club—the snake's head. My next favorite was the acrobatic tiger who would come out all done up in yellow. But after waiting and waiting, I found neither of them came on. Although the young *dan* had gone off, she was followed straightaway by a young *sheng* played by someone who was not at all young. Too tired to do it myself, I asked Guisheng if he would go and buy me some beancurd broth. He came back after a little while and reported, "None to be had. Deaf old guy who sells it has gone home already. There *was* some in the daytime. Had two bowls myself. How about a ladle of water?"

I declined. Propping myself up in a sitting position, I continued to watch, though I couldn't have told you just what I was watching. Little by little, the actors' faces began to take on a very strange cast and then their bodies all slid together into a single, one-dimensional blur. Most of the younger children began to yawn and the older ones, having long since stopped watching the stage, were simply chatting among themselves. It wasn't until a clown dressed in a red jacket was tied to a pillar and horsewhipped by an old greybeard that everyone came to life and, amid much laughter, started watching again. I thought it quite the best thing we'd seen all night myself.

But then an old *dan* came on stage. Now, old *dan* roles had always turned me off more than any other, especially when they *sat down* to sing—and sing, and sing. As I glanced around and noticed how down-at-the-mouth all my friends looked, I realized that their feelings were no different from my own. At first, the old woman didn't do anything except pace back and forth, singing as she went. But then she suddenly made a beeline for an armchair at center stage and plunked herself down in it. Now I was really worried! Shuangxi and the others started muttering and cursing under their breath too. I contained myself as best I could. After quite some time, she raised one hand and I thought she was going to get up, but then she slowly put it back down again and went right on singing. A few of us began letting out one impatient sigh after the other, while the others just started to yawn.

Finally Shuangxi had had enough. "Come sunrise, she'll probably still be at it. What do you say we call it a day?" Everyone agreed with that right off. With the same lively enthusiasm as when we had set out, three or four people rushed to the stern, picked up the poles, and pushed us out several yards until they had enough leeway to turn the boat bow-for-stern. Still cursing the old *dan,* they placed the oars at the ready and set off in the direction of the pine forest.

It would seem that we hadn't been watching very long after all, for the moon had not yet set. Once we were clear of Zhao Village, it loomed unusually bright in the night sky. As I looked back, the stage appeared just as it had when we arrived: the faintly discernible abode of Daoist Immortals, bathed in a halo of torchlight that shrouded it like the sunset glow of evening. The sounds that now wafted to my ears were once again the melodious strains of a flute, making me suspect that the old *dan* at long last had made her exit, but I was too embarrassed to ask my friends to take me back.

Before long we had left the pine grove far astern. We were making fairly good time at that, but the darkness continued to thicken and you could tell that we were already deep into night. Cursing and laughing by turns, my friends discussed the actors, rowing hard and fast all the while. The water slapped against the bow much louder than when we had come. Like a great white fish with a cargo of children on its back, our boat leaped through the breaking whitecaps. Even a few old men who were fishing at night stopped their own boats to watch and to cheer us on.

By the time we were within a mile of Flatbridge, however, we had slowed down considerably. The rowers explained that they hadn't had anything to eat in quite some time. What was more, they had squandered too much energy when we first started back, and were paying for it now.

This time it was Guisheng who came up with a good idea. "Why not boil up some *arhat* beans?"[14] He pointed out that we already had firewood aboard and that since this was the peak of the season, all we had to do was steal a few limas and we'd be all set. Everyone agreed it was a wonderful idea, and we immediately drew in to the bank and tied up. The fields were packed with dark glistening pods.

Shuangxi, first to jump to the bank, now yelled, "Hey Ah-fa, this side belongs to your family and that side belongs to Old Six-one.[15] Which side should we steal from?"

The rest of us jumped down as Ah-fa answered, "Hold on a minute while I check them out." Bending down, he went from one field to the other feeling the beans. At last he stood up straight and said, "Let's take them from my family. Our beans are the biggest!" Upon securing his permission, the boys immediately scattered through the field. Each of them made off with a good double handful and tossed them into the boat. Shuangxi cautioned us against taking any more lest Ah-fa's mother discover the theft and give us all a good tongue-lashing. Whereupon, everyone went over to Gramps Six-one's fields and stole a good double handful from him as well.

A couple of the older boys now rowed the boat leisurely downriver while some others went into the cabin to make the fire. The younger lads and I were assigned the shelling. Before long the beans were done. Letting the boat drift where it would, we all gathered round and ate them with our bare fingers. When we had finished them we rowed off again, washing our utensils and dumping the pods as we went so as to obliterate every trace of our crime. But Shuangxi was still worried. He pointed out that Eighth Gramps was an old man who kept a close check on things and was sure to notice that we'd used his salt and firewood. He'd give us a

---

14. "*Arhat* beans" *(luohan dou)*, is a Shaoxing dialect for the kind of lima that is known elsewhere as *can dou*. An *arhat* is a saint or perfect man in Hinayana Buddhism.

15. According to customs governing naming practices in and around Shaoxing, it is probable that when Six-one was born, his grandfather was sixty-one. Six-one would then have acquired this name in honor of his grandfather.

good scolding for it too. But after we discussed the ins and outs of it our conclusion was that we didn't have to worry about Eighth Gramps anyway. If he cursed us out over snitching a few measly beans, then we'd ask *him* to return that dried-out old cedar that he'd hauled away from the riverbank last year. Better yet, we'd call him "Eighth Old Scabby Head" right to his face.[16]

"We're all back! I told you so. Didn't I say I could guarantee everything would be all right before we left?" Shuangxi abruptly announced our arrival from the bow in a good loud voice.

I looked forward and saw that we were coming up on Flatbridge. There was someone standing at the foot of the bridge—my mother. Shuangxi had been shouting his remarks to her. I stepped out of the cabin as the boat neared shore. Once it was tied up, we all rushed pell-mell onto the bank. Mother was a bit put out nonetheless. She said that it was already past the Third Watch and demanded to know where we had been all this time.[17] Having gotten that off her chest, however, she immediately melted and with a big smile invited everyone back to our place for a snack of crispy-rice.

They all said they'd already had a snack, were asleep on their feet, and had better get to bed. Each going his own way then, my young friends all went home.

It must have been around noon when I got up the next day. I didn't hear a word about the Eighth Gramps salt-and-firewood incident. In the afternoon, as usual, I went fishing for shrimp.

"Shuangxi, you little devil, you and your friends made off with some of my beans yesterday, didn't you? Didn't do much of a job at pickin' either. Tramped down a whole bunch of good plants!" I raised my head and saw Gramps Six-one poling a boat in our direction. He was obviously coming back from selling his beans at market, for there was still a pile of unsold ones in the middle of the boat.

"That's right. We were treatin' a guest. At first we didn't even want *your* beans. Hey! Now look what you've gone and done! Scared all my shrimp away!" Shuangxi answered.

Catching sight of me, Gramps Six-one stopped poling and smiled. "Treatin' a guest, huh? And so you should too." Then to me, "Brother Xun, was the opera pretty good last night?"

---

16. Like Ah Q, he has ringworm scars.
17. The hour would have been around midnight.

I nodded and said, "Yes."

"And were the beans pretty good too?"

I nodded again, "Yes, very."

Much to my surprise, Gramps Six-one now seemed actually *grateful* for the theft. Quite full of himself, he held up his thumb and said, "It takes a city lad with book-learnin' like yourself to know a good thing when he sees it! I'm very careful about pickin' out the sprouts I plant. Go through them one by one. Country people round here can't tell what's good and what's bad. They even say my beans aren't as good as other people's. I'm gonna send some over to your mom this very day." He picked up his pole and punted on by.

When Mother called me to dinner, there was a big bowl of boiled *arhats* on the table. Good as his word, Gramps Six-one had sent them over. Later on I heard that Old Gramps had praised me to the skies when talking to Mother. "If he's this smart this young, later on he's sure to win a *Zhuangyuan!*[18] Ma'am, your future happiness is guaranteed, guaranteed!" But when I ate the beans, they weren't nearly as good as the ones I'd had the night before.

As a matter of fact, down to this very day, I have really never eaten beans as good as those I had that night, nor have I ever seen such fine opera either.

OCTOBER 1922

18. The *Zhuangyuan* was the highest possible "pass" on the civil service examinations.

WONDERING WHERE TO TURN

New Year's Sacrifice

When you come right down to it, the wind-up of the old Lunar Year was what the end of a year really should be. To say nothing of the hubbub in the towns and villages, the very sky itself proclaimed the imminent arrival of the New Year as flashes of light appeared now and then among the grey and heavy clouds of evening, followed by the muffled sound of distant explosions—pyrotechnic farewells to the Kitchen God.[1] The crisper cracks of fireworks being set off close at hand were much louder, and before your ears had stopped ringing, the faint fragrance of gunpowder would permeate the air. It was on just such an evening that I returned to Lu Town. I still called it home even though my immediate family was no longer there, a circumstance that forced me to put up at Fourth Old Master Lu's place. Since he is my clansman and a generation above me, I really ought to call him "Fourth Uncle."

An old Imperial Collegian and follower of Neo-Confucianism,[2] he seemed little changed, only a bit older than before, though he still had not grown a beard as one might have expected. Upon seeing me, he recited the usual social commonplaces; commonplaces concluded, he observed that I had put on weight; that observation having been made, he began to denounce the new party. I knew, however, that this was by no means intended as an indirect attack

First published in the Shanghai periodical *Eastern Miscellany,* vol. 21, no. 6, in March 1924.

1. Toward the end of the twelfth lunar month, the kitchen god of each household, King Stove (Zao Wang), ascended to heaven and reported the doings of the family to the Jade Emperor. A paper image of the god was burned (the ascension) and he was given a royal firecracker farewell to ensure that he would have nothing but good news to report about the family.

2. "Imperial Collegian" *(jiansheng)* might refer to someone actually placed in the Imperial College *(guozijian)* at Beijing, or to someone, like Fourth Uncle, who had been proclaimed "qualified" to be there. The title could either be earned through examination or bought. *Neo*-Confucianism is the school of Confucianism, somewhat puritanical and heavily influenced by Buddhist metaphysics, which dominated scholar-official circles in China from 1313 onward, the year when it was declared the orthodox ideology for interpretation of the classics in the civil service examinations. Its authority went virtually unchallenged until 1905, when the examination system was officially abolished.

on me, for by "new" he had meant the reformers of twenty years back, people like Kang Youwei.[3] Even so, as we continued to chat, my words and his never seemed to jibe and before long I found myself alone in his study.

I got up quite late the next day, and after taking lunch, went out to visit some relatives and friends. I spent the third day in exactly the same way. They did not seem much changed either—a bit older, that was all. In every household people were busily preparing for the ceremony known as the "New Year's Sacrifice."[4] In Lu Town this was the most important of all the ceremonies conducted at the end of the year. With great reverence and punctilious observance of ritual detail, people would prepare to receive and welcome the gods of good fortune, and to ask them for prosperity during the coming year.

Chickens and geese would be killed; pork bought; and the meats washed with a diligence and care that left the arms of the women red from the soaking. Some women kept on their locally made bracelets—braided strands of silver—even as they washed. On the last day of the year, once the meats were cooked, chopsticks would be thrust at random into the various dishes prepared from them. This was the "ritual offering" which would bring down bountiful blessings during the new year. At the Fifth Watch, just before dawn on New Year's Day, the various dishes would be set out, candles lit, incense burned, and the gods of good fortune respectfully invited to descend and enjoy the feast. The actual execution of the ceremony was exclusively the province of men.

Once the ceremony was completed, then of course still more firecrackers would be set off. Year by year, family by family, so long as people could afford the expenditure, the ritual had always been performed in this manner. And this year, of course, was no exception.

The sky grew ever darker. By afternoon it had actually begun to snow. From horizon to horizon, blending together with the soft mists and general atmosphere of urgent activity, snowflakes as

---

3. Kang Youwei (1858–1927) was among those reformers at the turn of the century who sought to modernize China while retaining the imperial government. At the time this story is set (somewhere between 1919 and 1924), people of the narrator's age and educational background would have considered Kang Youwei outdated and reactionary.

4. *Zhufu,* the ceremony described in this story, was unique to the area around Lu Xun's native Shaoxing.

large as plum blossoms danced through the air, catching Lu Town off balance and throwing it into a state of hopeless disarray.

By the time I got back to Fourth Uncle's study, the roof tiles were white and the study so brightened by the reflected light of snow that the red ink-rubbing hanging on the wall stood out with unusual crispness. The rubbing consisted of the single character meaning "long life" and had been written by Venerable Founder Chen Tuan.[5] There had been a pair of scrolls flanking it, but one of these had fallen off the wall and now lay loosely rolled up on the long table under the rubbing. Its mate still hung on the wall and read: *Having completely penetrated the principle of things, the mind becomes serene.*[6] Aimlessly I went over and rummaged through the pile of old-fashioned stitched books on the desk by the window: an incomplete set of the *Kang Xi Dictionary,* a copy of *Collected Commentaries to "Reflections on Things at Hand,"* and a copy of *A Lining to the Garment of the "Four Books."*[7] Then and there I decided to leave the next day. Furthermore, when I thought about how I had run into Sister Xianglin on the street the day before, I realized it would have simply been impossible for me to remain in Lu Town with any peace of mind.[8]

It had happened in the afternoon, immediately after I had paid a visit to a friend of mine on the east side of town. Leaving my friend's place, I caught sight of Sister Xianglin down by the riverbank. Her eyes were intense and focused on me. I could tell she wanted to have a word.

Among the people I had run into on this visit, I can safely say that no one had changed as much as she: the grey hair of five years back was now entirely white. No one would have taken her for the

---

5. A historical figure of the Five Dynasties period (907–59) who lived as a mountain recluse and, according to the tradition, became a Daoist Immortal.

6. An important Neo-Confucian concept divided the universe into form, or principle *(li),* and substance *(qi).* Contemplation of "forms" led to serenity (the influence of Buddhist meditation is apparent) and would eventually result in enlightenment. The narrator, we should remember, views these ideas as outmoded claptrap.

7. The dictionary was compiled under the reign of the Kang Xi emperor (1661–1722), hence its name. *Reflections on Things at Hand (Jinsilu)* is a collection of writings by four Neo-Confucians of the Northern Song (960–1126); it has been translated into English by Wing-tsit Chan (New York: Columbia University Press, 1967). *A Lining to the Garment of the "Four Books"* is a Qing Dynasty (1644–1911) commentary on the *Four Books* of Neo-Confucianism: *The Analects of Confucius, The Mencius, The Great Learning,* and *The Doctrine of the Mean.*

8. "Sister" *(sao)* is a polite term of address for married women.

woman of forty or so that she was. Her face was sallow with dark circles around the eyes, and what was more, even the expression of sadness that she used to wear had now disappeared altogether. Her face seemed to be carved of wood. Only an occasional eye movement hinted that she was still an animate creature. In one hand she carried an empty bamboo basket; a broken bowl lay inside it—empty. With the other hand she supported herself on a bamboo pole that was taller than she and had started to split at the bottom. It was obvious that she had become a beggar, pure and simple. I stood still, waiting for her to accost me and ask for money.

"So, you've come back," she began.

"Yes."

"Just the man I've been lookin' for. You know how to read books. You've been out there in the world and must've seen a thing or two. Now tell me . . ." A bright light suddenly glowed in her heretofore lifeless eyes. Never imagining that she would begin by saying this sort of thing, I just stood there in astonishment.

"Tell me . . ." She came a few steps closer, lowered her voice as though sharing a secret, and continued in tones of great urgency: "Is there *really* a soul after a body dies?"

I was aghast at the question. When I saw how her eyes were riveted upon me, I became so fidgety you would have thought that someone had thrown a handful of thorns down the back of my gown. I was even more on edge than when, back during my school days, a teacher would pop an unexpected question, look straight at me, and wait for the answer.

I had never really cared one way or the other about whether souls existed or not, but that was not my problem. My problem was what would be the best answer to give *her* right then and there? I hesitated for a moment to give myself time to think. I knew that people in these parts did, as a rule, believe in ghosts, but now *she* seemed to doubt—or perhaps "hope" would be a better word—seemed to hope that they existed, and yet, at the same time, seemed to hope that they did not. Why add to the suffering of a poor woman already at the end of her rope? For her sake it would probably be best to say that they did exist.

I hemmed and hawed: "Well, perhaps they do. Probably. The way I see it—"

"Then there's gotta be a hell too, right?"

"What! A hell?" Taken off guard by the question, I became evasive. "Well, logically, I suppose there ought to be, but then not necessarily either. Who has the time to bother about that sort of thing anyway?"

"But if there *is,* then dead kin are all gonna meet again, right?"

"Hmmmm . . . Let's see . . . Your question . . . your question is . . . uh . . . will they meet again?"

At this point I began to see that, for all the good it did me, I might just as well have remained uneducated, for despite all my stalling, despite all my brainwracking, I had been unable to stand up to three questions posed by this simple woman. Suddenly I turned timid and searched around for a way of nullifying whatever I had said up to this point. "Well, you see . . . To tell the truth, I can't say for sure. As a matter of fact, I can't even say for sure whether there are souls or not." Taking advantage of a lull in her persistent questioning, I strode away and beat a hasty retreat to Fourth Uncle's house.

Anxious at heart, I began to mull it all over in my own mind. "That may well have been a dangerous sort of answer to have given her," I thought to myself. "To be sure, it's probably just because everyone else is so caught up in preparations for the New Year's Sacrifice that she's become so keenly aware of her own isolation—but still, could there be anything more to it than that? Could it be that she has had some sort of premonition? If there *is* anything more to it and something regrettable happens as a result, then I shall be partially responsible because of what I said . . ."

By the time I got to this point, I couldn't help but laugh at myself. After all, what had happened was nothing more than a chance occurrence and could not possibly have any great significance. Yet, against all reason, I had insisted on analyzing it in painstaking detail. Was it any wonder that certain people in educational circles had accused me of being neurotic?[9] What was more, I had told her in no uncertain terms that I couldn't "say for sure," nullifying everything I had said before. "Even if something *does* happen," I thought, "it will have nothing to do with me."

Can't say for sure—what a wonderfully useful expression! Dauntless youngsters, wet behind the ears, will often plot a course

9. This reflects charges that were leveled at Lu Xun himself, who, at the time he wrote this story, was working in the Ministry of Education and teaching part-time as well.

of action for an indecisive friend, or even go so far as to help someone choose a doctor. When things don't turn out well, then of course they've only succeeded in making enemies.

If, on the other hand, you conclude everything you say with a *can't say for sure,* you always remain comfortably free and clear no matter *how* things turn out. After meeting with Sister Xianglin on the street that day, I began to appreciate the necessity for some such formula. I hadn't been able to get along without it even when talking with a simple beggar.

Nonetheless, I continued to feel uneasy. Even after a good night's sleep I couldn't get her out of my mind. It was as though I had a premonition of disaster. The wearisome atmosphere of my uncle's study melded with the gloom of the snow-filled skies to intensify my anxieties. "Might as well leave and go back into the city tomorrow," I thought to myself. "Shark's fin cooked in clear broth costs only a dollar a bowl at the Fuxing—good food at a bargain price.[10] Wonder if it's gone up by now? The friends I used to go there with, of course, have long since scattered to the four winds, but I can't afford to pass up that shark's fin soup even if I do have to eat alone . . . Well, I'm definitely going to clear out of here tomorrow, come what may."

I had often seen things that I hoped wouldn't turn out the way I anticipated, begin, one after the other, to turn out exactly the way I was afraid they would. Now I began to worry that this business of Sister Xianglin would fit the mold. And sure enough, strange things began to happen. Toward evening, I heard people discussing something-or-other in the inner rooms. Before long, the conversation ended, and all I could make out was the sound of Fourth Uncle pacing back and forth. He began to yell. "Not a minute sooner and not a minute later, had to pick exactly *this* time of year! You can tell from that alone what bad stock we're dealing with!"

At first I was merely curious as to what it was all about, but then I began to feel downright uneasy, for Fourth Uncle's words seemed to have something to do with me. I poked my head out the door, but there was no one around whom I could question. I was on pins and needles until just before supper, when a temporary servant, taken on for the holidays, came into my room to make tea. I finally had my chance.

---

10. "Clear broth" means there is no soy sauce in the recipe.

"Who was Fourth Old Master so mad at just now?"

"Sister Xianglin, who else?" Brief and to the point.

"What *about* Sister Xianglin?" I asked apprehensively.

"She's aged away."[11]

"Aged away?" My heart constricted into a tight knot and felt as though it would jump out of my body. The color probably drained out of my face too, but from beginning to end, the servant kept his head down and tended to the making of the tea, unaware of my reaction. Forcing myself to be calm, I continued with my questions.

"*When* did she die?"

"When? Last night, or maybe it was today. I can't say for sure."

"What did she die of?"

"*What* did she die of? Poverty, what else?" He answered in flat, unemotional tones; still not raising his head to look at me, he left the room.

Surprisingly, however, my own agitation turned out to be but a momentary thing, for right after the servant left, I felt that what was bound to happen had already come and gone. Without even having to resort to a *can't say for sure* or adopting the servant's formula for dismissing the whole thing—*Poverty, what else?*—I gradually began to regain my composure. And yet, I still felt an occasional pang of guilt.

With Fourth Uncle in stern attendance, dinner was served. I wanted to learn more about Sister Xianglin's death, but I knew that although Fourth Uncle had read that *ghosts and spirits do but natural transformations of the two powers be,*[12] he still harbored many superstitions and would not, under any circumstances, be willing to discuss anything related to sickness or death as the time for the New Year's Sacrifice drew near. If such subjects had to be broached, then one would be expected to employ a substitute language of roundabout phrases in discussing them. Unfortunately, I did not know the proper phraseology and therefore, although there were several moments when I thought about asking something, in the end I didn't. As I looked at the stern expression on my uncle's face, it suddenly occurred to me that he might well be

11. It would be unlucky to pronounce a word meaning "die" during the New Year period, hence the circumlocution.

12. The two powers are *yin* and *yang* (the female and male principles in nature); the quotation is from *Reflections on Things at Hand,* the work whose commentary lies on Fourth Uncle's desk (see n. 7).

thinking that I, too, "not a minute sooner and not a minute later, had to pick exactly *this* time of year" to come and disturb his peace of mind, and that I too was "bad stock." Deciding that I had better set his mind at rest as soon as possible, I told him I would leave Lu Town in the morning and go back to the city. He made a very perfunctory bow in the direction of trying to dissuade me. We finished the meal in gloomy silence.

Winter days are short. Snowy skies shorten them even more, and thus by the time our meal was over, the shades of evening had long since enshrouded the entire town. By lamplight on this New Year's Eve, people were bustling about in every home as they prepared for the following day.

Outside the windows of those same homes, however, all was lonely silence. Large snowflakes fell on a blanket of white that was already piled thick on the ground. I even seemed to hear a faint rustling sound as they touched down, a sound that made me feel the silence and loneliness all the more intensely. As I sat there in the yellowish glow of an oil lamp, my thoughts turned to Sister Xianglin.

With nothing left, with no one to turn to, she had been tossed onto a garbage heap like a worn-out toy that people are tired of seeing around. And yet, until only a short time before, Sister Xianglin had at least managed to maintain her physical form even amid the refuse. People happy in their own lives had no doubt thought it odd that she chose to continue such an existence.

Well, now at last Wuchang had swept her away without leaving the slightest trace.[13] I didn't know whether souls existed or not, but in the world we live in, when someone who has no way to make a living is no longer alive, when someone whom people are sick of seeing is no longer around to *be* seen, then one cannot say that she has done too badly, either by herself or by other people. Sitting in silence, listening to the faint rustle of snowflakes, and thinking these thoughts, gradually and quite unexpectedly I began to feel relaxed.

13. Wuchang (the name means literally "nothing is permanent") was a deity who, despite a rollicking sense of humor, played the role of grim reaper. A local Shaoxing saying went: "When you see Wuchang arrive, you'll not be long alive" *(Wuchang yidao, xingming nantao)*. Lu Xun devoted a reminiscence to Wuchang and even included some of his own sketches of him. This is included in *Zhaohua xishi* (Dawn Blossoms Plucked at Dusk). A translation appears in *Selected Works of Lu Hsun* (4 vols.), vol. 1, pp. 377–386. Translated by Yang Hsien-yi and Gladys Yang. Peking: Foreign Languages Press, 1956–1960.

As I sat there, the bits and pieces of Sister Xianglin's story that I had either witnessed or heard about secondhand came together and painted a portrait of her life.

* * *

She did not come from Lu Town.

At the beginning of winter one year they decided to change maids at Fourth Uncle's place. And so it was that Old Lady Wei, acting as go-between, led a new servant into the house.

Hair tied back with a piece of white wool, she wore a black skirt, a blue lined jacket with long sleeves, and over that a sleeveless vest of light blue. She looked to be twenty-six or twenty-seven and was on the whole rather pale, though her cheeks were rosy. Old Lady Wei called her Sister Xianglin and said she was a neighbor of her mother's. Because her man had died, Sister Xianglin had come out to look for a job. Fourth Uncle frowned at that, and Fourth Aunt knew the reason: he objected to hiring a widow. But at the same time she also noted that Sister Xianglin looked quite presentable, seemed sound of limb, and what was more, kept her eyes submissively averted and said nothing at all—very much the hardworking servant who knows her place. And so it was that despite Fourth Uncle's frown, Fourth Aunt decided to give her a try.

During this trial period, from one end of the day to the other, Sister Xianglin worked so hard that one would have thought being unoccupied depressed her. Moreover, she was quite strong, easily a match for any man. And so on the third day things were finally settled: Sister Xianglin would be taken on as the new maid at five hundred coppers a month.

Everybody called her Sister Xianglin. No one asked her family name, but since the go-between was from Wei Family Hill and had said that Xianglin lived close to her mother's place, it is safe to assume that Sister Xianglin's name was Wei too. She did not like to talk much; when people asked questions of her she would speak, but even then she did not volunteer very much.

Back where she had come from, she had had a very strict mother-in-law, and a brother-in-law who was only ten, just big enough to gather firewood. She had lost her husband back in the spring. Ten years younger than she, he had been a fuel gatherer too. Bit by bit this came out over a period of two weeks or so. That was all anyone knew of her.

The days passed quickly, but Sister Xianglin's pace slackened not one whit. She was very fussy about her work, to which she gave her all, but was not in the least particular about the food she ate. People began saying that over at Fourth Old Master Lu's place they had hired a maid who was more capable than a hardworking man.

And when the end of the year came, she single-handedly cleaned the entire house, straightened up the yard, killed the geese and chickens, and worked straight through the night to prepare the ritual offering that would assure the Lu household of blessings in the year to come. That New Year, Fourth Uncle was actually able to get by without hiring any part-time help at all. Despite all these demands on her energies, Sister Xianglin seemed quite contented. Traces of a smile began to appear at the corners of her mouth, and her face began to fill out as well.

Just after the New Year, she came back from washing rice down by the river one day with all the color drained from her face. She said that she had seen a man skulking around off in the distance on the opposite bank, a man who looked a lot like an elder cousin of her husband. She was afraid he might well be looking for her. Fourth Aunt was a bit suspicious, but when she tried to get to the bottom of things, Sister Xianglin immediately clammed up. When Fourth Uncle heard about it, he frowned and said: "Doesn't look good. She's probably a runaway." Before long, Fourth Uncle's conjecture was confirmed.

A few weeks later, just as everyone was gradually beginning to forget the incident, Old Lady Wei suddenly reappeared. She had in tow a woman who looked to be somewhere in her thirties. This, she announced, was Sister Xianglin's mother-in-law.

Although the woman looked like a hillbilly, she had a certain natural poise and was a good talker as well. After the usual formalities, she apologized for the intrusion and announced she had come to fetch her daughter-in-law back. She pointed out that it was now Beginning-of-Spring, a busy season for farmers. Since everyone back home was either too young or too old, they were shorthanded and in sore need of Sister Xianglin.

"Since it's her mother-in-law who wants her to go back, what can we say?" opined Fourth Uncle.

Sister Xianglin's wages were totalled up: one thousand seven hundred and fifty coins. When she first started to work, she had told Fourth Aunt to keep the money for her and had not touched any of it. Now the entire amount was handed over to her mother-in-law, who also took care to gather up all of Sister Xianglin's clothes. By the time the mother-in-law had thanked everyone and gone on her way, it was already noon.

It was not until some time after they had left that Fourth Aunt cried out in alarm: "The rice! Wasn't Sister Xianglin preparing the meal?" Fourth Aunt was probably a little hungry by then and had remembered the lunch. Thereupon she and Fourth Uncle went to look for the rice basket. She tried the kitchen first, then the hall, and finally Sister Xianglin's bedroom—no trace anywhere. Fourth Uncle went outside to look, but didn't see it anywhere out there either. It was not until he had gone all the way down to the river that he caught sight of the rice basket, neatly placed on the bank, a head of cabbage still beside it.

According to some people who saw what happened, a white-canopied boat had moored on the river that morning, the canopy closed tightly all the way around so that no one could tell what was inside. At the time nobody had taken any particular notice of it anyway. But then later on, when Sister Xianglin had come down to wash the rice, two men had jumped out just as she was about to kneel down on the riverbank. One of them had grabbed her in his arms and, with the help of the other, dragged her into the boat. Sister Xianglin had screamed a few times, but afterwards there was no sound at all. They had probably gagged her. Soon after that, two women emerged from the boat. One of them was Old Lady Wei. No one had recognized the other. A few villagers had tried peeking through the canopy, but it was so dark inside they weren't able to see very clearly. They had, however, made out Sister Xianglin's form lying on the floor, all tied up.

"Despicable! But still . . ." said Fourth Uncle.

Fourth Aunt had to boil the luncheon rice herself that day. Her son, Ah-niu, made the fire. After lunch, Old Lady Wei came back again.

"Despicable!" said Fourth Uncle to her.

"What in the world do you think you're doing? You've got your nerve coming here again," said Fourth Aunt angrily as she washed the ricebowls. "You were the one who brought her here to us, and then you turn around and join up with those people to come and snatch her away! And what about all the commotion you kicked up in the neighborhood while you were doing it? What are you trying to do, make a laughing stock of our family?"

"Aiya . . . aiya, I was really taken in. I made a point of gettin' back to you today to get this cleared up. Okay then, Sister Xianglin comes to me lookin' for a place. Now how was I to know that it was behind her mother-in-law's back? Let me tell you, Fourth Old Master and the Missus, I'm just as sorry as I can be. All said and done, I slipped up and wasn't as careful as I should've been. Now I've gone and done wrong by two of the best clients I've got. Lucky for me that you've always been bighearted, understandin' folks, not the kind to get picky with ordinary folks like me. Well, never you mind. I'll get you a *really* good maid this time to make up for it . . ."

"But still . . ." said Fourth Uncle.

And thus ended the Sister Xianglin affair. Before long, she was entirely forgotten.

* * *

Only Fourth Aunt ever mentioned her again, and that was only because she was not happy with any of the maids she hired afterwards. Most were either lazy or the kind who would try to eat you out of house and home—and some were both. When exasperated with one of them over this or that, she would often say to herself: "I wonder how she's doing now?" What she really meant was that she hoped Sister Xianglin would somehow come back. By Newstep of the following year, however, she had given up all hopes of that.[14]

Toward the end of Newstep a comfortably tipsy Old Lady Wei showed up at Fourth Uncle's place to wish everyone a belated Happy New Year. She said she had gone back to Wei Family Hill to spend a few days with her parents, and this was why she was late in coming to pay her respects. In the course of the conversation, of course, the subject of Sister Xianglin came up.

"Sister Xianglin?" began Old Lady Wei expansively. "Her turn for good luck's rolled round again. Long before that mother-in-law of hers ever came over here to snatch her away, she'd fixed it up to marry her off to the sixth son of the He family over in He Family Hollow."

14. Newstep *(xinzheng)* is the period that includes the first fifteen days of the lunar year.

"Aiya! What kind of mother-in-law would *do* a thing like that?" asked Fourth Aunt in shock.

"Would you listen to that! Dear, dear lady, you really *do* sound like a rich-family wife! Up there in the hills, for poor families like us, it's no big deal. Sister Xianglin had a younger brother-in-law up there, you know. Well, he needed a wife too, right? If they hadn't married Sister Xianglin off, where would they have come up with the money to get him a bride? That mother-in-law of hers is one sharp cookie. A real planner too, that one. That's how come she married Sister Xianglin off to somebody way back in the hills. Now if she'd sold her to somebody right there in the village, how much money would *that* bring? But you're not gonna find too many girls willin' to marry way back into the hills. That's why she came out of the deal with eighty strings of cash in hand! Just think, the wife she got for her younger son only cost her fifty. Take out the cost of the weddin' and stuff, and she still had more'n ten strings to the good. Now that's what I'd call plannin', wouldn't you?"

"And did Sister Xianglin actually go along with it?"

"What's that got to do with it? Fuss? Sure, anybody'd put up some sort of fuss. But in the end they just get hog-tied, stuffed into a bridal chair, and carted off to the man's house.[15] As a rule, all you've gotta do then is slap on a weddin' cap, force 'em through the ceremony, then lock 'em up in a room with the new man, and that's that.

"But Sister Xianglin was somethin' else—kicked up a rumpus the likes of which nobody'd ever seen. Folks said it was more than likely 'cause she'd worked in a family that had book learnin' and wasn't just your run-of-the-mill widow bein' remarried. Let me tell you, Missus, us go-betweens have seen a lotta this kind of stuff. When second-timers marry, some'll scream and holler; some'll try to do themselves in; some'll raise such a ruckus after they get to the groom's place that you can't even get 'em through the ceremony; you'll even find some who'll bust up the weddin' candles.

"But Sister Xianglin topped 'em all. Hear tell she wailed and cursed every step of the way. By the time they got her there, she'd shouted herself so hoarse she couldn't even talk. They had to drag her out of the bridal chair. But even with two strong men and her

15. A bride would be sent to her new home in a sedan chair supported between long poles that were carried on the shoulders of two bearers.

brother-in-law thrown in, all holdin' onto her for all they were worth, they *still* couldn't get her through the ceremony. Then when they let their guard down for just a split second—Aiya, may Buddha preserve us!—before anyone knew what was up, she slammed her head on the corner of the incense table. Made a hole so big the blood just gushed out. They slapped a couple handfuls of incense ash on the hole and wrapped her head in some red cloth. But even with all that they still couldn't stop the blood. Clear up to the time when they got her—and they had everybody fallin' over everybody else tryin' to do it—got her and the groom into the bride-room and locked it from the outside, she kept cursin' for all she was worth. *Aiya!* That was really, really . . ." She shook her head, looked down, and stopped there.

"And then what happened?" Fourth Aunt went on with her questions.

"The way I heard it, she didn't get up the next day," answered Old Lady Wei, raising her eyes.

"And then?"

"Then? Well, then she got up. Toward the end of the year she had a kid, a boy. He was two this New Year's.[16] Past few days when I was at my folks' house, someone went out to He Family Hollow and saw the two of 'em. The kid was nice and chubby and the mom was all filled out too. Better yet, now she's got no mother-in-law over her. She's got a good strong man who knows how to work, and the house is theirs free and clear. Her turn for good luck has rolled around again for sure!"

After that, Fourth Aunt never mentioned Sister Xianglin again.

* * *

But one year in the fall—it must have been a New Year or so after Sister Xianglin's "turn for good luck rolled round again"—to everyone's complete surprise, there she stood once again in the main hall of Fourth Uncle's house. Her bamboo basket, shaped like a water chestnut, lay on the table, and her small bedroll was under the eaves outside. She was much the same as she had been the first time: hair tied back with a piece of white wool; black skirt

---

16. His age would be counted as "one" immediately at birth and "two" at the following New Year.

and blue lined jacket with long sleeves; and sleeveless vest of light blue. But her cheeks had lost the slightly rosy touch that had once relieved her general pallor. She kept her eyes averted; the spirited gleam that once had lit them was now gone, and traces of tears showed in their corners. Just as the first time, too, it was Old Lady Wei who led her in. Assuming an exaggerated air of compassion, the old woman prattled on and on.

"*Like a bolt out of the blue*—there really is somethin' to those words. That man of hers was a husky young guy. Who would've ever expected a young horse like that would lose his life to typhoid. As a matter of fact, he *did* get over it, but then later on he went and ate a bowl of cold rice, and it came onto 'im again. Luckily he left a son behind and Sister Xianglin's someone who knows how to put in a good day's work. Gatherin' firewood, pickin' tea, raisin' silkworms—no problem. She should've been able to hold things together. Who would've even thought that with spring almost over there'd still be wolves comin' round the village. Well, with no rhyme or reason one *did* come along, and dragged her son right off.

"Now she's got nothin' left but herself. Her brother-in-law came and took the house back. Drove Sister Xianglin out.[17] She's really at the end of her rope now. Nothin' left for it but to come here and see if her old employers can help out. The good part is that she's got nothin' to tie her down now. As luck would have it, the Missus is lookin' for a maid right now, and so I decided to bring her over. I thought since Sister Xianglin knows her way around the place, it'd be much better for the Missus to get *her* back than to have to break in someone new . . ."

"I was real dumb, real dumb," began Sister Xianglin as she raised her expressionless eyes. "All I knew was that when it snows and the wild animals can't find anything to eat up there in the hills, sometimes they'll come into the villages. But I didn't know they could show up in springtime, too. I got up bright and early, opened the door, filled a little basket with beans, and told our Ahmao to go outside, sit by the door, and shell 'em. He always minded, did everything I told him. Well, he went out and I went to the back of the room to split firewood and wash the rice. I

17. Sister Xianglin was not driven out so long as her son, a blood heir to her dead husband's family, was still alive.

put the rice in the pot and was gettin' ready to steam the beans on top. 'Ah-mao!' No answer. I went out and all I saw was beans scattered all over the ground, but our Ah-mao was nowhere to be seen.

"Now it wasn't like him to go and play at other kids' houses, but I asked all over anyway. Sure enough, nobody'd seen him. That's when I got good and worried, begged folks to go out and make a search. Right down till the bottom half of the day, they looked everywhere. Finally, they came to a holler and found one of his little shoes hangin' on some brambles. They thought he was a goner then for sure, that most likely he'd met up with a wolf. They kept on goin' and sure enough, there he was, lyin' in the den of a wolf. His belly was open and his insides all eaten out. Still had that little basket clutched tight in his hand." She kept on talking, but now she was sobbing so that she could no longer get an entire sentence out.

At first, Fourth Aunt had been somewhat hesitant, but after hearing out Sister Xianglin's own telling of what had happened, she too became a bit red-eyed. She thought for a moment and then told Sister Xianglin to take her blanket and bedroll to the servant's room. As though just relieved of a heavy burden, Old Lady Wei heaved a sigh of relief. Sister Xianglin also looked more relaxed than when they had first arrived. Without waiting to be shown the way, she took the basket and bedding to her room and once again Sister Xianglin worked as a maid in Lu Town.

To be sure, the family still called her Sister Xianglin, just as they had before, but her situation was far different this time. She had not been back more than a few days or so when her employers noticed that she was not so quick on her feet as she had once been and that her memory had gone downhill too. Furthermore, from one end of the day to the other, there was never so much as the trace of a smile on her corpselike face. When talking to her now, Fourth Aunt revealed considerable dissatisfaction in her tone of voice.

When she first came back, Fourth Uncle frowned as might well have been expected, but in view of the difficulties he and his wife had endured in finding a good replacement, he did not seriously oppose her return. However, he did warn Fourth Aunt privately: "People like her may seem quite pitiable, to be sure, but one must remember that they do have a deleterious influence on the morals of society.[18] While it may be permissible to let her help out with the housework, she must have absolutely nothing to do with the family sacrifices. You will have to prepare all the sacrificial offerings yourself; otherwise they will be tainted and our ancestors will not accept them."

In Fourth Uncle's house, the family sacrifices had always been the most important event of the year by far, and always in the past Sister Xianglin had been busiest during the period when they were conducted. This year, however, she had not been given a thing to do. Of her own volition, she took a table and placed it in the center of the room, tied the tableskirt around the edge, and even remembered to arrange the chopsticks and winecups just as she had done before.

"Sister Xianglin, *leave those alone!* I'll set the table!" Fourth Aunt cried out in alarm. Completely at a loss, Sister Xianglin drew her hands back, and then went to fetch the candlesticks.

"Sister Xianglin, *put those down!* I'll get them." Again the tone of voice was one of alarm.

Aimlessly she walked around the room for a bit, but since there was nothing for her to do, she finally walked out the door in a state of utter bewilderment. The only thing she was allowed to do during this entire day was to sit by the stove and tend the fire.

The people in the village still talked with her and called her Sister Xianglin, just as they had before, but their tone of voice had changed and the smiles on their faces had turned cold. When she met up with them, she paid no heed to any of this but simply stared off into space and recited that same story, which she could not put out of mind either by day or by night.

"I was real dumb, real dumb. All I knew was that when it snows and the wild animals can't find anything to eat up there in the hills, sometimes they'll come into the villages. But I didn't know they could show up in springtime, too. I got up bright and early, opened the door, filled a bamboo basket with beans, and told our Ah-mao to go outside, sit by the door, and shell 'em. He always minded, did everything I told him. Well, he went out and I went to the back of the room to split the firewood and wash the rice. I put the rice in the pot and was gettin' ready to steam the beans on top.

---

18. Fourth Uncle is a hidebound traditionalist: a widow would be bad enough, but a remarried widow is simply beyond the pale of decency.

I yelled, 'Ah-mao!' No answer. I went out and all I saw was beans scattered all over the ground, but our Ah-mao was nowhere around. Then I got really worried. I begged people to go out and make a search. By the bottom half of the day, some of 'em came to a holler and found one of his little shoes hangin' on some brambles. They thought he was a goner then for sure, that most likely he'd met up with a wolf. They kept on goin' and sure enough, there he was, lyin' in the den of a wolf. His belly was open and his insides all eaten out. Still had that little basket clutched tight in his hand." At this point tears would be streaming down her face and her voice broken with sobs.

Her story was actually quite effective, for by the time she got to this point, even the men would put aside their smiles and wander off in embarrassed silence, while the women would immediately shed their disdainful looks and, seeming to forgive her somewhat, would join their tears with hers.

The few old ladies who had not heard Sister Xianglin tell her sad tale in the streets and alleyways would make a special point of running her down so that they, too, might have a chance to hear her heartrending recitation. When Sister Xianglin reached the point where she began to sob, then they too would release tears that had been welling up in the corners of their eyes, sigh for a bit, and then walk away, contentedly evaluating the details of her story in a great flurry of chatter.

Sister Xianglin told her tragic tale over and over again. Before long everyone in town knew it down to the finest detail. Even in the eyes of the most pious old Buddhist ladies, not so much as the trace of a tear was anymore to be seen. Later on, it even got to the point where everyone could recite it word for word. And so it was that people eventually grew so sick of hearing her story that their heads ached at the mere mention of it.

"I was real dumb, real dumb," she would begin.

"Right, all you knew is that when it snows and the wild animals can't find anything to eat up there in the hills, they'll come to the village." They would cut her off immediately and get away as quickly as possible.

Stunned, she would stand there, mouth agape, and stare after their retreating forms. And then she would walk away as though she too felt there wasn't any point to it. And yet, against all reason, she still wanted to tell people the story of her Ah-mao. She began searching out opportunities to bring it up: whenever anyone mentioned a small basket, or beans, or someone's child, she would try to fit her story into the conversation. Whenever she saw a two- or three-year-old, she would look at the child and say, "Oh, if only our Ah-mao was still alive, he'd be just about that big too . . ." The child, in turn, would usually be frightened by the look in her eyes, grab its mother's clothing, and pull her away. At this point, Sister Xianglin would again be left standing alone, and finally she too would sense the awkwardness of the situation and wander away.

After a while, everyone became aware of this quirk of hers, and whenever there was a child in the immediate vicinity, someone would look at her with a smile that was not really a smile and ask, "Sister Xianglin, if your Ah-mao was still livin' he'd be just about that big too, wouldn't he?" By now everyone had long since chewed and savored the taste of her tragedy, had long since worked it into pulp, flavorless and ready to be spit out. She may not have been aware of this herself, but she did sense something cold and sharp in their smiles and knew there was no point in speaking. She would simply glance at them, but utter not one word in reply.

Lu Town had always celebrated the New Year, and this year was no exception. Things began to pick up after the twentieth day of the twelfth lunar month. But this year, even after they had taken on a temporary male servant, there was still too much to do at Fourth Uncle's place and too little time to do it in. And so it was that Mother Liu was hired to lend a helping hand. As a pious Buddhist who kept to a vegetarian diet, however, she believed in preserving life and refused to butcher the chickens and geese. She was willing to help only with the washing of the sacrificial utensils. At this, the busiest time of the year, not being allowed to do anything except tend the fire, Sister Xianglin found herself almost completely idle.

And so it was that she was sitting by the stove one day, watching Mother Liu work. A light snow was beginning to fall. As though talking to herself, she sighed and said, "I was real dumb, real dumb . . ."

"There you go again, Sister Xianglin," said Mother Liu, looking at her impatiently. "Okay, then, let me put it to you this way. Wasn't it at that second weddin' that you bashed in your head and got yourself that scar there?"

"Uh, uh . . ." Sister Xianglin became evasive.

"Okay, then let me try another one on you. Since you went to all that trouble, how come you finally gave in?"

"Who, me?"

"Yeah, you. I think way down deep you must'a wanted to, or else—"

"Now wait just a minute, you don't know how strong he was."

"Don't believe a word of it. I just can't see how a woman as strong as you are couldn't hold him off if you wanted to. Down deep you *wanted* to give in, and then you turn around and lay it on his bein' strong."

"Well, I'd . . . I'd just like to see *you* try and hold him off." Sister Xianglin smiled.

Mother Liu roared with laughter, making the corners of her mouth go back so far that her deep wrinkles shrunk together and transformed her face into a walnut. Her wizened little eyes glanced at the scar and then fixed Sister Xianglin with such a stare that she became quite ill-at-ease, stopped smiling, turned away, and gazed at the snow.

"Sister Xianglin, you really came out on the short end of the stick on that one," said Mother Liu enigmatically. "If you'd only put up more of a fight, or just bashed your brains out and been done with it, you'd have been all right. But now? Without even gettin' to spend two years with that second man, you've ended up committin' a big sin. Just think, later on when you die and go to the underworld, the ghosts of those two men are gonna fight over you. Which one will you give yourself to then? Yama, Great King of the Underworld, will have only one choice—saw you in half and give each of 'em his piece. The way I see it, you've really gotta . . . Well, I think you've gotta find some way of guardin' against that as soon as you can. Why not go to the temple and donate money for a doorsill. Then that doorsill will be your body. Thousands'll step on it and tens of thousands'll walk over it. That way you'll make up for all your sins and you won't have to suffer after you die."

At the time, Sister Xianglin said nothing in reply, but in all likelihood she was extremely depressed, for the dark circles around her eyes when she got up the next morning bespoke a sleepless night. After breakfast, she made her way to the temple at the west end of town and asked if she could donate a doorsill. At first, the priest in charge was adamant in his refusal. It was only when Sister Xianglin became emotional and was on the verge of tears that he reluctantly agreed. The price was set at twelve strings of cash, a thousand to the string.

Since everybody had long since become bored with the story of Ah-mao, she had not been able to find anyone to talk to in a long time. But now, once word of her conversation with Mother Liu spread abroad, people began to take new interest. Once again, they would stop her on the street and inveigle her into a chat. Now of course, in view of the new wrinkle that had been added, people's interest focused entirely on the scar.

"Sister Xianglin, how come you finally gave in?" one of them would ask.

"What a shame you had to bash your head in for nothin'," another would chime in while staring at her scar.

Aware of their smiles and tone of voice, she probably realized they were making fun of her, and so she would just stare at them without saying a word. Later on, she got so that she would not even turn her head when people called her.

Bearing that scar, which everyone now considered a mark of shame, tight-lipped and silent from morning to night, Sister Xianglin ran the errands, swept the floor, prepared the vegetables, and washed the rice. It was not until a year was almost out that she took from the hands of Fourth Aunt all the wages she had let accumulate and exchanged them for twelve Mexican silver dollars. She asked for time off to go to the west end of town. Then, well within the space of time it takes to eat a meal, she was back. She appeared relaxed and happy, and there was even an unaccustomed spark of life in her gaze. She seemed in very high spirits as she told Fourth Aunt how she had just donated a doorsill at the Earth God's temple.

When the winter solstice came and it was time to carry out the ancestral sacrifices, she became particularly energetic. Seeing that Fourth Aunt had already set out the sacrificial foods, Sister Xianglin got Ah-niu to help her move the table to the center of the hall. Then, with complete self-assurance, she went to get the winecups and the chopsticks.

"Sister Xianglin, *leave those alone!*" shouted Fourth Aunt frantically.

Sister Xianglin jerked back her hand as though it had been

scorched. Her face began to darken. Nor did she go and fetch the candlesticks. She just stood there, utterly lost. It was only when Fourth Uncle came with the incense and told her to get out of the way that she finally left the room. The change in her this time was immense. The next day there were again deep circles around her eyes and she was more listless than she had ever been before. What was more, she became very timid: she was afraid of the night; she was afraid of dark shadows; she was afraid of people, even her own employers. In everything she did, she was as skittish as a mouse away from its nest in daylight. Often she would just sit motionless and blank, lifeless as a wood-carved doll. Before half a year was out, her hair began to turn grey and her memory slipped dramatically, even to the point where she often forgot to wash the rice.

Sometimes, with Sister Xianglin right there in the room, Fourth Aunt would say, as though issuing a warning: "Wonder what's come over Sister Xianglin? It really would have been better not to keep her when Old Lady Wei brought her back."

But such warnings had no effect. She stayed the same, and it was painfully obvious that there was no hope she would ever again become the alert and nimble Sister Xianglin of old. They thought of getting rid of her at this point, of sending her back to Old Lady Wei, but while I was still in Lu Town, at any rate, this remained just talk. Looking back, though, it is apparent that they must have let her go sometime later on. But was it right after leaving Fourth Uncle's place that she became a beggar, or had she gone back to Old Lady Wei first? There was no way to tell.

* * *

Startled into wakefulness by the loud roar of fireworks going off close by, I focused my eyes on a yellow patch of light the size of a human head—the glow of the oil lamp. I heard the sharp and rapid *pow-pow pow-pow-pow* of entire strings being set off. Fourth Uncle's family was indeed in the midst of celebrating the New Year and I realized it must have been close to the Fifth Watch. In my drowsiness I was also vaguely aware of the faint but continuous sounds of various other kinds of explosions going off all around me in the distance, sounds that wove together into a skyful of dense and resounding clouds. Thickened by flakes of snow, they held all of Lu Town in their enfolding arms. Wrapped in this comforting symphonic embrace, I too was filled with a deep sense of well-being and felt wholly free of worldly cares. All the worries and concerns that had plagued me from morning till night the day before had been totally swept away by the happy atmosphere of the New Year. I was conscious of nothing except that the various gods of heaven and earth were enjoying the ritual offerings and all the incense that burned in their honor. Comfortably tipsy by now, they staggered through the sky and prepared to shower the people of Lu Town with infinite blessings.

FEBRUARY 7, 1924

Upstairs in a Wineshop

While making a trip from north China down into the southeast, I detoured a bit to visit the area where I was born and had grown up. And so it was that I arrived in S-town. It was the midst of winter and a recent snowfall had rendered the landscape bleak and clear. S-town was only ten miles from my home town, less than half a day by boat, and I had once put in a year here teaching school.[1]

A comfortable sense of freedom from my normal round of duties gave such impetus to the nostalgia that assailed me that I ended up checking into a place called the Luosi, a hotel that had not been here back in my teaching days. Since S-town wasn't very large to begin with, I quickly made the rounds on foot as I hunted up a few former colleagues I thought might still be around. It turned out, however, that they had long since scattered to who-knows-where. Then I sauntered over to see the school where I had taught. It had so changed, in both name and appearance, that it no longer felt the least bit familiar. Thus, before two hours were out, my initial homecoming enthusiasm had waned completely. I decided that my detour had been a waste of time and rather regretted having come.

The Luosi rented rooms but sold no food. Meals had to be ordered in from the outside, and the one I got was as tasteless as sawdust. Outside my window, withered moss clung to a stain-mottled wall above which there was nothing to relieve the monotonous pallor of the leaden sky, a pallor emphasized by the light snow that had begun dancing in the wind.

Since I hadn't eaten enough lunch and had nothing to occupy

First published in the Shanghai periodical *The Short Story Magazine*, vol. 15, no. 5, dated May 1924.

1. Lu Xun spent the years 1902–1909 as a foreign student in Japan. Upon his return to China, he taught physiology and chemistry for a year at the Zhejiang Normal School in Hangzhou, some thirty-odd miles from his native Shaoxing. Then during the period 1909–1911, he was engaged as a teacher and dean of studies in the Shaoxing High School. In many of his writings, "S-town" stands loosely for Shaoxing and its environs. The stories, of course, are fictional and reflect only in an approximate way the actual events of Lu Xun's life.

my time, my thoughts turned quite naturally to the *Gallon,* a little two-storied wineshop where my face had once been a familiar one. It occurred to me that this new hotel couldn't be far from it. I locked my door, went outside, and headed off to find the *Gallon.* It wasn't that I wanted to get intoxicated, but simply that I wanted to escape, if only for a moment, that awful nothing-to-do feeling that so often besets the traveler.

It was still there too—the same battered old sign, the same cramped and dingy downstairs room. From the manager on down, however, there wasn't a single person I recognized. As far as the *Gallon* was concerned, I had been transformed into a newcomer.

Nonetheless, I walked over to the corner of the room, placed my hand on the bannister, and climbed the stairs I had trod so many times before to the little room on the second floor. Just as I remembered, there were five small tables. The only change was that the latticed window at the rear had been torn out and replaced by a pane of glass.

"A catty of Shaoxing.[2] To eat? Ten fried beancurd cakes, and don't skimp on the hotsauce!" Saying this to the waiter who had followed me up, I made straight for the table under the back window. Since the room was empty, I was free to pick the best seat—a lofty perch by the window from which I could look down on the abandoned courtyard out back. As I think back on it, that yard probably didn't belong to the wineshop. I had gazed down on it many times before, and sometimes in snowy weather just like today's, too. But now, to forgetful eyes that had become accustomed to the scenery of north China, there were things in that courtyard well worth marveling at. Several old plum trees were doggedly blossoming in the midst of the snow as though oblivious to the rigors of winter, and next to a pavilion that had long since collapsed, a camellia showed more than a dozen red blooms against thick, dark green leaves. Fire-bright against the snow, it stood there in all its grandeur, passionate and proud, seeming to scorn the wanderer's willingness to have ventured so far from home. At this point, I suddenly recalled how moist the snow is here in my homeland. It glistens brightly and will stick to any-

2. Shaoxing is famous for the manufacture of the liquor that bears its name. The local distillery is a present-day tourist attraction.

thing, nothing like the dry powdery snow of north China that flies up and fills the sky with a white mist whenever the wind picks up.[3]

"Wine . . . for . . . the . . . guest," said the waiter slowly as he arranged cup, chopsticks, winepot, bowl, and saucer. The Shaoxing had arrived. I turned back toward the table and poured myself a cup. It occurred to me that while it was true the north wasn't my home, the south wasn't my home anymore either, for I was treated as a guest here too. No matter how the dry snow of the north scattered in the wind, no matter how the moist snow of the south clung to things—none of that had anything to do with me. Somewhat dejected at the thought, I took a very satisfying sip of wine. The flavor was authentic, and the beancurd cakes were done to a turn, but the hotsauce, sad to say, was watery and weak. The people of S-town have never understood what a spicy cuisine is all about.

Perhaps because it was only the afternoon, no aroma of wine permeated the shop. Even after I had downed my third cup, the upstairs was still empty, save for myself and four unoccupied tables. Gazing at the abandoned courtyard outside, I began to feel even more lonely. And yet, I really didn't want anyone to join me either. And so, when I heard footsteps on the stairs, I could not help but feel irritated. I didn't regain my composure until I saw that it was only the waiter. Sitting there alone, I drank two more cups of wine.

The next time, the footsteps were far too slow to be those of the waiter. I was sure that another patron had arrived. I waited until I thought he must have reached the landing and then, somewhat apprehensively, raised my head to get a good look at this alien companion of mine. I rose from my seat with a start. I had never imagined it would prove to be an old friend—that is, if he would still let me call him that. No doubt about it, the man who had come up was an old schoolmate of mine. After graduation, when I was a teacher, he had once been my colleague too. The only thing about him that had really changed was his movement: he had become noticeably sluggish, nothing like the forceful and agile Lü Weifu I had known in years gone by.

"Weifu, is that you? I never expected to meet you here."

---

3. Lu Xun had previously mentioned this peculiarity of northern snow in "Some Rabbits and a Cat."

"What, can that really be you? Who would have thought . . ."

I invited him to sit down. To my surprise, he actually seemed to hesitate a bit before joining me. My first reaction was simply to consider his behavior a bit odd, but then I began to feel somewhat saddened and even offended. I studied him more closely: same disheveled hair, same long squarish face, but grown old and thin. His spirits seemed subdued too—one might even have said enfeebled. Yes, beneath those thick black brows of his, the life had gone out of his eyes. And yet as he surveyed his present surroundings, the moment he caught sight of the abandoned courtyard, those eyes blazed with that same old flame with which he had once been able to transfix people. I had often seen that look in our school days.

"Well, Weifu," I began enthusiastically, albeit a bit unnaturally, "it must be a good ten years this time. A while back, I heard you were in Jinan, but I was too darned lazy to get a letter off to you."[4]

"Yes, well it was the same with me too. I'm at Taiyuan now.[5] Been there over two years already. Mother's with me. It was when I came back down here to get her that I discovered you'd long since moved away—disappeared without a trace."

"What are you up to in Taiyuan?"

"Family tutor in a fellow provincial's home."

"And before that?"

"Before that?" He fished a cigarette out of his pocket, put it between his lips, lit it, took a puff, exhaled, and then gazed musing into the cloud of smoke. "Didn't do anything really, except a bunch of stuff that didn't amount to anything. Actually, it's the *same* as having done nothing."

In his turn, he asked me about my own situation since we had last met. While I was setting it out for him, I told the waiter to bring another pair of chopsticks and a cup. I ordered another two catties of Shaoxing and passed my own over to him in the meantime. We had never stood on ceremony in the past, but now when it came to ordering the food, we outdid each other in insisting that "you order what *you* want" until things got so mixed up we couldn't tell who had ordered what. We had to depend on the

---

4. Jinan, capital of Shandong Province, is about five hundred miles north of the two friends' homeland.

5. Taiyuan, capital of Shanxi Province, is something more than seven hundred miles northwest of their homeland.

waiter's reading it back to us to determine that four dishes had in fact been ordered: beans cooked with fennel, jellied meat, fried beancurd, and dried black carp.

"As soon as I got back, I realized what an absurd figure I must cut," he said with a wan smile, holding his cigarette aloft with one hand and grasping his winecup with the other. "When I was a kid, I used to think that bees and flies were absurd and pathetic. I'd watch the way they'd light someplace, get spooked by something, and then fly away. After making a small circle, they'd always come back again and land just exactly where they had been before. Who could have imagined that someday, having made my own small circle, I would fly back too? And who would ever have expected that you would do the same thing? Couldn't you have managed to fly a little farther away?"

"Hard to say. I'm probably no different than you—just made my little circle before coming back," I answered with a smile as wan as his own. "But why have you flown back *this* time?"

"Just to do some more stuff that doesn't amount to anything." He downed a cup of wine with a single gulp, took several drags on his cigarette, and opened his eyes a bit wider. "Doesn't amount to a darned thing really, but I suppose it won't do any harm to tell you about it."

The waiter came upstairs with our order. When he had it all set down, it covered the whole table. Permeated with the warm aroma of cigarette smoke and fried beancurd, the little upstairs room now assumed a lively air. Outside the window, the snow was falling even thicker than before.

"You probably know I had a little brother who died when he was three and was buried out in the countryside. I can't even remember what he looked like now, but according to Mother, he was a lovable little guy who got along very well with me. Down to this very day, her eyes mist up whenever she speaks of him. Well anyway, this spring we got a letter from a cousin saying that the riverbank was eroding fast, and if we didn't do something pretty soon, his grave would slide into the river. As soon as Mother found out—she knows enough characters to read letters—she was worried sick. Couldn't sleep nights. But what could *I* do? No money, no time. I was helpless.

"The situation dragged on and on until finally I was able to take advantage of the New Year's vacation to come back down and rebury him." Draining another cup of wine, Weifu looked out the window. "When would you ever see anything like this up north—flowers blooming in all that snow, the ground underneath not even frozen?

"Well anyway, day before yesterday I bought a little coffin in town (I thought the original must have long since rotted away), picked up some cotton batting and quilts, hired four grave diggers, and set out to rebury him. Suddenly I began to feel very positive about the whole thing. Now I actually *wanted* to dig up the grave, wanted to have a look at the dead bones of the little brother who had once been so close to me. I'd never quite had such feelings before in my entire life.

"When we got to the gravesite, sure enough, the river water had eaten away at the bank until it was less than two feet from the mound. And what a pitiful little grave mound it was, too. No one had added any dirt to it for over two years, and it was pathetically flat. With an air of command, I stood there in the snow, pointed at it, and gave the order: 'Open it up!' Coming from me, such an authoritative command had an incongruous ring, for I'm a very run-of-the-mill kind of man, not at all accustomed to telling people what to do. But the grave diggers didn't seem to find anything in the least odd about my giving commands. They simply started digging.

"Once they had the mound open, I went over and looked inside. As I had expected, the coffin was almost gone—transformed into shreds of rotting wood. Heart beating wildly, I carefully brushed aside what was left of it, so that I might be able to see my brother. To my surprise, however, there was nothing there, absolutely nothing! The quilt he'd been wrapped in, the clothes he'd worn, his skeleton—all gone. I had always heard that the hair is the last part of the body to rot. 'Perhaps there's still some hair left,' I thought to myself as I knelt down and sifted through the dirt around the place where I thought the pillow must have been. Nothing there either. He had disappeared without leaving a trace!"

I noticed that Weifu's eyes were slightly red, but immediately realized that this signaled nothing more than the fact he had had too much to drink. While we were talking, he had eaten next to nothing but had continued to down cup after cup of wine, and must have long since gone through a good catty or more. The alcohol seemed to put new life into him, both physically and spiritually. He was now beginning to resemble the old Weifu I used to know. Swinging around in my chair, I ordered another two catties of wine; then I turned back and, sitting directly across from my old friend, listened in silence as he continued.

"Actually, at that point, I really didn't have to go through with it. I could simply have smoothed the grave over, sold the coffin, and that would have been the end of it. To be sure, trying to get rid of a coffin like that would have looked a bit peculiar, but as long as I didn't ask too much, I'd probably have been able to sell it back to the store where I'd bought it. At the very least, I'd get enough for a drink or two. But I didn't even try.

"Instead, I spread the quilt out in the new coffin just as I had originally planned, took some dirt from the spot where my brother's body had lain, wrapped it in cotton batting, and put the resulting package inside the quilt. Then I had the coffin moved to the graveyard where my father is buried. I had them bury it next to him. This time I had the coffin enclosed in bricks to make a good tight seal. Had to spend most of my day yesterday supervising the workmen. At any rate, it's over and done with, and at least I've done enough to pull the wool over Mother's eyes and set her mind at rest.

"Hey, why are you looking at me like that? Do you blame me for being so different from the old Lü Weifu who lives in your memory? I can understand your feelings. I too can still remember how it was when we were young, how we used to go to the City Temple together and yank the beards off the statues of the gods, and how we'd often argue the whole day about this or that way of reforming China, until we got so worked up we even came to blows. But now, I am as you see me—a man who goes through the motions of living without taking anything seriously. Sometimes it occurs to me that if my friends from back then were to see me now, they'd disown me. But I am what I am." He fished out another cigarette, dangled it between his lips, and lit up.

"I can tell from your eyes that you still have hopes I'll do something to realize some of our old ideals. Though I'm much more insensitive than I used to be, I can still sense some things by the way a man looks at me. And I'm grateful for your faith in me too. But at the same time, it makes me anxious for fear that when all is said and done, I'll let down those old friends who, like you, continue to think well of me to this very day."

He paused in his recitation, took several drags on his cigarette, and then resumed in slow, measured tones: "Only today, just before I came here to the *Gallon,* I did something else that didn't amount to anything, but at least it was something I wanted to do. It had to do with an old neighbor of ours by the name of Changfu. He was the boatman who lived on the east side of our place. Had a daughter named Ah-shun. You probably saw her now and then when you used to come by to see me. But she was so young back then that you probably didn't give her a second glance. Didn't turn into any great beauty when she grew up, either—just an ordinary kind of oval face that was a bit drawn and somewhat on the sallow side. But those *eyes* of hers! And those long lashes! The whites of her eyes were as clear as a cloudless sky at night. And I'm talking about a northern sky on a night when there's no wind. We have nothing to compare to it down here.

"Ah-shun was a very capable girl, too. Lost her mother when she was eleven or so. From then on, the care of her younger brother and younger sister fell entirely on her. And then of course, she had to attend to her father's needs too. She did it all, and she did it well. Knew how to save a penny, too. After she took over the management of the household, the family's finances gradually got onto a better footing. There was hardly a neighbor around who didn't have a good word for Ah-shun. Even Changfu would often say how grateful he was to have a daughter like her.

"Well, at any rate, when I was on the point of setting out to come back down here this time, my mother started thinking about Ah-shun. Funny what long memories old people have. She said she remembered a time when Ah-shun had wanted a red velvet flower to put in her hair. Seemed that she'd seen another girl wearing one and decided that she'd like one too. But she couldn't find any place that sold them. She bawled and bawled until Changfu finally gave her a beating. Went around with red and swollen eyes for a couple of days afterwards.

"Artificial flowers like that come from outside the province and if she couldn't find one even in S-town, then she certainly wouldn't be able to find it anywhere else. As long as I was coming down this way, Mother told me to buy her one somewhere along the way. Well that was one task I didn't mind in the least. As a matter of fact, I rather looked forward to it, for I honestly felt like doing something for Ah-shun myself.

"When I was down here the year before last to pick up Mother and take her back up north with me, I happened by Changfu's place one day and, somehow or other, struck up a conversation with him.[6] The upshot was that he invited me to stay for a snack, a bowl of cereal made out of buckwheat flour. He made a point of telling me they made theirs with white sugar. Think about that: a fisherman who's able to keep white sugar in the house can't be any pauper, that's for sure. As a matter of fact, you could say he must be eating rather well. Changfu kept pressing me to sit down until I couldn't very well say no. But I agreed only on the condition that he give me a small bowl. Well, he wasn't born yesterday and probably knew what I meant, so he said to his daughter: 'Ah-shun, you know these educated people—don't know what a real meal is, so make sure you use a small bowl. And don't hold back on the sugar either!'

"When she brought it out, I almost fell off my chair. That bowl was huge. There was easily enough in it to keep my mouth on duty the whole day. But then I saw Changfu's bowl and realized that mine really was small by comparison. I'd never eaten buckwheat cereal in my whole life and didn't find it exactly palatable when I tasted it now, but there was no denying it *was* sweet. Looking as casual about it as I could, I downed a few mouthfuls and was just about to set aside my bowl when I happened to catch a glimpse of Ah-shun standing over in the corner. I lost my nerve immediately, for she was watching me with a mixture of fear and hope, probably afraid that she hadn't made it just right, but at the same time hoping that I'd like it. I knew that if I left over half the bowl, she would feel terribly disappointed, and guilty as well.

"Through sheer will power, I widened my throat as much as I could and crammed that cereal down as fast as it would go, almost as fast as Changfu himself. For the first time in my life I understood what a painful thing forced feeding is. For unpleasantness, I could remember nothing that came even close—except, perhaps, once during my childhood when I had to eat a bowl of tapeworm medicine mixed with brown sugar.

"And yet I didn't mind in the least, for when Ah-shun came to take my bowl, that smile of utter satisfaction, which she was doing her best to hold in, more than repaid any discomfort I may have

6. In 1919 Lu Xun went back to Shaoxing from Beijing, sold the family property, and took his wife and mother north to live with him. This trip is also reflected in "Hometown."

suffered. Though I left feeling so bloated that I couldn't get to sleep that night and had one nightmare after the other, I still wished Ah-shun nothing but the best and hoped that, for her sake, the world would take a turn for the better. Almost immediately, however, I laughed at myself for entertaining such thoughts, for I realized that they were simply vestiges of the old dreams I'd entertained in days gone by. After that, I put her completely out of mind.

"I hadn't known that she'd once gotten a beating over an artificial velvet flower, but hearing my mother bring it up, my experience with the buckwheat cereal came back to mind and the memory of it made me especially diligent on Ah-shun's behalf. I searched the town over in Taiyuan without finding one. It wasn't until I got to—"

Shish! Outside the window, an accumulation of snow that had been weighing upon a camellia branch, bending it down into an arc, now slid to the ground as the branch stretched itself straight out, showing off its dark glistening leaves and blood-red blossoms. The leaden sky was even darker now and you could hear chirping everywhere: dusk was fast approaching and, unable to find any food on the snow-blanketed ground, birds now hurried back to their nests for the night.

"—until I got to Jinan," he continued after turning to look out the window, "that I managed to find velvet flowers. I had no idea whether they were like the one she'd taken a beating for, but they *were* velvet. And since I didn't know whether she preferred lighter or darker hues, I bought her a bright red one and a pale pink one.

"It was only this afternoon, right after lunch, that I went to look her up. Put off my departure a whole day just to do it. The house was still there, but as I looked at it, there seemed to be something that wasn't quite right. Dismissing that as my own subjective feeling, I walked closer and saw Changfu's son and second daughter, Ah-zhao, standing in the doorway. They were both grown now. Ah-zhao had developed into a young woman who looked nothing like her elder sister. Looked more like some sort of witch.

"When she saw me coming toward her, she shot inside like a bolt. I learned from the son that Changfu wasn't at home. 'How about your elder sister?' He immediately opened his eyes into a wide and angry stare and asked what business I had with her. He suddenly looked so vicious you would have thought he was a wild animal ready to pounce on me to tear the flesh from my body with bared fangs. Trying to smooth things over as best I could, I left in a hurry. I never have the guts to see things through any more . . .

"You probably don't know this, but I'm much more afraid of calling on people than I used to be. You see, now that I *know* what a contemptible wretch I am, I even despise myself. Sure, people may not come right out and *say* anything to me, but knowing how they must feel about me, what's the point in going to see them? Deliberately making them uncomfortable? Despite all that, I felt this was one task I had to see through. After wracking my brains for a while, I walked over to the firewood store diagonally across from their place. Old Granny Laofa was still there. She recognized me and, much to my surprise, invited me in. After we'd exchanged greetings, I explained why I had come back to S-town and why I was looking for Changfu.

"She sighed and said, 'Too bad Ah-shun wasn't lucky enough to get to wear your flowers.' Granny Laofa then told me the whole story, from beginning to end.

" 'It was probably around spring last year,' she began, 'that Ah-shun began lookin' all weak and pale. Later on, she took to cryin' a lot. When they asked her why, she wouldn't say. Sometimes she'd cry the whole night. Finally, Changfu couldn't take it anymore and blew his top. Cursed her out for stayin' an old maid too long, and said it was this that was makin' her crazy. Come fall, somethin' that started out as just a cold ended up gettin' so bad Ah-shun couldn't even get out of bed. Wasn't till a few days before she died that she finally told her dad what was really wrong. Said that for a long time she'd been the way her mother used to be—spittin' up blood and breakin' into night sweats. She'd hidden it all that time so as not to worry him.

" 'And then one night, her uncle, Changgeng, came round tryin' to borrow money—he did that a lot. He wouldn't take no for an answer. When Ah-shun wouldn't give 'im any, Changgeng gave a mean laugh and said, "Don't get so uppity there. I'm a helluva lot better than the man they've got picked out for *you!*" After that, Ah-shun got really down in the dumps. Such a modest girl she was. Rather than askin' round to get the facts about this man her dad was supposed to have picked out, she just bawled. Changfu finally found out how she'd been taken in by Changgeng and told her the truth about what a fine fellow he'd lined up for her. By then, though, the harm'd been done. You could tell she didn't really believe what her dad said because she came back with: "It's a good thing I'm in the shape I am, 'cause now it don't matter one way or the other."

" 'If the man he'd picked for her wasn't a match for Changgeng, that'd be enough to scare anybody to death! Not even a match for a *chicken thief*? What sort of excuse for a man would that be? I got to see her intended in person when he came to Ah-shun's funeral. Had nice clean clothes and wasn't all that hard to look at either. Tears in his eyes, he told everybody there how he'd poled a boat almost half his life. Scrimped and saved until he'd finally put enough by to buy himself a wife. And then she went and died on 'im. You could tell he was a good man and that all that stuff Changgeng had said was nothin' but a pack of lies. What a pity that Ah-shun should believe that bastard's crap and go lose her life for nothin'.' The old lady finished it all up by telling me: 'If you wanted to put it on anything, you'd have to put it on Ah-shun's bad fate.'

"Well, whatever the case, I was through with my part of it. But what was I to do with the flowers? I asked Granny Laofa if she would give them to Ah-zhao. Since Ah-zhao had treated me like a wild wolf or worse, I really didn't *feel* like letting her have them. So then why did I? Because that way I'd be able to tell Mother how delighted she was. What's it all amount to anyway? Right now, all I've got to worry about is muddling through till New Year's is over and then I can go back to teaching my *thus-spoke-the-Master* and *so-states-the-Poetry-Classic*."[7]

"You're teaching the *classics*? I asked in astonishment.

"Of course. Did you think I was still teaching ABCD?[8] At first I had two students, one studying the *Poetry Classic* and the other doing *The Mencius*.[9] Later on a third one joined us, a girl. She's reading *Maxims for Young Ladies*.[10] I don't even teach mathemat-

---

7. Italicized words translate the four-character phrase *ziyue shiyun*, a shorthand reference to classical learning. The friends, of course, consider all such erudition reactionary and useless. The "Master" is Confucius.

8. "ABCD" is shorthand for Western learning, and the original text prints it in roman type.

9. Mencius (372–279 B.C.) is sometimes referred to as the "St. Paul" of Confucianism, because without him no ongoing tradition would have grown and developed.

10. An anonymous text known in several different versions.

ics anymore. It's not that I don't want to, it's just that their fathers don't want me to."

"I never expected that you'd actually be teaching that kind of thing."

"That's what their fathers *want* them to be taught. I'm an outsider, so it's all the same to me. What's it all amount to anyway? All I have to do is muddle along as best . . ."

His entire face was flushed now and he seemed slightly inebriated. The gleam in his eyes, however, had subsided. I gave in to a light sigh and for the moment could think of nothing to say. There was a flurry of sound on the staircase as several newcomers crowded their way up. First in line was a short man with bulging jowls. Second, a tall fellow with a conspicuous red nose.

Others followed behind them, stomping up the stairs with such force that the whole building trembled. I turned and looked at Lü Weifu just as he also turned to look at me. I told the waiter to total up our bill.

"Does it give you enough to get by on?" I asked as I prepared to leave.

"Yes, it . . . To tell the truth, I get twenty a month and don't get by all that well."

"What do you plan on doing after this?"

"After this? I don't know. Just think, not a single one of the hopes and dreams we had back then has worked out, has it? I don't know anything anymore. I don't even know what tomorrow's going to bring, or even the next moment . . ."

The waiter came up and handed me the check. Not nearly so deferential as when I first arrived, he simply threw me a single glance and then, looking utterly uninterested, stood to one side and smoked while I took out the money to pay.

Weifu and I walked out of the wineshop together, but since his hotel lay in the opposite direction to mine, we parted at the door. As I walked off toward the Luosi, with the cold wind and snowflakes blowing against my face, I felt refreshed. Judging from the color of the sky, it was already dusk. Along with the surrounding buildings and streets, I too became woven into a pure white and ever-shifting web of snow.

FEBRUARY 16, 1924

A Happy Family

—In the manner of Xu Qinwen

"He writes only when inspired, and his works are like the rays of the sun, welling up out of an infinite source of light—not fleeting sparks struck from a stone. Only a man like that is a *true* artist, and only works such as *he* produces are true art. And me? What kind of work am *I* doing?" Having arrived at this point in his train of thought, he suddenly sat bolt upright in bed.

Previous to this, he had thought things over and had decided that he would have to write a potboiler in order to bring in enough money to make ends meet. He had also decided that he would submit it to the publishers of *Happiness Monthly,* since their rates were fairly generous. But if he were going to get them to accept it, then potboiler or no, it would still need some sort of theme. All right then, if it had to have a theme, then a theme it would have.

"Let's see, the greatest problem young people have on their minds today is . . . uh . . . Well there's probably a lot more than one. No doubt there's a whole string of them. Seems likely, though, that a lot of those problems ought to have *something* to do with love, marriage, and the family . . . Yes, those are the things a lot of the youth out there are down in the dumps about, the things they're discussing at this very moment. Okay, then, family it will be, but how will I treat it? Let's see . . . No, that won't do. Editors wouldn't accept it. Besides, what's the point in writing about anything unpleasant?" He jumped out of bed, walked the four or five steps to his desk, sat down, pulled out a piece of green-lined paper, and without the slightest hesitation—albeit in a manner that seemed to announce that he was wasting his great talents—wrote down the title of his story: "A Happy Family."

His pen abruptly screeched to a halt. He raised his head and stared at the ceiling as he prepared a place where this happy family

---

First published in the Shanghai periodical *The Ladies' Journal (Funü zazhi),* vol. 10, no. 3, dated March 1924. The attribution "In the manner of . . ." is explained in the author's own postscript to this story.

of his might be installed. "Beijing," he thought to himself, "will never do—dead as a doornail. Even the air in Beijing is dead. Could put up a high wall all around the happy family, but it still wouldn't be able to wall out all that dead air. Nope, just won't do. Jiangsu or Zhejiang? Trouble is people are worried about a civil war breaking out down there any day. And things are even worse in Fujian. How about Sichuan or Guangdong? No, there's fighting going on there this very minute. I've got it, Shandong or maybe Henan. Oh, oh . . . wait a minute, they'd get kidnapped there, and if one of them got kidnapped, I'd end up with a very *un*happy family. Rents are too high in the foreign concessions in Shanghai and Tianjin. Let's see . . . How about just putting them in another country altogether? Hold on now, this is getting ridiculous.

How about Yunnan or Guizhou then? No, they'd have a problem with transportation there." Wrack his brains as he would, he could not come up with a decent place for them to live. He was about to settle on a hypothetical place called *"A,"* but then he thought: "There are lots of people around who are dead set against using the letters of Western alphabets to stand for place names, or names of characters in a story. Probably be better if I don't do it on this one—safer that way. Okay then, where *will* I put them? How about the Chahar-Jilin-Heilongjiang area? —No, mounted bandits all over the place. Won't do either!" For the second time, wrack his brains as he would, he could not come up with a decent place for them to live. At this point he finally came to a decision: the locale for his "Happy Family" would just have to be that hypothetical place called *"A."*

"No matter how you look at it, my happy family will have to live in *'A.'* That much is non-negotiable. The family will simply consist of a couple—the master and mistress of their household. The marriage will be the *free* kind that they've undertaken themselves, rather than some traditional arranged thing worked out by the parents. They'll draw up a *contract* before the wedding. It will be very detailed with more than forty clauses in it, and that's precisely why there'll be such a conspicuous degree of equality between them, why they'll be so completely free. What's more, they'll both be highly educated, glamorous, and refined. Let's see now . . . returned students from Japan aren't that common anymore. All right, let them be returned students from the West. The master of the house will wear a Western suit with a stiff collar that's always white as snow. The wife's hair will always be freshly waved, light and fluffy as a swallow's nest. Her teeth will be locked in a perpetual ivory-white smile. But her clothes will be Chinese."

"No, no! That won't do! Twenty-five catties!"[1]

He heard a man's voice outside the window. Without thinking, he turned to look and was immediately aware of the window curtain hanging in front of his face. Streaming through it, the sun so dazzled his eyes that he couldn't see anything clearly and was conscious only of the sound of small bundles of wood being thrown to the ground. "Nothing to do with me." He turned back to his desk and went on with his own thoughts. "*What* twenty-five catties? — Well, since they're both very refined and glamorous, they'll be lovers of literature and the arts. From earliest childhood on, they've grown up in a happy environment, so they don't care for Russian fiction. Most Russian fiction talks about the lower classes and really wouldn't suit my happy family . . . *What* twenty-five catties? —Let's see, what kind of thing *do* they read? Byron? Keats? No, neither poet is really quite right for them and . . . I've got it! They read *An Ideal Husband.*[2] Haven't seen the book myself, but since even university professors are praising it, stands to reason that they'd go for it too. *She* reads it and *he* reads it too. They have his-and-her copies. One copy plus one copy makes two copies they have in the house, and . . ." He became aware that his stomach felt a bit empty. Putting down his pen, he put his elbows on the desk and supported his head between his hands, making it look like a world globe supported on twin pivots.

"The two of them are just sitting down to lunch. The table's spread with a snow-white cloth, and the cook is serving the meal, a Chinese meal . . . *What* twenty-five catties? —To hell with it. Why does the food have to be Chinese? Yes, they've decided on a Chinese diet because foreigners have said that Chinese food is the most sophisticated, tasty, and healthy food that one can eat. All right then, here comes the cook with the first course. Ah, but what *is* that first course?"

---

1. A catty is approximately equivalent to one and one-third pounds.

2. Not really "a book," this was the Chinese translation of Oscar Wilde's four act play by the same title. It was published serially in *New Youth* beginning with the second issue, Oct. 15, 1915.

"Firewood . . ."

He turned his head with a start and saw the mistress of his own family standing by his left shoulder, her peevish eyes riveted upon him.

"Well, what is it now?" From his point of view, she represented merely an intrusion inhibiting his literary creation, and he was more than a little put out with her.

"We've used up all the firewood and I bought a little more. The last time it was still ten catties for two-strings-four.[3] Today he wants two-strings-six. I think I'll give him two-five."

"Fine, fine. Two-strings-five."

"He says it's twenty-four and a half catties, but he's cheating. I think I'll pay him for twenty-three and a half, okay?

"Okay, okay, pay him for twenty-three and a half, then!"

"All right then, let's see: five fives are twenty-five, three fives are fifteen, and uh . . ."

"Let me do it. Five times five is twenty-five; three times five is fifteen, and uh . . ." He couldn't do it in his head either. After a moment or so, he snatched up his pen in exasperation and on that same sheet of paper that was headed "A Happy Family" began to do a draft of the bill. After quite some time he lifted his head.

"Five-strings-eight!"

"In that case, I don't have enough. I'm still eight or nine short."

He pulled open the desk drawer, grabbed up all the loose coins with one hand, twenty or thirty at least, and put them all in her outstretched palms. Only after he had watched her go out the door did he turn back toward his desk. His head was so jam-packed with crisscrossed pieces of firewood he thought it was going to burst: 5, 5, 25—a chaos of arabic numerals was indelibly stamped across the front of his brain. He took a deep breath and exhaled with great force, as if by doing so he might clear his head at once of firewood, calculations, and arabic numerals. And, as a matter of fact, his mind did feel much relaxed, and he was able to return to the fantasy world of his own thoughts.

"But what *kind* of Chinese food? It wouldn't do any harm to have them eat something a bit on the exotic side. Things like *Slippery Fried Pork* or *Shrimp Roe* or even *Sea Slugs* are really a bit too run-of-the-mill. I'll not settle for anything as common as that.

3. There were one hundred coins on a full string of cash. Two-strings-four would be 240 cash.

No, I'll say that what *they* like to eat is *Battle of the Dragon and Tiger!* But just what is *Battle of the Dragon and Tiger* anyway? I've heard some say it's a combination of snake meat and cat meat, some sort of Cantonese delicacy served only at large banquets. But I've seen it listed on menus in Jiangsu restaurants too, and I'm pretty sure Jiangsu people don't eat snake meat *or* cat meat. I'll bet it's really what what's-his-name said: frog and eel. Where will I have the master and mistress of my happy family come from? Who gives a hoot anyway? When you come right down to it, eating a bowl of snake and cat meat—or maybe it's frog and eel—will create a happy family image no matter *where* they come from. At any rate, the first course is definitely going to be *Battle of the Dragon and Tiger,* and that's that.

"All right then, at this point there is a platter of *Battle of the Dragon and Tiger* set nicely in the middle of the table. They pick up their chopsticks at precisely the same moment, point at the platter, beam at each other, and say:

'My dear, please.'

'Please, you eat first, my dear.'

'Oh no, please, you!'[4]

"At precisely the same moment they thrust their chopsticks toward the plate and, still in unison, clamp down on bits of snake meat between the tips, and then—no, no, no! No matter how you look at it, snake meat is a bit bizarre. Better make it eel. Okay, that settles it. My *Battle of the Dragon and Tiger* is going to be made from frogs and eels. At precisely the same moment, they pick up morsels of eel that are exactly the same size . . . Five fives are twenty-five and three fives . . . *Forget* about that! —At precisely the same moment, they put the pieces into their mouths and—" Though he tried to block it out, he kept wanting to turn around and see what was going on behind him. He was conscious of a great deal of activity back there, because people had gone tromping past two or three times already. Despite the noisy confusion, however, he doggedly pursued his own train of thought. "This all seems a bit too much. How could such a family even exist? But why does my train of thought keep getting derailed like this? At this rate, I'll never be able to work up my theme, promising as it is. Maybe I don't have to use returned students. A couple

4. In the original text, this imaginary dialogue between the story characters is printed in English.

who'd been educated right here in China would do just as well. Okay, but they'll still both have to be college graduates, refined and glamorous—*very* refined. The man is a writer. The woman's a writer too, or perhaps an admirer of writers. Or how about having the woman be a poet and the man, someone who admires poets and sincerely respects the fairer sex to boot? Or perhaps—" At last he could bear it no longer and finally turned his head.

There, against the side of the bookcase behind him, a stack of cabbages had appeared: three heads on the bottom, two in the middle, and one on top, piled into a perfect letter *"A,"* staring him straight in the face. He gasped in surprise, felt his face suddenly flush as though pricked by pins, and was conscious of thousands of needles jabbing lightly against his spine. "Hyoooo . . ." With a long sigh he managed to blow back this attack of pins and needles and get back to his own thoughts. "*My* happy family will have a commodious house. There will be a storeroom for cabbages and such. The master of the house will have a separate study, lined with bookcases and—it goes without saying—no cabbages anywhere near them. The shelves will be filled with Chinese and foreign books. Prominent among them, of course, will be *An Ideal Husband*—his-and-her copies. There'll be a separate bedroom with a yellow brass bed, or maybe to keep things on the simple side, they'll make do with one of those big elm monstrosities made in Prison Factory One. It's going to be very clean under that bed too!" His glance shot immediately to the area under his own bed.

The firewood had been used up, but a straw rope still lay there, lazily stretched out and looking for all the world like a dead snake.

"Twenty-three and a half catties—" He feared an endless river of firewood was about to burst through the door and flow under the bed. The pieces inside his head seemed to begin rustling again, too. He quickly stood and went over to close the door. No sooner had his hand touched the door, however, than he thought better of it, for such an act would be a bit too precipitous. He contented himself with letting down the grimy door curtain instead. It occurred to him that this act was no less than a master stroke of diplomacy, for by holding to the *Doctrine of the Mean,* he had equally avoided both the insecurity of an *open door policy* and the ill-considered haste of a *policy of isolation.*[5]

---

5. *Doctrine of the Mean* can be taken either as an ordinary conversational phrase or as the title of one of the *Four Books* of the Neo-Confucian school.

"The master of the house always keeps his study closed." He walked back to his desk and sat down. "When the mistress of the house has anything to discuss, she knocks on the study door first and enters only after the master has given his permission. Now that's really the right way to do things. Even if she has come to discuss literature, the mistress still knocks first. One thing you can be sure of is that she never comes barging in with a bunch of cabbages. *'Come in, please, my dear.'*[6] But what happens when the master of the house doesn't have the time for a chat about literature? Can I have him just up and ignore her? Just sit there listening while she keeps banging away at the door? No, that probably won't do. Maybe it's all written down somewhere in *An Ideal Husband.* I'll bet that's one hell of a book. If I get paid for this story, I'll go out and buy a copy myself."

WHACK!

He sat bolt upright, knowing from experience that this was the sound of his wife's hand coming down on the head of their three-year-old daughter.

"In *my* happy family—" He heard the child's wails but continued to sit bolt upright in his chair, doggedly pursuing his thoughts. "—children will come late, quite late. Or perhaps it would be better for them to have none at all. Then there'd just be the two of them with absolutely *nothing* to tie them down. Better yet, how about having them live in a hotel where everything would be taken care of for them, absolutely nothing to—" He heard the wails grow louder, stood up, and slipped through the door curtain. "The reason that Marx was a great man is that even in the midst of his children's crying and wailing he was still able to complete *Das Kapital.*" He walked through the other room, opened the storm door, and was immediately struck by the strong smell of kerosene. Face down, the child was lying to the right of the door. Upon seeing her father, she immediately broke into another loud wail.

"It's all right, don't cry. There's Daddy's good girl. Don't cry."

He took her up in his arms, turned around, and saw that the mistress of the house was still standing on the left side of the door. Ramrod straight, hands on her hips, filled with the rich vitality of rage, she looked as though she were ready to do a set of calisthenics.

"Even a child like you tries to make my life miserable! Don't

6. Italicized words are English in the original text.

know how to help out, just know how to mess things up! You would have to go and knock over the kerosene lamp, wouldn't you? What do you think we're going to use for light tonight?"

"Okay, okay, don't cry." He relegated the trembling sound of his daughter's sobs to the back of his mind and, gently stroking her head, carried her back to his desk. "There's a good girl." At this point he set her down on the floor, pulled out his chair, and maneuvered her until she was standing between his knees. "Come on now, be a good girl. Don't cry. Daddy'll do *cat-washing-its-face* for you." He raised his hands, stretched his neck way out, stuck his tongue out in the direction of his palms and pretended to lick them. Then, palms toward his face, he traced circles with first one hand and then the other.

"Hah, hah! Flower, Flower!" She chortled.

"Right, right, just like our cat, Flower."

He did a few more circles for good measure. Though she was all smiles as she watched, tears still clung to the corners of her eyes. It suddenly occurred to him that this lovable, innocent little face—though somewhat smaller in outline—looked exactly as her mother's had just five years before, especially the crimson lips. It had been on just such a clear and bright winter's day as this that she had listened while he vowed to overcome all obstacles and sacrifice everything on her behalf. She had smiled at him, just like this, with tears clinging to the corners of her eyes. And now, daughter between his knees, he just sat there in a daze, as though he had possibly had a bit too much to drink.

"Ah, those adorable lips," he mused.

The door curtain was suddenly raised, and the firewood delivery began. Coming to with a start, he focused his eyes and saw that the tears were still hanging at the corners of his daughter's eyes. As she stood there watching him, her little crimson lips were slightly parted just as her mother's had been. "Lips . . ." He glanced away and saw that the firewood was coming in. "I'll bet that later on you'll be *five fives are twenty-five-ing* it too," he thought to himself. "Worse yet, you'll have those same peevish eyes." He angrily snatched up the green-lined draft paper bearing the title of his story, the same paper that was covered with his calculations. He scrunched it up several times to make it soft and then used it to wipe his daughter's eyes and nose. "There's Daddy's good girl, you go and play now," he said, pushing her away. At the same time he wadded the draft paper into a tight little ball and testily threw it into the wastebasket.

Immediately, however, he felt a twinge of guilt, turned and watched his daughter walk forlornly out the door. The sound of wood being delivered rang in his ears. Trying to pull himself together, he turned back to his desk, closed his eyes, managed to banish a jumble of stray thoughts from his mind, and sat there looking calm and collected.

An oval black flower with orange center appeared at the left corner of his left eye and floated rightward across his line of sight until it disappeared. Next came a bright green one with dark center. And then a group of six cabbages rose majestically before him and stacked themselves into a gigantic "A."

FEBRUARY 18, 1924

Postscript

Last year, after reading Xu Qinwen's "The Ideal Mate" in the literary supplement to the *Morning Post,* I conceived the idea for the present story. Moreover, I thought it would be well to use Xu's style in the telling of it. However, it still remained just an idea. Then yesterday the idea came to mind again, and since I happened to have nothing else to do at the time, I wrote it out. Toward the end, however, my story seems to have gone off the track and become a bit too glum. Generally speaking, I believe that Xu's ending is not so somber as this one. But even so, on the whole, I cannot but say that my story is still "in the manner of."[7]

7. In most editions of Lu Xun's works, this postscript does not appear at all or is relegated to obscurity among the notes. When the story first appeared in *The Ladies' Journal,* however, the postscript was appended to the main body of the text. Xu Qinwen had written "The Ideal Mate" *(Lixiang de banlü)* to satirize what he saw as a ridiculous way of thinking, represented by a contest he had seen announced in *The Ladies' Journal* calling for essays on the topic of the ideal mate. Xu's story is a first-person narrative that begins with the arrival of the narrator's friend, who tells him about the contest in question. The narrator then suggests that his friend describe *his* ideal mate while the narrator carefully notes down what he says. The rest of Xu's tale consists of the narrator's record of what his friend says, reported with overtones of sarcasm and humor.

Soap

Bathed in the slant rays of the setting sun, Siming's wife sat with her back to the north window. She and her eight-year-old daughter, Xiu'er, were busily pasting paper coins for the dead. All of a sudden she heard the heavy steps of someone wearing cotton shoes and realized that Siming had just come in. She did not look up, but rather kept right on with her pasting.[1] The sound of his cotton shoes grew louder, closer, until finally she was aware that her husband was standing right next to her and that she could not help but turn around and look. Back bent forward, shoulders hunched high, he was struggling to retrieve something from the depths of the lapel pocket of the full-length gown he wore beneath a sleeveless jacket.

With many a twist and turn, he eventually succeeded in recovering a hand from the depths of his clothing. It held a small rectangular package of sunflower green, which he handed to his wife. No sooner had she taken it than she was aware of an odor she could not quite identify but that was something like an olive. She saw there was a sparkling gold seal on the wrapper along with a few fine-lined bouquet patterns. Xiu'er bounded over straightaway and was about to grab it away for a better look, but Siming's wife immediately pushed her away.

"Been shopping?" she asked, looking at her husband.

"Uh-huh," he answered, looking at the package in her hands.

At this juncture the sunflower green package was opened. Underneath the outside wrapper was a layer of very thin paper. It proved to be sunflower green as well. Only when this second layer was peeled away was the object itself revealed at last: it too was sunflower green and carried a few bouquets of fine-lined patterns, just like those on the outer wrapper. Now one could tell that the thin second layer of paper was actually rice colored. The odor,

---

"Soap" first appeared in two installments published in the literary supplement to the Beijing *Morning Post,* dated March 27 and March 28, 1924.

1. Tinfoil was pasted to paper squares, designs were stamped onto the foil, and then the coins were cut to size and strung together so as to resemble real strings of cash. This money was burned and thereby conveyed to the afterworld, where it would be used by the dead.

which Siming's wife could not quite identify but was something like an olive, grew heavier.

"Well now, this is really good soap," she said, deeply inhaling the aroma of the package. She lifted it to her nose with all the loving care one might exhibit when handling a baby.

"Uh-huh. I want you to use it from now on."

She saw his lips move to form these words but noted that his eyes were fixed on her neck; she seemed to sense a touch of warmth in her cheeks. On occasion, she herself had been conscious of a certain roughness when she ran her fingertips over her neck, especially in the area behind her ears. Actually, she had long since realized that this was the accumulated dirt of many years, but had never particularly minded it. Now, however, under Siming's close scrutiny and face to face with that sunflower green cake of soap with its exotic scent, she could not control that warmth—it grew and grew until it reached the base of her ears. At this point she resolved that after supper she would take that cake of soap and give herself a thorough scrubbing.

"Well, when you come right down to it, there are certain places you can't get all that clean just using soap pods," she said to herself as much as to anyone else.[2]

"Ma, let me have that!" Xiu'er stuck her hand out and grabbed at the sunflower green paper. Her younger sister, Zhao'er, who had been outside playing, also came running up. Siming's wife promptly pushed both girls away. She wrapped the thin inner wrapper around the soap, and then the green outer one around that. Bending over, she placed the package in the topmost cubbyhole of the washstand, checked to make sure it was not going to fall out, and then went back to pasting coins.

"X-u-e-c-h-e-n-g!" Siming, apparently having just remembered something or other, stretched out his voice and called his son. That task completed, he sat down in a high-backed chair across from his wife.

"Xuecheng!" she helped along. Then she broke off her pasting, cocked an ear and listened expectantly: not the barest hint of a response. Seeing her husband floundering there, awash with impa-

2. In the countryside, acacia pods were widely used in place of soap.

tience, she could not help but feel a bit guilty. Cranking her voice as high as it would go, she yelled: *"Shuan'er!"*[3]

This last call proved eminently effective and the *squeak squeak* of approaching leather shoes was soon heard. Before long Shuan'er stood before her. He was wearing a T-shirt. Glistening beads of sweat dripped down his fat round face.

"What were you doing that you didn't hear your dad calling you?" she demanded reproachfully.

"I was practicing my Eight Trigram Boxing."[4] He immediately turned and faced Siming. Standing straight as a writing brush, he looked directly at his father as if to say that he was ready to do anything expected of him.

"Xuecheng, what is an *e-du-fu?*"

"*E-du-fu?* That means a woman who's considered a battle-axe, doesn't it?"

"What an asinine answer!" Siming waxed more than a little wroth. "Am *I* a woman?"

Frightened, Xuecheng retreated a step or two and stood at an even more wooden attention. Although he sometimes thought his father walked a lot like the old men you see in Beijing opera, he had never thought of him as a woman. He knew there must be something terribly amiss about the answer he had given.

"*E-de-fu* is a woman who's a battle-axe! Now that's something I would never have known if I weren't lucky enough to have you around to tell me, would I? This wasn't Chinese, dummy! This was deviltalk! Now let me ask you again: What does *e-du-fu* mean? Do you know or don't you?"

"I . . . I . . . I *don't* know." Xuecheng was even more distressed.

"Hah! Wasted all that money sending you to one of those newfangled academies and you don't even understand a simple English expression. Isn't it fortunate that I picked an academy that touts its 'equal emphasis on speaking ability and listening comprehen-

---

3. This is the son's auspicious name, designed to protect him from the dangers of childhood. The *shuan* means "tied to"; the *er,* "son." His name then connotes being firmly "tied to life." See "Medicine," n. 1 for a very similar name.

4. A regimen combining exercise and martial art. Though now popular both in the West and in China, it is important to remember that Lu Xun regarded this and similar traditions as superstitious claptrap. Trigrams are the traditional combinations of unbroken (male) and broken (female) lines used for divination in conjunction with the *Book of Changes*.

sion'! They haven't managed to teach *you* a solitary thing. The boy who said this was even younger than yourself—couldn't have been more than fourteen or fifteen, but *he* was already able to *chit-chit chat-chat* in English for all he was worth. Yet you don't even understand a simple expression when you *hear* it. And then you've got the nerve to stand there and tell me: 'I don't know'! You go look it up this instant!"

Responding with a *yessir* from somewhere in the depths of his throat, Xuecheng respectfully withdrew.

"The students nowadays are really something," Siming said expansively, after some time had passed. "They give meaning to the word 'insufferable'! Back in the Guangxu period[5] I was one of the staunchest advocates of setting up these modern academies, but never in my wildest dreams did I ever imagine they would go this far off the track. They are forever talking about 'liberation' and 'freedom,' but they teach nothing about solid learning. The only thing they *do* teach is how to play the fool! I don't mind telling you I've put down quite a little money on educating Xuecheng —wasted, every last penny of it.

"I went to a lot of trouble getting him into one of those academies where they claim to blend Chinese and Western learning, where they boast of teaching their English 'with equal emphasis on speaking ability and reading comprehension.' Now, you'd think a program like that would be fairly good, wouldn't you? Hah! In it for a year already and still doesn't even know what *e-du-fu* means. I'll bet they have them reading and memorizing out of dead books, just the same way it's always been. I'll say it now and I'll say it straight out. We ought to close down every last one of them!"

"You're right. It really would be better to close them all," said Siming's wife sympathetically, while continuing to paste paper money.

"Being girls, Xiu'er and her sister don't have to worry about going to any 'academy,' or whatever they want to call them. What business do girls have going to school anyway? That's what Ninth Gramps used to say back when everybody was opposed to education for women. I even attacked him for it, but now I can see that the old folks had the right idea after all. Just think about it—now you can actually see girls walking out on the streets in *broad day-*

---

5. Penultimate reign period of the Qing dynasty, 1875–1908.

light, one group after another![6] And as if that weren't enough to affright the eyes of any proper man, they've taken to bobbing their hair! Those hairbobbers are enough to make a man's blood boil! In plain words, I can make some allowances for soldiers and bandits acting the way they do, but the ones who are *really* throwing this country into chaos are those modern girls! They ought to be given a good lesson, they—"

"Right! It's not enough that men cut off their queues and start looking like Buddhist monks, now the girls have to go cutting their hair and trying to look like nuns."

"Xuecheng!"

Holding a thick little gilt-edged book in both hands, Xuecheng hurried in and offered it respectfully to his father. He pointed to a line on the page and said, "This sounds a little bit like it. It says . . ."

When Siming took the book into his hands and looked at it, he realized it was a dictionary, but the tiny words were printed left to right across the page, not top to bottom in the traditional Chinese way. He frowned, held the book up to the light of the window, squinted, and began to read the line that his son had indicated. "*Name of a mutual aid society established in the eighteenth century.* Hmm . . . no, that's not it. How do you pronounce it?" he asked, indicating the "devil word" before him.

"E-te-fu-luo-si."[7]

"No, no, no, that's not it!" Siming suddenly waxed indignant again. "Now this time pay attention to what I'm saying. It was a bad word, a curse word—a word used to swear at someone like me. Now do you get the idea? Okay then, go look it up!"

"What's going on here? You come at the boy with a riddle out of nowhere and then expect him to know exactly what you want. You have to give him more to go on if you expect him to be able to find it." Seeing Xuecheng's predicament, his mother had begun to feel sorry for the boy and said this, in part, to make peace between father and son, but also because she was beginning to feel a bit put out with her husband.

"It all happened while I was at the *Broadprofit* buying the soap today," said Siming with a sigh. He turned and looked at her.

6. Except on holidays or other special occasions, women of the scholar-gentry class never left the family compound. Wives were referred to as "inside people" *(neiren)*.

7. Odd Fellows, i.e., the Chinese transliteration representing the Independent Order of Odd Fellows.

"There were three students there buying things too. And me? Well, from their point of view, of course, I probably did seem a bit fussy. I looked at six or seven different brands, but they were all over forty cents a cake, so I didn't buy any. There were some other brands for as little as ten cents, but they weren't even worth taking home—no scent. I decided my best course would be to strike a happy mean, and so I picked out that green one at twenty-four cents.

"Now the clerk there was a stuck-up little snob to begin with and had long since started making faces at me, but what really got my goat were those bratty young students laughing and winking at each other while talking that 'devil language.' Later on, when I wanted to tear a package open before paying out my good money for it—all wrapped up like that in foreign paper, how can you tell what the goods are like?—that little snob of a clerk not only refused to let me, but became totally unreasonable and said a lot of nasty stuff that there was no call for. Then those rotten young students all chimed in with *their* talking and laughing. What I want Xuecheng to look up is something that the youngest in the group said. You can tell it must have been something bad because he was looking at *me* when he said it; besides, the rest of them all started to laugh too."

At this point Siming turned his head and faced Xuecheng. "All you have to do is go hunt it up in the 'bad words' section. Now hop to it!"

Responding with a *yessir* from somewhere out of the depths of his throat, Xuecheng respectfully withdrew.

"And yet people still go on clamoring about 'New Culture' this and 'New Culture' that. Haven't brats like those in the store this afternoon been 'cultured' just about enough?" Fixing his eyes on the roof beam, Siming unwound and let go. "There's no morality in society, there's no morality among the students, and if we don't come up with some solution pretty soon, China will be done for! You can't possibly imagine how *shameful* that was!"

"What was?" asked his wife off-handedly.

"The *filial girl,* that's what!"[8] He turned his eyes toward her and continued in tones of high seriousness. "It all happened down-

8. Showing filial respect to one's parents and loyalty to one's ruler was the basis of Confucian social ethics; hence "filial girl" *(xiaonü)* and "filial boy" *(xiaozi)*—or "filial daughter/son"—were standard epithets of moral approbation.

town. There were two beggars. One of them was a girl, eighteen or nineteen by the looks of her—actually it's very unseemly for a girl that age to be begging, but begging she was. The other one was an old lady of sixty or seventy. She was blind and her hair was white. They were sitting on the ground under the eaves of the dry goods store begging from passers by. Most people said she was a filial girl and that the old woman was her grandmother. As soon as the girl got a little something, she'd immediately give it to the old woman, preferring to starve, herself, than to see her grandmother go hungry. And do you think anyone was willing to give alms to a girl as filial as that?" Siming nailed his wife with a probing stare as though testing her degree of sophistication in regard to the ways of the world.

She didn't answer but simply stared back at him as though awaiting his explanation.

At length he answered his own question. "Hmmph! They were not! I watched for a long time but only saw one person give so much as a single penny. The rest just stood around in a big circle and even had the gall to make fun of her. Worse yet, there were two bums in the crowd who had no scruples at all. One of them actually had the gall to say to the other: 'Ah-fa, don't be put off because the goods are dirty. All you've gotta do is buy a couple cakes of soap, give her a good old *rub-a-dub-dub,* and you'd have yourself a pretty nice piece there!' "

"Hmmph!" Siming's wife lowered her head. After a bit she spoke in measured tones: "Did *you* give any money?"

"Who, me? No. I had only a few pennies in my pocket and I'd have been too embarrassed to give her those. You have to remember she was no *ordinary* beggar, and—"

"Hmmph!" Without waiting for him to finish, she slowly stood up and went into the kitchen. The dusk of evening had noticeably thickened; suppertime had arrived.

Siming also stood. He went out into the courtyard. It was brighter outside than in the house. Xuecheng was over by the corner of the wall practicing his Eight Trigram Boxing, for such was the paternal learning Siming had passed on to his son. Taking advantage of the leisure afforded by that period when day begins to blend into night, Xuecheng had dutifully devoted himself to Eight Trigram Boxing on a daily basis for close to half a year now.

Nodding his head ever so slightly in parental approval, Siming put his hands behind his back and paced back and forth at his own leisure. Before long the broad leaves of the only potted evergreen in the courtyard disappeared yet another time into the darkness and stars began to glimmer among the white, burst-catkin clouds. Night had begun.

At this juncture, without conscious effort on his own part, Siming began to brim with emotion. He felt he was on the threshold of some great enterprise: perhaps he would single-handedly launch a campaign against the depravity of modern students, or possibly issue a declaration of war against the corrupt society that surrounded him. His spirits assumed an increasingly martial air. His pace grew longer. The sounds that issued forth from beneath his cotton shoes grew louder and louder until the hen and her chicks, long since asleep in their cage, again began to *cluck-cluck cheep-cheep.*

Lamplight appeared in the living room now, a beacon fire beckoning everyone to supper. The whole family crowded close together around the table in the center of the room. The lamp stood at the foot of the table while Siming occupied the head in solitary majesty. His was the same round, plump face as Xuecheng's, but two additional lines of moustache had been brushed on just above the lips.

Sitting there by himself, surrounded by the vapors rising from the hot food, Siming looked very much like the God of Wealth receiving sacrificial offerings of food in a temple. The left side of the table was occupied by Siming's wife along with her daughter, Zhao'er; the right was taken up by Xuecheng and his sister, Xiu'er. Chopsticks sounded against bowls like a heavy rainfall. Though no one spoke, it was indeed a very lively dinner.

And then Zhao'er knocked over her rice bowl, spilling liquid over a good part of the table. Siming opened wide the thin slits of his eyes and fixed her with a stare that he took back only when she was on the verge of tears. Now he thrust his chopsticks out over the table to fetch that cabbage-heart that had earlier caught his eye —but it was nowhere to be seen. Glancing round, he discovered that Xuecheng was in the process of stuffing it into his wide-open mouth and had to content himself with a bit of leaf instead.

"Xuecheng," he asked, looking his son directly in the eye, "have you found that phrase yet?"

"What phrase? Oh, not yet."

"Hmmph! Look at him! No learning, no understanding—the only thing he knows how to do is eat! Why can't you be like that *filial girl?* There she was reduced to begging and she still managed to be completely filial to her grandmother. Rather do without, herself, than let that granny of hers go hungry. But how would you modern students be expected to know anything about that! You've got no respect for anything. Later on you'll end up just like those bums—"

"Well, come to think of it, there *is* one that could have been it, but I can't be sure. I think maybe what they said was *e-er-te-fu-er.*"[9]

"Yes, yes, that's right! That's it! It sounded something like that, something close to *e-du fu-le.* What's it mean anyway? You're part of that modern student gang too, you must know."

"What's it mean? Umm, I'm not too sure about the meaning."

"Nonsense! You're trying to put something over on me. Every last one of you is no damned good!"

"Even Heaven will not beat anybody when they eat," quoted his wife, breaking her silence. "What's gotten into you today, going around flying off the handle all the time, keeping it up right through our dinner, too! How much do you *expect* children to understand?"

"What are you saying?" Siming was just about to put her in her place too, but when he turned around he saw that his wife's cheeks had tightened up like two little drums and had changed color as well; the light darting out from the triangles of her eyes was enough to strike fear in the heart of any man. He immediately took another tack and said: "I wasn't flying off the handle. I was just letting Xuecheng know that there are certain things he's got to learn to understand."

"How could he *possibly* understand what's on *your* mind?" Now she was really hopping. "If he knew what's on your mind, he'd have long since taken a lantern and gone out to hunt down that *filial girl!* Luckily, you've already bought her *one* cake of soap, so all we'd have to do is to go buy her another and then we could—"

"Nonsense! It was the *bum* who said that."

"I'm not so sure. All we'd have to do is get another cake of soap,

9. Transliteration of the English "old fool."

give her a good *rub-a-dub-dub,* serve her up to you on a silver platter, and then peace would reign in the world once again."

"Just what do you think you're talking about anyway? What's *my* buying soap got to do with anything? I only bought it because I happened to remember you didn't have any and—"

"It's got a *lot* to do with it, if you ask me. You didn't buy that soap for anyone else but that 'filial girl.' Well, for all I care, you can just take it yourself and go do your own *rub-a-dub-dubs* on her. I don't deserve it, and I don't want it! After all, I don't want to steal any glory from that wonderful beggar girl of yours!"

"Just what under the sun do you think you're talking about? You women!" Siming backed off from the subject as best he could. His face was now moist with perspiration, making him look something like his son after a practice session of Eight Trigram Boxing. Siming's perspiration, however, was probably mostly caused by the hot rice he had just swallowed.

"And what about us women? We're a darned sight better than you men. When you aren't cursing out eighteen-year-old girl students, you're singing the praises of eighteen-year-old girl beggars, and there's nothing good on your minds in either case. *Rub-a-dub-dub* indeed! Absolutely shameless!"

"How many times do I have to tell you that it was the *bum* who said that?"

"Oldman Siming!" From the darkness outside, a booming voice bellowed Siming's name.

"Oldman Daotong, is that you?[10] I'll be right there!" Like a prisoner who has just received a reprieve, Siming recognized the explosive voice of the widely renowned He Daotong and happily shouted a welcome to his friend.[11] "Xuecheng, hurry! Go fetch a lantern and show Old Uncle He into the study."[12]

Xuecheng lit a candle and showed Daotong into the study on

10. "Oldman" *(weng)* is a respectful term of address used among friends; as used by these middle-aged friends, it lends a slightly pretentious tone to their exchange.

11. The name Daotong is written the same as a traditional Confucian term meaning "orthodox transmission of the Dao." The effect is similar to that created in English if we should name a man "Orthodoxy Jones," but since all Chinese names have meanings that are more or less understandable, it is not quite so strong. Further, since the surname He can also mean "what," He Daotong's whole name can be understood as "What kind of orthodoxy is this?"

12. "Old Uncle" is a respectful term of address commonly used in reference to older friends of one's father.

the west side of the house. Bu Weiyuan had come with him and tagged along close behind. "Sorry I didn't get out right away to greet you properly. Please forgive me." Still chewing his food, Siming clasped both hands before him and saluted his friends. "How about sharing a little ordinary home cooking with us?"

"We've already taken the liberty of eating before you." Weiyuan trotted up, also clasping his hands before him in salute. "We've hurried over here this very night to settle on the topics for the Eighteenth Essay and Poetry Contest of our Society for the Improvement of the Social Mores. Isn't tomorrow the seventeenth?"

"What? Is today the sixteenth already?" asked Siming with surprise.

"Just look at what an old muddlehead you are!" bellowed Daotong.

"Then we'll have to get our topics over to the newspaper office this very night, so they'll be sure to come out in the morning paper."

"Well, I've drafted a topic for the essay. See what you think." As he spoke, Daotong fished out a strip of paper from among the things he'd brought along, all tied up in a handkerchief, and handed it to Siming.

Siming strode over to the candle, unfolded the paper, and read it aloud, word by word:

> ALL CITIZENS OF THE NATION UNITE IN A SINGLE VOICE TO CALL UPON OUR GREAT AND EXALTED PRESIDENT TO ISSUE A SPECIAL PROCLAMATION REQUIRING THAT THE CONFUCIAN CLASSICS BE HONORED ABOVE ALL OTHER WORKS AND THAT THE VIRTUOUS MOTHER OF MENCIUS BE PUBLICLY WORSHIPPED IN ORDER THAT THE PRESENT DETERIORATION OF MORALS MAY BE CURBED AND OUR NATIONAL HERITAGE MAINTAINED.[13]

"Marvelous, marvelous! But don't you think it might be just a bit long?" asked Siming.

13. It is difficult to convey the satire of Lu Xun's burlesque prose in Daotong's composition. Though this parallel is inexact, its flavor may be suggested if we imagine a group of American citizens petitioning the president of the United States to issue an official proclamation honoring the Bible above all other books and instituting public worship of George Washington's mother, in order to fend off the "moral deterioration" of society and to preserve the tradition of the "good old red-white-and-blue."

"Nothing to worry about!" bellowed Daotong. "I've counted the words and indeed there will be no need to pay anything in excess of our usual advertising fee. But what are we to do for a poem topic?"

"The subject for the poem?" As he spoke, Siming was enveloped by an aura of such high-minded seriousness that one almost could have reached out and grabbed a handful of it. "I have just the thing: 'Ballad of a Filial Girl.' It's something that really took place too. We ought to make her story widely known so that she may serve as a model to others. It all happened when I was downtown today. I—"

"Hold on a minute, you can't use that," Weiyuan interrupted, summarily dismissing Siming's suggestion with a wave of his hand. "I saw her too. Now, in the first place, she was probably an outlander. I couldn't understand her accent at all and she couldn't follow me either. Who knows where she comes from. Everybody said she was a *filial girl,* but when I asked her if she knew how to write poetry, she shook her head. Now if she only knew how to write poetry, you'd have yourself a good idea there."

"But loyalty and filial piety are important virtues all the same. Surely we can make allowances for her not being able to write poetry. Besides she—"

"No, no, my friend. There you're quite wide of the mark!" Weiyuan opened his hand wide and, waving it back and forth in continuous negation, trundled across the space that separated them. "People like that are only interesting in the event that they happen to know how to write poetry."

"I say we use it," said Siming, pushing him away. "We'll add a little something by way of explanation and turn it in. First off, we'll be able to publicize her example; and what's more, we'll be able to seize the opportunity to criticize present social mores and point the way to change. What's society coming to these days anyway? Do you know, I stood to one side and watched for a good long time and didn't see a soul give that filial girl so much as a penny? If that doesn't prove that people don't have feelings anymore then I don't know—"

"Hold on there, Oldman Siming!" Weiyuan came bearing down on him once again. "Do you know what you're doing? As the saying goes, you're *bad-mouthing baldheaded men in front of a monk.* You see, *I'm* one of the ones who didn't give her anything. It was just that I didn't have anything on me at the time."

"Don't be so sensitive, Oldman Weiyuan." Siming pushed him away once again. "Your case, of course, must be viewed in a different light. I had no intention of including you in what I said. Now let me finish!

"A goodly crowd had gathered around the two women, but the people in that crowd showed no respect at all for the old woman or the girl. They just used the two of them as the butt of their jokes. And as if that weren't enough, there were two bums in the group with no moral scruples whatsoever. One of them actually had the gall to say to the other: 'Ah-fa, don't be put off because the goods are dirty. All you've gotta do is buy a couple cakes of soap, give her a good old *rub-a-dub-dub,* and you'll have yourself a pretty nice piece there.' Now I ask you, my friends, what kind of animal would it take to—"

"Hah, hah, hah! Couple cakes of soap!" Daotong's laugh suddenly exploded with a boom that left one's ears ringing. "Buy a couple cakes of soap—hah, hah, hah!" he bellowed.

"Oldman Daotong! Stop that bellowing!" yelled Siming in shocked astonishment.

"*Rub-a-dub-dub!* Hah, hah, hah!"

"Oldman Daotong!" Siming yelled again, assuming a very stern air. "We're talking about a serious matter. What's gotten into you? Are you bound and determined to give us all headaches with that unseemly guffawing of yours?

"Now pay attention to what I'm saying. We'll go ahead and use the two topics we've just discussed, but we'll have to run them over to the newspaper right now, so that they'll be sure to come out in the morning edition. I'll have to beg out on that little chore, I'm afraid, and trouble you two gentlemen to deliver them."

"Certainly, that's no problem," came Weiyuan's immediate response.

"Hah, hah, hah! Give her a good *rub-a-dub-dub* . . . Hee, hee—"

"Oldman Daotong!!!" shouted Siming angrily.

Taken aback, Daotong finally stopped his laughing. After they had finished drafting the explanations, Weiyuan copied everything onto good stationery and, accompanied by Daotong, prepared to hurry over to the newspaper office. Siming picked up the candle and saw them out the gate.

Having seen his friends off, Siming walked back toward the living room. He stopped just outside, but then, after a moment's hesitation, stepped manfully over the threshold. As he entered the room, the first thing that greeted his eyes was the small, rectangular package of sunflower green that contained the soap. It had been placed in the middle of the small square table that stood in the center of the room. Encircled by bouquets of fine-lined patterns, the gold seal in the center of the package glittered brightly in the lamplight.

At the lower end of the table, Xiu'er and Zhao'er were squatted down at play; Xuecheng was seated on the right-hand side, thumbing through a dictionary. And then as his eyes adjusted to the room, Siming discerned the features of his wife seated in the shadows not far from the lamp. In what light there was he could see that her face was perfectly wooden, betraying no emotion whatsoever. Not looking at anything in particular, she stared straight ahead.

"*Rub-a-dub-dub,* shameless, absolutely shameless . . ."

Siming seemed to hear the faint voice of Xiu'er behind his back, but when he turned to look, there was no sign that she had said anything at all. Zhao'er, however, was still scratching her cheek with two small fingers.[14]

Feeling that the living room was no place for him, Siming blew out the candle and strode out into the courtyard. His mind somewhere else, he began pacing heavily back and forth: *cluck-cluck-cluck, cheep-cheep-cheep,* mocked the hen and her chicks. Siming abruptly lightened his step and tiptoed away. After some time, the lamp in the living room moved into the bedroom. The jade disk of the full moon appeared among the clouds. Its light covered every inch of the courtyard with a great seamless white sheet.

Siming felt more than a little melancholy. Like the *filial girl,* he too seemed to have become a *subject in distress with no place to turn for succor.*[15] He was alone and totally forsaken. It was extremely late that night when he finally got to sleep.

---

14. This description suggests the conventional Chinese gesture meaning "Shame on you!"

15. Based on a passage from the Regulations of a King chapter of the *Book of Rites (Li Ji),* where four categories of unfortunate subjects of the realm are named: (1) orphans, (2) old people with no children, (3) widowers, and (4) widows. If taken together, the Chinese characters that represent the names of the first two categories *(gu* and *du)* form a compound Chinese word meaning "isolation." *Gudu zhe* or "one who is isolated" is the Chinese title of the story translated below as "The Loner."

Next morning, the soap was honored with an opportunity to serve in its official capacity. Siming got up later than usual and saw his wife bent over the washstand, rubbing her neck. Soap bubbles were piled high behind her ears like the froth on a large crab's mouth. Compared to the thin tenuous layer of bubbles that used to appear when she used soap pods, the difference was as great as that between Heaven and Earth. After that day, a certain fragrance always clung to the body of Siming's wife, a fragrance one could not quite identify but that reminded one of an olive. One day before half a year was out, that particular fragrance was suddenly replaced by another. Everyone who was exposed to it said it was something like sandalwood.

MARCH 22, 1924

The Eternal Lamp

On an overcast spring afternoon the atmosphere of Luckylight Village's only tearoom is charged with excitement as the faint sound of a low-pitched voice lingers in everyone's ears: *"Put it out!"*

Of course this is by no means to say that the entire village is aware of it, for the people who live here are not much given to going out. Whenever they do, they are sure to consult the *Yellow Almanac* to make sure the entry for that day does not read: *Not favorable for going abroad.* If it does not, and they actually do go abroad, then to assure themselves of encountering good fortune, before wending their ways toward their actual destinations, they first take a few steps in that direction whence the *Almanac* says the God of Good Luck is to be sought on that particular day.[1]

And so it is that the only people sitting in the tearoom (tough-minded souls not kept indoors by such taboos) are a few of the younger set who pride themselves on being enlightened. In the minds of the rest of the hibernating villagers, however, every last one of them is a prodigal son bent on bringing his family to ruin. And now the atmosphere of this very tearoom is charged with excitement.

"Still the same way?" asks Triangle Face, lifting his teabowl.

"Way I hear it, he's still the same," answers Square Head. "Still does nothin' but say, 'Put it out!' And the look in his eyes gets wilder all the time. Damn him! He'll be the bane of our village yet. Don't take him too lightly, either. We really oughta think up some way of gettin' rid of him."

"What's so hard about that? After all, he's only a . . . What a bastard! When the temple was goin' up, *his* ancestors gave to it too, but now he wants to blow out the Eternal Lamp in that very temple! How's that for an example of posterity gone to pot? Let's go to the district police and bring charges against him for bein' *unfilial.*" Brimming over with public-spirited self-righteousness,

"The Eternal Lamp" was published serially in the literary supplement of the Beijing *Republican Daily News,* March 5 to March 8, 1925.

1. Promulgated annually by the imperial court, the *Yellow Almanac* (because it was printed on yellow paper) established the agricultural seasons for the year.

Kuoting makes a fist and brings it down hard on the table, causing the cover of a teabowl that is not squarely placed to flip over and clatter against the tabletop.

"We can't do that. By law it takes a parent or an uncle on the mother's side to charge a kid with bein' unfilial," objects Square Head.

"Trouble is, he's only got one uncle and that's on his *father's* side," comments Kuoting, the edge of his enthusiasm immediately dulled.

"By the way, Kuoting," Square Head suddenly queries in a loud voice, "how was your luck at mahjong yesterday?"

Kuoting opens his eyes wide, gives Square Head an icy stare, but offers no reply. At this point, fat-faced Zhuang Qiguang cranks up his voice and begins to sputter: "If he blew out the Eternal Lamp, what kind of village would our Luckylight Village be? There just wouldn't be a 'lucky light' village any more, that's all. And don't all the elders say that *that* lamp was lit by Emperor Wu way back in the Liang Dynasty and that it's been handed down to us without ever goin' out since then—not even durin' the times of the Long Hair Rebellion?[2]

"Have you ever noticed," Zhuang clicks his tongue in admiration, "the beautiful emerald glow of that flame? Why, all the strangers who come by our way make a special point of stoppin' off just to see it. They all praise it." He clicks his tongue again. "It's soooo . . . beautiful! Now what in the world's gotten into him to go and stir up all this commotion over it?"

"Well, he *is* crazy. You mean you hadn't figured out he's bonkers?" asks Square Head with an ill-disguised note of contempt.

"Can't all be as smart as you," replies Zhuang, his face beginning to sweat.

"Way I see it, best thing's to pull that same old trick on 'im again," puts in Fifth Auntie Hui, proprietress of the tearoom as well as its only waitress. So far she has merely listened in, but now, sensing that the talk is veering away from the object of her own concern, she abruptly puts an end to their petty bickering and brings the conversation back to the main theme.

"What old trick?" Zhuang Qiguang's voice sounds puzzled.

---

2. Emperor Wu (464–549) of the Liang dynasty was one of China's most devout and enthusiastic patrons of Buddhism. The Taiping rebels (1850–64) were also known as the "Long hairs" because they undid their queues and let their hair fall down around their shoulders.

"Didn't he go off once before, same way as now? Well, his old man was still alive then. And we pulled a trick that cured him."

"What trick? How come I don't know about it?" Zhuang Qiguang is more confused than ever.

"How would you know about it? You were still a small-fry back then, only knew how to suck a tit and shit your drawers. Even *I* was somethin' different back in those days. You shoulda seen my hands back then, all soft and tender, smooth as—"

"You're still all soft and tender, even now," observes Square Head.

"Go blow it out your ass!" The smile on Fifth Auntie Hui's face belies the angry expression in her eyes. "Don't talk such foolishness. We're dealin' with serious business here. He was still pretty young then, too. You know that old man of his wasn't exactly all there himself. Be that as it may, I hear tell it all started one day when his granddad took him to the village temple and told him to pay his respects to the Temple God, the God of Plagues, and the Guardian God of the Temple Gate. He got scared, wouldn't worship, and hightailed it outta the place. He's been kinda weird ever since that day.

"Later on he got to be the way he is now. You know how whenever he meets anybody, he always starts right up talkin' about ways to put out the Eternal Lamp over there in the main hall of the temple. Says that once the lamp's out, there'll be no more locusts and no more epidemics. To hear him talk, you'd think it was real serious stuff, important as all get out. His runnin' outta the temple like that when he was a kid was prob'ly 'cause an evil spirit got into 'im and was afraid of meetin' all those good spirits face to face.

"Take us, for instance. Would we be afraid of seein' the old Temple God? Hey, your tea's gettin' cold. Let me pour a little hot water in. Now where was I? Oh, yeah. Well, later on he broke into the temple and tried to blow out the lamp. His old man doted on him so much, he just couldn't bring himself to lock 'im up. Remember how, later on, the whole village got ticked off and went to have it out with his old man? But nothin' came of that, either.

"Luckily that croaked ghost of a husband of mine was still alive and kickin' then, and he's the one who came up with the idea.[3]

3. Tough women of this village sometimes referred to a deceased husband in this way. —Author's note.

They wrapped a heavy quilt around the lamp so the main temple hall was pitch black. Told him the light had been blown out! They took 'im there to see for himself."

"Ha, ha! Not half bad. It'd take a man like your husband to come up with somethin' like that." Triangle Face lets out a sigh that would seem to indicate boundless admiration.

"Why go to all that bother?" Kuoting asks pugnaciously. "Just kill the bastard and get it over with. Bah!"

"Can't do that." Fifth Auntie Hui looks at him in surprise and summarily negates his suggestion with a grand sweep of her hand. "No way we can do that. After all, his granddad used to go around with a seal in his hand, didn't he?"[4]

Kuoting and the others quickly glance at each other and realize that there really *is* no good way of handling the situation other than to follow the ingenious scheme that Fifth Auntie Hui's "croaked ghost of a husband" once came up with.

"After we tricked him that time, he was okay!" She begins to pick up the tempo of her recital as she wipes a few drops of saliva from the corner of her mouth with the back of her hand. "He was perfectly okay! Never went into the temple again and never said nothin' about it again for years and years. I don't know exactly how it happened this time, but it wasn't too many days after he'd seen a temple fair that he went crazy again. Yup, he's exactly the same way he was last time. Passed by here after lunch and I'm sure he was headed for the temple. You guys oughta go over and talk it over with his uncle, Fourth Master, and see if it wouldn't be a good idea to play that same trick on him again. After all, the Eternal Lamp *was* lit by the fifth younger brother of the Liang family, wasn't it?[5] Don't they say that if the lamp ever goes out, this here tract of land we're on will turn into ocean and we'll all turn into mudfish? You'd better hike on over there and talk to Fourth Master right away, otherwise—"

"We'd better go on over to the temple first and have a look-see," Square Head suggests as he strides grandly out the door. Kuoting and Zhuang Qiguang follow quickly after him.

Last to leave the teashop, Triangle Face pauses at the door,

---

4. She means that he once held a substantive official appointment. —Author's note.

5. Unlettered Fifth Auntie Hui hears "Emperor Wu of the Liang dynasty" as "the fifth younger brother of the Liang family." The two epithets are homophonous *(Liang wudi)*, although the Chinese characters for the sounds are different.

turns and announces: "Guess you'll have to put it all on my tab this time. Fuckers!"

Fifth Auntie Hui nods her agreement, goes over to the east wall of the shop, picks up a piece of charcoal from the floor, and draws two more lines underneath a triangle on the wall, a triangle beneath which a goodly number of such lines are already inscribed.

* * *

The village temple comes into sight in the distance. Just as they expected, several people are gathered there—the madman himself, two adults who have come to see the fun, and three children.

But the temple gate is closed tight.

"Good, the gate's still shut," observes Kuoting in a pleased tone.

As Kuoting and the others approach, the children grow bolder and gather in closer around the madman. The madman, who has been standing and looking at the gate, now turns and faces them.

He is the same as ever—a pale, square face, raggedy blue cotton gown, and in the large eyes under the bushy brows, there glows a strange flickering light. He is a man who can stare and stare at you without blinking. His eyes are a mixture of sadness and indignation, touched with fear. Two bits of rice stalk are stuck to his short hair, probably stealthily placed there from behind by the children, for now when they see them, the children all draw in their necks and stick out their tongues, sharing in a private joke.

The adults stand still, each looking into the other's face.

It is Triangle Face who finally steps forward and demands: "And just what do you think *you're* doin'?"

"Trying to get Old Blackie to open the gate," he answers in low, genial tones, "because that lamp has got to be blown out. All those gods have got to go, too—old Blue Face with the three heads and six arms; Triple Eye; Tall Hat; Half Head; Bull Head; and Hog Tusk. Got to get rid of them all! If the lamp is blown out, we won't be plagued by locusts anymore, and we won't have any more epidemics of trench mouth either."

"Ha, ha! How dumb can you get!" Kuoting laughs derisively. "If you blow out the Eternal Lamp, there'll be more locusts than ever and *you'll* come down with a good case of trench mouth yourself.

"Ha, ha!" Zhuang Qiguang joins in Kuoting's derision.

A bare-chested boy takes a reed he has been toying with, carefully aims it at the madman, and suddenly opens his cherrylike little mouth to issue a *POW!*

"You'd better head on home now." Kuoting's voice is louder now. "If you don't, your uncle's gonna break every last bone in your body. If you're worried about the lamp, *I'll* blow it out for you. Come back in a couple of days and see for yourself!"

The light in the madman's eyes grows brighter and he rivets Kuoting with a stare so intense it causes the latter to avert his gaze.

"*You* blow it out?" The madman smiles mockingly, and then continues decisively. "No! I don't need you. I'll blow it out myself and I'll do it now!"

Immediately deflated, Kuoting looks as unsteady as someone who has just come off a good drunk. Now it is Square Head who stands forward. His words come slowly. "You've always been a reasonable kinda guy up to now, but this time you've really gone off the deep end. Let me clue you in and you'll see it for yourself. It's like this: What if you *did* blow out the Eternal Lamp? Wouldn't all those bad things you talk about still be around? Don't be so half-baked. Your best bet's to go home and get yourself some sleep!"

"I know they would still exist as well as you do." A sinister smile suddenly appears on the madman's face, and just as quickly it vanishes. "But it's all I can do for right now." His tones are low and serious. "I'll get that lamp out of the way first. Things will go a little easier after that. I'm going to blow it out right now—all by myself!" He turns as he speaks and pushes at the temple gate with all his might.

Kuoting is furious. "Just a damn minute! Aren't you from these parts yourself? Are you bound and determined to turn us all into mudfish? Go home! There's no way you can get it open anyhow. And there's no way you can blow out the Eternal Lamp either! Now why don't you just go on home!"

"I *won't* go home! I'm going to blow it out once and for all!"

"Impossible! There's just no way you can get that gate open!"

". . ."

"There's no way under the sun you can get that gate open!"

"Then I'll do it some other way." He calmly turns around and surveys them.

"Hah, we'll just see what other way you can come up with!"

". . ."

"There's no way under the sun you can get that gate open!"

"I'd like to see what other way you can come up with!"

"I'll set it on fire."

"What?" Kuoting suspects he hasn't heard him right.

"I'LL SET IT ON FIRE!"

Like a crisp peal of chimes, silence rings out through the air and then draws back into itself again, immobilizing every living thing in its wake. After a few moments, however, several heads come together in mouth-to-ear conclave, and then after another few seconds, pull apart again and begin moving toward the village.

Two or three of them come to a stop once again a slight distance away. Zhuang Qiguang's voice can be heard shouting from outside the wall at the rear gate of the temple. "Hey, Blackie, things are all fouled up out here. Keep the gates locked tight! Did you hear me, Blackie? Keep things locked up good and tight! We're gonna go figure out what to do and then we'll be right back!"

The madman, however, takes no heed of any of this. His frenzied eyes quickly search the ground, the sky, and even the bodies of bystanders, as if trying to find some means of starting a fire.

* * *

After Square Head and Kuoting, fast as shuttles on a loom, have threaded in and out the gates of several leading families, the whole of Luckylight Village is suddenly galvanized into action.

In the minds and ears of many of the villagers there echoes a frightening threat: *I'LL SET IT ON FIRE!* But, of course, there are still other minds and ears belonging to villagers in a deeper state of hibernation who are still oblivious to that disturbing voice. The atmosphere of the entire village is charged with tension nonetheless, and anyone conscious of it is ill at ease, as though afraid that he himself might turn into a fish at any moment and the whole world come to an abrupt end. Of course, people are vaguely aware of the fact that it is only Luckylight Village that will actually be destroyed, but in their minds, it would seem, Luckylight Village *is* the whole world.

Before long the leading actors in this drama are forgathered in the guest hall of the madman's paternal uncle, Fourth Master.

In the place of honor sits Guo Laowa, a man as eminent in virtue as rich in years, with a face already wrinkled like a wind-dried orange. He keeps tugging at wisps of beard on the lower part of his chin as though intent on pulling them out by the roots. "Forenoon . . ." Now he lets loose of the white strands and slowly continues with phrase-at-a-time deliberation. "When Old Fu out at the West End had a stroke, his son . . . his son said . . . said it was because something had disturbed the Earth God. You can tell from this, Fourth Master, that . . . that in the future . . . when anything inauspicious happens . . . it'll be a wonder . . . be a wonder if people don't come here to your place. Yes, they'll come . . . looking for you. Spells trouble."

"Do you really think so?" Fourth Master also tugs at a few grey catfish whiskers on his upper lip. However, as he continues talking, he seems not at all worried: "Retribution for his father's sins—that's what it is. When his father was alive, *he* didn't believe in the Bodhisattvas either. I didn't see eye to eye with him on that, but there wasn't a thing I could do to change him, and he was my own brother. What do you expect I'll be able to do now?"

"I think there's only one . . . one thing to do. Yes . . . only one. Tomorrow . . . tie him up and . . . and take him to the city. Put him in the City Temple and leave . . . leave him there overnight . . . overnight, so that the evil spirits . . . evil spirits will be driven out of him."

On the basis of the merit they have acquired in attempting to protect the entire village, Kuoting and Square Head have for the first time in their lives gained admission to Fourth Master's guest hall, a place that under normal circumstances they would not easily have seen. Moreover, they have even been treated to tea. Earlier, after following Guo Laowa in and making their report, they paid attention only to the fine tea they had been served, and even after draining their bowls, still remained silent. But now at this juncture Kuoting suddenly expresses an opinion. "That's way too slow. The temple's still under guard, you know. We've gotta decide right now what we're gonna do! If he really sets the temple on fire—"

His lower jaw trembling, Guo Laowa twitches with fright.

"If he really sets it on fire—" Square Head tries to horn in.

"—then," shouts Kuoting, drowning him out, "we'll really be in the soup!"

A young girl enters and pours more tea. Kuoting stops talking at once and eagerly takes up his bowl. Suddenly his entire body twitches. He puts the bowl down much faster than when he took it up. Licking his lips, gingerly he takes the cover off the bowl, quickly sets it to one side, and starts blowing on the tea.

"It's bad enough what he's doing to himself, but then *I* get dragged into it too." Fourth Master lightly taps his fingers on the table. "Posterity like that would be better off dead."

"Yeah, he really would be," Kuoting agrees, raising his head from his bowl. "Matter of fact, folks over at Liang Village did kill an unfilial son last year. Decided 'forehand they'd all start beatin' on him at exactly the same time so you couldn't tell who'd hit 'im first. Know what? When it was all over, nobody got in trouble for it."

"Another time, another place," observes Square Head.

"Won't do us any good here and now. There are people watchin' him anyway. We've got to come up with somethin' right away quick. The way I see it . . ."

Guo Laowa and Fourth Master both eye Kuoting respectfully.

". . . the way I see it, best thing would be to lock him up someplace for the time bein'."

"That actually is a sound plan." Fourth Master nods his head slightly in agreement.

"Sound plan!" agrees Kuoting.

"That actually . . . is a sound . . . a sound plan," opines Guo Laowa. Let's have him hauled over here . . . over here to your place, Fourth Master . . . right now. You had better . . . better get a room ready. And don't forget to . . . to provide it with . . . a lock."

"Room?" Fourth Master throws his head back, ponders a bit, and says: "But I don't *have* a room I can spare. Besides, there's no telling when he'll finally get well, and—"

"Well then . . . just use . . . use his own room," suggests Guo Laowa.

"Our Liushun," says Fourth Master, waxing solemn and sad, his voice slightly trembling, "is going to take a wife in the fall, so I'm afraid that . . . Just think of it, old as my nephew is, he still doesn't know how to do anything except go crazy. He shows no inclination to set up a family and establish himself in an occupation. Now it is true that my younger brother, his father, did after all live out his allotted span in this world, and even though he was not entirely that solid, still, I cannot let his family line be cut off."

"That goes without saying!" A trio of different voices harmonizes to express the same sentiment.

"If Liushun has sons, what I'd really like to do is give my nephew the second one for adoption. But, gentlemen, can I simply up and ask for my daughter-in-law's son, just like that?"

"Impossible!" A trio of different voices harmonizes to express the same sentiment.

"And as for the ramshackle room we are talking about, I certainly don't begrudge him that, nor does Liushun. But to take one's very own child and give it away just like that—I'm afraid we can't expect a mother to be so openhanded."

"That goes without saying!" A trio of different voices harmonizes to express the same sentiment.

Fourth Master falls silent. The members of the trio look back and forth at one another.

"Every day I hope and pray that he'll improve," says Fourth Master slowly after a somber but short-lived silence, "but he never does. It's not so much that he doesn't get better as it is that he doesn't *want* to get better. I'm at the end of my rope. Perhaps we'd better do something similar to what this gentleman suggests—lock him up so he doesn't harm anyone or disgrace his father's memory. Perhaps that would be best, and perhaps that way I will be doing the right thing by his father after all."

"That goes without saying," observes Kuoting, obviously moved. "But what about a *room?*"

"Aren't there any vacant ones in the . . . in the temple?" asks Fourth Master haltingly.

"Why, yes!" says Kuoting, beginning to catch on at last. "Yes. On the west side, just as you go in the main gate, there's an empty one. Better yet, there's only a tiny square window in it and it's got big thick up-and-down window bars. He'd never be able to pry them loose. Perfect!"

Guo Laowa and Square Head suddenly put on pleased expressions too. Kuoting blows his tea a bit more, puckers his lips, and begins to drink again.

* * *

Even before the advent of dusk, peace has been restored to the world. Perhaps everyone has simply forgotten the whole thing, for not only have the original worried expressions of early afternoon disappeared from every face, but even the relieved ones that later replaced them are also gone without a trace.

Of course there are many more footprints in front of the village temple than usual, but before long they will begin to disappear too. Since the temple gate has been locked for the past few days, the children have not been able to get inside to play, and so this evening they are especially pleased at finally being allowed to get into the courtyard again. After supper some of them run back to the temple to play.

"See if you can guess this one," says one of the biggest children. "I'll say it again:

A white topped boat,
With bright red oars,
Paddles across to opposite shores,
Rests a bit, enjoys the view,
Finds some snacks and eats a few—
Even sings some opera too."

"What could that be with 'bright red oars'?" asks a girl.

"Let me tell you, it's a—"

"Hold on, hold on!" says one child with a scabby scalp. "I've guessed it. A riverboat!"

"A riverboat!" a bare-chested lad agrees.

"A *river*boat?" scoffs the child who has just recited the riddle. "A riverboat is *poled,* not rowed. Besides, can a riverboat sing opera? You'll never get it. Let me tell you—"

"Hold on, I know . . ." says Scabby Scalp.

"Hah! You'll never, never, never guess it. Let me tell you. It's a goose."

"A goose!" says the girl, laughing. "A goose with red oars!"

"But how do you figure it's a white-topped boat?" asks the bare-chested lad.

"I'LL SET IT ON FIRE!"

With a start, the children suddenly remember the madman and focus their attention on the west room. They see one of his hands latched onto a window bar while the other claws at the wood. A pair of fiery eyes flashes from between the bars.

The silence lasts only an instant before it is broken by Scabby Scalp, who suddenly lets out a yell, breaks into a run, and heads for the gate. The other children run out too, shouting and laughing as they go. The bare-chested lad points the reed he is carrying back in the direction of the madman. From his panting, cherrylike little mouth issues a crisp *POW!*

And then all is silence. Night falls and brighter than ever the emerald glow of the Eternal Lamp fills the temple hall, lights up the gods in their niches, shines out into the courtyard and on into the darkness behind the wooded window bars of the west room.

Once outside the temple, the children stop running, join hands, and make their leisurely way homeward. Smiling, they put their voices together and sing, making up the words as they go along:

A white topped boat
rests across the moat.
Blow it out, do, do, do,
and sing some opera too.
Burn it down, clown, clown, clown,
burn it, burn it, do, do, do.
And here are some snacks for you,
and a little opera too.

MARCH 1, 1925

A Warning to the People

At this time of day, on a certain street in the western suburbs of the *Realm of the Highest Good,* there is not the slightest hint of activity.[1] Although the fiery rays of the sun are not yet shining straight down, a shimmering glow radiates from the gravel and a cruel heat fills the air, everywhere proclaiming the dominion of midsummer. Several dogs loll out their tongues. Beaks hanging open, even the black crows up in the trees are panting. But there are, of course, exceptions: far off in the distance comes the faint sound of two copper cups being struck together, reminding people of chilled prune juice, making them almost feel cool; the intermittent punctuation of those lazy and monotonous metallic sounds renders the silence even more profound.[2]

Mute, save for the sound of their own footsteps, rickshaw pullers hurtle forward as though trying to escape the merciless sun.

"Hot baozi! Fresh from the steamer!"[3]

A fat boy of eleven or twelve narrows his eyes, draws his mouth to one side, and calls out before a storefront on one side of the street. His voice is already hoarse and somewhat sleepy as well, as though hypnotized by the long summer day.

Betraying not the slightest trace of steam, twenty or thirty *baozi* and *mantou* lie cold on a rickety table at his side.[4]

"Hey, hey, hey! Get your hot mantou, get your hot baozi!"

Like a rubber ball that has been thrown hard against a wall and bounces back again, Fat Boy suddenly bounds to the other side of the street. At precisely that moment two men come to a stop next to a telephone pole facing Fat Boy and the street behind him. One is a thin, sallow-faced policeman in pale yellow uniform, a saber

---

First published in the second issue of the Beijing weekly *Fragments (Yusi),* dated April 13, 1925. Lu Xun and his brother Zhou Zuoren founded *Fragments* to create an outlet for their own writings as well as the writings of their followers. For the title's meaning see n. 6, p. 23.

1. "Realm of the Highest Good" is a traditional literary epithet for Beijing.

2. Hawkers of prune juice bang metal cups together to announce and advertise their product.

3. Steamed bread rolls with meat and vegetable filling.

4. Steamed bread rolls without filling.

at his side. In one hand he holds a rope, the other end of which is tied round the arm of a man wearing a long blue cotton gown beneath a sleeveless white vest. A brand new straw hat with turned-down brim hides the man's eyes. But Fat Boy is short, so that when he raises his eyes, his gaze meets that of the prisoner, who seems, in turn, to have his eyes focused on the boy's head. Fat Boy hastily lowers his gaze and looks at the white vest where he sees line after line of Chinese characters, large and small, that he cannot read.

In no time at all, the trio is partly surrounded by a large semicircle of spectators. By the time a bald-headed old man adds himself to the group, there are already very few places left. These are occupied straightaway by a red-nosed fat man who is so wide that he takes up space enough to accommodate several people, forcing the straggling latecomers to content themselves with positions in a second row, whence they are obliged to thrust their heads between the shoulders of those standing in the row in front of them.

Baldy is now standing roughly in front of the man in the sleeveless white vest and bends over to study the characters written on it. He begins to read them aloud: "Mmm . . . all the . . . uh . . . in eight . . . and, eh . . ."

Fat Boy, noticing that White Vest is now engaged in a close study of the shiny bald head that has presented itself before him, joins him in these researches but discovers nothing more than two patches of grey hair alongside the ears of an otherwise stark-naked head. Apart from those patches, however, he detects nothing remarkable about the specimen. In the back, an old amah with child in arms avails herself of the opportunity thus presented to crowd in closer and view the prisoner over the top of Baldy's back. Suddenly fearful lest he lose his place, however, Baldy stands up straight even though he hasn't finished reading the vest. And so it is that Baldy now looks directly into White Vest's face: beneath the brim of a straw hat, half a nose, a mouth, and a sharp chin.

Like another rubber ball that has been thrown hard against a wall and bounces back again, a schoolboy bounds up, one hand clamping a white cotton cap to his head, and begins to bore his way into the clump of humanity before him. But when he reaches the third (or perhaps it is the fourth) layer of spectators, he encounters something of truly monumental proportions, something that is not to be budged. He looks up: there, poised atop a pair of blue pants, appears the rear slope of a fleshy mountain down which there descends a cascade of perspiration. Realizing the impossibility of moving it, he turns right and follows his way around Blue Pants' waist.

Fortunately, just as he comes to a dead end, amidst all that flesh, he discovers a patch of light—an empty place! He lowers his head and is on the verge of squeezing through when a voice is heard asking, "What did you say?" and the buttocks below the waist of the blue pants mountain shift to the right, instantly stopping up the empty space. The patch of light disappears as well.

Nonetheless, the schoolboy finally manages to brush past the saber hanging at the side of the policeman and emerges into the open area in front of the crowd. Startled, he looks about and surveys his new situation. A semicircle of humanity surrounds this open space; the place of honor is taken by a man wearing a white vest. Standing to one side there is a bare-armed fat boy; behind the boy there stands a red-nosed fat man. Now the student vaguely begins to recognize the nature of that magnificent obstacle that impeded his progress a moment or so before; he marvels at the sight and now gazes with admiration at the red-nosed fat man from afar. Fat Boy, having noticed the schoolboy as soon as the latter had squeezed his way out of the crowd, cannot keep himself from following in the direction of the schoolboy's gaze. And now as he turns his head to seek out the object of the schoolboy's admiration, he is confronted by a very plump breast, around the nipple of which several long hairs protrude.

"What crime has he committed?"

Everyone looks at the questioner with stunned surprise: it is a husky, workingman type who has, in the most deferential of tones, just posed his question to the bald-headed old man.

Uttering not so much as a peep in reply, Baldy opens his eyes wide and nails the worker with a stare that forces the latter to lower his gaze in submission. The worker waits a few seconds and then makes so bold as to look up again: Baldy is still pop-eyed and staring. What's more, now it seems that *everyone* is pop-eyed and staring.

The worker feels increasingly ill at ease, as though he himself has committed the crime. Finally he retreats a few steps, turns, and slips away. A tall man with a parasol moves in and takes his place, at which point Baldy swings his head around to look at White Vest again.

Tall Man begins to bend at the waist, so as to get low enough to view White Vest's face from beneath the brim of the straw hat, but then, unaccountably, he stands up straight again, forcing the people behind him to crane their necks; one skinny fellow cranes his head up so high that his mouth drops wide open, making him look like a dead perch strung on a line.

Without warning, the policeman raises his foot. Immediately, all eyes are glued to this foot in surprise. Then he puts the foot down again. Eyes come unglued and resume watching White Vest. Tall Man suddenly bends forward again, still intending to peek under the turned-down brim of that straw hat. But then, just as suddenly, he stands back up, raises one hand on high, and begins to scratch his scalp for all he is worth.

Baldy is out of sorts. He senses some sort of disturbance going on behind him. What's more, a *chomp chomp chomp* sound assails his ears. He knits his brows together and turns around to look: very close to his right shoulder a dark hand is holding half of a large *mantou* and is in the midst of stuffing it into the mouth of a face that looks like a cat's. Baldy does not say anything, but simply turns back around and begins to study White Vest's new straw hat.

Like a clap of thunder, something suddenly collides with the crowd. Even Fat Man, who looms like a mountain across the horizon, cannot help but lurch forward. At the same time an arm that yields nothing to others of its own girth thrusts itself out past Fat Man's shoulder, its five fingers spread wide. *SLAP!* The hand belonging to the arm comes down across Fat Boy's cheek.

"Havin' a good time fer yerself, huh, little fucker?"

As the slap descends, this question is uttered by a face, even rounder than that of a Happy Buddha, located somewhere behind Fat Man.

Fat Boy stumbles four or five steps but does not fall. One hand to his cheek, he pivots around with a mind to squeezing through the crack there to the left of Fat Man. The latter, however, recovering from his lurch, now steadies himself, shifting his buttocks to one side in the process, thereby blocking up the space. "What's going on?" he snarls.

Like an animal fallen into a trap, Fat Boy panics for a moment. Then he breaks in the direction of the schoolboy, pushes him to one side, and charges through the crowd. The schoolboy turns around and follows in his wake.

"Darned kids!" There must be at least five or six people who express this sentiment.

By the time equilibrium is reestablished and Fat Man goes back to looking at White Vest's face, he discovers that White Vest has now raised his eyes, too, and is staring back at his own chest. Fat Man quickly lowers his head and looks down: seeing a pool of sweat in the sunken pit between his breasts, he wipes it away with the palm of his hand.

Within this new equilibrium, however, there still seems to be something or other not quite in balance. At the time of the disturbance, the old amah with the child had looked first to one side and then the other to see what was going on, and had inadvertently bumped her "Suzhou beauty" against the nose of a rickshaw man standing by her side.[5] The man had pushed at her but his hands had landed on the child, who performed an about-face in her arms and clamored to be taken home. Old Amah, having stumbled for a step or two, has recovered her balance. She turns the child back around so as to make him face White Vest, now directly in front of them. She points at the vest. "Look, look! Isn't that fun?"

Suddenly an inquisitive, student-type head wearing a hard straw hat pokes itself into this space and puts something on the order of a watermelon seed into its mouth. The jaws close and crack the seed open; the seed is chewed, the head withdrawn. The vacancy thus created is filled at once by a sweat-covered oval face, generously caked with grime.

Tall Man with Parasol is angry now, too. He drops one shoulder lower than the other, knits his brow, and turns to glower at Dead Perch, now situated behind that shoulder. The warm breath exhaled by such a large mouth would be difficult to endure at any time, much less in midsummer. Baldy has just raised his head to inspect four white characters inscribed on a red board nailed to the telephone pole. He seems to find them intriguing. Fat Man and the policeman are both studying the sickle-shaped points of Old Amah's shoes.

"Bravo!" From somewhere or other, several voices join in a cheer. Aware that something or other has just happened, the sum

5. A particular style of combing the hair into a knot or bun, originally popular in Suzhou.

total of all heads present upon this occasion turns collectively around. There is even some degree of motion on the part of the policeman and his prisoner.

"Baozi! Fresh from the steamer! Hey, hey, hey! Come and get your hot baozi . . ." Across the street Fat Boy cocks his head to one side and calls. His tone is long and sleepy.

And on the street, rickshaw pullers hurtle mutely forward as though trying to effect an immediate escape from the merciless sun overhead. Everyone is on the verge of disappointment. Fortunately, however, when they make a visual inventory of their immediate environs, they discover a rickshaw man who has just taken a hard fall about ten doors down the way. He is only now climbing back to his feet.

The circular formation immediately disintegrates into a chaos of feet walking toward the accident. Fat Man has to stop and rest under a locust tree before he is halfway there. Walking faster than Baldy or Oval Face, Tall Man is first to approach the rickshaw. Still sitting in the rig, the passenger is unharmed. Although the rickshaw man himself is now completely back on his feet, he still rubs at his knees. Smiling broadly at the fun, four or five people have already gathered round the puller and his fare.

"You okay?" asks the passenger as the rickshaw man prepares to go on.

He nods, picks up the shafts, and pulls the rickshaw away. Faces now wreathed in disappointment, everyone watches him move down the street. At first they know which rickshaw it is whose puller just took the spill, but then as it mixes with the other rigs, they are no longer sure.

Once again the street is quiet. A few dogs loll out their tongues and pant. In the shade of the laurels, Fat Man watches a dog's abdomen rapidly *rise-and-fall* and *rise-and-fall.*

Holding the child in her arms, Old Amah scurries along under the eaves of the stores. Fat Boy squints hard, stretches his voice out long, and shouts in sleepy tones: *"Hot baozi! Hey, hey, hey! Fresh from the steamer!"*

MARCH 18, 1925

The Venerable Schoolmaster Gao

On this particular day, from morning until afternoon, his time had been spent on primping before the mirror, reading *A General Textbook of Chinese History,* and looking things up in *Liaofan's Shorter History*—clearly confirming the wisdom of the saying *Once you learn to read, Misery takes the lead.*[1] Now, suddenly, he began to realize there were quite a few things in this old world that he resented, and what was more, resented with an intensity he had never felt before.

First off, it occurred to him that your average parents do not properly look after the welfare of their children. As a child, for instance, he had loved to climb the mulberry tree out in the backyard and eat the berries. His parents, however, failed to foresee the potential danger involved, so that he eventually fell out of the tree and cracked his head open; as if that weren't enough, they hadn't taken him to a really good doctor either. The upshot was that down to this very day he carried an ineradicable reminder of the experience at the tip of his left eyebrow. He had disguised it as best he could by letting the hair in that area grow long, so that he could comb it down slantwise over his temple. Despite his best efforts, however, people could still detect the sharp silhouette of that childhood scar.

No matter how you looked at it, that scar did constitute an imperfection. And what if the girls at school caught sight of it? It couldn't help but make them disdain him. With an angry sigh, he put down the mirror.

Close behind on his list of gripes was the gall of the man who had edited *A General Textbook of Chinese History* in not taking the classroom teacher into account when putting this text together. Though some of it did tally with *Liaofan's Shorter History,* there were large chunks that didn't, so that it was impossible to weave the two books together into any kind of coherent lecture.

First published in the Beijing weekly *Fragments,* no. 26, dated May 11, 1925. Lu Xun and his brother Zhou Zuoren founded *Fragments* to create an outlet for their own writings as well as the writings of their followers.

1. The *Shorter History* of Yuan Liaofan (1573–1620) is an abbreviated chronological history. The quoted verse comes from a poem of Su Dongbo (1036–1112).

The Venerable Schoolmaster Gao glanced at a slip of paper that had been left in the textbook, and his smouldering resentment against the teacher who had quit halfway through the course was fanned into a full blaze, for the note read: *Begin at Chapter Eight —The Rise and Fall of the Eastern Jin Dynasty* [317–420]. If that clod hadn't already finished lecturing on the Three Kingdoms Period [220–65], Gao himself wouldn't have had nearly so much difficulty preparing. He knew the Three Kingdoms Period up one side and down the other: *The Triple Oath of the Peach Garden, Kong Ming Borrows Arrows, Zhou Yü Thrice Angered, Huang Zhong Beheads Xia Houyuan at Dingjun Mountain,* and any number of other such incidents. Why, he had such a bellyful of stuff like that, he wouldn't be able to spit it all out even in a whole semester![2]

And if it had only been some later period—let's say the Tang Dynasty [618–907]—well, then you had material like *Qin Qiong Sells His Horse.*[3] Yes, he could have told stories like that in a pretty entertaining way, too. But no! It couldn't be the Three Kingdoms or the Tang, it had to be that damned Eastern Jin right in between! Once more, Gao sighed in exasperation; and once more too, he made a dive for *Liaofan's Shorter History.*

"What's this I hear, old buddy? Wasn't enough for you to admire all those young foxes from a distance, now you've wormed your way into the school for a closer look!" At the same time, a hand described an arc over his shoulder and tried to pull his chin around. Knowing full well that the man who had sneaked up behind him could be none other than his old friend and card-playing crony Third Huang, Gao tensed his neck muscles and wouldn't let his head budge. Only the week before, he had played cards, attended the opera, and sallied out to drink and womanize with this old friend.

---

2. All of these episodes are contained in the popular historical novel *Romance of the Three Kingdoms.* Such material was the traditional stock-in-trade of storytellers and popular playwrights. In a Western setting, a character like Gao might consider familiarity with Dickens' *Tale of Two Cities* and Hugo's *Ninety-three* sufficient qualification for offering a course on the French Revolution.

3. Qin Qiong was a military hero who helped the first Tang emperor found the new dynasty. Again, Gao's knowledge is derived from a wealth of popular fiction. Unfortunately for Gao, storytellers have not taken an equal interest in the Eastern Jin.

Now, however, the Venerable Schoolmaster Gao decided that, all things considered, Third Huang was really a rather lowlife type with nothing much to recommend him, for in the interim Gao had published an article in the *Great China Daily News* entitled "The Duty of Every Citizen in the Chinese Republic to Aid in the Study and Systematization of Our National Heritage."[4] People were talking about it wherever you went, and hard on the heels of its publication, Gao had been engaged as a history teacher in the *Academy for Young Ladies of Character and Ability.* As a result, our Venerable Schoolmaster Gao was not about to turn his head for anyone the likes of Third Huang. Trying to look as respectable as he could under the circumstances, Gao assumed a stern expression and said: "Quit your horsing around. I'm preparing my lecture . . ."

"Come off it. Didn't you tell our mutual buddy Old Bo that the only reason you wanted to teach there in the first place was to have a chance to size up all the foxes in class?"

"Don't believe all the crap Old Bo puts out!"

Third Huang sat down next to the desk and glanced at the chaos all over the top. His gaze immediately fell on a bright red appointment card that lay half open between the mirror and a clutter of books. He grabbed it up and read it word by word with wide-open, appraising eyes.

Be It Respectfully Requested That:
The Venerable Schoolmaster
ORKY GAO
Serve as HISTORY INSTRUCTOR at this Academy to
Teach FOUR HOURS PER WEEK at exactly
THIRTY CENTS PER HOUR, Salary to be Calculated
Strictly According to Time.
With all Due Deference and Courtesy,

HE-WAN SHUZHEN
Principal
Academy for Young Ladies of Character and Ability

4. The political position implied by this title ("Let us understand the past before we take any rash action in the present") was espoused by the so-called National Heritage School *(guocui pai)* during the 1920s. This position was anathema to Lu Xun. As he saw it, the real goal of those who encouraged study of the past was to get young people to bury their heads in books, so that they would have neither the time nor the energy to look around them, see what was going on in the present, and take steps to change it.

Summer of this Thirteenth Year
of
The Republic of China
Auspicious Day, Chrysanthemum Month

Effective Immediately[5]

As soon as he had finished the letter, Third Huang was brimming with impatient questions. "Who is this *Orky Gao?* You? Changed your name?"

The Venerable Schoolmaster Gao's only reply was a superior smile. He had, in fact, changed his name. But how was he to explain the profound significance of such a step to this card-playing lout? Third Huang wasn't up on the New Learning *or* the New Art and Literature either. He had never even heard of the Russian literary giant Gorky. Hence Schoolmaster Gao did not deign to respond, except for that superior smile.

"Hey, hey, what's going on here, old buddy? Don't go getting yourself mixed up in idiotic stuff!" Third Huang exhorted, putting down the appointment card. "Since the opening of those modern schools for boys, things have already gotten far enough out of hand. Why do they want to go messing around with *girls'* schools? How far is all this going to go before we see an end to it? And why should you stir up trouble for yourself by joining in? It's not worth it . . ."

---

5. The Chinese transliteration for (Maxim) Gorky (1868–1936) is Gao-er-ji. Our pretentious and ignorant schoolmaster takes this transliteration of a foreign name and misreads it as a Chinese one. Since Chinese people give the surname first and the given name second, the schoolmaster assumes that Gorky must be surnamed Gao (Gor-) with the given name Erji (-ky). Then to show that he is a disciple of this famous Russian writer—and he probably knows little more about him than do his card-playing cronies—he alters the given name slightly, making it Erchu. His choice was probably based on the Chinese compound word meaning "foundation," *jichu.* Since the *ji* of *jichu* is part of Gao Er*ji,* he reasoned that it would be appropriate to use the *chu* of *jichu* to indicate his discipleship, thus becoming Gao Er*chu.*

The principal's double surname shows that she (Wan Shuzhen) is married to a man surnamed He. Playing with names is one way of making oneself appear more sophisticated or romantic than in real life for people all over the world; this was particularly true for the Chinese intelligentsia during the May Fourth period. The wording of the letter marks Principal He-Wan Shuzhen as utterly conservative: though the solar calendar has been in use for over a dozen years, the letter is dated according to the old lunar calendar system, replete with poetic appellations for the ninth month (Chrysanthemum Month) and the first day of the month (Auspicious Day). The letter also employs the old-fashioned "schoolmaster" *(fuzi)* in preference to the more modern "teacher" *(jiaoyuan).*

"And what makes you the expert? Besides, Mrs. He is so anxious to get me, she won't take no for an answer." Because Third Huang had maligned the school and because Gao had just glanced at his watch, noting that it was already two thirty (just half an hour before class), our Venerable Schoolmaster was more than a little put out with his friend. He shot Third Huang a glance that clearly conveyed his mounting annoyance.

"Okay, okay!" Always sensitive to people's feelings, Third Huang now took a different tack. "Let's get down to serious business. The eldest son of Mao Zifu from Mao Family Village has blown into town. He's come looking for a geomancer to help them pick a gravesite. But that's beside the point. The thing is that he's got a good two hundred barby-cooks[6] on him, and so I'm getting up a foursome for tonight. The other three will be myself, Old Bo, and you. It's the chance of a lifetime, old buddy, so don't blow it. You just *have* to be there. The three of us will clean him out like he's never been cleaned before!"

"Old Buddy" (the Venerable Schoolmaster Gao, that is) muttered something or other, but gave no clear answer.

"You've got to be there, you've just got to! I still have to run over and set it up with Old Bo. It'll be at my place. Believe me, Mao's young dumb-dumb son is a lamb in the woods just waiting to be fleeced. We'll shave him clean as a whistle. It's in the bag. Now if you'll just let me have those mahjong tiles of yours—the marked ones—I'll be on my way."

The Venerable Schoolmaster Gao slowly stood up, walked to the head of his bed, took down the box of tiles, and handed the box to Third Huang. Then he glanced at his watch: two forty! Third Huang *is* a man who knows how to get things done, he thought to himself, but still he's got no business coming over here and knocking the new schools when he *knows* that I'm teaching in one of them, and he's got no business disturbing me just before I go to class, either. "Let's talk about it tonight," he answered coldly. "I've got to go to class now."

Giving *Liaofan's Shorter History* one last frustrated glance, Gao picked up the textbook and thrust it into his briefcase. Then, with much care and precision, he donned a newly bought hat and headed out the gate with Third Huang. Once outside, he length-

6. "Barbarian cookies" was slang for the silver coins that came into China from abroad.

ened his stride so that, one after the other, his shoulders began to swing purposively forward and back like the ends of the crossbar on a carpenter's drill. In less time than it takes to tell, he had left Third Huang far behind him.

* * *

Upon arrival at the academy, Gao handed one of his newly printed name cards to the hunchbacked gatekeeper. He heard a *this-way-please* and followed the gatekeeper inside. Having made only two turns, they arrived at the Faculty Preparation Room, which doubled as the academy's reception hall. Since Principal He was not at the school, it was the grey-haired Dean of Studies who greeted him. This turned out to be the celebrated Wan Yaopu whose poetic name was "Server at the Incense Table of the Jade Emperor."[7] He was, at that time, in the midst of publishing some of his poetry in the *Great China Daily News* under the title "At the Altar of the Immortals." This series purported to be an exchange of verses between Wan Yaopu and a certain female immortal.

"Aiya! Old Gentleman Yaopu! A real pleasure, a long *anticipated* pleasure!" Yaopu cupped one hand inside the other and pumped them both up and down in salutation. In bowing, he put his knees and hips through a half dozen bends so deep that one would have thought he were about to kneel at Gao's feet any minute.

Thereupon they sat down as a school servant, looking more dead than alive, brought in two cups of hot water. The Venerable Schoolmaster Gao looked at the clock on the opposite wall. It still had only two forty, half an hour behind his own watch.

"Aiya! I was just thinking of Old Gentleman Orky's masterpiece, that article called . . . uh . . . called . . . Yes, that's it, the one called 'On Everyone's Duty to Preserve the National Essence.'[8]

7. The Jade Emperor is the supreme Daoist deity. This particular poetic name is borrowed from the Tang dynasty poet Yuan Zhen (779–831), who once described himself using the same epithet in his poem "Boasting to Bai Juyi of My Island Abode."

8. During the early stages of the May Fourth Movement, an ultraconservative group of intellectuals identified themselves as defenders of the "national essence" *(guocui)* and argued that in the wake of the economic, military, and cultural pressures brought to bear by foreign powers, China's national salvation lay in preserving her own distinctive essence. Lu Xun condemned this group as hypocritical (because they really wanted to preserve institutions such as concubinage and their own privileged social positions) and argued that the real question was not whether the Chinese could preserve their national essence but whether that so-called essence could preserve the Chinese people.

There's an article that gives real meaning to the expression 'brief and to the point.' It's also a good example of what people have in mind when you hear them praise a piece of literature with the saying 'You get something new out of it no matter how many times you read it.' Every young person should be made to take your article as a text. Yes, indeed! Your article's an ideal text for the young, a *perfect* scripture for the up-and-coming generation! The humble servant you see standing before you, Old Gentleman Orky, is also something of an aficionado of the writing brush. However, I am just a dabbler and would certainly never make so bold as to compare myself to your worthy person." He did an encore of his hand pumping and then continued in conspiratorial tones: "I belong to a group called The Sacred Altar of the Writing Sands, a group that communicates with one of the immortals on a daily basis. Your humble servant often exchanges poetry with her himself. Why doesn't Old Gentleman Orky honor our little group with his presence someday too? The immortal's name is Flowerheart Pearl. Judging from what she says, she must be a flower spirit who has been exiled to the Realm of the Red Dust.[9] There's nothing she likes better than exchanging poetry with well-known literary men.[10] She'd be certain to look with great favor on a scholar like Old Gentleman Orky. Haha! Haha!"

For his part, however, the Venerable Schoolmaster Gao was in no position to expound grandly on the subject of immortals: his preparation on "The Rise and Fall of the Jin" had been skimpy to begin with, and by now he had already forgotten a good part of what precious little there was. Rising zigzag through the troubled waters of his present frustration, broken fragments of thought began to surface in his mind as he sat there: CLASSROOM DEMEANOR MUST BE STERN / SCAR ON FOREHEAD MUST BE HIDDEN / DON'T GO TOO FAST WHEN READING FROM THE TEXT / APPEAR OPEN AND POISED WHEN LOOKING AT STUDENTS.

But at the same time, he was vaguely aware of bits and pieces of Yaopu's monologue sandwiched in between these thoughts: "Presented a water chestnut . . . *Tipsily mounting the Blue Phoenix,*

9. A conventional epithet for the visible world.

10. Such "exchanges" would take place through a form of automatic writing, in which two people held a short horizontal bar from which a stick was suspended, its tip resting on the surface of a pan of sand. When her name was invoked, Flowerheart Pearl would communicate with the group by using that stick to write characters in the sand.

She ascends into the azure clouds—What a transcendent line! Old Gentleman Zheng Xiao must have invoked her spirit five times before she favored us with a poem . . . *A red sleeve brushing the Milky Way, Oh say not* . . . And then the Flowerheart Immortal said . . . Must be the first time Schoolmaster Orky has . . . That is our botanical garden."

"What, what?" The sight of Yaopu's pointing finger suddenly jolted Gao free of his own tangled thoughts. Following along in the direction indicated, he shifted his line of sight to a small plot of open land outside the window. There were four or five trees growing there. A single-story building sat on the far side.

"Those are our classrooms," said Yaopu, continuing to point. "The students are quite well behaved. Other than going to class, they devote themselves entirely to sewing—"

"Yes, yes, I see." Schoolmaster Orky was in desperate straits and hoped against hope that Yaopu would shut up, so that he would have an opportunity to collect himself and turn his thoughts to "The Rise and Fall of the Eastern Jin."

"Unfortunately, you'll find a few of them who want to write poetry, but we're not about to tolerate that. We've no objection, of course, to their participating in the movement for modernization, but writing poetry is certainly not an appropriate activity for young ladies from proper families. Flowerheart Pearl doesn't think too much of girls' schools either, says they blur the distinction between the sexes. She tells me the official circle up there in Heaven is not too pleased with them either.[11] Your humble servant has had several fruitful discussions with her on this very point."

Hearing the bell ring, Orky suddenly leapt to his feet.

"That's nothing to worry about. It's only the end-of-the-period bell. Sit back down for a bit."

"But I'm sure that Old Gentleman Yaopu must have many pressing tasks to attend to. Please don't put yourself out on my account, just because—"

"No, I'm not busy, not busy at all! Now, as your humble servant sees it, promoting the education of girls is in harmony with worldwide trends; however, if it's not done just right, it can all too easily go to extremes. As your humble servant sees it, the reason the offi-

11. The organization of the Daoist heaven was similar to that of the traditional Chinese state, replete with emperor, ministers, and court officials.

cial circle up in Heaven has expressed its displeasure is to warn us that we ought to nip any erroneous tendencies in the bud.

"If, however, the responsible parties will take the preservation of our national essence as their goal and march straight down the road—the middle of the road—toward it, neither veering too far to one side nor to the other, then nothing will go amiss. What is your opinion on the matter, Old Gentleman Orky? Do I have the right view of it or not? The Flowerheart Pearl Immortal thinks that my position is, as she says, 'not without its merit.' Haha, haha!"

The school servant brought two more cups of hot water, but just at that point the bell rang again. Only after he had pressured Orky into taking a few sips, however, did Yaopu slowly stand up and lead him across the botanical garden to the classrooms.

Heart thumping wildly, Gao stood by the lectern. As he looked out, half the room seemed taken up by fluffy black hair. Yaopu fished out a letter from the pocket behind the lapel of his robe and carefully unfolded it. Glancing at it now and then, he addressed the students.

"This is Schoolmaster Gao, Schoolmaster Gao Orky, a famous scholar. His essay 'The Duty of Every Citizen in the Chinese Republic to Aid in the Study and Systematization of Our National Heritage' is so well known as to need no introduction. Furthermore, according to the *Great China Daily News,* Schoolmaster Gao, prompted by high regard for the character of that Russian literary giant Gorky, has changed his own given name to Orky as a token of his respect. The appearance of this man on the literary stage is surely a stroke of good fortune for the Chinese world of letters. As a result of Principal He's repeated invitations, and out of the goodness of his own heart, Gao Orky now deigns to join our school as a teacher of history."

Schoolmaster Gao suddenly felt forsaken. Yaopu was nowhere to be seen. There he was, all alone, stranded in front of the class. There was nothing for it but to take his position behind the lectern, bow to the students, and try to collect himself. Remembering his resolve to assume a severe demeanor, he slowly opened the text and began lecturing on "The Rise and Fall of the Eastern Jin."

Tee hee! It seemed there was someone out there trying to disguise a giggle.

Venerable Schoolmaster Gao's face flushed as he hurriedly consulted the text to see if he had read something the wrong way. No, there was the heading plain as the nose on your face: "The Eastern Jin Satisfied with Partial Sovereignty Over the Country," just the way he had read it. He peeked out over the top of the text. There was nothing amiss there either: half the room was still taken up by fluffy black hair. Suspecting the giggle was merely a function of his own present state of hypertension, he pulled himself together again, fixed his eyes on the text, and slowly continued.

At first, his ears made him aware of the words that were coming from his mouth, but then gradually they tuned out and he no longer knew what his mouth was saying. By the time he got to "The Ambitious Plans of Shi Le,"[12] he heard nothing but a swelling flood of laughter that now burst through the dikes of lips no longer able to contain it.

He just *had* to take another peek. The scene before him had almost totally changed: half the room was now taken up by eyes and just under the eyes, by petite equilateral triangles, a pair of nostrils growing in each and every triangle. What was more, eyes and triangles rushed together in a deep, roiling, glittering sea that surged massively forward and threatened to engulf him. Just in that split second when he peeked, however, the wave suddenly transformed itself back into half a roomful of fluffy black hair.

He averted his own eyes with the same immediacy as that which had led the students to avert theirs. From that point onward, he no longer dared let his gaze stray from the text. Finally, when he couldn't take it any longer and just *had* to look at something, he raised his eyes and contemplated the ceiling: the lines of a perfectly circular, decorative ridge were discernible in the center of a yellowed surface that had obviously once been white. While he looked, the circle suddenly came to life: it expanded and then it contracted, pulsating so rapidly that his head began to swim from watching it.

He knew, however, that if he lowered his eyes to classroom

12. During the period 304–439, competing barbarian groups in north China ruled over a bewildering array of short-lived kingdoms. One of these was Zhao, established by the Jie people. In 329 the Jie general Shi Le (274–333) mounted a revolt against the government, in part because he thought it had become too sinified. The new, more tribal regime that he established was thereafter known as the Later Zhao, to distinguish it from the sinified Former Zhao.

level, there would be no avoiding that terrible sea of eyes and nostrils, and so he had no choice but to shift his line of vision back to the textbook with lightning speed. By now he had already gotten to the Battle of the Fei River and the defending general, Fu Jian, was about to become so paranoid about the power of the Eastern Jin forces that, observing their mountain lair from afar, he would take "every blade of grass and every tree to be a soldier."[13]

Though the Venerable Schoolmaster Gao continued to suspect the students were still laughing up their sleeves at him, he kept a stiff upper lip and braved on. He lectured; he lectured; and then he lectured some more. He felt as though he had been at it forever, but that damned bell still hadn't rung. He couldn't keep glancing at his watch, for the girls would surely despise him for that. Before long he found himself explaining "The Sudden Rise of the Toba." After that came the chart showing "The Rise and Fall of the Six Dynasties—Compared," something he was totally unprepared to talk about since he had not expected to get that far today. He knew it would look a bit shoddy to dismiss the class before the bell, but what else was he to do?

After some hesitation he announced: "Since this is our first day, we'll just stop right here." With a slight bow in the direction of the girls, he stepped down from the lectern and slipped out of the classroom.

Tee hee hee!

He seemed to detect some giggling behind him and could almost see the laughter welling up out of that deep sea of nostrils. Thoroughly disconcerted, Schoolmaster Gao stepped into the botanical garden and strode manfully back toward the Faculty Preparation Room.

A sudden blow to the head so stunned him that *A General Textbook of Chinese History* dropped from his hand and fell to the ground. He stumbled back a few paces, focused his eyes, and saw that the leaves on the branch he had just now walked into were still trembling. The Venerable Schoolmaster Gao bent over and picked up his book. Immediately next to the place where it had landed, a small wooden sign was stuck into the ground.

---

13. The Battle of the Fei River took place in the present Anhui Province in the year 383.

MULBERRY

Genus: Mulberry

Once again he seemed to hear giggling behind him and could almost see the laughter welling up from that sea of nostrils. With great embarrassment, he raised his hand and felt the painful lump beginning to rise on his forehead. The Venerable Schoolmaster made a beeline for the Faculty Preparation Room.

The two cups of hot water were still there, but the servant who looked more dead than alive was nowhere to be seen and there was no trace of Yaopu, either. The Faculty Preparation Room's gloomy interior was only relieved by the brightness of Gao's brand new briefcase and the splendor of his newly acquired hat. He saw that the clock on the wall showed only three forty.

* * *

For quite some time after returning to his room, Schoolmaster Gao would feel his entire body flush with a sudden heat, and for no apparent reason; he was also subject to sudden flashes of anger. In the end, he began to feel that the new schools really were about to ruin the general morality and that it would, in truth, be better to close them down—especially the girls' schools. What was the point in educating girls anyway? An appeal to female vanity, pure and simple.

Tee hee!

The faint sound of laughter lingered in his ears, made him even angrier, and confirmed him in his resolve to resign. He would write a letter to Principal He this very night. All he would need to say was that he had been afflicted by some sort of foot disorder. And if she tried to get him to stay on anyway? What then? Well, he just *wouldn't,* that's all. *Who can tell WHAT kind of trouble these girls' schools will eventually get themselves into? Why implicate myself by joining ranks with them? It's just not worth it!*

With a decisive air, Gao removed *Liaofan's Shorter History* from his desk, pushed the mirror off to one side, folded up his notice of appointment, and was just about to sit down when he discovered there was something else not quite to his liking either: that appointment card was just too damned red. He grabbed it up and shoved it into one of the drawers along with *A General Textbook of Chinese History.*

Now he had his desktop arranged just the way he wanted: everything was cleared from it save for a mirror. The arrangement proved much more restful to the eyes. And yet, somehow or other, Gao still didn't feel right. It was as though half his soul were missing. Immediately realizing what the trouble was, he put on his red-tasseled autumn cap and went straight over to Third Huang's place.

"Well, if it isn't the Venerable Schoolmaster Gao Orky himself!" said Lao Bo in a loud voice.

"Oh, go blow it out your ass!" Gao Orky frowned and rapped Lao Bo across the top of the head.

"Finished teaching? How did it go? Any real foxes?" asked Third Huang eagerly.

"I've no intention of staying on. Who can tell *what* kind of trouble these girls' schools will get themselves into before they're done. There's really no point in decent people like ourselves getting mixed up with them."

Plump as a stuffed dumpling, the Mao family's pride and joy came through the door.

"Aiya! A real pleasure, a long anticipated pleasure!" Throughout the room, hands were cupped one inside the other and pumped up and down in salutation while knees and hips, one set after the other, were worked into bends so extreme that one would have thought their owners were about to kneel at the feet of the Mao family's young hopeful at any moment.

Pointing at the Venerable Schoolmaster Gao, Lao Bo explained to the Mao lad: "This is brother Gao Ganting of whom I've told you so much."

"Aiya! A real pleasure, a long anticipated pleasure!" The eldest son of the Mao family pumped his hands for Gao's benefit and even threw in a nod of the head.

On the left side of the room, angled away from the wall, a small square table had long since been set out. While greeting his guests, aided by a young servant girl, Third Huang placed four chairs around the table and arranged the mahjong tiles. Four tall candles were placed at the corners of the table and lit; four players took their places.

Silence reigned supreme, broken only when ivory tiles struck against the red sandalwood table and sent one crisp *clink* after another reverberating through the stillness of the early night.

Despite a fairly good run of tiles, the Venerable Schoolmaster Gao continued to be upset by a certain feeling of righteous, public-spirited indignation. Ordinarily he was able to put things out of mind quite readily, but this time it was different. Today he just could not rid himself of the thought that there was real cause for worry over the state of the world.

Though the pile of chips before him grew ever taller, it still wasn't enough to relieve him of this anxiety, or make him look on the bright side of things.

But the state of the world, after all, is never static. And so it was that in the course of time, the Venerable Schoolmaster Gao began to feel that things were actually improving after all. But this feeling came very late in the evening, after they had already finished the second round. The Venerable Schoolmaster Gao was holding a pure-color hand at the time.[14]

MAY 21, 1925

---

14. A winning hand, similar to the royal flush in poker.

The Loner

I

Wei Lianshu and I were fairly close for a while. As I think back on it, our friendship was somewhat unique—it began and ended with a funeral.

It was in S-town that I first ran into him.[1] Long before I met Wei, I had often heard people speak of him. They described him as something of an oddball: though his training had been in biology, he was employed as a history teacher in the local middle school; though he treated those around him with apparent indifference, he loved to involve himself in other people's affairs, and did so rather frequently; and though he was fond of saying that the family system ought to be destroyed, whenever he received any salary he would immediately send it back home to his grandmother. Wei Lianshu was the subject of interest in a variety of other respects as well; in sum, for the people of S-town, he provided something to talk about.[2]

One autumn when I had nothing in particular to do, I put up for a while at the home of relatives on Coldstone Mountain. They were named Wei, too, and were in fact clansmen to Lianshu. However, they understood him even less than outsiders did and would speak of him as though he were a foreigner. "Not like us," they would observe.

That he was not like them was not in the least surprising either, for though the attempt at mass education had been going on for two decades, Coldstone Mountain still could not boast so much as a single primary school. Lianshu was the only one from any of the mountain villages thereabouts who had gone away and been educated; thus in the eyes of the villagers he really *was* quite different. He was also the object of their envy and they claimed he had made a great deal of money.

Unlike most of the other stories in *Wondering Where to Turn,* "The Loner" had not been published elsewhere first. The Chinese expression that forms the basis of the title is explained in "Soap," n. 11.

1. Lu Xun often uses the name "S-town" to suggest his hometown, Shaoxing.

2. The character of Wei Lianshu is, in part, based on Lu Xun's friend Fan Ainong; see the Introduction.

At the end of fall that year, dysentery swept through the mountain villages. I was in danger myself and briefly considered going back to town. I heard that Lianshu's grandmother had contracted the disease and due to her advanced age was in grave danger; worse yet, there was not a single doctor on Coldstone Mountain. Lianshu's household, if you could call it that, consisted of nothing more than himself and this grandmother. With the help of a hired man, grandmother and grandson had always lived rather simply. Lianshu had lost his parents as a very young boy and it was his grandmother who raised him. From what I heard, she had gone through no little hardship in doing so, but was now at last secure and happy in her declining years. And yet there was a certain hushed and lonely air to their household too, for Lianshu had neither wife nor children. I daresay this was also one of the reasons people thought him "not like us."

By land, Coldstone Mountain was a good hundred *li* from S-town, where Lianshu taught at the middle school; and even by water it would be seventy.[3] If someone were sent to town to fetch him back, it would be at least four days before he could reasonably be expected to appear. In such a small out-of-the-way place, the old woman's illness was an important event that everyone would hear about. And so by the very next day, the news that she was failing fast and that the grandson had been sent for had already thundered through every household in the village. By the Fourth Watch that same day, however, she had breathed her last.[4] Her last words were: "Why won't you let me see Lianshu?"

Clan elders, close relatives, the old woman's maternal relatives, as well as people who were not intimately involved, gathered together and packed an entire room in solemn conclave. They estimated that by the time Lianshu arrived, it would be time to proceed with the encoffining ceremony. Since the *longlife box* and *longlife clothes* had long since been prepared, there was nothing to worry about on that score.[5] The first and foremost problem facing them now was how to deal with the *burden-inheriting grandson,* for they assumed he would be sure to try and introduce new wrin-

3. The distance measured by one *li* is about one-third of a mile.

4. The night was traditionally divided into five watches: I, 7–9; II, 9–11; III, 11–1; IV, 1–3; and V, 3–5.

5. Italicized words for the casket and burial clothes are conventional epithets.

kles into both the mourning rituals and the funeral ceremonies.[6] After proper deliberation, they established three principles from which they were determined not to budge: (1) he was to wear the customary mourning white; (2) he was to prostrate himself before the casket; and (3) he was to call in Daoist and Buddhist priests to perform the customary funeral ceremonies.

In short, everything would be done as it had always been done. That settled, they further agreed that they would meet once again in the main room of the house on the day Lianshu returned so as to present a united front. They would engage him in a rigorous and stern parley in the course of which each individual clan member would speak so as to add to their collective strength.

Licking their lips in anticipation of the coming confrontation, the rest of the villagers eagerly awaited news of Lianshu's arrival. They all knew that he was one of those "new party" people who "ate off foreign religions" and had never talked reason in his whole life.[7] To the villagers, it seemed more than likely that a fight would break out between Lianshu and his relatives, or if they were lucky, maybe they would get to see some other completely outlandish thing that they could not even anticipate as yet.

According to what I later heard, it was afternoon when Lianshu arrived home. He had barely had time to walk through the door and bow toward his grandmother's coffin when the clan elders began setting their prearranged stratagem into motion. They called him into the main hall and after a lot of polite chitchat, worked into the main theme. With half a dozen mouths and as many tongues, each speaking in support of the others, they so overpowered Lianshu with the force of their voices that he was unable to say anything. Finally, when they had said everything they had to say, silence filled the room. Every last pair of eyes stared apprehensively at Lianshu's lips.

There was not the slightest change in his expression as he answered quite simply: "Anything you say is fine with me."

Burdens were lifted from every heart there that day, for this was something they had not anticipated; in the twinkling of a thought, however, those same burdens returned, and with even greater

6. Since his father was dead, Lianshu had "inherited" the burden of supervising the family's funeral arrangements; the term *chengzhongsun* was specific to the situation.

7. The villagers use "new party" as a cover term to describe all modernizers; to "eat off a foreign religion" is to make a living by toadying to foreign missionaries.

weight than before, for they felt that Lianshu was still acting far too much "not like us" and this gave them fresh cause for concern. The other villagers were quite disappointed when they heard about his behavior. "That's strange!" they commented as they passed the news around. "He said, 'Anything you say is all right with me.' Let's go see what's up." Actually, if everything were "all right" with him, then everything would be exactly as custom prescribed and there could be nothing "up" in the first place, but nonetheless they wanted to go see. In high spirits they filled the main hall of the house just as dusk was descending. I was among those who went to see "what was up." I had sent some incense and candles on ahead. By the time I arrived, Lianshu was already putting the burial clothes on the corpse.

He was a small, energetic man whose disheveled head of hair conspired with thick black eyebrows and a heavy beard to render half his face darkly invisible, and in the midst of all that darkness glowed two eyes. He dressed the corpse so skillfully and meticulously that one would have thought him a professional undertaker. All those who were watching sighed in admiration. However, according to the old and established precedents of Coldstone Mountain, at times like these relatives could always be expected to find fault, and find fault they did. Lianshu bore it in silent good humor, immediately responding to criticism by making whatever changes were requested, and without the slightest sign of displeasure. A white-haired old lady standing in front of me sighed in admiration.

Then came the ritual prostrations; then the ritual wailing while the women chanted Buddhist prayers; then the laying-in; then still more ritual prostrations and then more wailing, until the last nail had been hammered into the coffin. After a brief moment of silence and immobility everyone suddenly started stirring again. One could readily tell they were rather surprised, and dissatisfied as well. I, too, could not help but feel that something was radically wrong, for from beginning to end, Lianshu had not shed a single tear. He had just sat there on the mourner's mat, eyes glowing in the midst of the darkness that was his face.

And thus the encoffining was completed in an atmosphere of surprise and dissatisfaction. Everyone milled around uneasily as though ready to break up and go home as soon as Lianshu gave the word. But he still sat there on the mourner's mat deep in thought. Then quite suddenly tears began to stream down his cheeks. Sounds broke from his throat and came together in a long wail which sounded like the howl of a wounded animal, like a wolf on a deserted plain howling into the depths of night—sorrow and fury mixed with pain.

Within the customary categories of mourning ceremonies there was no place for such a display, and hence the relatives neither anticipated it nor knew how to react to it. After a moment's hesitation, one or two went forward and pleaded with him to stop. More and more joined them until a small crowd had gathered. But Lianshu sat immobile as a mountain and continued to wail.

There was nothing the mourners could do but break up and leave. Lianshu continued to weep for a good half hour or so, and then just as suddenly as he had begun, he stopped. Without in any way acknowledging the presence of a few lingering mourners, he headed straight for home. Later on someone went to spy on him and came back to report that Lianshu had gone straight into his grandmother's room, flopped down on her bed, and gone to sleep.

Two days later, the day before I was to go back to town, I heard the villagers talking about something or other in such excited tones that you would have thought they had seen a ghost. They said that Lianshu planned to burn most of the furniture so that his grandmother would have the use of it in the afterworld, and to hand the rest of it over to the maid who had served his grandmother in life and had seen her through all the funeral arrangements in death. What was more, he was going to let this maid live in the house for as long as she pleased. His close relatives and more distant clansmen reasoned with him until they were blue in the face, but he simply would not be talked out of it.

It was probably more curiosity than anything else that moved me to drop by on my way back to town to offer my condolences. Lianshu came out wearing unhemmed white mourning clothes. His expression was as detached and indifferent as ever. I expended quite some effort in condoling with him over his loss and exhorting him to face the future, but other than grunting in agreement now and then, his only response was to thank me for my "good intentions."

2

The third time we ran into each other was at the beginning of winter that same year. It was in a bookstore in S-town and we nodded to each other, recognizing at least the bare fact of our acquaintance. But it was only toward the end of that year—after I lost my job—that we became really close, for it was during this period that I started to visit him. In part, of course, this was a function of my being bored and having nothing better to do; in part it was also because I had heard that Lianshu, though normally cold and aloof, could be quite warm to people who were down on their luck. The world is filled with unpredictable *ups* as well as downs, however, and people *down* on their luck are not likely to remain that way over a long period of time. Hence Lianshu seldom kept friends over a long period of time either. But when I sent my name card in, he proved worthy of his reputation, for he received me immediately.

His living room consisted of two adjoining rooms. There was no furniture to speak of—just a table, some chairs, and a few bookcases. Although people said he was one of those "new party" fanatics, there were few modern books on the shelves. Lianshu was already aware that I had lost my job, and yet once we had exhausted all the usual host-guest clichés, we could not manage anything more than sitting and facing each other in a silence that gradually began to weigh on both of us. I simply sat there and watched as he puffed nervously on his cigarette; only when the butt was short enough to burn his fingers did he throw it on the floor.

"Have a smoke," he said abruptly while reaching for a second one himself.

I took one and smoked along with him. I talked of teaching and of books, but the atmosphere still felt just as oppressive as before. Just as I was thinking of leaving, I heard a chaos of voices and footsteps outside. Four boys and girls barged in. The eldest was eight or nine, the youngest four or five. Their hands, faces, and clothes were quite dirty. They were ugly. Nonetheless, a happy glow immediately appeared in Lianshu's eyes. He hurried to his feet and walked into the adjoining room. "Big Liang, Second Liang, so you've both come too! I've bought the harmonicas you asked for yesterday!"

The children crowded in and in less time than it takes to tell, crowded back on out again, each blowing away on a harmonica. As soon as they were outside, however, a fight broke out and one of them started to bawl.

"Each of you gets one harmonica. They are all exactly alike, so there's no need to fight over them!" Lianshu enjoined, following along behind.

"Who does all *that* crew belong to?" I asked.

"The landlord. They're motherless, only a grandmother to look after them."

"Is the landlord all by himself?"

"Yes. It must have been three or four years ago that his wife died, and he hasn't taken another—otherwise he'd never have been willing to rent out his spare rooms to a bachelor like myself." He grinned sarcastically as he spoke. I itched to ask *why* he was still single but because I did not feel I knew him that well, in the end I did not.

When I did get to know him, Lianshu turned out to be quite a conversationalist. He had lots of ideas about all kinds of things; what's more, they were often startlingly good. But some of the people who came to visit him were hard to take. Most of the latter had read Yu Dafu's short story "Sinking," and often referred to themselves as "unfortunate youths" or "superfluous men."[8] Arrogantly draping themselves over his furniture like great indolent crabs, they would moan, sigh, knit their brows, and smoke their cigarettes.

And then there were the landlord's children, forever fighting amongst themselves, knocking over the china, and begging for snacks until it made your head swim. Yet as soon as Lianshu set eyes on them, he would cease to be his usual cold self and treat them as though they were more precious to him than his own life. Someone told me that once when Third Liang came down with measles, Lianshu was so wrought up that his normally gloomy face managed to take on an even darker hue. Unexpectedly it turned out to be such a light case that even the children's grandmother treated the intensity of Lianshu's concern as a subject for lighthearted jests.

He seemed to sense that his intense concern for children was a little too much even for me, for one day he made a special point of finding just the right time in our conversation to explain to me that "children are always good. They're so innocent."

"That's not entirely true either," I responded in an offhand way.

---

8. A semi-autobiographical short story exposing the inner feelings and sexual frustration of a Chinese student in Japan. It has been translated by Joseph S. M. Lau and C. T. Hsia in *Twentieth-Century Chinese Stories,* ed. C. T. Hsia (New York & London: Columbia University Press, 1971), pp. 3–33.

"But it is. Among children you won't find the evil dispositions you do among adults. The evil they grow into—the kind you so often attack—is the result of environment. It wasn't there in the beginning. In the beginning there was only innocence. I think this is the only reason we have for holding out any hope for China."

"No, you're wrong. If there were no roots in the children to begin with, how would the fruit appear after they've grown up? Take a seed, for instance. It's precisely because the seed contains the potential to produce branches, leaves, flowers, and fruit that these are able to appear once the tree has matured. How could these things come out of nothing?" I was full of such Buddhist arguments. Because I was unemployed and had nothing better to do, I had followed in the footsteps of those political bigwigs who keep to a vegetarian diet and go in for Buddhist philosophy once they have been thrown out of office. I too was reading Buddhist sutras. I didn't really understand the principles behind Buddhism, of course, but that didn't keep me from running on and on.

In the end the only thing I accomplished was to get Lianshu good and mad. He scowled at me but didn't say anything. I couldn't tell if it was because there was nothing he *could* say or whether he felt I wasn't worth arguing with. His attitude toward me was much colder than I had seen it in a long, long time. In utter silence he smoked two cigarettes. By the time he had started on the third, the only thing left for me to do was to leave, and I did.

It wasn't until three months later that the air between us finally cleared. Forgetfulness no doubt played a good part in helping us get over our misunderstanding, but the fact that an "innocent" child glared at him with murderous enmity played its part too. The experience made him conclude, perhaps, that *some* allowance could be made for my presumptuous and irreverent view of children, though this of course is nothing but conjecture on my part.

On the day the air cleared, after a few drinks at my place, he raised his head a bit and announced in a melancholy air: "It was really strange. On the way to your place just now, I saw a child on the street with a reed in his hand. He pointed it at me and shouted, 'Kill!' Just a kid, barely old enough to walk—"

"It's simply the result of a bad environment."

The words were no sooner out of my mouth than I regretted them, but my friend had apparently not taken offense. He kept on drinking cup after cup of wine while firing up cigarette after cigarette as well.

"Hey, I almost forgot to ask," I said, changing the subject as best I could. "Since you don't go around visiting people very often, what got into you today that you came to see me? Though we've known each other for more than a year now, this is the very first time that you've come to my place."

"I was about to bring that up myself. Make sure you don't come over to my place for the next few days. I've got some very repulsive people staying with me, an adult and a child. Don't act like human beings, either of them!"

"An adult and a child? Who?" I was puzzled.

"My cousin and his son. Hah! The kid's just like his old man."

"Come to town to see you and take in the sights?"

"No. Says he's come to talk things over with me. Wants me to adopt his son."

"What? Adopt his *son*?" I couldn't help raising my voice. "But you're not even married yet, right?"

"They know I'm not going to *get* married either. Doesn't make a bit of difference. What they're really after is that ramshackle house of mine up on Coldstone Mountain. You know me. Soon as I get any money, I spend it. That house is the only bit of property I have. I'm letting an old working woman live up there. It seems that my cousin and his son have decided to devote their lives to running her off the place."

The icy sarcasm of his voice sent chills down my spine. Nonetheless I tried to put a better face on things. "Your clansmen can't be as bad as all that. Just a bit old-fashioned in their ideas, that's all. How about when you wept at your grandmother's funeral? Didn't they all gather round and do their best to comfort you?"

"That's nothing. You should have seen their enthusiasm when they gathered round to comfort me when my *father* died and they were trying to push me into signing the house over to them." He stared into space as though recreating that scene in his mind's eye.[9]

"Well, when you come right down to it, the crux of the whole matter is that you don't have any children of your own. Come to think of it, why is it that you've never taken a wife?" I had finally found the rudder I needed to steer the conversation.

He looked at me in surprise. And then, after a bit, stared down

9. Lu Xun's brother, Zhou Zuoren, said that Lu Xun once used these very words to describe how his own great uncle tried to cheat him of the family property in Shaoxing when their father died in 1897.

at one of his knees. He began to smoke, but let my question go unanswered.

3

But even in such utterly humdrum surroundings Lianshu would not be allowed to live in peace. Anonymous attacks on him gradually began appearing in the local papers and rumors about him began circulating in educational circles as well. These were no longer the anecdotes of old that used to be passed around as amusing topics of conversation, but rather vicious bits of gossip intended to do him real harm. I realized this was because he had recently taken to publishing his own opinions about things in newspaper columns here and there, and so I did not pay much attention to it, for I knew there was nothing the people of S-town disliked more than a man with the temerity to publish no-holds-barred opinions. They would be sure to find some way of doing him in behind his back. That's the way things had always been in S-town, as Lianshu himself well knew.

One day that spring I heard that his principal had fired him. The news shook me up a bit. It was not that the residents of S-town were behaving any more badly than usual—they had always been that way—it was just that I had always hoped against hope that people in my immediate circle of friends would be lucky enough to be spared.

At the time I had more than enough to do worrying about making my own living. Besides, I was busily negotiating for a teaching position that fall in Shanyang and couldn't afford the time to call on him. It wasn't until three months or so after he had been sacked that I was free enough to pay him a visit, but somehow or other, even then I still didn't.

While downtown one day I happened to stop at a used bookstand and noticed with a start that one of the items on sale was a Jiguge first edition *Key to the Shiji*.[10] It was Lianshu's. Though he was fond of books, Lianshu was by no means a real collector and a

---

10. Mao Jin (1599–1659), the Ming dynasty scholar and printer, gave the name Jiguge to the studio from which he edited and published books. Jiguge editions were prized even during Mao Jin's lifetime. Burton Watson has translated much of the *Shiji* under the title *Records of the Grand Historian of China*. The *Key to the Shiji (Shiji suoyin)* is a multivolumed commentary by Sima Zhen of the Tang dynasty.

treasure like this would have constituted the centerpiece of his modest library. He would never have parted with it unless hard pressed. Could he have gotten *that* poor in three short months? On the other hand, it was true that he spent his money as fast as he made it and never had any savings to fall back on. Still . . . I bought a bottle of wine, two bags of peanuts, two smoked fish-heads, and set out to pay Lianshu a call.

His door was closed. I called his name a few times. No answer. Perhaps he had gone to sleep. Rapping on the door, I called even louder.

"Probably gone out!" Obviously annoyed by the racket I was making, a fat woman with triangular eyes thrust her grey head out a window from across the way and shouted just as loudly as I had. She was the grandmother of Big Liang and the other children.

"Where did he go?" I asked.

"Where did he go? Who knows? Where *could* he go? Just stick around a while, he's never very long."

I pushed open the door and entered his living room. *If you don't see a friend for even a day, three years' worth of changes may have come into play*—there's a lot to that saying, for Lianshu's room was now empty and forlorn. Little furniture was left, and the bookshelves were virtually bare—nothing but a few foreign works that you couldn't have given away in a place like S-town. The round table still stood in the center of the room, the same table around which had gathered, so often in the past, mixed assemblages of the landlord's dirty, brawling children, melancholy young men who had taken the burden of the world upon their shoulders, and self-proclaimed geniuses born ahead of their times. The table now stood abandoned and functionless, a light layer of dust covering its top. Putting down the wine bottle and paper bag, I pulled out a chair and sat facing the door.

It was not very long before the door opened and someone slipped, like a shadow, silently into the room—Lianshu in the flesh. Perhaps it was because of the fading light of dusk, but he seemed somehow darker than before, though the expression on his face was the same as ever.

"Oh, so *you're* here. How long have you been waiting?" He seemed rather pleased to see me.

"Not long," I replied. "Where have you been?"

"Nowhere, really. Just wandering around."

He pulled out a chair and sat down at the table. We began drinking. We talked a bit about how he had come to be out of work. He didn't want to dwell on it, however, for he considered his joblessness something one might easily have expected, and besides, it was the kind of thing he had encountered many times in the past anyway. As usual, he drank his wine cup after cup after cup. And, as usual again, he held forth at some length on the topics of society and history. I don't know why exactly, but at just that point I happened to glance over at his empty bookshelves and remembered having seen his Jiguge first edition *Key to the Shiji* on sale. I was suddenly engulfed by melancholy and loneliness.

"How bare your living room looks . . . Not many visitors lately, huh?"

"None. Since I'm in such a down mood they know it wouldn't be much fun to come by anyway. Someone who's depressed really does make others feel uncomfortable. After all, no one goes to a park in the winter." Then quite suddenly he raised his head, looked at me, and asked, "You still haven't managed to land a steady job yourself, have you?"

Though I knew he was already a bit tipsy, I still couldn't help feeling slightly offended. As I was about to reply, he cocked his head as though he had just heard something; then he grabbed a handful of peanuts and headed outside. I could hear Big Liang and the others shouting and laughing outside the door.

No sooner had he gone out than the voices died away as the children ran from him. Lianshu chased after them, tried to talk with them, but they did not answer. Silent as a shadow, he slipped back into the room again and put the peanuts back into a paper bag.

"They won't even take food from me," he said in low tones as though mocking himself.

Although I felt sick at heart, I forced a wan smile and said, "Lianshu, I think you go around *trying* to make things difficult for yourself. You take too dim a view of your fellow man. You—"

He tried to cut me off with a cold laugh, but I wouldn't have it.

"You're not going to get off that easily. I'm not done yet. You probably think that those of us who occasionally visit you come only because we're bored and don't have anything else to do, that we *use* you as a convenient way to pass an idle hour. Am I right?"

"Absolutely not! Well . . . perhaps I think that way sometimes

—either that, or you're looking for an amusing story to pass along to your friends."

"Well, you're dead wrong. People aren't like that. It's *you.* You're the one who's spun yourself into a tight little cocoon. You should try to look on the bright side of things," I concluded with a sigh.

"Perhaps. But answer this for me: where did all the silk for that cocoon come from? Besides, you'll find lots of others like me in this world—my grandmother, for instance. Though I don't have any of her blood in my veins, it looks as though I may well have inherited her fate anyway. It doesn't really matter though, for I've shed my tears in advance for that fate—and for hers as well—a long, long time ago."

My mind's eye immediately went back to his grandmother's encoffining ceremony. And now I pounced on the opportunity to ask: "I've never understood. Why did you weep so inconsolably when—"

"When my grandmother was encoffined? That's right, you wouldn't understand." He lit the lamp and went on in flat tones devoid of feeling. "I'll bet our friendship owes itself to the way I wept that day too. You've no way of knowing this, but that grandmother of mine was my father's *step*mother. His own mother died when he was only three." Musing to himself, Lianshu drank his wine in silence and finished a smoked fish-head. "Back then *I* wasn't aware of this either—except that even as a child, I felt there were certain things that just didn't make any sense.

"My father was still alive and we were well enough off so that during the first month of the lunar New Year we'd hang up paintings of the ancestors and provide them with lavish sacrifices. I loved to gaze at those paintings of my ancestors all dressed up in their finest clothes. Couldn't get enough of it. An elderly maid would always hold me up to one of the paintings, point, and say: 'This is your very own grandmother. Pay your respects to her so she'll help you grow up good and fast and make you healthy as a lively young tiger.'

"Since I already *had* a grandmother, I couldn't figure out how I had come to have this second one who was said to be my 'very own.' On the other hand, I rather liked the looks of this 'very own' grandmother too. Unlike the grandmother who lived with me now, she wasn't old. This grandmother was young and pretty. She wore a gold-bordered dress and had on a cap festooned with pearls.[11] She looked just about the same as my mother in *her* wedding picture. As I looked at her, she looked back. What's more, a smile gradually gathered at the corners of her mouth. I knew she must love me very much.

"But I loved the grandmother I had now too, the grandmother who sat by the window day in and day out doing her needlework. And I kept right on loving her even though I often felt there was something cold about her, something that made her different from other boys' grandmothers. You see, no matter how much I'd try, I was never able to coax even a smile from her, never able to get her into a playful mood.

"As the years went by, bit by bit I began to draw away from her. This had nothing to do with her increasing age or the fact that I knew she wasn't my 'real' grandmother. It was just that seeing her sit like that year in and year out doing all that needlework like a machine of some sort was, as you can well imagine, enough to put off a growing boy. While I changed, she remained exactly what she had been: she did her needlework, she looked after me, and in her way she continued to love me too. To be sure, she seldom smiled, but then she never scolded me either. She went on like that right up until my father died. And afterwards, if anything, she became even *more* the needlework machine because at that point we were almost entirely dependent on what she did just to make ends meet. And she slaved away at it for all she was worth right up until the time I entered the academy . . ."

The oil was almost gone and the light in the lantern died down. Lianshu stood, took a galvanized iron oilpot down from a bookshelf, and filled it.

"Coal oil's gone up twice this month alone," he commented, adjusting the wick. "Things are getting tougher every day . . . All things considered, her final years weren't all that bad—she lived a long time too—and so there was no real reason for me to weep the way I did at the encoffining. There were certainly enough other people weeping for her at that ceremony anyway, wouldn't you say? Even those who had done their best to do her in while she was alive wailed for all they were worth, or at the very least, managed to look as sad as possible.

---

11. Lianshu describes a traditional wedding costume.

"Well, right in the midst of all their wailing, somehow or other, my grandmother's life appeared before my eyes in miniature—a human life composed entirely of isolation, an isolation she had fashioned with her own hands, an isolation she had put into her mouth and chewed on like a cud over the years. But more than that, I felt there were many people like her in the world, and it was for all those people that I wept so bitterly. But as I think back on it now, a good part of it was probably also because I tended to think too much with my heart and not enough with my head.

"Your way of viewing me now is the way I viewed her then, but I was wrong. For in all truth, I have to admit that from as far back as I can remember, I *myself* was one of those who drew away from *her* . . ."[12]

Cigarette between his fingers, Lianshu became silent and lowered his head, lost in thought. The lamp flickered weakly.

"What a hard thing it is to die and have no one to mourn you," he said as though talking to himself. After a brief pause he raised his head and looked at me. "From the looks of things, you've got all you can do just to take care of yourself. But even so, I've got to find *some* sort of work right away."

"Don't you have any other friends you could ask to help out?" At the time there was nothing I could do for him—or myself, for that matter.

"As a matter of fact, there probably *are* a few, but they're in the same boat I am."

By the time I took my leave of Lianshu and went outside, the moon was directly overhead. It was an exceedingly silent night.

---

12. According to Zhou Zuoren, the character of Lianshu's grandmother is based on Lu Xun's own grandmother. During his childhood, Lu Xun had been especially close to this ill-treated woman. It is likely that his awareness of her unhappy life accounts, in part, for the strong note of feminism in his writing. Her unfortunate position in the family resulted from two circumstances: (1) though she gave birth to a daughter in 1868, she bore no sons; (2) she was the second wife of Lu Xun's grandfather (his first wife died soon after giving birth to Lu Xun's father) and suffered almost total neglect while her husband enjoyed the sexual favors of his concubines in Beijing, where he served as an official. As a young boy, Lu Xun, like Lianshu, had once been told abruptly that this woman was not his "real" grandmother and then was shown a picture of his grandfather's earlier wife. Zuoren has said that the words Lianshu uses in reminiscence here are the very ones Lu Xun often used himself to describe the unhappy lot of his grandmother. When she died in 1910, Lu Xun also supervised her funeral.

4

The school situation in Shanyang was anything but ideal. After two months I still had not received a single penny of my salary and even had to cut down on cigarettes. But the school staff, all the way down to petty clerks making no more than fifteen or sixteen dollars a month, accepted their fate with cheerful equanimity. Toughened on the forge of poverty, these clerks continued to push their lean and haggard bodies through the routines of the day. And if in the course of their work, a person of rank happened to drop by, they would rise from their seats with a great flurry of respect, giving the lie to that old saw: *The people will well mannered be, Only when fed sufficientlie.* Whenever I saw them pop out of their seats like that, somehow or other I would always think of the request Lianshu had made of me just before I left.

Indeed, just before I left for Shanyang, his prospects for making any kind of livelihood were bleaker than ever. Poverty often showed its face in the things he did. You could tell by looking at him that he had already lost his accustomed reserve. Hearing that I was about to leave, late one night he dropped by for a visit. At first he was reluctant to speak. Then, in a hesitant voice, he said: "I wonder . . . I wonder if you might . . . might be able to work something out for me when you get there . . . even a twenty- or thirty-dollar-a-month job as a copyist would do. I . . ."

For the moment I could not think of anything to say. I was shocked to hear that he was prepared to sink so low.

"I . . . I have to go on living a bit longer—"

"I'll see when I get there. I'll do all I can."

Such was the offhand promise I made that day. Later on in Shanyang, I would often hear my voice forming those words while Lianshu's image floated before my eyes and he told me in that faltering voice: "I have to go on living a bit longer." At such times, I would run all over my new school and recommend him wherever I thought there was any hope of a position. But what use was it? There were more people looking for jobs than there were jobs to be had. I would usually be granted a few polite phrases of apology which I would then relay to him by mail.

As the first semester drew to a close, my situation grew even more intolerable. Some of the local Shanyang gentry put out a weekly called *Principles of Learning*. Attacks on me—anonymous of course—began to appear in its pages. They were cleverly phrased so as to make readers think I was trying to incite a student movement, and my efforts to get Lianshu a job were interpreted as an attempt to import a crony who would immediately enlist in my cause.[13]

Given the situation, the only thing to do was—nothing. Other than going to class, I simply holed up in my room and kept out of people's way. Sometimes I was afraid of even letting cigarette smoke escape through the cracks in my window for fear I would be suspected of inciting a student movement. And of course, at this point there was absolutely nothing I could do for Lianshu. Things dragged on like that right into the middle of winter.

It had been snowing all day and on into the night. Outside, everything was silence, a silence so deep one could almost hear it. Sitting by the light of a tiny lamp, I closed my eyes and sat motionless. I imagined the snowflakes outside, floating down and thickening into a white carpet that would spread as far as the eye could see. Suddenly I was back home. Everyone was busily preparing for the New Year. I was a child again out in the backyard with my friends, making a Buddha out of snow. We fashioned the eyes from two lumps of jet black coal. Suddenly those eyes became Lianshu's eyes!

"I have to go on living a bit longer." The same tones again.

"But why?" I asked myself without thinking. The question was no sooner out of my mouth than it sounded ridiculous, even to me, but it did pull me out of my reverie. I sat upright in my chair, lit a cigarette, pushed the window open, and looked out. Just as I had imagined, thick snow was falling and blanketing the ground.

I heard someone knocking at the gate. Before long someone came into the courtyard. I could tell by the familiar footsteps that it was no visitor, only the servant who did odd jobs around the compound. He pushed open the door to my room and handed me an envelope about six inches long. Though the characters were scribbled in a very cursive style, I immediately recognized the two words FROM WEI and realized it was Lianshu's letter.

This was the first I had heard from him since leaving S-town.

---

13. In May of 1925 Lu Xun and six other professors at Beijing Women's Normal School issued a declaration supporting the students against the authoritarianism of the school administration. An article in the *Contemporary Review* accused Lu Xun and his colleagues of "secretly inciting a student movement."

Well aware of what a poor correspondent he could be, I was not at all surprised at not having heard from him for so long. Even making allowances for that, however, from time to time I did feel somewhat put out with him for not letting me in on what he was doing. But when I received this letter, without any reason I could put my finger on, I felt that something must be wrong. Hurriedly ripping open the envelope, I discovered that the letter proper was written in the same cursive and somewhat frenzied style as the address.

> —— Shenfei:
>
> What form of address should I use with you? I have left it blank. Fill it in with whatever you please. Anything will be all right with me.
>
> I have had three letters from you since you left, but I have not answered a single one. The reason is simple enough: couldn't afford to buy stamps.
>
> Perhaps you would like to know a little of how things have gone with me since we last met. Well, let me give it to you simply: *I have failed!* I used to think I was a loser a long time back, but back then I really wasn't. It's only now that I have become a real loser. Back then, when there was someone who wanted me to go on living and when I *myself* wanted to go on living, it seemed that I couldn't. Yet now, when there's absolutely no need to go on living any longer, I . . .
>
> But *should* I?
>
> Lured into a deathtrap, the one person who wanted me to go on living a bit longer back then wasn't able to survive either. And who was the killer? No one knows.
>
> How quickly come the changes of life! During this past half year, there has been a time when I was close to begging. Actually, it would be fair to say that I really *was* a beggar. But I still had things I wanted to accomplish and for that reason I was quite willing to beg, to go cold and hungry, to be lonely, and to suffer. Back then I would have done anything rather than die and pass into oblivion. See what great power was exerted by that single individual who wanted me to live a bit longer!
>
> But that power is gone now, gone with the person who produced it. On the one hand, I don't feel that I deserve to go on living. —How about other people? Do they? No, they don't deserve to, either. —But on the other hand, I'm perversely intent on doing just that to spite all those who would rather see me dead. Fortunately, the only one who wanted to see me sur-

vive and have a good life is already dead, so there's no one left around to be hurt no matter what I do now. I couldn't have brought myself to hurt someone like that, but now even that person is gone.

And how is it with me now? Well, now I am unimaginably happy and exceedingly content, for I have already done all those things I used to despise, all those things I used to stand against. And I have rejected and desecrated every last thing I used to hold dear, everything I used to stand for. I am a real loser. And yet, I stand victorious!

You'll probably think I've lost my mind, or perhaps you'll think I'm on my way to becoming some sort of hero or great man. No, it's none of that. The whole thing's quite simple really: I've recently become aide-de-camp to a divisional commander at a salary of eighty dollars a month.[14]

Shenfei . . .

I leave it to you to decide what monster I've become. Any label you deem appropriate will be all right with me.

You still remember, no doubt, the living room I used to have, the one we first met in—the one we said goodbye in too, for that matter. I'm still using it, but everything in it is new now: new guests, giving me new presents and singing me new praises. You'll also find new people, newly engaged in worming their ways into my good graces to improve their positions. There are new kowtows and new bows, new card games, new finger-guessing games,[15] new icy stares and evil hearts—and also new sleepless nights and a new spitting of blood . . .

In your last letter you said you weren't too happy with your teaching position. How would you like to become an aide-de-camp too? Just say the word and I'll set it up. As a matter of fact, in a place like this, you'd do well even if you signed on as a lowly gatekeeper. You would still enjoy new guests giving you new presents and singing you new praises. You would . . .

It's snowing hard outside. How's the weather there? Although it's already very late at night as I write, I am quite alert, for I have just spit up some blood and that's brought me pretty much awake.

---

14. It was traditional for bright young men from Shaoxing to serve civil or military governors as their advisors (*guwen,* here translated as aide-de-camp). Lianshu is, no doubt, serving on the staff of one of the notorious and powerful warlords who were the de facto rulers over much of China at this time. Both friends would regard serving a warlord as capitulation to the forces of reaction and a betrayal of their ideals.

15. A kind of drinking game.

> It occurred to me that since last autumn, you've written me three letters one after the other—quite surprising when you think of it—and so I felt I really had to send you some news of myself. I hope you won't be too shocked.
>
> Most likely I'll not write again. You've long been familiar with this quirk of mine. When are you coming back? If it's soon, we'll probably get to see each other again. On the other hand, when you come right down to it, we're on different roads now, so why don't you just forget me. Accept my heartfelt thanks for so often trying to find me employment in the past, but now you had better forget me. Besides, I am already "well."[16]
>
> LIANSHU
> DECEMBER 14TH

After I had read his letter—hastily the first time and line by line the second—though I wasn't "shocked," it did make me uncomfortable. And yet, at the same time, the unpleasant feelings his letter occasioned were not without a slight admixture of relief. Well, a job's no longer a problem for him at any rate, I told myself, and that's one less burden for me, even though I was never able to do anything for him at this end anyway.

Little by little, I began to forget him. His face no longer haunted my memory as it once had. But then, less than ten days after I received his letter, the S-town gentry group that published *Fundamentals of Scholarship* began mailing out its weekly again. It wasn't the sort of thing I usually read, but since it had already come in the mail I opened it and glanced through it. By means of that paper Lianshu was brought into my consciousness once again, for it often contained poems and articles related to him, bearing such titles as "Visiting the Honorable Lianshu on a Snowy Night" and "An Elegant Gathering in the Study of Aide-de-camp Lianshu."

In the paper's "Chitchat" column there appeared an old story related to Lianshu that I remembered having once heard passed around as a joke at his expense. Now, however, it was no longer a joke but rather an "amusing anecdote" told with keen relish,

16. Apparently an allusion to "Diary of a Madman," where the protagonist is considered "well" once he joins the cannibalistic society that surrounds him by assuming an official appointment.

implying that *One who's fated to honors bear, will always do the thing that's rare.* I don't know why exactly, but even though the newspaper articles kept reminding me of him, the actual *look* of his face faded more and more from my memory. And yet, across the miles, I began to experience an almost physical kinship with Lianshu that grew closer and closer with every passing day. Quite often, and for no apparent reason, I would experience an uneasiness that I was at a loss to explain, and it would be accompanied by a barely perceptible trembling in my own body. Fortunately, that autumn *Fundamentals of Scholarship* stopped coming.

But just as one weekly paper ceased to be a source of annoyance, another, our own Shanyang *Principles of Learning,* took up the slack by publishing a long article entitled "The Factual Basis of Gossip," in which it was said that certain stories related to various local gentlemen were currently receiving wide circulation among fair-minded and impartial members of the local gentry. Since I was one of those "gentlemen" about whom stories were circulating, it behooved me to be extra careful. As was my habit, I continued to guard against any smoke escaping through the cracks in my window, but in addition to being a downright nuisance, having to be *that* careful with regard to personal behavior keeps one constantly busy too. In fact, it took so much effort that I had no time for anything else, and so, of course, I no longer had the leisure to think of Lianshu. In sum, I succeeded in putting my friend completely out of mind.

Despite all the time and effort expended, however, I wasn't able to hold onto my job even down to the summer vacation. I left Shanyang at the end of May.

5

From Shanyang I went to Licheng, and then to Taigu, bouncing around from pillar to post for the better part of a year. But try as I might, I couldn't find any work and resolved to return to S-town. I arrived on one of those early spring afternoons when it looks as though it wants to rain but can't. Everything was shrouded in grey. There was an empty room in the place where I used to live and so I settled in there. I had begun to think about Lianshu on the way back and decided to go see him after supper. Taking along two packages of the steamed cakes for which Wenxi is justly famous,[17] I walked my share of wet streets and yielded the right of way to my share of imperious canines sprawled across my path before finally arriving at Lianshu's place. There was a lot of light coming from inside. As soon as one rises to aide-de-camp, I thought to myself, even one's house begins to brighten up. Pleased with my own humor, I chuckled. As I neared the house, I saw a patch of white at the side of the gate—a paper notice pasted aslant.[18] Big Liang's grandmother must have died, I thought, as I stepped over the threshold and made my way inside.

In the light that illuminated the courtyard, I spotted a casket. Someone in military uniform stood to one side of it—a soldier. I made out someone else standing there talking to him. Taking a closer look, I saw that it was Big Liang's grandmother. There were several coarse-looking fellows in short jackets scattered about the courtyard, apparently with nothing to do. At the sight of all this, my heart gave an involuntary start. The old woman turned and stared at me.

"Aiya! You're back! Why couldn't you have made it a few days earlier?"

"Who . . . who's gone?" I asked, even though I was fairly sure of the answer.

"Bigman Wei. He's been gone since the day before yesterday."

I looked around. Lit by a single lamp, the living room was sunk in somber shadows. A white funeral scroll was hung in the middle room while Big Liang, Second Liang, and the others were gathered outside.

"He's in there," said Big Liang's grandmother, pointing as she walked over to me. "After Bigman Wei received his appointment, I rented him the middle room as well. He's laid out in there now."

In front of the mourning curtain that hid my friend from view, there were two tables, a long narrow one and a square one. About ten bowls of food were set out on them. No sooner had I lifted my foot over the doorsill than two men in long white gowns appeared out of nowhere and barred my way. With eyes opened so wide they looked like dead fish eyes, they fixed me with two suspicious stares. I hastened to explain my relationship with Lianshu to them. But it was not until Big Liang's grandmother came in and

17. Wenxi is a county in Shanxi Province.

18. This would be the conventional way of announcing a death in the family.

vouched for everything I said that their muscles began to relax and their eyes gradually softened. Silently they signaled their permission for me to go forward and pay my respects.

As I bowed to my old friend, a voice suddenly burst out sobbing somewhere near my feet. When I composed myself and looked down, I saw a child of about ten lying prostrate on a mourner's mat. He was dressed in white and around his head, which was shorn close enough to appear almost bald, a hank of linen was tied. In the course of exchanging social commonplaces with the two men, I discovered that one of them was Lianshu's paternal first cousin—his closest living relative—while the other was a distant nephew. I asked them for one last look at the deceased. They did their best to talk me out of it, saying that I would be doing them "too great an honor." But I finally convinced them and they opened the curtain so that I might have one last look at my friend.

The Lianshu I encountered this time, of course, was dead. But to my amazement, despite the crumpled jacket and trousers, despite the bloodstains on the lapel, and even despite the pitifully emaciated face, his basic features were *exactly* as they had been in life. Mouth and eyes were closed in calm repose, as though he were sleeping. It was almost enough to make me put my hand to his nostrils to see if he might still be breathing.

Everyone was deathly still, the living as well as the dead. Finally I withdrew. His cousin approached me again. Determined to accord the proper formal courtesies to all mourners, he told me that when his "humble cousin" had been called to "join the ancients" in the prime of life with an unlimited future before him, this call had not only visited catastrophe upon the "bereaved clan," but had subjected even friends to great anguish as well. Exhibiting an ability for courteous speech seldom encountered among hill people, he managed through all of this to convey the impression that he was *apologizing* for Lianshu. Then he fell silent, and once again everyone was deathly still, the living as well as the dead.

Feeling at loose ends, but not particularly sad, I went out into the courtyard and struck up a conversation with Big Liang's grandmother. From her I learned that the encoffining ceremony would soon begin (they were only waiting for the arrival of the *longlife clothes*) and that all those born in the years of the rat, horse, rabbit, or rooster would have to keep away while the coffin was being nailed up. She was quite full of herself and the words flowed out in a torrent: she spoke of Lianshu's illness, of how it had been with him when he was alive, and even supplied some criticism of her own.

"Let me tell you, after that man made it big, he was a totally different person. Went around with his nose hiked up in the air, proud as a peacock. When he talked to you, he didn't act like an old fuddy-duddy egghead anymore either. Remember how he used to go round with his mouth sewn up all day? About all I ever got out of him was an 'Honored Madam' whenever he clapped his eyes on me. But after his luck turned and he hit it big, he took to calling me 'Old Dingbat'! Haha—he was really something! When people'd give him some good Xiangjü herbs for tonic, he wouldn't use them himself.[19] He'd just toss them into the courtyard—right here where we're standin' now—and yell, 'Here, Old Dingbat, you take them!' After his luck turned, there were so many people runnin' back and forth around here that I let him have the middle room too. That's when I moved over here into the side room myself. The rest of us always used to laugh and say he was livin' proof that *When someone's boat comes in, He's sure to go far out.* If you'd only come a month earlier, you'd have been here in time to see all the fun yourself. Two days out of three, there'd be a party. You'd hear all this talkin' and laughin' and singin'! He and his friends would be in there drinkin' their heads off and slammin' down the mahjong tiles to beat the band. Sometimes you'd hear them recitin' little poems they made up too. You name it, they did it!

"He used to be more afraid of kids than kids were of their own old man. Whenever there were any around, he'd always bow down at their feet. Well, not too long back, he did an about-face on that one too. Got so he was able to talk with them and even horse around a bit. Big Liang and my other kids really liked him. Whenever they had a spare minute, they'd run over to his room. He had all kinds of ways of teasin' them too. Like if a kid wanted him to buy somethin', Adjutant Wei would made the kid bark like a dog or whack his head on the ground in a good loud kowtow. Haha, things were really jumpin' around here then! Month before last, when Second Liang wanted money for shoes, Adjutant Wei

19. The specific herb mentioned is *zhu:* rhizome (or rootlike subterranean stem) of atractylodes. Xianjü is a county in Zhejiang Province.

made him do three head-whackers. Second Liang's still wearin' em too—good as new."

A man dressed in a long white mourning gown came out and the old woman stopped talking. I asked her about the nature of Lianshu's illness, but she didn't seem to know too much about it. She said that he'd probably started getting thin a long time back, but because he was always going around as happy as a lark, no one had noticed. It hadn't been until just over a month ago that she first heard about his coughing up blood. As far as she knew, he hadn't gone to see a doctor, either. A little after that, he took to his bed, and then, just three days before he died, he lost his voice and couldn't say a single word. At that point, a relative of his from up on Coldstone Mountain had trekked all the way down to S-town just to see him. He had asked Lianshu if he had any savings but couldn't get a word out of him. The relative had thought Lianshu was faking it. And yet there were those who said that people dying of consumption sometimes really do lose their voices before they go—who's to say?

"But Adjutant Wei was a bit strange, even for me," she said in suddenly lowered tones. "Wouldn't save a penny—went through his fingers like water. Thirteenth Bigman even thought *we* got somethin' out of him, but we didn't get beans. He just spent his chuckle-headed way straight through it with no rhyme or reason. Take buyin' things. He'd buy somethin' today, and then sell it off tomorrow, or maybe even break it in the meantime. I don't know *what* he thought he was doin'. By the time he died, he didn't have a single thing. He'd gone through it all. Otherwise things wouldn't be so bare and quiet around here today . . .

"Clowned around all the time and never thought of anything practical that'd be good for himself. So I started doin' his thinkin' for 'im, and tried to set 'im on the right path. At his age he should've been thinkin' about setting up a family, and what with his money and position, it would've been easy enough to do, too. On the off chance that he couldn't find a girl to suit 'im for a wife, there would have been no harm in buyin' a couple of concubines for starters. After all, people should put up a good front and go through life as though they really mean it. But as soon as I'd start in, he'd laugh and say, 'Do you always worry over other people's love lives like this, Old Dingbat?' You can tell from that how he always liked to play the fool and didn't know how to take friendly advice the way it was given. If he'd listened to me early on, he'd never have ended up like this—down there in Hell all by himself, gropin' around in the dark. If he'd listened to me, at least he would've been able to hear the weepin' voices of a few relatives now . . ."

A shop clerk arrived with a bundle of clothes on his back. Three relatives fished some underwear out of it and disappeared behind the funeral curtain. Before long it was raised: the underwear had already been changed and now they were putting on his outer garments. Much to my surprise, they started with a pair of light brown army pants with very broad stripes running down the seams; next came the coat with its bright, shiny epaulets. I have no idea as to what rank they denoted or how Lianshu had come by them. Now a pair of brown leather shoes was placed beside his feet and a papier-mâché saber at his waist. Beside his face, which had now grown so dark and bony it looked like a pile of twigs, they laid a gilt-edged hat.

The three relatives held onto the side of the coffin, wept a spell, then dried their eyes and wiped away their tears. The child with the hank of hemp tied round his head withdrew along with Third Liang—probably both born in a rat, horse, rabbit, or rooster year.

As one husky fellow picked up the coffin lid and was about to put it on, I moved in closer for a final look at my friend, who was about to take leave of me forever. He lay there quite peacefully in the ill-fitting uniform. His eyes were shut, his mouth closed. The faint traces of an ice-cold smile seemed to play at the corners of his mouth as though he himself were sneering at what a ridiculous corpse he made.

As the sound of the first nail being driven into the casket broke the air, several people broke into simultaneous wails. Those keening voices were more than I could bear and I withdrew into the courtyard. Once set in motion, my feet kept on of their own accord, and before I knew it I was already out through the main gate. I gazed up into space. The thick clouds had parted and a round moon was hanging there, scattering sober and passionless beams on the world below.

I hastened along as though trying—and unsuccessfully, at that —to muscle my way out from under some great burden weighing down from above. Something in my ears was struggling to get out.

It wrestled and tussled and at long last broke free. It was rather like the howl of a wounded animal, a wolf on a deserted plain howling into the depths of night—sorrow and fury mixed with pain.

And then my heart began to lighten. Completely at ease now, I walked forward through the moonlight on the damp cobblestone road.

FINISHED ON OCTOBER 17, 1925

Mourning the Dead

—Handwritten notes of Juansheng

If I am able, I shall commit my sorrow and remorse to paper, for her sake as well as my own.

How lonely, how empty this dingy little room off in a forgotten corner of the Hometowners' Club![1] Where has the time gone? To think that a whole year has passed since I first fell in love with Zijun. How perverse the workings of fate that *this* should be the only vacant room at the club on my return. Everything is now as it was then—the same broken window, and outside the window the same half-withered locust and old wisteria; inside, the same square desk, the same slatboard bed, and the same faded wall. Lying alone here in the depths of night just as I did before we began living together, even *I* am the same. It is as though all the days of this past year had never been, as though I had never moved out of this dingy little room to set up a small and hope-filled household of my own on Goodomen Lane.

A year ago, however, the loneliness and emptiness were not so disheartening, for then they carried with them a cheerful note of expectancy as I awaited Zijun's arrival. The crisp sound of high heels would suddenly come breaking over the brick pavement and rouse me to life. Soon I would see her—a pale dimpled face, slim white arms, striped cotton blouse, and black skirt. She would show me fresh new leaves she had brought in from the withered old locust outside the window, and she would give me some of the lilac-hued wisteria blossoms that hung cluster after cluster from the ironlike trunk of the old tree.

And now? Only the loneliness and emptiness remain. Zijun will never return. Never!

First published in *Wondering Where to Turn.*

1. The *huiguan* of the Chinese text were hostels where people from the same area stayed while away from home; occasionally *huiguan* served as housing for people with the same occupation. In Beijing, Lu Xun lived in the Shaoxing Club (Shaoxing Huiguan) from 1912 until 1919.

* * *

When Zijun was not in my room, I never saw anything I looked at. Sometimes, out of utter boredom, I would grab the book nearest to hand and start reading. Literature, science, whatever—it was all the same to me. I'd read and read, and then it would suddenly dawn on me that though I had gone through more than ten pages, I could recall nothing of what I'd read.

My sense of *hearing,* on the other hand, grew increasingly acute. I could make out quite clearly all the footsteps passing back and forth outside the main gate of the compound; then, amidst the others, there would come the sound of Zijun *tap tap tapping* ever closer. But all too often, steps that I had thought were hers would gradually fade until they disappeared into the swell and rhythms of countless others.

The cloth-soled shoes of the servant's son made a sound that I learned to loathe, for it was nothing like Zijun's; but I hated even more the leather-soled sound of the young fop in the next courtyard, who was forever smearing his face with cold cream, for the sound of his steps was all too much like Zijun's.

Had her rickshaw overturned? Had she been hit by a trolley? Beset by such worries, I grabbed my hat and decided to go to her place. But just as I was on the point of leaving, I remembered how her uncle had once warned me to keep away and had called me ugly names. Suddenly the sound of her footsteps began to close in, each louder than the last. By the time I had gotten up and run out to greet her, she was already passing the wisteria—her face dimpled into a smile, a sure sign that she had not been subject to abuse from her uncle. I breathed a sigh of relief.

Once inside, we silently stared into each other's eyes. And then, gradually, the room began to fill with the sound of my voice. I spoke of the despotism of the family system, of destroying old customs, of the equality of the sexes, of Ibsen, of Tagore, of Shelley . . . Eyes agleam with childlike curiosity, Zijun smiled and nodded her head. I pointed to a copperplate engraving of Shelley on the wall. I had clipped it from a magazine because it was the most handsome likeness of the poet I'd been able to find. Zijun gave it a cursory glance and then lowered her head in obvious embarrassment. In this, as well as some other regards, she had not yet completely freed herself from the shackles of traditional morality. Afterwards, it occurred to me that it might be well to replace the engraving with a commemorative portrait of Shelley drowning at sea, or perhaps a picture of Ibsen. I never got around to it, however, and now I do not even remember what has become of the Shelley I originally had there.

* * *

"I belong to myself! None of them has any right to interfere in my life!"

Several moments of silent deliberation had preceded this declaration and it was delivered in calm, clear, decisive tones. We had been seeing each other for half a year at the time, and had just been discussing her uncle—with whom she lived here in the capital—as well as her father back home. By then I had long since explained to her my own ideas about everything under the sun, had told her all there was to tell of my own background, and had even shared my character defects, holding back very little. What was more, Zijun had sympathetically *understood* everything I had said. Therefore, when the above declaration came, it stirred me to the depths of my being and continued to echo in my ears for days afterwards. I was happy beyond words: now I knew that Chinese women were *not* the helpless, hopeless lot our pessimists would have us believe, and I was confident that a glorious dawn lay on the horizon for them in the not-too-distant future.

As I walked her out to the front gate that day, as usual, we kept a good ten paces apart; as usual, too, the old devil with the catfish moustache held his face so close to his drab and dirty window as we passed his room that the tip of his nose flattened into a pancake; and as usual again, when we reached the outer courtyard, the face of the young fop who was forever plastering himself with vanishing cream appeared behind his bright and sparkling windowpane. Walking with poise and pride, eyes straying neither to one side nor to the other, Zijun didn't notice either of them. After saying goodbye, I returned to my room with the same proud and poised bearing.

"I belong to myself! None of them has any right to interfere in my life!" This uncompromising mentality was even more firmly rooted in Zijun than it was in me. How could old Flatnose or

Even Juansheng realizes he can't

young Vanishing Cream possibly hope to intimidate a young woman of Zijun's caliber?

* * *

By now, I can no longer clearly remember exactly *how* I made my pure and passionate declaration of love. Why speak of it now? Even then, immediately after it was over, the whole scene blurred out of focus so quickly that when I attempted to recall it later that very night, virtually nothing remained save a few disjointed fragments. And by the time we had been living together for a month or so, even those bits and pieces had slipped irretrievably into the dreamy waters of oblivion. The only thing I clearly remembered was that ten days or so *before* I made my proposal, I sat down and planned the whole thing out—from the posture I would assume while speaking right down to exactly which words I would say first and which I would reserve for last.[2] I had even thought through what I would do in the event that she refused. When the time came, however, all my planning was to no avail, for in my nervousness—without thinking—I actually dropped to one knee, just the way I had seen them do it in movies. Later on, whenever I thought of my actually having done such a thing, I was mortified. Yet, perversely, that is the only fragment of the entire scene that was indelibly emblazoned on the screen of my memory.

I was unaware of my own words at the time and didn't pay a great deal of attention to Zijun's either. I simply knew that she had accepted, and that was enough. And yet I do vaguely recall her face momentarily paling and then flushing a deeper red than I'd ever seen it before—or since. Her childlike eyes glowed with the poignancy of joy, and though she did her best to avoid my gaze I detected a glimmer of surprise and bewilderment in those eyes as well—like a bird trapped in a room, she seemed to be looking for an open window through which to fly away. When all is said and done, the only thing I knew with any degree of certainty was that

---

2. Replete with a panoply of elaborate ceremonies, traditional weddings were preeminently family affairs often having little or nothing to do with the individual wishes of the bride or groom. Young, liberal intellectuals of the May Fourth period flouted the traditional claims of family to exercise free choice in the selection of their marriage partners. They had no institutionalized way of doing it—hence Juansheng's ludicrous attempt at staging the scene.

she *had* accepted, though I couldn't have told you exactly what she said to express that acceptance.

Zijun, on the other hand, remembered everything *I* had said down to the very last comma. In her own mind, she went over the words I had used so many times that it became a *text* for her, one that she committed to memory and could recite with drop-of-the-hat fluency.

She was able to describe my *actions* too, so vividly and in such detail one would have thought she was watching a motion picture of the scene as she spoke, a film I could not see and one that, unfortunately, included that particularly sophomoric frame I so longed to forget. Late at night, when everything was quiet, time after time she would review it all like a student going over old lessons. Like a student, too, I was often questioned on it, tested, and even ordered to repeat everything I had said during my proposal. As though tutoring a "D" student, Zijun often had to supplement the things I left out, and to correct what little I did manage to remember.

As time went by, the number of these review sessions gradually decreased. But whenever I saw her staring off into space, lost in her own thoughts, her expression growing more and more tender, her dimples deepening, I would know she was in the midst of rerunning that same old film. I would secretly wince at the thought that she would soon see that most ludicrous scene once again. At the same time I knew, of course, that that particular scene was precisely the one she most wanted to see and that she would not rest content until she had seen it, for even though *I* thought it utterly fatuous, she saw nothing ludicrous in it whatsoever. In retrospect, I realize that Zijun saw it the way she did because her love for me was passionate and pure.

Our happiest time together was at the end of spring this past year. It was also our busiest. Although physically I was constantly on the run looking for a place to live, mentally I was serene. New anxieties soon came along, however, and shattered that serenity, so that my mind soon rivaled my body in activity. For the first time, Zijun and I allowed ourselves to be seen together on the streets. Aside from a couple of visits to the park, most of our expeditions were undertaken for the express purpose of finding a place to live. I was often conscious of the stares we attracted: some were inquisitive, others derisive; some lascivious, and still others downright contemptuous.[3] It was only by dint of summoning up all the defiant pride I could muster that I was able to keep myself from shrinking back before the onslaught of all those eyes. Zijun, on the other hand, was not in the least intimidated. Unhurried and confident, she would walk through the streets as though they were empty.

Finding a place to live was far from easy. Most of the time, people would manage to find some pretext or other to turn us away, although occasionally it was we who turned a place down because it did not suit our needs. It wasn't that we were choosy, it was just that we were sometimes able to tell at a glance that *this* place was not for us. Of course, that was only at the beginning; later on, our sole criterion was that the landlord be willing to rent to us at all. After looking at more than a score of places, we finally came across one where we thought we could make do, at least for the time being—two rooms on the south side of a small compound on Goodomen Lane.[4] Even though he was a petty bureaucrat, this landlord-official of ours turned out to be broad-minded enough to accept us. He occupied the center and side rooms, where he lived rather simply with his wife, a baby daughter not yet a year old, and a maid hired in from the countryside. As long as their baby did not cry, our small household promised to be quiet as well as pleasant and secluded.

We made do with simple furnishings, but even so, their purchase used up more than half the money I had scraped together to set up housekeeping. In order to raise more, Zijun sold a pair of earrings along with the only gold ring she owned. I tried to stop her, but seeing that she was bound and determined to do it, I did not press things. I realized that unless she contributed something of her own to this little home of ours, she would never feel comfortable living in it.

She had long since broken with her uncle, so infuriating him in the process that he no longer recognized her as his niece. One after the other, I too had to break with several friends who, under the guise of loyalty, warned me against my present course, but who—

3. The chances were good that a young couple out looking for a place to live on their own would be doing so without the blessing of either family. Such a pair would be considered by conventional onlookers to exemplify the height of immorality.

4. Rooms on the northern side of the compound would have been preferable since they would face south and get more sun.

if the truth be known—were either projecting their own fears onto me, or were simply jealous. Our losses on both sides, however, were more than compensated for by the resulting simplicity of our lives.

Though it was close to dusk when I would get off work, and though the rickshaw pullers seemed bent on seeing how long they could take to get me home, still at the end of each day that glorious moment finally arrived when Zijun and I would stand face to face once again. First we would stare silently into each other's eyes, and then in a flood of conversation we would pour out our innermost feelings. And then we would fall silent again. We would lower our heads and appear to be utterly lost in deep thought; actually we would be thinking about nothing at all—such was the depth of our intuitive mutual understanding. Gradually, and with total comprehension, I learned to read her like a book, both body and soul. In the course of three weeks my knowledge of Zijun grew ever deeper as I peeled away layer upon layer of those things that had stood between us, things I had previously congratulated myself on understanding but which had actually stood as barriers of misunderstanding. That, after all, is what true barriers really are.

Zijun grew livelier by the day. I discovered that she did not care much for flowers. I bought her two little potted plants at a temple fair, but after going unwatered for four days they withered and died—after all, I did not have the time to look after everything myself. She did, however, like animals. In this enthusiasm she had perhaps been infected by the landlord's wife, for before a month was out, our family was suddenly increased by four little chicks who ran around in the courtyard along with the dozen or so others that belonged to the landlord's wife. Amazingly, the two women easily distinguished which chicks belonged to which family. Soon after that, Zijun bought a Beijing pug at a temple fair. As I recall, the dog already had a name when Zijun got it, but she gave it another, "Shadow." Though I never liked the name, I called it that too.

I soon discovered that love is something that must be constantly renewed, constantly nurtured, and constantly recreated. When I shared this insight with Zijun, she nodded her head in loving and sympathetic understanding. What peaceful and happy nights those were!

* * *

Our serenity and happiness began to thicken and to set as though they had been poured into a mold.

Back in the Hometowners' Club we had had our occasional misunderstandings and differences of opinion, but once we moved into Goodomen Lane, even these disappeared. Seated across from each other in the lamplight, it was only in reminiscence that we could savor that renascent joy we had been used to feeling when making up after a quarrel.

Zijun began to fill out and a lively glow appeared on her cheeks. At the same time, however, she began getting busy—terribly, terribly busy. She was so taken up with household chores she no longer had time to chat, much less read or go for a walk. We often said that we ought to hire a maid.

This situation, of course, bothered me as much as it did Zijun. When I would come home in the evening, I would often detect a troubled look in her eyes. But what bothered me even more was that now she did her best to hide it with forced smiles. Fortunately I was able to get to the bottom of it—her discomfiture was due to squabbling with the landlord's wife, and the chicks were the fuses that set the squabbles off. A family needs a place of its own. Our present situation was quite intolerable.

The pattern of my life was set. Six days out of seven, I would go from home to the government bureau where I was employed, and then from the bureau back home again. At the office, I would sit before my desk and copy official letters and official documents, and when that was done I would copy some more letters and documents. At home the pattern was to sit with Zijun or help with the cooking by firing up the stove, boiling the rice, or steaming the *mantou.*[5] It was during this period of my life that I first learned how to cook rice.

The food I got was much better than anything I'd had back at the Hometowners' Club. Although Zijun had no particular talent for cooking, she threw herself into it heart and soul, and in the face of such dedication I could not very well *not* participate in her daily culinary tasks. By doing so, of course, I was demonstrating my own willingness to share the bitter along with the sweet. Yet

---

5. Steamed bread rolls about the size of a small fist.

from one end of the day to the other, she worked so hard that her face was constantly covered with perspiration and her short hair was usually stuck to her forehead. The skin on her hands began to grow rough. And on top of everything else, she had Shadow and the chicks to feed too.

"I can go without eating, but we simply can't have you working so hard," I admonished her one day. She said nothing in reply, but when she glanced at me I saw that she was hurt. I had no choice but to drop the subject, and she continued to work as hard as ever.

* * *

On the eve of the Double Ten,[6] the blow I had anticipated finally arrived. I was sitting on the sofa with nothing to do while Zijun washed the dishes. There was a knock on the door. I answered. A messenger from the bureau handed me a mimeographed slip of paper. As I took it over to the lamp for a better look, I already had a good inkling as to what it was. Just as I had thought:

TO WHOM IT MAY CONCERN:

BY ORDER OF THE BUREAU CHIEF, Shi Juansheng

NEED NO LONGER REPORT FOR WORK.

DRAFTED IN THE SECRETARY'S OFFICE

THIS NINTH DAY OF OCTOBER

Even while I was living at the Hometowners' Club, I had expected something like this would eventually happen, for I knew that the bureau chief's son and the young fop who was forever smearing his face with vanishing cream were gambling pals. It was a foregone conclusion that Vanishing Cream would pass on rumors that were bound to reach the chief's ears. As a matter of fact, I was rather surprised that I had gone *this* long without getting the sack.

6. October 10, anniversary of the 1911 Republican Revolution.

I really should not characterize what happened as a "blow" either, for I had long since considered the alternatives that would be open to me when it finally came: I could hire myself out as a copyist, I could take a position as a family tutor, or—though it would be much more difficult work—I could even do a few translations. Publishing them should not prove too difficult, I thought, for I was fairly well acquainted with the editor-in-chief of *Freedom's Friend* and had corresponded with him only a month or so back. Despite all these solid precautions, however, my heart pounded violently as I read the dismissal slip. Getting the sack was bad enough but Zijun's reaction to it disturbed me even more, for upon learning the news, my ordinarily fearless Zijun looked downright worried. Could it be that she had actually gone timid on me of late?

"Doesn't mean a thing! We'll find something else to do, that's all; we'll . . ." she offered bravely.

I don't know how it happened exactly, but though she continued speaking, her voice began to fade in my ears and the light from the lamp began to dim as well. What ridiculous creatures we human beings are that such trifles should have the power to influence us right to the very core of our beings.

We stared at each other in silence for a moment and then gradually began reviewing our alternatives. In the end we decided that the first order of business was to economize. At the same time, I would put a few lines in the classifieds, offering my services as copyist or tutor. I would also write to the editor-in-chief of *Freedom's Friend* explaining my present difficulty and asking him to let me do a translation for his magazine in order to tide me over in this time of need. "No sooner said than done! Let's set out on that new road this very minute!" Turning to the table, I pushed a bottle of sesame seed oil and a saucer of vinegar out of the way so as to clear a workspace. Zijun carried the lamp over and set it down. First I drafted the advertisement; next I selected one of my foreign books to translate—because I had not opened a single volume since moving, they were all covered with dust. Finally I began the letter.

I hesitated a long time before writing that letter because I couldn't decide how to word it. As I lifted my pen from the paper to think a bit, I caught sight of Zijun. In the weak light of the lamp, she looked quite depressed. I would never have suspected that such an insignificant trifle could work such a change in my normally resolute and fearless Zijun. It must have been that she actually *had* grown more timid of late; what's more, it was obvious that this timidity must have been coming on her for a long time, for she could not possibly have grown so fearful overnight. Thinking about all this, I was more confused than ever. The image of a more idyllic life suddenly appeared before me, the life we had lived back in the Hometowners' Club. But as I tried to bring the image into focus, it faded away in the murky lamplight. After quite some time, the letter was finally drafted. It was a rather long one and writing it had apparently drained me—it would seem that *I* must have been growing faint-hearted and weak of late as well. Having decided that we would place the ad in the classifieds and send out the letter first thing next morning, without thinking we both raised our arms at exactly the same moment and stretched. Though nothing was said, Zijun and I sensed a common spirit of fortitude and tenacity welling up within us.

Suddenly we began to see hope for our future.

* * *

Though well calculated to destroy us, this external assault had had the opposite effect of imbuing us with new spirit. My life at the bureau had not been much to begin with anyway. I was like a wild bird trapped in the cage of a birdseller who always gives it just enough feed to maintain life, but never enough to grow strong on; as the days wear on, the bird's wings atrophy so that even if it is let go, it can no longer fly. Now at least I was free of the cage before I had forgotten how to flap my wings. From this point on I would soar through new stretches of sky.

* * *

I did not expect any overnight miracles from the advertisement, of course, but I was surprised to find that doing the translation was more than I had bargained for. No sooner had I set my hand to it than scores of knotty problems began cropping up in passages I had previously read and *thought* I had understood. Nonetheless I rolled up my sleeves and put my nose to the grindstone. Before half a month was out, the worn and dog-eared pages of a dictionary, one that had been fairly new when I began, offered mute testimony to my diligence, a diligence inspired by the fact that the editor-in-chief of *Freedom's Friend* had assured me he would never sit on a good manuscript.

Unfortunately, I lacked a quiet space to work in. Moreover, Zijun was not as quiet as she used to be, or as sensitive to my needs. The room was forever a chaos of bowls and dishes, and coal smoke from the stove hung heavily in the air, making it impossible for me to keep my mind on my work. Of course, I had only myself to blame for not being able to afford a home with a study. But as if the bowls, dishes, and coal smoke weren't enough aggravation, then there was Shadow; and as if Shadow weren't enough, then there were the chicks; and as if the chicks weren't enough, then they had to go and grow into *chickens* and thereby provide even shorter fuses for the quarrels between our family and the landlord's.

And then, too, there was the never-ending round of meals. It seemed that Zijun's sole function in life was to buy and prepare food. She fed me so that I could make money, then used that money to feed me some more so that I could make more money. On top of all that, of course, she had to feed Shadow and the chickens too. She seemed to have forgotten things she once would have known instinctively, for apparently it didn't occur to her now that in calling me to sit down and eat, she often interrupted my train of thought. I attempted to make her aware of this on several occasions by glowering at her during dinner, but every time I did she went right on chewing for all she was worth, completely oblivious to my angry glare.

It took a good five weeks before I was able to get it through to her that my work simply could not be subject to the restrictions of her meal schedules. And after I did, she was probably put out with me, though she said nothing. After that, my work proceeded much more rapidly and before long I had translated some fifty thousand words. All I had to do was polish it a bit and send it off to the editor-in-chief of *Freedom's Friend,* along with two essays I happened to have on hand. Meals, however, continued to be a problem. It was not so much that I had to eat my food cold—given Zijun's meal schedule, there was no way to get around that. Rather, there simply was not enough of it, not even for my present appetite, which had been substantially diminished since I had begun my regimen of holing up in the house the entire day, working my brain while my body idled. Sometimes there was not even enough rice. The reason, it turned out, was that she fed it to Shadow, occasionally even giving him the mutton that we so rarely had the money to afford. Her explanation was that the landlord's wife had been making fun of Shadow for being so pitifully thin, and that sort of criticism was more than she could bear.

While Shadow was fed *before* me, the chickens, I learned after a prolonged period of observation, got my leftovers. Just as Huxley had been able to determine "man's position in the universe" in the wake of a long course of scientific study,[7] I too, over a period of time, researched my way to enlightenment regarding *my* position within our family—somewhere between the dog and the chickens.

* * *

Later on, after much urging on my part and much opposition on hers, one by one the chickens were transformed into mealtime delicacies. With fresh poultry on the table every day, Zijun, the dog, and I lived off the fat of the land for almost two weeks. To tell the truth, it was not really all that "fat" either, for the chickens, having long received nothing but a few grains of *gaoliang* for their daily fare, were downright scrawny. After we had consumed the last of them, our household was noticeably more peaceful. Zijun, however, was quite depressed and often became so glum and listless that she stopped talking. How easily people change, I thought to myself.

After a while, we were so pressed for money we could no longer afford to keep the dog. The time had already passed when we might reasonably have hoped for rescue by mail, and Zijun had long since run out of the tidbits she'd employed to coax Shadow to walk on his hind legs or sit up and cross his paws in a formal greeting. Furthermore, winter would soon be upon us and even buying fuel for the stove would present us with difficulty enough. As a matter of fact, it had long since become apparent that Shadow's food was more of a burden than we could bear. To keep him any longer would be simply beyond our means.

---

7. Thomas Huxley's (1825–1895) *Evolution and Ethics* was translated into Chinese by Yan Fu (1853–1921) in the 1890s and rapidly became the common coin of discourse among intellectuals.

Had we attached a price tag to the dog and taken him to a temple fair, we probably could have turned a profit on him, but neither of us had the heart to do it.[8] In the end, I wrapped a piece of cloth around his eyes so he could not see, took him out beyond the city limits, and turned him loose. He tried to follow me and I had to push him into a deep ditch before I was able to shake him. As soon as I got home, I felt a sense of relief and freedom. When I noted Zijun's expression, however, I was shocked. I had never seen her look as utterly dejected as she did that day. It was over Shadow, of course, but why should this have affected her so intensely? I hadn't even told her the part about shoving him into the ditch.

By nightfall, in addition to looking dejected, she seemed to have turned ice cold as well.

"How strange you look, Zijun, what's come over you today?" I couldn't help but ask.

"What do you mean?" She didn't even turn to look at me.

"But the expression on your face, you—"

"It's nothing . . . nothing at all."

Judging from her gestures as well as the things she was saying, I finally perceived what was going on within Zijun: she had come to the conclusion that I was a hard-hearted man with no real feelings. No feelings? If it weren't for my feelings for *her,* I'd probably be on my own making a fairly good living for myself. To be sure, because of my own pride I'd never had much to do with my family's circle of friends here in the capital. And since moving to Goodomen Lane, I'd gradually become estranged from every last one of my own acquaintances as well. Yet all I'd have to do was break out of here, go to some other place, and the road ahead of me would still be wide open.

Didn't she know I was only enduring the miseries of my present life for *her* sake? And for that matter, if it hadn't been for her sake, why would I have gotten rid of Shadow? One day as we were talking, I found occasion to hint at all of this. As I spoke, Zijun nodded her head as if she understood, but if one were to judge from her subsequent actions, it's obvious that she must not have realized what I was driving at. Or perhaps she hadn't taken me seriously.

The cold room and Zijun's icy expression were so oppressive

8. The buyer might well have purchased the dog as meat.

that I no longer felt comfortable at home. But where was I to go? To be sure, I had no icy looks to contend with out on the streets or in the park, but the winter's wind soon proved to be something to reckon with too. Just as my skin was about to crack, I finally found a haven in the Popular Library. You didn't have to buy tickets to get in and they had two iron stoves set up in the reading room. Granted, the coal was more dead than alive, but even the *sight* of those two stoves was enough to make a man feel warm.

There was nothing worth reading—the old books were shot through with outworn and stale ideas, and there were no new ones. Fortunately I wasn't there to read. A dozen or so other people would often gather there as well. They were thinly clad and had, like myself, come for the stoves. Nevertheless, we all made a pretense of reading so as to have an excuse for staying. That library suited my purposes perfectly, for out on the streets I still ran the risk of running into people who knew me and becoming the object of contemptuous glances; inside the library, at least, I was safe from such unpleasant surprises. Besides, my acquaintances would mostly be gathered around other iron stoves in their offices or around earthen ones at home.

Though there was nothing for me to read, the sheer fact of being there provided me with some time to think. As I sat by myself with nothing to do, I began to realize that for the better part of a year now, I had neglected every last essential of human life for the sake of love alone—blind love. First of all, I'd forgotten about the business of making a living. A man has to be able to make a living before he can provide a place for love to dwell. Though I wasn't what I used to be by a long shot, I still had faith that new roads would always open up for a man who knew how to struggle.

And now the room and all the other patrons gradually faded from my consciousness as new visions rose before my eyes: a lone fisherman in the midst of towering waves; a soldier in his trench; a man of high rank riding in his motorcar; a speculator on the stock exchange; a bold bandit deep in his mountain lair; a professor behind his lectern; a political activist at dusk; a thief in the depths of night. And Zijun? Zijun was not part of these visions, for she had lost her courage. Her sense of grief and indignation had shrunk to the scope of worries about a dog; the only thing capable of holding her spellbound now was cooking. The wonder was that *physically* she had not grown either weak or thin.

The library started to get cold. The few broken chunks of more-dead-than-alive coal had finally burned out. It was closing time—time once again to go back to Goodomen Lane and suffer an evening of Zijun's icy looks. Of late, I had occasionally seen a warm expression appear on her face, but surprisingly this had only added to my miseries. There was one night in particular when her eyes suddenly filled with that childlike glow I hadn't seen in so very long. Smiling happily, she spoke fondly of the life we'd had back at the Hometowners' Club. Once in a while, however, her face betrayed another emotion—fear. Knowing that my indifference toward her, which had recently begun to outstrip her own coldness toward me, was the cause of that fear, I strained to assume a warm demeanor and forced myself to say things that I knew would comfort her. However, no sooner was the smile on my face, no sooner were the words on my lips, than both words and smile were transformed into utter emptiness, an emptiness that immediately reverberated throughout the room and then came echoing back as a cruel and mocking laugh.

Zijun must have heard it too, for from that time on she entirely lost her accustomed calm and seemed constantly assailed by feelings of apprehensiveness—feelings, though she tried her best to disguise them, that were betrayed by her face. Now she began treating me with much more affection and warmth. I wanted to come straight out and tell her how I felt, but somehow was never able to work up the courage. And then on one occasion when I finally *could* have, that childlike gleam appeared in her eyes again and I just didn't have the heart to do it. Instead, I forced a smile, which immediately transformed itself into another cruel and mocking laugh, one which swept me off my own platform of indifference and calm.

* * *

Once again Zijun began to put me through those sentimental reviews of our courtship. She devised new test questions to gauge my feelings for her, forcing me to give comforting and hypocritical answers. With every word I spoke, I composed a rough draft of hypocrisy in my heart, and as the pages rapidly accumulated, I found it increasingly difficult to breathe. In the midst of my miseries, I often thought of the great courage it takes to speak the truth. At the same time I knew full well that if I habitually resorted to hypocrisy as the easy way out, I would never be able to carve out a new path for myself. What was more, I might just as well have never lived!

One bitterly cold morning, I detected a look of resentment on Zijun's face such as I had never seen before. Perhaps that is only the way I interpreted it, but at any rate it was a look that infuriated me. In the privacy of my heart I scoffed at her, for it was clear to me now that her entire discipline of new thought and all those brave liberal words she had learned to voice were, in the end, empty—and that *she* was not even aware of it.

She no longer read anything. Furthermore, she had obviously forgotten that the single most important thing in life is survival. It matters little whether a couple marches down the road hand-in-hand or advances separately, but if one of them hangs upon the other's coattails, then even the bravest of warriors will be disastrously encumbered and both will be destroyed.

I came to the conclusion that our only hope was to separate. If only Zijun herself would work up the resolve to leave. Suddenly I caught myself contemplating her death. I instantly castigated myself for even having such a thought and was filled with remorse. Fortunately it was early morning and I still had plenty of time to devise some way of breaking the truth to her. Whether or not I'd be able to blaze a new trail for myself would hang entirely on the outcome of today's conversation.

I began rather casually by talking about literature. I quickly moved to the topic of foreign authors and their works—more specifically, *Nora* and *The Lady from the Sea*.[9] First I praised Nora's decisiveness, and then . . . In sum, I said exactly the same sort of thing I had said at the Hometowners' Club the year before. But *now* everything I said seemed an empty sham. As I listened to my own words, I had the eerie feeling that there was a mischievous child standing behind me, maliciously mimicking everything I said.

---

9. *Nora* is better known to English-speaking audiences as *A Doll's House*. Since both these Ibsen (1828–1906) plays take free choice of marriage partners as a theme, their translations into Chinese were enormously popular with young intellectuals. While Nora, no longer content to play the doll, or puppet, role in which she has been cast, leaves her husband at the end of the play, the heroine of *The Lady from the Sea* decides to remain with her spouse before the final curtain falls. Her decision is made, however, only after her husband has given her the freedom to leave if she chooses.

Paying close attention, Zijun kept nodding her head in agreement. Then she fell silent. In bits and pieces, I limped to the end of my piece. At long last even the echo of my voice disappeared into the emptiness of the room.

"I see," she said quite simply, and then fell silent again. "But," she asked after a bit, "how about *you,* Juansheng? I have the feeling that recently there has been a change in you. Has there? I . . . I want the truth."

While I had beaten around the bush, Zijun had come straight to the point. For a moment I was thrown off balance by her head-on approach. Then quickly collecting myself, I described the situation as I understood it and laid out suggestions as to the best way of handling it. I particularly stressed the need for us to take new roads and make new lives for ourselves so that we did not both go down to destruction.

As the conversation approached its conclusion, I spoke in very decisive tones: "What's more, now you've got nothing to hold you back! You're free to advance again without any fear. You want the truth. That's as it should be. People weren't meant to live in hypocrisy. Well, let me give you the truth then—yes, there has been a change in me. I . . . I'm no longer in love with you! Actually it's much better for *you* this way, for now you can go ahead and do whatever you choose without having me to worry about . . ."

As I spoke, I anticipated the worst, but when I had finished there was nothing but silence. Then an ashen pallor swept across Zijun's face and she looked as though all life had suddenly been drained out of her—then, just as suddenly, she revived and that childlike gleam began to sparkle in her eyes again. She looked around the room like a hungry child searching for its mother. Her frightened eyes constantly shifted their gaze as she desperately sought to avoid mine.

I could not bear to look at her any longer. Fortunately our conversation took place after opening time at the library, and, bracing myself, I bolted out into the cold air and made my way straight to it. Leafing through a copy of *Freedom's Friend,* I was surprised to note that my essay had actually been published. That put some life back into me. There are many roads still open to me, I thought to myself, but not if I go on living the way I am now.

* * *

Once or twice I tried going to the homes of some old acquaintances with whom I'd long since lost touch. Although their places were well heated, I still couldn't shake the gnawing chill that night after night went to the very marrow of my bones as I lay curled up in a knot in a room much colder than ice.

Nor could I shake off the needles of ice that numbed my soul as well. There were still many roads open to me, I thought to myself; after all, I hadn't forgotten how to flap my wings as quickly as all that. I suddenly caught myself imagining her death but then instantly condemned myself for having such thoughts, and was filled with remorse.

In the library, I often saw a brilliant flash illuminating a new road that lay stretched out before me. I imagined Zijun bravely coming to her senses as she resolutely strode forth and left our icy home. And on her face one could not detect the slightest trace of rancor or resentment. At such times I felt light and free as a drifting cloud. Above me would appear a blue sky; below, deep mountains and vast oceans. I would see towering skyscrapers; battlefields; motorcars; the stock exchange; bright sunny streets bustling with people; and deep black nights. I had a genuine premonition that this new life of mine was not far off.

* * *

At long last we made it through the difficult winter, and a Beijing winter at that. Yet it was only a matter of time. We were like a dragonfly fallen into the hands of a mischievous child who ties it round the waist with a thread, plays with it to his heart's content, and then goes on to torture it as well. To be sure, as it lies struggling on the ground, the dragonfly can count itself lucky to be still alive—but it is only a matter of time.

I had already sent three letters to the editor-in-chief of *Freedom's Friend* when I finally received a reply. The envelope contained two credit slips, one for twenty cents, the other for thirty. I'd spent *nine* cents in postage alone just trying to dun payment out of him. I'd gone hungry. And what did I have to show for it? Nothing.

And then, what I expected might happen, finally did.

* * *

Winter was on its way out and spring on its way in. Since the wind was losing some of its bite, one day I lingered on the streets after closing time at the library and it was already dark when I arrived home. As usual, I felt depressed on my way back to Zijun; as usual again, the sight of our gate further depressed me and I slowed my steps. At last I went inside. The fire had not yet been lit for supper. I groped for a match, lit it, and looked around. An eerie silence pervaded the room. Just as I was beginning to wonder what was wrong, the landlord's wife appeared at the window and beckoned me outside.

"Zijun's father came today and took her back," she reported quite simply. Stunned, I stood there speechless.

"And she went with him?" I managed to ask at last.

"Yes."

"Did . . . did she offer any explanation?"

"No. Just said she was leaving and to tell you when you got back."

I refused to believe it, and yet the room *was* unusually silent and empty. I looked all around but saw nothing save a few pieces of broken-down furniture lurking in the gloom, their crisp lines offering mute testimony that they were incapable of concealing anyone.

Now my thoughts took a different tack and I hunted around for any note or letter she might have left, but there was nothing. Neatly grouped in one place on the table, however, I found salt, pepper, flour, half a head of cabbage, and a few dozen dollar coins —the sum total of what we had to live on. Deliberately and with consideration, Zijun had left it all there as a silent injunction for me to take it and use it to go on living as long as I could.

And then, from all sides, everything seemed to crowd in on me until I was forced to flee out to the courtyard, where I was engulfed by darkness. Shadows cast by lamplight appeared on the paper window of the landlord's living room. As I listened to him and his wife laughing and playing with their little daughter, I began to collect myself a bit. And now, in the midst of this heavily oppressive atmosphere, gradually—and indistinctly at first—the faint outlines of an escape route began to appear: deep mountains and great marshes; the stock exchange; a sumptuous feast beneath electric lights; trenches; the blackest of black nights; the stabbing of a sharp knife; and silent footsteps . . .

Feeling somewhat more relaxed and at ease, I considered the problem of travel expenses.

* * *

As I lay in the room that night, the future I anticipated for myself unfolded before my closed eyes scene by scene, coming to an end just before midnight. Suddenly in the darkness I seemed to see a mound of food and then Zijun's pallid face floating before me. Her childlike eyes gazed imploringly into my own. But no sooner had I regained my composure than her image disappeared again.

Once again my heart felt very heavy. Why had I not been able to put up with it for a few more days? Why had I been in such a terrible hurry to tell her the truth? Now that she knew the truth, from here on out her life would consist of nothing but the moralistic austerity—crueler than the fieriest rays of the sun—of a father who would forever hold her in his debt, and the judgmental stares —colder than ice or snow—of everyone else. Apart from all that, her life would become a void. Shouldering the burden of emptiness that I had thrust upon her, she would have to walk this so-called road of life in an atmosphere of moralistic austerity and judgmental stares. A terrifying prospect! And when at last she came to the end, her only reward would be a grave with no stone to honor her.

I should not have told Zijun the truth. Since we had loved each other once, I should have gone on offering up my daily tribute of empty lies. How could I seriously maintain that truth was anything of value when it became such a heavy burden to Zijun? Lies, to be sure, would only have been another kind of emptiness, but even so, as she neared the end of her road, a burden of lies would certainly be no more onerous than the terrible freight of truth she had to carry now.

I had thought if I told her the truth, she would be able to move forward once again with no misgivings about the past, with that same resolution and determination she had shown when we first decided to live together. I was wrong. The courage and fearlessness she had mustered back then both derived their strength from love.

Lacking courage to shoulder the burden of hypocrisy, I had placed the heavier burden of truth on Zijun. Falling in love with me had condemned her to bear that burden as she walked the so-called road of life in an atmosphere of moralistic austerity and judgmental stares.

Catching myself thinking of her death again, I realized that I was a coward who had no place among the strong, be they truth-tellers *or* hypocrites. And to think that, through all of this, Zijun had only hoped that I would go on living as long as I could . . .

* * *

I wanted to leave Goodomen Lane, to get away from that eerie silence and emptiness. "If only I can get out of here, it will be as though Zijun is still with me," I said to myself. "At least if I'm still in town, it's just possible that one day, quite unexpectedly, she'll come and visit me just the way she used to when I was at the Hometowners' Club."

Nothing had come of all the requests I'd made and all the letters I'd written, so I had no choice but to turn to my family's circle of friends, people I had heretofore been too proud to call upon. I went to see a friend of my uncle's—a boyhood schoolmate of his—whom I hadn't seen in a very long time. As a youth, he had been selected as an outstanding exemplar of both literary and moral attainment and presented at the capital as a candidate for the special palace examinations. He had been in Beijing ever since and had a very wide circle of friends and acquaintances.

Perhaps it was the threadbare clothes I wore, but his gatekeeper was rather contemptuous and it took quite some talking before I managed to get myself shown in. Although my uncle's friend still recognized me, he treated me coolly—it turned out he knew everything about my relationship with Zijun.

"To be sure, it will not do for you to stay here in the capital," he said coldly after I had asked him to help me find a job someplace else. "But where else *can* you go? It's not going to be easy, you know. By the way, that—what should I call her?—that *girlfriend* of yours is dead, you know."

I was speechless.

"Can that be *true?*" As I began to recover from the initial shock, the words came out without my thinking.

"Of course it's true. My servant, Wang Sheng, comes from the same village she does."

"But . . . but . . . *how* did she die?"

"Who knows? She's dead, that's all."

I can no longer remember how I took my leave of him or how I got back to my own room. I knew that he was not a man to lie, that Zijun would never again come and visit me as she had the previous year. Though she was willing to bear the burden of emptiness I had thrust upon her, to go on walking this so-called road of life in an atmosphere of moralistic austerity and judgmental stares, she had not even been able to do that. No, she had been fated to destruction, engulfed by the truth of the loveless world I had given her.

I was enveloped by a vast emptiness and deathly silence. In the blackness of the night before my eyes, I seemed to see the face of each and every person who had ever died for lack of love, and to hear their cries of pain and despair.

* * *

I still hoped for something new to come, something nameless and unexpected. Yet day after day there was nothing but deathly silence.

I no longer went out as much as I used to. I would just sit or lie in that vast emptiness while the silence slowly ate away at my soul, a silence that would, on occasion, tremble and hide itself away, providing cracks in its own continuity through which would flash images of hope—nameless, unexpected, and new.

One dreary morning when the sun proved too weak to free itself of the clouds and even the air seemed tired, the twin sounds of breathing and light footsteps caused me to open my eyes. I looked around. The room was empty as ever, it seemed, but then I caught sight of a tiny animal curled up on the floor. It was covered with dirt and looked emaciated, half-dead. I took a closer look. My heart skipped a beat as I jumped out of bed. Shadow was back.

My departure from Goodomen Lane wasn't simply due to the icy stares I received from my landlords and their maid—it was mainly because of Shadow. There were still a good many roads open to me, of course, and I had a fair idea of what they were, too. Sometimes I would even catch a glimpse of one of them right before my eyes, but I still did not know how to take that first step.

After weighing various possibilities, I decided that the Hometowners' Club was about the only place that would still have me. And so here I am. Run-down room, slatboard bed, half-withered locust and wisteria—all that still remains, but the person who had brought hope, happiness, love, and life itself into this room is gone forever. There is nothing left but emptiness, an emptiness that I have bought with the truth.

* * *

There are still many roads open to me, and since I remain in the realm of the living, eventually I will have to choose one of them. But I have yet to discover how to take that first step. Sometimes I see a new road rushing grayly toward me like a great, wriggling serpent. I wait and wait, watching it approach, but then just as suddenly as it appeared, it disappears again into the darkness.

These early spring nights are as long as ever. Sitting here, utterly bored, I remember a funeral procession I saw on the street this morning. Paper people and paper horses led the parade while keening voices that sounded more like singing brought up the rear. For the first time, I understood the wisdom of it all—how relaxed, how simple, and how very final.

And then Zijun's funeral procession appeared before my eyes. All alone, she was carrying that heavy burden of emptiness down a long and gloomy road, only to fade suddenly into the atmosphere of moralistic austerity and judgmental stares that surrounded her.

I hope there really are such things as ghosts and spirits. I hope there is a hell, too. For then I shall seek her out, and one day, even if it be in the midst of roaring flames, I will tell her of my sorrow and remorse and beg her forgiveness—or else be engulfed by the raging flames that will incinerate my body, consuming all my sorrow and remorse.

In the midst of the howling winds and searing flames, I would take Zijun in my arms, beg her forgiveness, and perhaps bring her some happiness . . .

* * *

But all these thoughts are even more vacuous than the new roads that appear and then disappear again into the darkness. All that I actually possess at the moment is this early spring night—

and it is so long, so very, very long. Since I must remain in the land of the living, I will eventually find a new road for myself. In committing my sorrow and remorse to paper, for her sake as well as my own, I am taking the first step down that new road.

I have nothing but a keening voice that sounds like singing with which to see Zijun into her grave, with which to bury her in the realm of all that is past and forgotten. And forget her I must. For my own sake, I must even forget *how* I consigned her to the realm of all that is past and forgotten.

I must take the first step and make my way silently down that new road, hiding the truth within my heart's deepest wound and taking falsehood and forgetfulness as my guides.

FINISHED ON OCTOBER 21, 1925

Brothers

There was never any official business to take care of at the Bureau of Public Welfare. Today, as was their custom, the few clerks sat around the office chatting about family affairs. Qin Yitang, holding the stem of a waterpipe in one hand, was coughing so hard he couldn't catch his breath, and his colleagues had no choice but to stop talking until he did. At length he raised his flushed and swollen face and spoke, still trying to catch his breath: "And yesterday they went at it again. Fought all the way from inside the house right out to the front gate. No matter how I bellowed, I still couldn't stop them." Beneath scattered strands of grey whiskers his lips still trembled. "Number Three said the loss Number Five took on public bonds could not be counted as a family debt and that Number Five ought to make good the sum himself."

"See, it's always over money," observed Zhang Peijun expansively, rising from a dilapidated divan, his deep-set eyes radiating benevolence. "I've never been able to understand why brothers of the same family should get so petty about what's yours and what's mine. After all, it all amounts to the same thing in the end anyway, doesn't it?"

"Ah, but where can you find another pair of brothers like you and *your* brother, Zhang Peijun?" asked Qin Yitang.

"The only difference is we don't divide up the family property like that. What's mine is his and what's his is mine. Ideas about *money* and *property* never enter our heads in the first place. That's why we never had any trouble. Whenever I hear of a family about to split up, I make it a point to tell them how it is with me and my brother and plead with them not to be so picayune. If you'd just help them straighten out their thinking, Mr. Qin—"

"I can't do any good," said Mr. Qin, shaking his head.

"It probably wouldn't work out at that," observed Wang Yuesheng as he gazed with admiration into Zhang Peijun's eyes. "Don't find many like you and your brother around. I've never

---

The story was first published February 10, 1926, in the third issue of the fortnightly *Wilderness (Mangyuan)*. The present translation was first published, in slightly different form, in the first issue of *Renditions* (Autumn 1973).

seen the likes of it. Why there's simply no trace of a selfish thought in either one of you. That's a very rare thing."

"Fought all the way from inside the house right out to the front gate," mumbled Qin Yitang.

"Your younger brother as busy as ever?" asked Wang Yuesheng.

"Yes, he still spends eighteen hours every week in class and has to correct ninety-three compositions on top of that. It's more than one man can handle. You know he's been out on sick leave the last couple of days. Has a temperature. Probably a touch of cold."

"Now that's something you really have to watch," said Yuesheng in tones of utmost seriousness. "This morning's paper said there's a seasonal epidemic making the rounds right now."

This unexpected intelligence gave Peijun quite a start. "Epidemic of *what?*" he asked anxiously.

"I'm not all that clear about it myself. Some kind of fever or other, I think."

Peijun strode off in a hurry to the reading room. Yuesheng sighed and followed Peijun's flying figure through the door with admiring glances. Then he directed his attention to Mr. Qin: "There aren't many brothers like that around anymore. Why those two are like a single individual. If *all* brothers were like that, how would family trouble get started in the first place? I wish I could learn—"

"Said that money lost on public bonds couldn't be treated as a family debt," continued Mr. Qin bitterly as he slipped the touchpaper (with which he had just lit his waterpipe) back into its holder.

For a short while the office sank into silence, a silence soon broken by Peijun's footsteps in the hallway and the sound of his voice summoning the office boy. Stammering, voice trembling as he spoke, Peijun sounded as if on the brink of some great disaster. He told the office boy to phone Dr. Putisi[1] and tell him to head for Zhang Peijun's place at the Tongxing Apartments to pay a house call.

At this point Yuesheng realized that Peijun must be really worried: to be sure, he had always been aware of Peijun's faith in Western medicine, but he also knew that Peijun lived on a limited

1. Transliteration of a German name.

income which he spent quite frugally. And yet, in spite of all this, he had just now sent for the best known and most expensive doctor in the area. Yuesheng realized it must be something terribly serious. He went into the hall and saw Peijun, pale as paper, standing to one side and listening attentively as the office boy made the call.

"What's the matter?"

"The paper says . . . says that what's going round is scarlet . . . scarlet fever! When I left home for the bureau this afternoon, that's just what my brother Jingfu's face was like—red all over. What? The doctor's gone out on his rounds already? Ask them . . . ask them to try and get him by phone. Tell him to come right away—the Tongxing Apartments."

He waited while the office boy completed the call, then rushed into the office to fetch his hat. Caught up in Peijun's excitement, Wang Yuesheng rushed back into the office after him.

"If the chief checks in, tell him I'm taking a few days' leave. Say that someone's sick at home and I've gone for a doctor," he said, nodding his head with a singular lack of coordination.

"You just go along and tend to your brother. Don't worry about a thing. It's quite possible the chief won't check in today anyway," said Yuesheng.

* * *

When he got out to the street, it didn't even occur to him to shop around for the least expensive ride the way he usually did. As soon as he spotted a fairly strong puller who looked as though he could really handle a rickshaw, he asked the price, clambered aboard, and without further ado said: "Okay. I'll pay whatever you ask, but get me there in a hurry!"

As usual, the apartments were peaceful and quiet; as usual, too, the houseboy sat outside playing the *huqin.*[2] When Peijun entered the bedroom, he felt his heart begin to pound still harder, for his brother's face was even more flushed than before and he was gasping for breath. Peijun reached out and felt Jingfu's forehead—red hot!

"Wonder what I've got? Nothing serious, is it?" Jingfu asked.

---

2. A two-stringed instrument played with a bow whose hairs pass between the strings.

The anxious look in his eyes showed that he too felt something was not quite right.

"Nothing to worry about . . . probably just a cold," said Peijun, dodging the question. Ordinarily he was an implacable enemy of superstition, but this time even *he* felt there was something "unlucky" about Jingfu's appearance and tone of voice; it was as though the patient himself had some sort of premonition. Such thoughts made Peijun even more uncomfortable, and he hastened out of the room. In a low voice he summoned the houseboy and bade him call the hospital, to ask if they had located Dr. P yet.

"Yes, I understand. They haven't found him yet," the boy said into the mouthpiece.

By this point, no matter whether he sat or stood, Peijun was on pins and needles. However, in the midst of all this anxiety, his thoughts took a new tack. Suppose it wasn't scarlet fever after all? Since no one seemed able to get hold of Dr. P, then how about Dr. Bai? For, although Bai Wenshan, who lived in the same apartment complex, was only a practitioner of traditional Chinese medicine, he might at least be good for identifying the disease.[3] Peijun remembered uneasily that he had in the past often attacked traditional Chinese medicine in the course of an argument with Dr. Bai. What was more, Dr. Bai might well have heard that Peijun was trying to telephone the German doctor . . . In the end, however, he went on over to fetch Dr. Bai.

Strange to tell, Bai Wenshan did not seem to mind in the least. He immediately donned his tortoiseshell dark glasses and came straight over to Jingfu's room. He took the pulse, carefully scanned Jingfu's face, and then loosened his clothing to take a look at his chest. Perfectly calm and collected, Dr. Bai then took his leave and returned to his own quarters, with Peijun following close behind.

He asked Peijun to sit down, but didn't seem inclined to say anything more. Peijun couldn't prevent himself from asking straight out: "Wenshan, esteemed elder brother, what's wrong with my little brother?"

"*Hongbansha*. See for yourself—the spots have already come out."

---

3. Lu Xun himself was a harsh critic of traditional Chinese medicine.

"Then it's not scarlet fever!" Peijun's spirits began to lighten a bit.

"The Western doctors call it 'scarlet fever,' but we Chinese doctors call it *hongbansha.*"

This made Peijun's hands and feet turn cold and clammy once again. "Can it be cured?" he asked, spirits sinking.

"It can. All depends on your family's luck."

Peijun came out of Bai Wenshan's apartment so thoroughly confused that he himself could not have explained how it was that he had actually gone so far as to ask Bai for a prescription. Passing the telephone, Peijun remembered Dr. P, and he called the hospital again. They said they had located Dr. P, but that he was very busy and probably wouldn't be able to see Jingfu until very late that day, or possibly even the next morning. Peijun told them it was imperative that Dr. P see his brother today.

When he went to his brother's bedroom and lit the lamp, he saw that Jingfu's face was more flushed than ever and that even more spots had appeared than before, spots that were redder than the earlier ones. The eyelids were puffed up as well. On pins and needles, Peijun sat down to wait. As the night grew ever quieter and his vigil ever longer, the honking of every horn in the street struck his ears with heightened clarity. Once, for no really good reason, he simply assumed that one of those honks belonged to Dr. P's car and jumped up to go out and greet him. But long before he reached the front gate, the car had driven past. He turned about sluggishly and made his way back through the courtyard. A bright moon had climbed high in the western sky and now was casting the ghostly shadow of a neighbor's locust tree before him, a shadow that eerily intensified his already deep sense of melancholy.

Suddenly a crow cawed. This was a sound that Peijun was ordinarily used to hearing, for there were three or four nests in that locust tree. But *this* time, strangely, he was nearly frozen with terror. Trembling, he crept to his younger brother's room and saw Jingfu still lying there, eyes closed. Now his brother's whole face seemed bloated. He wasn't sleeping and had probably heard his elder brother's footsteps, for he suddenly opened his eyes; the light from those eyes flickered in an unnatural and anguished way.

"Was it a letter?"

"No, no. It was me." The sound of Jingfu's voice startled Peijun and it was a second or so before he could collect himself. "It . . . it was me," he stammered. "It was me, I . . . I thought it would be a good idea if we called in a Western doctor, so you'd get better a little sooner. He hasn't come yet . . ."

Without making any response, Jingfu closed his eyes again. Peijun sat next to the desk that stood before the window. All was silence save for the hurried breathing of the patient and the *tick-tock* of an alarm clock. Again, all at once the sound of a horn in the distance raised him to a peak of alertness. Peijun listened as it drew closer, closer—until it seemed to be right outside the gate. Then just when he thought it was going to stop, he heard the receding sound of the motor as the car went past. This experience was repeated so many times that Peijun soon became familiar with the various sounds made by all kinds of horns: someone whistling; someone passing wind; a woman sobbing; a dog barking; a duck quacking; a cow lowing; the clucking of a startled hen; a roll of drums . . . Peijun berated himself that he hadn't previously paid sufficient attention to the peculiarities of Dr. P's horn, so that he would be able to identify it now.

The lodger across the way hadn't yet come home. He had, no doubt, gone to the Beijing opera as usual, or perhaps to one of those tea gardens that double as brothels. It was so late now that the sounds of the cars began to fade away. The paper window glowed white with the bright silvery light of the moon.

The boredom of waiting gradually sapped Peijun's alertness and he no longer heard the horns. Fragmented images, exploiting his temporary state of psychological lassitude, worked their way up to the surface of his consciousness. For the moment he seemed to *know* that Jingfu had scarlet fever and furthermore, that he was going to die of it. In that case, what would he do about the family finances? Could he support the entire family all by himself? He could, of course, move to a small town, but even then, with prices going up all the time . . . Besides, he had three children of his own. Add Jingfu's two to that and it would be difficult to make ends meet, much less send them all to school. Suppose he could only afford to send one or two of them to school: well, if that were the case, his own son Kang'er was the brightest of the lot. But if he sent Kang'er, then everyone would criticize him for treating his brother's children so shabbily . . .

And what about the funeral? He didn't even have enough to buy wood for the coffin, much less ship the body back to their hometown down south. For the time being, he'd have to bury it in a pauper's field.

The sound of footsteps approaching in the distance made Peijun jump up and walk outside: only the lodger across the way.

"O-u-r l-a-te em-per-or . . . da-da dum-dum . . . at Bai-di Ci-ty . . . dump dee-da-da . . ." The man was singing snatches from a popular Peking opera. Hearing this light, happy humming, Peijun felt first disappointed, then indignant—so indignant that he almost ran across the way to give the lodger a piece of his mind. But before he had time to do that, he caught sight of the houseboy approaching, a storm lantern held high in one hand. Its light revealed a shiny pair of shoes following along behind him, and in the faint glow above the shoes Peijun could make out a large man with white face and black beard. This had to be Dr. Putisi.

He ran up to the doctor as though he had just stumbled onto hidden treasure, and then led him to the sickroom. The two men stood together before Jingfu's bed. Peijun reached for a lamp and held it up so that the doctor could see.

"He has a fever, Doctor . . ." said Peijun catching his breath.

"When . . . did . . . it . . . begin?" Hands thrust into his trouser pockets, Dr. P spoke slowly, in halting but precise Chinese, while staring straight at the sick man's face.

"The day before yesterday—no, it was the day before that—no, it was the day *before* the day before that."

Dr. P didn't utter a sound. He took Jingfu's pulse in a perfunctory fashion and asked Peijun to hold the lamp closer, so that he might get a better look at the face. He also asked that the quilt be drawn back and the patient's clothing loosened. After he had taken a close look at Jingfu's body, he thrust out one finger and felt his stomach.

"Measles," said Dr. Putisi in a low voice, as if talking to himself.[4]

"Measles?" Peijun's tone was so ecstatic that his voice seemed to quaver slightly.

"Measles."

"Just plain ordinary measles?"

4. Dr. P uses the English word.

"Measles."

"Do you mean to tell me you've never had measles, Jingfu?" While Peijun was happily asking his brother this question, Dr. P had already started moving toward the desk, and now Peijun followed him. Dr. P placed one foot on the chair that stood before the desk, grabbed a sheet of paper from the top, fished a stubby pencil from his own pocket and scratched several words onto the paper, words that were not easy to read. Clearly, this was the prescription.

Peijun took it from the doctor's hand and said: "I'm afraid the druggists are all closed today."

"Tomorrow . . . will . . . do. Give it to him . . . tomorrow."

"Will you come back to see him again tomorrow?"

"There's no need . . . for me to see him . . . again. Just don't let him eat anything sour . . . hot . . . or anything too salty. After the fever has . . . gone down . . . take a urine sample and . . . send it over to my hospital. I'll examine it. And that . . . will be that. Put it in a . . . clean glass . . . bottle. Write his name . . . on the outside."

Dr. P said all this while walking out to the front gate; he also accepted a five-dollar bill from Peijun, and thrust it into one of his pockets. Peijun saw him all the way out to the street and didn't turn away until after the doctor had gotten into his car and driven off. As he came back through the gate, Peijun heard a *moo moo* sound behind him, and only then did he discover that Dr. P's horn was really something like the lowing of a cow. There's not much use in knowing that now, he thought to himself.

Back inside the apartment, even the lamplight seemed happy. Peijun felt as though he had everything under control. Peace and quiet reigned on all sides—and yet, somehow, his heart still felt empty. He handed prescription and money to the houseboy, who had followed him in, with instructions to fill it at the Mei Ya Pharmacy first thing in the morning. Dr. P had specified this pharmacy in particular, saying that Mei Ya alone sold consistently reliable drugs.

"The Mei Ya Pharmacy on the east end! That's the one you have to go to. Remember—the Mei Ya!" Peijun aimed his remarks at the houseboy's back as the latter strode away.

The courtyard was filled with moonlight white as silver. The singing neighbor had gone to sleep and all was silence save for the rhythmic and happy *tick-tock* of the alarm clock on the desk. Even the breathing that came from the sickbed was smooth and almost inaudible now . . . Peijun sat down and before long started to feel happy again. "So, old as you are, you mean to tell me you've actually never had the measles before?" he asked his brother, in the astonished tones of one who has just witnessed a miracle.

". . ."

"You wouldn't remember yourself. Only mother would know the answer to that one."

". . ."

"And she's not here . . . So you've never had the measles! Ha, ha, ha!"[5]

* * *

When Peijun woke up in his own bed, back in his own room the next morning, the sun had already begun to shine in through the paper window, and now it poked into his sleepy eyes. He couldn't rouse himself right away, however, for his limbs felt powerless; besides, there was still some cold and clammy sweat on his back. Suddenly, from out of nowhere, he saw a child standing before his bed, her whole face dripping with blood. He was just about to strike her when in a flash this image faded away and he was once

5. Speaking of the plot, an old friend of Lu Xun's has remarked:

> Most of it consists of experiences that Lu Xun went through himself. It was probably sometime around the end of spring or the beginning of summer in 1917. He and his younger brother, Zuoren, were both living in the Bushu Study of the Shaoxing Hostel in Beijing. Zuoren suddenly developed a temperature. There was an epidemic of scarlet fever going through Beijing at the time. More than that, one of our colleagues at the Ministry of Education had died during just such an epidemic the year before. All this made Lu Xun especially apprehensive and he called in a German doctor by the name of Di-bo-er [transliteration of a German name] for a diagnosis. Only then did he discover that it was actually nothing more than measles. The next day when he came to work at the Ministry [of Education], Lu Xun was in exceptionally good spirits and recounted to me in great detail how slow Dr. D had been in coming and how quick he had been in making his diagnosis. And then he said, "To think that Qimeng [Zuoren], old as he is, has never had the measles." (Xu Shoushang, *Wo suo renshi de Lu Xun* [The Lu Xun I Knew] [Beijing: People's Press, 1952], p. 62)

again sleeping alone in his own room, with no one else around. He pulled the cover from his pillow and wiped the perspiration off his chest and back. Then he got into his clothes and walked from his own room into Jingfu's. On the way he saw his opera-loving neighbor in the courtyard rinsing out his mouth—from appearances it must be very late. Jingfu had awakened, too, and lay upon his bed, eyes wide open.

"How do you feel today?" Peijun asked.

"A little better . . ."

"Hasn't the medicine come yet?"

"Not yet."

Peijun sat down next to the desk, facing the bed, and observed that Jingfu's face was not so flushed as it had been yesterday. But now his own head, on the other hand, felt a bit dizzy, and dream fragments began to flicker and glitter once again as they bobbed up to the surface of his consciousness.

He saw Jingfu lying just as he was lying now, but he had become a corpse, and Peijun was preparing the body for burial. All by himself, Peijun was carrying the coffin on his back, *all the way from outside the front gate right into the house.* The place looked much like their old home down south, and he recognized several very familiar-looking people who were standing off to one side praising Peijun's brotherly devotion to Jingfu . . . He had issued orders that Kang'er, as well as his younger brother and younger sister, were all to attend school. But there were two *other* children, who were wailing and begging to be allowed to attend school too.

Peijun was harassed to the limits of endurance by all their howling and yet, at the same time, he was deliciously aware that he was now in possession of the highest authority and virtually infinite power. With the palm of his hand, now grown to three or four times its normal size and hardened into steel, he struck out at the face of Hesheng, one of his brother's children.

The assault of these dream fragments so frightened Peijun that he was on the point of getting up and running outside, but in the end he didn't move at all. He tried to repress them, to forget them, but like goose quills swirling around in water, after a few turns they would float to the surface again.

Hesheng, face all bloody, came into the house weeping. He

jumped up onto the sacrificial altar.[6] Following behind the child was a cohort of people, some of whom Peijun knew, and others he didn't. He realized they had all come to attack him.

"I'd certainly never sink so low as to turn a deaf ear to the promptings of my own conscience," he told them. "Don't be taken in by the lies of a mere child." He heard his own voice saying these things.

Hesheng was next to him now, and Peijun raised his steely palm once again . . .

Suddenly he awoke. He was exhausted, and his back still felt cold. His younger brother lay before him, and although Jingfu's breathing was a bit hurried, it was even. The alarm clock on the desk seemed to tick with redoubled vigor.

Peijun turned to face the desk: it was covered with a thin layer of dust. Letting his eyes wander over toward the paper window, he saw that the number on the wall calendar was 27.

The houseboy came back with the medicine and was carrying a small bundle as well.

"What is it?" Jingfu asked as he forced his eyes to open.

"The medicine's come," Peijun answered, just having wakened from a semiconscious state himself.

"No. I mean the bundle."

"Don't worry about that just now. Just take your medicine." Having given Jingfu his medicine, Peijun picked up the bundle and said: "Suoshi sent it over. It must be that copy of *Sesame and Lilies* you wanted to borrow."[7]

Jingfu reached out and took hold of the book. As soon as he had looked at the cover and felt the gold lettering on the spine, he put

---

6. Presumably, to report to his dead father the injustice he now suffers at the hands of his uncle. Even the psychological parts of this story reflect Lu Xun's feelings toward his younger brother. In a book of reminiscences, Zuoren once recalled:

> After I recovered from my illness Lu Xun talked about it one day, remarking that it was quite a joke my having had measles at that age. Then he added something to this effect: 'At the time I was scared out of my wits and an unworthy thought cropped up in my mind—I thought that this time I would have to look after your family for sure.' This same thought was expressed toward the end of the story "Brothers." (Zhou Zuoren, *Zhitang huixiang lu* [Reminiscences of Zhou Zuoren] [Hong Kong: The Ting Tao Press, 1970], pp. 320–23)

7. A collection of essays and lectures by John Ruskin (1819–1900).

it down by his pillow and, not making a sound, closed his eyes again. After a short silence, he announced in a happy tone of voice: "When I begin to feel a bit better, I'm going to translate some of it, send it in to the Cultural Press, and make a little money. Wonder if they'll take it . . ."

* * *

On this particular day, Peijun made his way in to the Bureau of Public Welfare much later than usual. It was almost afternoon. The office was filled with smoke from Qin Yitang's waterpipe. Spotting Peijun from a distance, Wang Yuesheng came running out to greet him. "So you're here! Is your little brother better already? I thought it was nothing to be concerned about. After all, there's an epidemic of *something* or other every year. Nothing to worry about. Our old and honored friend, Qin Yitang here, and I were just thinking about you. We both wondered what could be the matter that you hadn't turned up yet—but now, here you are. That's just fine. But look at you! You look more or less as though . . . There's no doubt about it, you look a bit *different* from yesterday.

To Peijun also, both the office and his colleagues were rather different from what they had been yesterday—somehow unfamiliar despite the fact that everything was, at the same time, familiarly the same: the broken coathook, the spittoon with a chipped-out lip, the chaos of dust-covered case reports, the dilapidated divan with a missing leg, and Qin Yitang lounging upon it, waterpipe in hand, coughing and sighing as he shook his head from side to side, intoning: "Same as always, they fought all the way from inside the house right out to the front gate."

"And that's exactly why," chimed in Yuesheng, "I think you ought to tell them about Peijun, let them take a lesson from him and *his* brother. Otherwise, they'll be the death of you yet, old man."

"Number Three says the loss Number Five took on public bonds cannot be counted as their joint responsibility, and that Number Five ought himself to . . . ought to . . . ought to . . ." Yitang was now doubled over coughing.

"As the saying goes, people *are* different," said Yuesheng, turning away to face Peijun. "Well then, is anything at all wrong with your brother?"

"Nothing serious. Doctor says it's measles."

"Measles? That's right. Come to think of it, I've heard it's rampant among the children hereabouts. Three kids living on the same courtyard with me all have it. Absolutely harmless! And to think you got so worked up about it yesterday that even we outsiders couldn't help but be moved by your concern. Nothing like fraternal affection, as they say."

"Was the bureau chief around yesterday?"

"Made himself scarce as hen's teeth. All you have to do is go sign in for yesterday, and nobody will be the wiser."

"Said that Number Five ought to make good on it himself," Yitang droned, as much to himself as anyone else. "These public bonds really do great harm to people. Can't make heads or tails of them myself, but it seems that anyone who touches them ends up taking a beating. And yesterday, by the time evening rolled around, they were at it again. Fought all the way from inside the house right out to the front gate. Number Five said since Number Three has two more children in school than he does, that means Number Three has gotten more out of the public funds too. Got so mad—"

"The whole thing gets more and more muddled all the time," said Yuesheng in despair. "And that's why, when I see a brother like you, Peijun, I respect you so much. I put you up on a pedestal, as they say. It's the honest truth—I swear it. It's not just something I say to your face, to flatter you."

Peijun didn't respond, but spotting a messenger who had just come into the office with some item of official business to transact, he rushed over and took the document from him. Yuesheng followed Peijun, stood behind him, and read aloud from the document now in his hands: "*Citizen Hao Shangshan and others, in order to maintain the public health and promote the general welfare, hereby petition the Bureau of Public Welfare to immediately order its branch office to arrange a casket for, and bury the body of, an unidentified male who dropped dead in the eastern suburbs.*
—You let me take care of that," said Yuesheng. "Why don't you just take off a bit early. I know you must be worried to death

about your brother. Why, you two are as affectionate as 'pied wagtails on the moor,' as the saying goes."[8]

"No!" Peijun held onto the document. "I'll take care of this one myself." Yuesheng didn't press the point.

Peijun was apparently in a very calm state of mind as he proceeded toward his own desk where, eyes still on the petition, he reached out and removed the somewhat corroded brass cover from the top of his inkbox.

NOVEMBER 3, 1925

8. Based on a line from the *Poetry Classic.*

Divorce

"Happy New Year, Uncle-wood!"[1]

"How ya doin', Eighty-three? Happy New Year!"[2]

"Happy New Year! Ai-girl's with you too, huh?"

"Hey there, Gramps-wood!"

Setting off an explosion of voices, Zhuang Wood-three and his daughter Ai-girl had just clambered down into the boat as it made its stop at Magnolia Bridge. A few of the people behind the voices clasped both hands together, pumping them up and down in salutation. At the same time, four places on the benches along either side of the boat were vacated. Returning all the greetings, Zhuang Wood-three sat down and propped his long bamboo pipe against the gunwale of the boat. Ai-girl sat on her father's left, arranging her two sickle-shaped feet into a figure eight[3] that pointed straight over at Eighty-three, who was seated just across from her.

"Goin' to town again?" asked a man with a crabshell face.

"Nope." Gramps-wood sounded a bit depressed today, but his dark brown face was so wrinkled you couldn't sense the change just by looking at him. "We're just making a jaunt over to Chong Village."

His reply silenced the entire boat. Everyone turned and stared at father and daughter.

"Still over Ai-girl's business, is that it?" After a long pause, Eighty-three now began the interrogation.

"Yup, still over her. Be the end of me yet. We've been caught up in that ruckus a good three years now. I've lost track of the num-

---

First published in the Beijing weekly *Fragments,* no. 54, dated November 23, 1925.

1. Peasant names were invented in a bewildering variety of ways, reflecting the popular culture and local customs of the particular region. In traditional China people believed that a harmonious balance of the five elements (earth, water, fire, metal, and wood) was essential to personal well-being; it is possible that Uncle-wood's name illustrates this belief. Since he is later referred to as Wood-three, he was probably the third child born to his family. Elsewhere he is sometimes addressed affectionately as Gramps, depending on the age of the speaker.

2. In and around Shaoxing, a newborn child is often named after the actual age of the father, grandfather, or great grandfather at the time of birth. The tradition persists even today. I am indebted to Peng Xiaoling of the Lu Xun Museum in Beijing for this information.

3. The Chinese character for eight *(ba)* is written 八.

ber of fights we've had with them, and the number of times we've made peace afterwards, but there's still no end in sight."

"Are you all gonna meet at Old Master Wei's house this time too?"

"Yeah. He's tried to settle things a couple of times already, but I've never gone along with it. This time the Wei folks are havin' a New Years family get-together. Even Bigman Seven from town's gonna be there."[4]

"Bigman Seven?" Eighty-three's eyes popped wide at that. "So Bigman Seven's gonna say his piece too! Well, in that case of course . . . Uh . . . Matter of fact, you could say we got pretty even with them last year when we pulled their stove down.[5] Besides, come to think of it, wouldn't be much fun for Ai-girl even if she did go back." At this point Eighty-three lowered his eyes.

"Now just hold on there a minute, Brother Eighty-three. I'm not exactly itchin' to go back there in the first place!" Ai-girl raised her eyes with indignation and threw back her head in a display of defiant pride. "I'm fightin' because I'm flat-out mad, that's all. Just think of it, that young pig shackin' up with that pretty widow, and then thinkin' he could dump me. I'd just like to see him try and get away with that. And then that *old* pig he calls a father sides right in with him and *he* wants to dump me too. Fat chance! And so *what* if Bigman Seven's there? Are you gonna tell me that just 'cause Bigman Seven is in tight with the district magistrate, he's forgot how to talk people-talk like the rest of us? Whatever Bigman Seven is, ain't no way he can be as thick-skulled as Old Master Wei. 'The best thing would be to dissolve the marriage,' that's all Old Master Wei knows how to say! Matter of fact, I'm *glad* of the chance to tell Bigman Seven exactly what I've been putting up with the last few years—see what *he* says about who's got the right of it!"

Overwhelmed by Ai-girl's shower of invective, Eighty-three could say nothing in reply. And now the only sound heard in the boat was the gentle *slap slap* of the bow against the water. Silence reigned supreme as Zhuang Wood-three reached out, took up his

4. He is the seventh born into the Wei family, and has achieved a degree of social distinction, hence "Bigman Seven."

5. According to Zhou Zuoren, when families became entangled in a feud back in Shaoxing, the final act of the victorious family was to shove a long pole into the brick stove of the defeated one, and to jimmy it up and down until it collapsed.

pipe, and filled the bowl. A fat man who sat diagonally across from father and daughter fished out a flint from inside his pocket and fired up a tiny bit of tinder, which he then pressed into the bowl of Wood-three's pipe.

"Bli-dja, bli-dja," said Wood-three nodding his head.[6]

"We haven't met before, it's true, but I've known about you a long time, Uncle-wood," said the fat man respectfully. "Is there a single soul in all eighteen of the three half-dozen villages hereabouts who *hasn't* heard what happened? We've all known, for a long time now, how that Shi lad left your girl to shack up with that young widow. When you and your six sons went over there and flattened their stove last year, everybody said they had it coming. A man like you, who's welcome in all the richest homes around, a man who walks the earth with big, proud steps—why should you be scared of the likes of them?"

"Now you're a man after my own heart, Uncle," said Ai-girl with enthusiasm, "even though I don't know your name."

"Name's Wang Degui," the fat man promptly responded.

"Try and brush *me* off? No way! I don't care if it's Bigman Seven, Bigman Eight, or Nine, whatever—I'm still gonna raise hell like they've never seen it raised before! Won't stop till I've wiped out their whole damn clan! Old Master Wei's tried to talk me down four times already and *couldn't,* right? Why, even Dad started gettin' itchy palms when he heard how much they were gonna give to settle, and then—"

"What the hell do you think you're doin'?" Wood-three scolded his daughter in subdued tones.

Crab-face joined the conversation: "But I hear tell the Shi family threw a big shindig for Old Master Wei last New Year's."

"That won't cut any ice at all," objected Wang Degui. "If he lost his senses over a little New Year's dinner, then think what'd happen if somebody threw him a real Western feast! Men like that, who *read the classics and understand morality,*[7] they always deal with people fair and square. When everybody else gangs up to do a

---

6. A shortened form of "obliged" or perhaps a contraction of "obliged to you." —Author's note.

In Chinese, Wood-three says *"Dui, dui."* Lu Xun's note explains that this is either a clipped form of *duibuqi, duibuqi* (Sorry to bother you—lit., I can't face you) or a contraction of *dezui, dezui* (I've troubled you—lit., I'm the one to blame).

7. A well-known phrase describing Confucian scholars.

man dirt, they're the ones who come out and stand up for 'em. They don't care who's gonna offer them a banquet or who isn't. Always fair and square. Master Rong from my own village just came back from Beijing at the end of the year. Now there's a man who's been around and seen a thing or two, not like us country hicks. Way he tells it, the person with the most clout up that-a-way is Madam Guang. Tough and—"

"Everybody off for Wang-family Jetty!" yelled the boatman as the craft slowed to a stop.

"Wait for me! Wait for me!" The fat man now seized his pipe and jumped nimbly up onto the jetty. Walking rapidly forward so as to keep abreast of the departing boat, he nodded at his fellow passengers and shouted, "Bli-dja, bli-dja!"

The *slap slap* of the water was clearly audible once again against the new silence. Eighty-three began to fall off into a nap. His mouth, which was pointed toward the pair of sickle feet just across from him, began to hang open. The voices of two old women in the bow could be heard intoning Buddhist prayers. Prayer beads in hand, they now looked momentarily at Ai-girl, looked at each other, then pursed their lips and nodded.

Eyes wide open, Ai-girl stared up at the canopy that covered the center section of the boat, no doubt imagining how she would raise hell "like they'd never seen it raised before" until she had "wiped out their whole damn clan" and had finally gotten both "Young Pig" and "Old Pig" helpless in her hands. In all of this Old Master Wei didn't so much as enter her thoughts. She'd seen him a few times before—nothing but a little runt with a cannonball head. You could find lots just like him in her very own village. To be sure, the villagers' skins were a lot darker, she conceded to herself, but that was the only difference.

The tobacco in Zhuang Wood-three's pipe had long since been consumed and now, as he continued to draw on the mouthpiece, a steady *bip bip bip* issued from the burning tars at the bottom of the metal bowl. He knew that as soon as they passed Wang-family Jetty they would come to Chong Village. Off in the distance, the Confucian temple at the edge of the village was already in sight. He had been to Chong Village many times before, and in his view it was nothing to write home about; the same was true of Old Master Wei. Wood-three recalled the day Ai-girl had come back from Chong Village in tears, and then remembered how rotten his son-in-law and all the other-in-laws had been, and how later on they had openly taken advantage of his daughter and himself. These familiar scenes from the past began to unfold before his eyes. This time, however, he did not smile with satisfaction when he came to the getting-even scene. The sight of the collapsing stove did not evoke the bittersweet smile it usually had, for somehow or other the rotund figure of Bigman Seven suddenly sprawled across Zhuang Wood-three's mental horizon, throwing everything else askew.

The boat moved onward through the stillness of the countryside. While the sound of the women intoning their beads grew louder, everything else seemed to have accompanied Zhuang Wood-three and Ai-girl into the silence of their own thoughts.

"Uncle-wood, old friend, almost time to get off. We're comin' up on the temple already." By the time the boatman's voice had fully roused Zhuang Wood-three from his reverie, they were already squarely facing the Confucian temple.

Zhuang Wood-three disembarked, followed by his daughter, and together they walked past the temple and headed off toward the Wei house. Moving southward along the bank, they passed some thirty gates, took another little turn, and there they were. Long before arriving, they had noticed four black-canopied boats moored at the Wei family's place.[8]

When they had stepped in through the black lacquered gate, Wood-three and Ai-girl were shown into the gatehouse, which was already packed with two tables of feasting boatmen and farmhands. Ai-girl didn't dare look at them directly, but she did allow her eyes to rove just far enough to determine that no trace of Old Pig or Young Pig could be seen. By the time the servant brought out the New Year's Broth, Ai-girl had begun to feel hemmed in and uneasy, although she couldn't put her finger on the reason. "Just 'cause Bigman Seven's in tight with the district magistrate, that doesn't mean he's forgotten how to talk people-talk like the rest of us," she reassured herself. "Men who *read the classics and understand morality* always deal with people fair and square! I'm gonna tell Bigman Seven every last bit of what happened ever since I first

8. "Divorce" is set in Lu Xun's homeland in southeastern China, an area known as "water-country" *(shuixiang)* because most local travel is taken by way of canals that serve as streets.

came over to Chong Village as a daughter-in-law at fifteen, and then . . ."

She finished her New Year's Broth.[9] She knew the moment that would decide her fate was about to arrive. And sure enough, before long she and her father were following a farmhand through the main hall, making the turn, and walking through the door into the living room.

There were all sorts of interesting things to look at, but Ai-girl didn't have time for that. There were many different guests too, but Ai-girl saw only the flashing reds and blacks of the short satin jackets worn by the gentryfolk. And amid all those jackets, her eyes quickly found their way to one man—this was Bigman Seven, she was sure. Although he had the same cannonball head as Old Master Wei, his frame was larger and more imposing. His big round face was marked by two thin slits of eyes and two thin, jet black lines of moustache. The head was bald. But both head and face were sleek, ruddy, and so shiny that they shimmered in the light. This puzzled Ai-girl at first, but then, neatly and quickly, she worked out an explanation—he must have rubbed himself with lard.

"This is an *anus stopper.* The ancients placed it in the corpse's anus at the encoffining ceremony." Bigman Seven held what looked like an old fragment of stone in his hand. He scratched his nose with it twice as he spoke. "Unfortunately," he continued, "it is from a new excavation, but well worth acquiring nonetheless. Han Dynasty at the latest, I'd say. See this spot? That's the 'mercury stain.' "[10]

Several heads immediately clustered in the vicinity of the "mercury stain." One of them of course belonged to Old Master Wei, while several others were the proud possessions of the Young Masters. The latter had been so overshadowed by the imposing aura of Bigman Seven, however, that Ai-girl had not even noticed them at first.

She didn't understand what they were talking about, nor was she much interested. Nor did she have the nerve or inclination to

---

9. A preparation of glutinous (sticky) rice balls in sweet broth, presented as a festive treat at the end of the meal.

10. The Han Dynasty is traditionally dated 206 B.C.–A.D. 220. Mercury was put into corpses to inhibit decay. Jade pieces were inserted in the bodily openings for the same purpose.

go and investigate any old "mercury stain"—whatever that might be. She stole a moment to look round the room. The two people standing closest to the wall by the door right behind her were none other than Old Pig and Young Pig. Although she only caught a glimpse of them, she could tell they had aged considerably since half a year ago, when she had chanced to run into them on the street.

The meeting in the vicinity of the "mercury stain" suddenly adjourned. Old Master Wei took his anus stopper back, then sat down and rubbing it between his fingers, turned toward Zhuang Wood-three.

"Just the two of you, eh?"

"Yes."

"None of your sons came."

"Couldn't spare the time."

"Well, if it weren't for the fact that we still haven't been able to resolve this problem, there wouldn't be a need to trouble anybody during New Year's in the first place. I think you have all been squabbling just about long enough. Over two years now, isn't it? It's always a lot easier to get into a feud than to get out of one. Now Ai-girl can't get along with the Shi lad, and what's more, her in-laws don't like her to begin with. In view of all that, the way I see it, we'd still do well to go along with what I've said in the past: the best thing for everyone concerned would be to dissolve the marriage. In the past I've never seemed able to convince you of this on my own hook. Now, as everyone here knows, Bigman Seven is the fairest and squarest of men. And so I've asked him for *his* opinion. It turns out that he says exactly what I've been saying all along. However, he thinks that both sides ought to give a little. He's suggested that the Shi family add ten dollars to the settlement, bringing the total up to ninety dollars. Think of it, Zhuang Wood-three, *ninety* dollars!"

". . ."

"If you took the case all the way up to Old Uncle Emperor himself, you still wouldn't get a deal as good as that. Only a man like Bigman Seven would venture to come up with such a generous settlement."

Bigman nodded in agreement. The slits in his face opened into eyes, which now focused on Zhuang Wood-three. Ai-girl felt things were about to take a bad turn. She was truly astonished that her father, a man both feared and respected by all the folks inhabiting this coastal region, did not immediately stand up for her before Old Master Wei. She saw no reason for her dad to act in such a spineless way.

A little while earlier, while Bigman Seven was giving his speech about the anus stopper, Ai-girl hadn't understood very much of it, but as he spoke she did get the feeling he was rather a friendly and approachable person, not at all the awesome figure she had previously imagined.

"Bigman Seven," she began, "is not like us hicks. He's a sensible man who's *read the classics and understands morality.*" Her courage swelled as she spoke. "The Shi family did me wrong, and I had no one to turn to. As a matter of fact, I planned on hunting up Bigman Seven *myself* so's I could have a good heart-to-heart talk with him. I've been a model daughter-in-law ever since I married into that family. Always went around with my eyes down, obedient as could be. There wasn't a single, solitary rule about how a daughter-in-law should act that I didn't hold to, but those Wei people were all dead-set against me. All they had to do was clap eyes on me, and every last one of 'em would go on the warpath. And that year the weasel got their big rooster, they laid into me for not closin' the coop good! What really happened was, that damn old mangy mutt of theirs had popped the coop open with his nose while he was stealin' chicken feed. But Young Pig just up and clouted *me* across the mouth, without ever tryin' to figure out what really happened."

Bigman Seven looked at her.

"I knew there was more to this than met the eye," she continued. "It wouldn't have fooled anyone as smart as Bigman Seven either. People who *read the classics and understand morality* know just about everything. Well, as it turned out, Young Pig had been bewitched by that sleep-around slut of a widow, and he was just lookin' to come up with some way to get me out of the house. Now when I married into the Wei family, I was presented with the three gifts of tea and went through all six ceremonies, like a good girl's supposed to.[11] I was carried over there in a bridal chair, the way a proper wife should be! Did he think he could get rid of me

11. Tea was given to brides for its symbolic message: a tea bush, replanted, no longer produces seed; a remarried widow will no longer produce sons.

as easy as all that? Fat chance! They're gonna find out just who they're dealin' with before they're through with *me*. I don't care if I *do* have to go to law. If they don't do right by me at county level, I'll take it up to the prefecture, and if—"

"Bigman Seven is already familiar with everything you have brought up," said Old Master Wei looking up. "Ai-girl, if you don't turn back while you still can, you are going to pay for it. Why do you always have to be like this? See how smart your dad is, but neither you nor your brothers have the good sense to follow his example. Suppose you *do* go to law and take it up to prefectural level, do you mean to tell me the prefect won't ask Bigman Seven's opinion too? By then it will be a case of a *public matter handled according to the letter of the law,* and then we'll see how . . . Ai-girl, you simply can't—"

"I'll go for broke if I have to! Put my own life on the line and take everybody else down with me!"

It was only at this point that Bigman Seven, in slow and measured tones, began to offer his opinion. "It's not the kind of thing," opined Bigman Seven, "one puts one's life on the line about. Moreover, it is always a good idea for young people to be on the polite and amiable side. Politeness and amiability breed wealth, as they say. I have added an additional ten dollars and that is more than you had any reasonable right to expect in the first place. After all, by rights your in-laws only have to say the word, and out you go! And there's no point in worrying about whether things would be any different at the prefectural level either. Things would come out exactly the same whether you were in Beijing, Shanghai, or even overseas, for that matter. If you don't want to take my word for it, ask *him*. He's just returned from a foreign-run academy in Beijing." Bigman Seven now turned his face in the direction of a sharp-chinned Young Master and asked, "Am I right?"

"Right as right can be!" The sharp-chinned Young Master immediately straightened up and delivered his dutiful reply.

Ai-girl now felt completely isolated. Her dad hadn't stood up for her; her brothers hadn't dared to come; Old Master Wei was on her in-laws' side, lock, stock, and barrel; Bigman Seven obviously wasn't going to help; and the Young Master with the sharp chin, cowering before all of them just like a squashed bedbug, would go along with anything they said. But thrown for a loop though she was, Ai-girl was determined to fight one last round.

"What? Even Bigman Seven?" She feigned a look of utter astonishment and disappointment before continuing. "Well, it's only to be expected . . . It's because people like us with no schoolin' don't know how things are done. It's dad's fault for not knowin' how the world really works. Poor old guy doesn't even know which end is up. That's why Old Pig and Young Pig can shove him around any which way they please. They've learned how to run their buns off, ass-kissin' everyone in sight—"

The Young Pig, who had been standing right behind her, suddenly spoke up: "See for yourself, Bigman Seven, if she acts like this in front of *you,* you can guess what she was like back home. Kept things so stirred up even the pigs and chickens never got a decent rest. Always referred to my father as 'Old Pig' and whenever she had anything to say to me, it was always 'Young Pig' this or 'son-of-a-runaway' that."[12]

"What daughter of a slut who's made it with ten thousand men ever called *you* a 'son-of-a-runaway'?" Ai-girl wheeled around and fairly shouted the question. Then she turned back to Bigman Seven: "I've got a thing or two *I'd* like everybody to know about too. I suppose you think *he* was all sweetness and light with me, huh? Well let me tell you right now, every time he opened his mouth it was 'bitch' this and 'cheap trash' that. And after he hooked up with that little whore of a widow, he even started in on my ancestors, tellin' me to go fuck this one or go screw that one. Bigman Seven, you be my judge, wouldn't you say that I . . ."

Ai-girl suddenly shuddered with fear and stopped dead in her tracks, for she saw Bigman Seven roll his eyes heavenward and lift his face. At the same time, a high quavering voice issued forth from that orifice, surrounded by long thin strands of hair, that constituted his mouth.

"Co-o-ome hi-i-ther," Bigman Seven's voice droned the order out.

Suddenly Ai-girl felt her heart stop. Then just as suddenly, *thump-thump thump-thump,* it began beating again. It was as though the climax had passed and the whole situation had changed to something new—as though she had lost her footing and fallen into water while simultaneously realizing that the fall had been her own fault.

---

12. In other words, "bastard." —Author's note.

A man wearing a long blue gown under a sleeveless jacket came in just now and stood at attention before Bigman Seven. Quite erect, arms hanging straight down at his sides, he looked something like a rolling pin.

Throughout the guest hall *even crows and magpies had lost their voices.*[13] Bigman Seven set his mouth briefly in motion, but no one could make out just what he had said. His servant, however, had obviously heard it quite clearly; what was more, the sheer force of Bigman Seven's order seemed to bore into the marrow of his bones, causing his entire skeletal frame to respond with a spasmodic jerk. Fairly jumping out of his skin, the servant replied, "Yes, sir!" Taking two steps to the rear, he did an about-face and marched out the door. Ai-girl knew that something unexpected was about to occur, something she had absolutely no way of anticipating and therefore no way of guarding against. Only now did she fully realize just how formidable Bigman Seven really was. Had she properly understood this previously, she wouldn't have been so unrestrained, so coarse and vulgar.

Ai-girl now regretted her behavior of the past few moments and said without thinking: "Matter of fact, I always meant to go along with whatever Bigman Seven decided. It's just that I . . ."

And once again throughout the guest hall *even crows and magpies had lost their voices.* Though Ai-girl's words were as light and sheer as silk, Old Master Wei leapt from his seat as if catapulted by a clap of thunder. "Settled!" he shouted. "Bigman Seven is truly fair and Ai-girl is truly enlightened." Then he turned to Zhuang Wood-three. "Wood-three, old friend, since your daughter has already agreed, I don't think you can have any objections. I assume you have brought along the Red-Green Certificates as I suggested.[14] Well then, if both parties will just bring forward the documents, we can . . ."

Ai-girl saw her dad reach into the money belt fastened round his waist and take something out. The man who looked like a rolling pin came back in and handed Bigman Seven a lacquerware box. It was flat and shaped something like a turtle. Fearing things had taken a bad turn, Ai-girl quickly glanced at her father. He was

13. A conventional phrase of classical Chinese, used here to establish a satirical, mock-heroic tone.

14. Wedding certificates were traditionally printed on paper that was colored red and green.

over by the tea table opening a blue cloth package, and taking silver dollars out of it.

Bigman Seven pulled the head off the turtle and dumped something from inside the body onto the palm of his hand. Thereupon, the man who looked like a rolling pin took back the lacquerware box. Bigman Seven stirred one finger around in the substance on the palm of his hand, and then thrust that finger into and out of his nostrils several times. His nose and upper lip immediately turned a brownish yellow. His nose began to wrinkle as if he were about to sneeze.

While Zhuang Wood-three was still counting the silver dollars, Old Master Wei took some coins out of the pile not yet counted and slipped them back to the Old Pig. He then switched the positions of the two Red-Green Certificates and pushed them toward their original owners. "Why don't you take these back now. Wood-three, old friend, make sure you count carefully—money's no laughing matter. You—"

Ah . . . ah . . . ah-chooo! Ai-girl knew perfectly well that it was Bigman Seven sneezing, but without thinking she turned in the direction of the sound. There he stood, mouth hanging wide open, nose all wrinkled and cocked for the next one. In the fingers of one hand Bigman Seven clasped something that "the ancients used to place in the anus of a corpse" and was scratching the side of his nose with it.

After a great deal of difficulty, Zhuang Wood-three finally managed to finish counting up the money. Both parties picked up their Red-Green Certificates and put them away.

Postures began to relax, faces lost their tenseness, and in less time than it takes to tell the tale, an atmosphere of politeness and amiability reigned supreme throughout the Wei family's entire living room.

Seeing that both parties to the dispute seemed ready to take their leave, Old Master Wei breathed a sigh of relief. "Good! We've got it all settled at last," he said. "Well, I guess we don't have anything else to take up, do we? A Happy New Year to all! We can congratulate ourselves on having worked our way through a knotty problem. Leaving already? Why don't you all stay for a cup of New Year's Wine—it's a rare opportunity."

"Not this time. Put it away and we'll come back for some next year," said Ai-girl.

"Thank you, Old Master Wei. We won't have any. We still have some other things to tend to."

Speaking all at once, Zhuang Wood-three, Old Pig, and Young Pig withdrew from the Wei family's living room, each with marked gestures of deference and respect.

"What's this? Not even a parting drink of wine?" Old Master Wei aimed this remark toward Ai-girl, the last one out the door.

"No, maybe some other time. Thanks just the same, Old Master Wei."

NOVEMBER 6, 1925

About the Translator

William A. Lyell received his Ph.D. from the University of Chicago and is currently Associate Professor of Chinese at Stanford University. The author of *Lu Hsün's Vision of Reality,* he has also published numerous translations and articles related to modern Chinese literature.